FIELD OF FIRE

FIELD OF FIRE

MARC CAMERON

PINNACLE BOOKS
Kensington Publishing Corp.
www.kensingtonbooks.com

PINNACLE BOOKS are published by

Kensington Publishing Corp.
119 West 40th Street
New York, NY 10018

All Kensington titles, imprints, and distributed lines are available at special quantity discounts for bulk purchases for sales promotions, premiums, fund-raising, educational, or institutional use. Special book excerpts or customized printings can also be created to fit specific needs. For details, write or phone the office of the Kensington sales manager: Kensington Publishing Corp., 119 West 40th Street, New York, NY 10018, attn: Sales Department; phone 1-800-221-2647.

ISBN-13: 978-0-7860-3892-3
ISBN-10: 0-7860-3892-6

First printing: January 2017

10 9 8 7 6 5 4 3 2 1

Printed in the United States of America

First electronic edition: January 2017

ISBN-13: 978-0-7860-3893-0
ISBN-10: 0-7860-3893-4

For Julie

Thanks, Sis.

The art of war . . . is a matter of life and death, a road either to safety or to ruin.

—SUN TZU

Prologue

VOSTOK Satellite Imagery Reconnaissance Post
Khabarovsk, Russia, 11:05 A.M.

The dimly lit basement held nothing but conscripts and sad stories, none of which Junior Lieutenant Andre Bukin wanted to hear. Corporal Popovich knew this full well, and still the bony soldier beckoned Bukin to his flickering video monitor. Bordering on skeletal, he was one of twenty-four paste-white faces around the walls of the quiet room. As officer of the watch and a recent graduate of the Budyonny Military Academy in St. Petersburg, Bukin was absolutely certain he was smarter, stronger, and imminently better than any of the other two dozen men and women around him slouching in front of computer screens. He was a stern-looking man, with jet-black hair slicked backward like a young Joseph Stalin. A heavy brow and strong jaw added weight to his brooding manner and made him perfect for the job of overseer. His superiors saw his potential, and he took enormous pride in that.

Every soul Bukin supervised had been drafted into the Army for the term of a single year. Some were nearing the end of their service, but most were at the halfway point. It was called service, but was it really if served at the point of a sword? When their year was done, these minions would flee like prisoners paroled. No one expected much of them, and they gave no more than was expected.

Around the chilly room, computer fans hummed and keyboards clicked. In the rare event that any of the soldiers spoke, they did so in churchlike whispers. It was no secret that most kept a mobile phone resting on a thigh and hidden below the desk, content to play games and chat with friends on ICQ. For the most part, the conscripts watched their monitors, and Bukin watched them. It was all so mundanely perfect, the consistent work from which careers were made—until the idiot corporal raised his bony arm.

Nestor Popovich was a skeletal thing, barely out of his teens, with a shaved head that bore the many knots and scars of *dedovshchina*—the brutal hazing he'd received from more senior conscripts during basic training. His baggy blue coveralls appeared to be eating him alive.

"There is something in the river, Lieutenant," he whispered, when Bukin was close enough, dipping his scarred head toward the image on his screen. "Frozen, I think . . . but it is too early in the season . . ." Popovich rolled his chair back from the long metal counter with a squeak, giving Bukin room for a better vantage point. The boy looked up with obscenely naïve eyes.

Bukin studied the screen for a long moment, leaning in, then back, then in again. His breath quickened as it dawned on him what he was seeing. He toggled the keyboard to enlarge the image. He had to make certain his eyes were not playing tricks.

"Dead fish," Bukin gasped, taking an instinctive

step backward, distancing himself from the screen if not the situation. The horrific images from the satellite feed flickered against his slack jaw. He hooked a finger in the constricting collar of his uniform shirt, a futile attempt to get more air, and thought of how insane it was that a river of dead fish was about to cost him his career—or worse.

"Fish?" Popovich said, a little too loudly for Bukin's rapidly fraying nerves.

His head swimming, Bukin had to lean forward and rest his hands on the long counter to stay upright. It put the men elbow to shoulder, and he turned his head to stare at the corporal, seething inside. It was protocol to summon a superior in such instances, but Bukin hated him for it.

It was unlikely that the ignorant boy had any idea what he was even seeing, but the lieutenant knew too well. The events unfolding in real time on his screen sent audible waves of nausea gurgling through his bowels. Sweat trickled down his forehead and disappeared into the thick brow that formed a single, unbroken line overhanging his face.

The enlarged image on Popovich's screen showed thousands of bloated white bellies in the otherwise dark oxbows of an Arctic river, forming a shockingly pale raft against the green tundra and gray mountains.

The corporal pointed toward the images of crosshatched streets and drab concrete buildings that made up the Siberian port village on the shores of the Chukchi Sea.

"This is Providenya," he said.

Bukin shot a furtive glance around the dimly lit room as if Popovich had just divulged a state secret. No one looked up.

Bukin turned back quickly to lock eyes with the skinny conscript, narrowing his eyes in the unspoken but universal look from a superior officer that said, *Keep your mouth shut.*

Popovich shrank back, rolling his chair closer to his workstation. He clicked the computer mouse to overlay a map on the satellite image, zooming in more and bringing the river into sharper focus. Both men stared, their mouths hanging open.

"*Gemorróy*!" Popovich gasped. Literally, "*hemorrhoids!*"

Lieutenant Bukin thought it an apt description of the situation. He gnawed at the inside of his cheek, his mind spinning through the possibilities. A die-off near Providenya could mean only one thing.

The flight path of *Kosmos 2491,* one of the satellites responsible for over-watch of American military bases in Alaska also took it directly over the small settlement in the protected bay on the Russian coast, 3,500 kilometers northeast of the monitoring station where Bukin's sweat now dripped onto the metal counter. Along with the dead fish, the satellite feed clearly showed the gray and unremarkable concrete buildings of the old MIG 17 base across Providenya Bay. Most everyone in the Russian Army knew the lonely outpost had also been a depot for chemical weapons during the Soviet days. Official reports said it had been closed for over forty years. Strategically placed debris and the rusted hulks of several military planes on and around the airstrip indicated that the remote base had fallen into disrepair.

Bukin knew differently. From here on, discretion was not only a matter of state security; his life depended on it.

Corporal Popovich, still oblivious to the gravity of the situation, glanced up at his superior.

"There are so many, sir" he said. "What could have killed them?"

Bukin put a hand on the boy's shoulder, trying to sound like a father figure though he was no more than a few years older. "You must watch your words on this."

"With respect," the corporal said, "such a massive die-off will be difficult to conceal." The boy's hand shot to his open mouth. "Lieutenant, look!"

Bukin watched the screen in horror as a small skiff carrying six men moved upriver from the mouth of the bay. The man seated at the bow stood as they neared the fish, teetered there for a moment, then fell overboard, floundering in the water, apparently unable to swim. A moment later the others in the boat began to thrash wildly. Two more fell into the river. The remaining three lay sprawled on the deck of the boat, motionless. With no one to steer it, the skiff arced gracefully through the water to run itself up on a gravel bank mere feet from the drifting raft of bloated fish.

Bukin blotted the sweat from his hands on the front of his uniform trousers and placed them palms down on the countertop. A sudden flush of panic washed over him when he saw the glowing red clock below the video monitor. Standing bolt upright, he snatched a small notepad from the pocket of his tunic and ran a trembling finger down the list of times and numbers he'd taped to the back.

He found what he needed and grabbed up a black handset beside the monitor and dialed the number from the back of his notebook. Bukin hated the corporal for following protocol—and shortly, another officer would feel the same way about him.

He had ninety-one minutes until a U.S. Lacrosse

satellite made its first of two daily flights over Providenya. When it did, the Americans were sure to see the river.

Still hopelessly oblivious, Popovich used the computer mouse to move around the image, studying the old MIG 17 base.

"My girlfriend is Chukchi Eskimo," The corporal whistled under his breath. "She tells me crazy stories of Providenya. The townspeople do not speak of it much, but there are many secret things that go on there."

Junior Lieutenant Bukin held up his hand to quiet the idiot corporal, then cupped his hand around the telephone receiver to explain the situation in frenzied whispers. If the other conscripts noticed, or cared about what was going on, they didn't show it. The officer on the other end of the line explained in no uncertain terms how he wanted Bukin to proceed.

"Now?" the junior lieutenant whispered. "Here?"

The officer held firm with his order.

"Yes, Captain," Bukin said, feeling his future prospects drain away. "I understand. I will do so immediately." He replaced the receiver, trying to remain nonchalant as his hand dropped to the Makarov pistol on his belt and moved it to the pocket of his uniform tunic.

"I want to hear more about what your girlfriend has told you," Bukin said, offering the conscript a cigarette, hoping the boy didn't see his hands shake. He shot a conspiratorial glance around the room. "But we mustn't do it here. Let us step outside and discuss it in private. Bukin followed the foolish conscript out the door, his hand gripping the Makarov in his uniform pocket. His orders had been clear. *Those who spoke too much of Providenya must end up like the fish.*

GRU Regional Headquarters, Khabarovsk, 11:33 A.M.

"*Gemorróy!*" Colonel Ruslan Rostov spat into the telephone. His bald head glowed red, his broad face twisted as if frozen in the middle of a sneeze. Thick knuckles turned white around the handset. "How many dead?"

"At this point, twenty-seven, sir," Captain Evgeni Lodygin said, his voice characteristically deadpan. "I anticipate that number to go up as the spill moves downstream and enters the bay."

Rostov knew Lodygin to be exceptionally capable though he did have his little eccentricities. But for certain violent lapses in judgment with the occasional prostitute—whom no one would ever miss anyway—he was able to control his most unseemly appetites. There were times when a high-functioning psychopath could be a valuable commodity—a fact that Rostov had learned from experience.

The colonel bounced his fist on the desk in frustration. "How much was leaked?"

Lodygin cleared his throat, obviously stalling.

"How much?"

"The entire cache is missing," Lodygin said.

"Then this was no accident?" Rostov felt his career evaporating. The general would be furious. He hunched forward in his chair, dumbstruck. "Someone released the chemicals on purpose?"

"I fear that is exactly what occurred, Colonel," Lodygin said.

"The old fool dumped all his work into the river?" Rostov said, still processing the gravity of the situation. He felt as though he might begin to weep. "This will kill thousands. I will be summoned to Moscow . . ."

"That is the thing, Colonel," Lodygin said. "All the Novo Archangelsk is missing, but we have only found a dozen empty containers in Volodin's lab."

Rostov closed his eyes, steeling himself.

"How much stock was on hand?"

"He destroyed the records," Lodygin said. "Much of the stock has already been sent to secure storage in the vault, but there were at least three cases in the lab as of last week."

"Two full cases . . ." Rostov whispered. That meant two-dozen canisters of the most deadly gas known to mankind were unaccounted for. The news hit him like a sledgehammer in the guts, but as terrible at that was, he had the more immediate problem of the oncoming American satellite.

"Very well," he said. "We must focus on the immediate problem of the spill at this moment."

"Of course," Lodygin said. "The deaths would have been catastrophic had the water not diluted the compounds. Prevailing winds continue to blow in from the sea, toward generally uninhabited mountains. If the winds reverse, or begin to blow southerly the entire city would be affected."

Rostov groaned. Providenya was a far-flung outpost at the edge of nowhere—that's what made it perfect. But two thousand bloating bodies would be a difficult thing to conceal, even at the edge of the world.

"All but essential personnel have been ordered to remain in their quarters," Lodygin continued. "Those who must work outdoors are required to wear a protective suit and breathing apparatus. I've told local authorities across the bay that there has been a leak of chlorine gas from a shipping container. They are using the tsunami warning system to have everyone stay in their homes until ordered to do otherwise. So far no one has spoken of Novo Archangelsk."

"And you would be wise to keep quiet about it." Rostov exhaled slowly. Containment. Everything now was about containment. "What of the fish?" he said. "What do you intend to do about them?"

"Ah, the fish," Lodygin said, maddeningly smug. "My men are spraying them with black paint as we speak."

"Paint?" the colonel bellowed. He shoved the padded leather chair away from his desk, sending a ceramic coffee mug made for him by his fifteen-year-old daughter against the thin, institutional carpet, dashing it to pieces. "Paint, you say? How you were ever promoted to captain is a mystery to me. I am told the *Onyx 182* will overfly Providenya in sixty-three minutes and your most brilliant plan to conceal the fish is to spray them with black paint?

Onyx was a codename for the fifteen-ton American Lacrosse radar imaging satellite that passed over the Russian Far East twice every day.

"I assure you, Colonel, we will prove successful, but I am happy to institute your superior plan."

Rostov closed his eyes. He took a deep breath through his nose in an effort to steady himself before speaking.

"Captain Lodygin," he said. "Did it even occur to you that you will simply have a river full of dead fish covered in black paint? You would be wise to remember that American satellites are capable of counting the dimples on a golf ball at night and in bad weather."

"That is true enough." Lodygin gave a hollow cough, as if he was being forced to pay attention to something that bored him, his superior officer for instance. "But the Lacrosse passes over 650 kilometers above us, covering a large target swath with each pass. That is a great deal of area on which to spy encompassing many square kilometers of terrain. More clearly, the American satellites are so sophisticated that they have mountains of data to sift through. This makes it much easier to hide the golf ball you mention unless they have a specific reason to focus on it in particular."

"Very well," Rostov sighed. "But I will shoot you myself before I face a firing squad."

"Do we yet utilize firing squads?" Lodygin said, dead serious.

"I will reinstitute the practice myself for your benefit, Captain," Rostov said, his voice rising, "if you do not keep the Americans from seeing those fish! And arrest that fool Volodin. He's obviously responsible for the spill—and I want to know what he's done with the rest of it."

Rostov consoled himself by imagining what he would do to the doddering scientist. The Kremlin had forced the man on him with assurances that he was the best in the field of chemical weapons. And so he was, but he was also a nightmare. Once a gifted scientist, Kostya Volodin had begun to slip mentally. Worse yet, he appeared to have developed a conscience over chemical weapons. Rostov had reported this, but the general had made it clear—Novo Archangelsk was important to the Kremlin and to the President himself. The responsibility of keeping Volodin working fell squarely on Rostov's shoulders. Up to now, the greasy Lodygin had been doing just that, allowing Rostov to abstain from the gory details.

A sudden thought sent a new crop of sweat to the colonel's bald head. "He was not among the dead, was he?"

Lodygin remained silent.

Rostov screamed into the phone. "Do not dare tell me Volodin is dead!" He wiped frothy spittle off his lips with his forearm. "He must account for the missing gas."

"He has vanished," Lodygin said.

"What do you mean, vanished?" Rostov slapped the desk with his hand. This was possibly the only news worse than if the old bastard had died. "Are you saying he took the gas with him?"

"I do not know," Captain Lodygin said. "Corporal Myshkin informed me only moments ago. Apparently, a young woman with whom Volodin keeps frequent company has also gone missing."

"You are as close as can be to the end of the earth," Rostov said through clenched teeth. "Where could they have gone? Put Myshkin on speaker."

A shaky voice came across the line. "I . . . am . . . Corporal Myshkin, Colonel." If pale gray had a sound, this was it.

"You've searched the entire facility?" Rostov barked. "What of his apartment?"

"We have looked everywhere, Colonel," the boy stammered.

"Well, look again!"

"Yes, Colonel," Myshkin stammered. "The captain has placed men at his apartment, in the event he returns . . . but I fear he will not."

"And this girl?" Rostov snapped.

"Yes, Colonel," Myshkin said. "Kaija Merculief. We are watching her apartment as well. The neighbors inform us that she is a *night butterfly*, a prostitute, but that Dr. Volodin is her only customer. She is fifteen years of age—"

Rostov wanted to strangle someone with the phone

cord. His daughter was fifteen. "Kostya Volodin is an old man. You tell me he keeps company with a fifteen-year-old prostitute? Is that how you people amuse yourselves in Providenya?"

"No, Colonel," the corporal stammered. "I mean, I suppose Dr. Volodin does. In his defense, the girl looks much older than fifteen."

"Never mind," Rostov said. "I do not much care how old she looks. Find Volodin. Now. I want him back in his lab with the missing gas canisters within the hour. Your life depends on this, Myshkin. Am I clear?"

"Yes, Colonel, extremely clear, but . . ." The corporal's terrified gulp was audible over the phone. "I . . . I fear that is not possible. No one has seen the doctor since the last flight out of Providenya."

Rostov ran a thick hand across his face, thinking. "Are you there, Captain? Pick up the phone."

"Yes, Colonel," Lodygin said, still supremely smug, as if he were perfectly happy digging his own grave. The line was clearer now that it was off speaker and the sniveling Myshkin was gone.

Rostov took a long breath, working to relax his clenching jaw. "What does he mean, the last flight?"

"An air charter departed Providenya one hour and ten minutes ago."

"Tell me what you make of this, Captain." Rostov's voice rose with each and every word. He had abandoned any idea of calming down. "Because from where I sit, it looks as though the doctor hoisted a flag of warning to our enemies with this debacle in the river and then slipped away with the remainder of the gas under your watch."

"I will locate Dr. Volodin myself," Lodygin said, finally showing some sort of initiative beyond his inane plan to spray black paint on dead fish.

Rostov paused before answering. “This charter flight,” Rostov said. “Did it by chance go to Murmansk? I seem to remember the old fool having family there.”

“Not Murmansk, sir.” Captain Lodygin gave a quiet cough. “Alaska.”

PART I
CONSPIRE

The meaning of my star is war.
—Rudyard Kipling, *Kim*

Chapter 1

Near Anchorage, Alaska, 3:25 P.M.

Jericho Quinn knew an ambush when he saw one. He rolled the throttle of his gunmetal gray BMW R1200GS Adventure, leaning hard over into the second of a long series of S turns. Sometimes called the two-story bike of the motorcycling world, the big GS flicked easily on the twisty road. A chilly wind bit the tiny gap of skin between the chin of his helmet and the collar of his black leather jacket. Behind him, riding pillion, Veronica "Ronnie" Garcia squeezed with strong thighs, leaning when he leaned, moving when he moved as he negotiated the narrow, seaside road. Her soft chest pressed against his back, long arms twined around his waist.

Popping the bike upright on a straightaway, Quinn shot a glance in his side mirror and watched the grill of a dark panel van loom behind him. It came up fast, pressing aggressively on the winding two-lane that ran on the narrow ledge between mountain and ocean. Quinn bumped the throttle again and sped up, easing farther to the right and buying some distance while he considered any and all options that didn't end with him and Garcia as twin grease spots on the asphalt or Wile E. Coyoted into the mountainside.

The van accelerated, moving close enough that it filled Quinn's side mirrors with nothing but chrome grill. Just as he was about to swerve onto a gravel trail that cut off toward the ocean, he got a clear view of the guy at the wheel. A kid with a thick mullet haircut pressed a cellphone to his ear while gesturing wildly with the hand that should have been reserved for steering. Quinn kept up his speed but took the shoulder instead of the trail, allowing the van to barrel past before the next blind corner. For all Quinn knew, the guy never even saw him.

He'd ridden the Seward Highway south of Anchorage hundreds of times while growing up and knew there was a passing lane less than a mile ahead. Cell phones, sleepy drivers, drunks, turds with mullets—all made Quinn want to beat someone to death with an ax handle—but road rage had no place from the back of a motorcycle. No matter the traffic laws, the reality of physics dictated a right-of-way by tonnage if you wanted to stay alive.

"I'm proud of you, Mango," Garcia's sultry voice, spiced with a hint of her Cuban heritage, came across Quinn's Cardo Bluetooth headset as he flicked the leggy BMW back onto the highway proper. "You didn't even mutter when you yielded to that dude."

Quinn poured on more speed, sending up a tornado of yellow leaves from a tiny stand of birches along the road. "I'm not much of a mutterer," he said.

"Yeah, well," Ronnie chuckled, "you're not much of a yielder either."

Turnagain Arm, a narrow bay off the Cook Inlet of the Pacific Ocean, lay to their right, silty waters white-capped and churning as if her tremendous tides hadn't quite figured out which way to flow. Craggy peaks of the Chugach Mountains loomed directly to their left in a mix of rock, greenery, and waterfall that tumbled right to the shoulder of the winding road.

Quinn moved his neck from side to side, letting the adrenaline brought on by the idiot in the van ebb—and taking the time to enjoy the ride until the next idiot barreled up behind him. He flicked the bike around a basketball-sized rock that had come to rest in his lane. Here and there, great swaths of stone and shattered trees that had been bent and torn by avalanche, fanned down the mountainside, just beginning to heal from the previous winter.

Quinn could relate.

It felt good to be back—back in his home state, with a badge back in his pocket, and back on his bike with the woman he loved on the seat behind him. Along with the two guns and Japanese killing dagger that hid under his black leather jacket, he bore as many scars as the avalanche chutes that cut the mountains above him. Some of the wounds were still painfully raw.

Ronnie bumped the back of his helmet with the forehead of hers and worked in closer behind him, giving him a playful squeeze. She was a strong woman, just a few inches shorter than Quinn, with broad, athletic shoulders and strong, alluring hips. Far from fat, her Russian father had called her *zaftig*. Her ex husband—a man who wisely steered well clear of Quinn—described her as having a "ghetto booty." But if the powerfully aggressive BMW reminded Quinn of The Death Dealer's black warhorse, Veronica Dombrovski Garcia was no helpless maiden, cowering at the feet of a Conan or John Carter of Mars. She was a beautifully fierce warrior princess, clutching her own sword and flanked by pet tigers. Quinn's seven-year-old daughter had privately confided to him that Garcia looked an awful lot like Wonder Woman.

As strong as she was, Garcia's squeezes were considerably weaker than they had been, absent the ferocity they'd once possessed. It was understandable. Her treatment at the hands of sadistic captors had left both shoulders badly damaged, one requiring a lengthy surgery and months of physical therapy to repair. There had been concerns that she might not be able to use that arm again at all.

It would take a while, but Quinn was sure she'd heal, maybe only to ninety percent—but ninety percent of Ronnie Garcia was ten percent above any other woman Quinn had ever met. She pushed the limits being out of her sling, but he wasn't really in a position to admonish her.

Gripping the handlebars, Quinn rolled his own shoulders back and forth, feeling the tell-tale pop and grind of damaged gristle and working out some of the stiffness and after-effects of being shot by a Chinese terrorist just months earlier. Emiko Miyagi, friend and defensive tactics mentor, had done wonders with shiatsu massage and her specially designed, if incredibly painful, yoga routines. He could deal with physical pain. It was the thought of being incapacitated that haunted him.

The official written orders from the Air Force doc at Andrews had been to take it easy. But in an off-the-record chat, he'd told Quinn to work the injury until he started to "piss it off," and then dial back some. Riding the bike definitely pissed off his old wounds. He found the hyperawareness and attention to balance it took to negotiate the mountain roads and prosecute the tight turns on the leggy Beemer to be just what he needed to put a bow on his recovery process—both mental and physical. In any case, disobeying doctor's orders was part of his DNA. He'd been doing it for weeks, adding dead hangs and then pull-ups to his physical therapy regimen as soon as he could make a good fist. His old man had once lamented that Jericho could burn calories just sitting in the corner and looking mean. The older he got, the less that was true, so exercise was a necessity, injured or not.

Quinn knew he might not be a very good yielder, but he was a good healer. At nearly thirty-seven, the mending just took a little longer.

Both he and Garcia wore beaked Arai dual-sport helmets, his gray with an airbrushed paint job of crossed war-axes on the sides, hers canary yellow. Racing gloves and full black leathers protected them against an accidental dismount and the icy crispness of an Alaska autumn. Icon Truant motorcycle boots offered protection to his ankles but allowed him the freedom of movement to run should the need arise.

Though not a heavy woman by any stretch, Garcia was ample enough to make an extremely pleasant backrest. Her warmth seeped through Quinn's leather jacket, bringing with it an added layer of comfort against the chill and an excited happiness that he hadn't felt since his daughter was born.

Garcia gave him another playful squeeze. It sent a twinge of pain through Quinn's bruised ribs but he didn't care. His father had often urged him to lead the kind of life that bruised ribs. Now, as an agent for the Air Force Office of Special Investigations or OSI, he'd been assigned to work directly for the President's National Security Advisor—doing the things that needed the heavy hand of his particular skill set. He wasn't about to let a couple of old wounds—or some jackass with a mullet—stop him from enjoying this trip with Garcia. They'd been apart for far too long, and now he'd finally gotten her to his home state.

They'd been in Alaska for the better part of the week, going to the Musk Ox Farm and eating reindeer hotdogs in downtown Anchorage with his seven-year-old daughter Mattie. The two got along well enough that they shared whispered girl-secrets that they kept from him. To Quinn's astonishment, even his ex-wife Kim seemed at ease with the fact he'd brought his girlfriend up to spend time with his parents—an obvious final step before any more permanent arrangement.

The trip was never meant as a test, but if it had been, Garcia would have aced it. Every new place Quinn took her threw her into a state of childlike awe. If anything, she appeared to love Alaska even more than he did—which was saying something.

The pavement was still clear and dry but the mountains along the Seward Highway had been dusted by snow that same morning. This "termination dust" signified the end of Alaska's short autumn but gave the already breathtaking scenery an extra shot of beauty. Quinn couldn't remember the last time he'd wanted to impress anyone as bad as he wanted to impress Veronica Garcia. It was a difficult endeavor considering everything they'd been through together.

As if she knew he was thinking about her, Garcia moved even closer—if such a thing were even possible.

Quinn absorbed it all, flicking the BMW back and forth through a maze of rocks that had tumbled onto the road on the far side of a blind curve. Like Quinn, the bike was happiest when dealing with the rough stuff.

Garcia's husky giggle poured through the Cardo earpiece in his helmet. "She wiggles like a sassy woman."

"That she does," Quinn said, his lips pressing against the foam microphone. "But she doesn't wiggle herself. I wiggle her."

"You got that right—"

Always scanning, Quinn tensed at a sight a quarter mile up the highway, causing Garcia to stop mid-sentence.

He could tell by the way her body moved—or stopped moving—that she saw it right after he did.

A white Anchorage PD patrol car sat parked in a paved pullout overlooking the ocean. The driver's door gaped open and a uniformed officer crouched behind the back bumper. He was bent over the prone body of his partner, one hand on the downed man's chest, the other at the radio mic clipped to his lapel. A scant three hundred yards ahead on a long straightaway, a red pickup and a white Subaru sedan sped away, southbound, past the turnoff to the ski village of Girdwood.

Quinn slowed, using his left hand to unzip his jacket and reach inside to retrieve a black leather credential case. Pulling up on a fallen officer without ID was a good way to get shot.

The downed officer lay on his back, surrounded by shattered glass from the rear window. His eyes were open and he writhed in pain. A good sign, Quinn thought as he put his foot down to steady the bike and flipped up the visor on his helmet. A line of what could only be bullet holes stitched the side of the police car. The other officer, a younger man with the earnest look of a full-grown Cabbage Patch doll, glanced up at the sound of the approaching motorcycle. His big eyes narrowed with adrenalized intensity. He nodded at the sight of Quinn's OSI badge and returned to his radio traffic.

". . . medics code red," the officer said, calling in help for his injured partner.

The officer's earpiece had come unplugged and the steady voice of the dispatcher spilled out of his radio. "All units, 10-33 for 25-Bravo-2," she said, advising others on the frequency to yield to the officer's traffic.

The young officer continued with his description. "Two white male adults, one white female. They . . . it . . . I mean . . . the vehicle's still going south." His face was flushed, his voice a half an octave higher than it should have been.

Quinn recognized the wounded officer as Greg Sizemore, a man Quinn had gone to high school with. A patch on the shoulder of his navy blue uniform identified him as an FTO or Field Training Officer, which made his partner a trainee. New or not, the rookie was doing everything right by applying pressure to an apparent gunshot wound just above Sizemore's collar bone.

"Are both vehicles involved?" Quinn asked, nodding toward the tiny dots that were the pickup and the Subaru as they faded into the distance around a mountain curve.

"Only the white sedan," Sizemore said, grimacing at the pain from his wound. "The pickup came by just before the shooting. I think the white car must have passed him. Driver and . . . front passenger are both armed. Don't know about the girl in back."

Quinn felt Ronnie tap him on the shoulder. He scooted forward against the gas tank, giving her room to get off the bike. The bullet looked to have caught Sizemore just above his vest, probably destroying his collarbone. Blood seeped up through the rookie's clenched fingers but he appeared to have it stopped until an ambulance arrived. Ronnie peeled off her helmet, shaking out long black hair, and bent to help.

"You good for me to go get 'em, bud?" Quinn asked, looking at the downed officer.

"Hell, yes," Sizemore grunted, stifling a cough. "Sons of bitches shot me. Tear 'em up."

The rookie looked up at Quinn. "We have units responding from South Anchorage and a Trooper coming north from Summit Lake—"

"Tell them the man on the bike is a good guy," Quinn said, before flipping down his visor and giving the highway behind him a quick head check. A cloud of smoke rose from the BMW's rear tire as he rolled on the gas, falling in after the white Subaru.

The GS accelerated quickly, scooping Quinn into the seat as it ripped down the highway. He leaned hard, nearly dragging a knee as he rounded the first corner past the Girdwood cutoff. He pushed from his mind the fact that the only thing that kept him upright were the two rubber contact patches where his tires met the pavement, each about four square inches.

Chapter 2

Quinn's mind raced ahead of the bike, looking for rocks, vehicles jumping out from side roads, and any other obstacles that could send him over the side of the Seward Highway in a flaming ball of twisted metal and leather.

He toed the Beemer down a gear, feeling the aggressive pull of the engine. The speedometer on the GPS display between his handlebars climbed past ninety and then a hundred miles an hour. The Subaru moved fast, and the red pickup stayed tight on its tail, but Quinn began to gain ground the moment he left the downed officer.

Still a mile back, Quinn watched the red pickup move up as if to pass the little Subaru on a long straightaway. Instead of passing, the larger truck jerked to the right, untracking the sedan and sending it spinning out of control and slamming it against the mountain on the left side of the road. The red pickup flew past, smoke pouring from its rear tires as it skidded to a stop, and them began to back down the middle of the road toward the wrecked Subaru.

Quinn reached back with his left hand, feeling along

the metal cargo box until he found a one-liter metal fuel bottle.

He was still a little over a half mile behind the Subaru. At his present speed, the GS would close the distance in less than twenty seconds. It took Quinn a few of those precious seconds to flip the latches that held the fuel bottle in place, but he finally felt it snap and brought the bottle up by his handlebars, holding it tight in his left hand.

Ahead on the left, people began to boil out of the wrecked Subaru, surely stunned. They'd shot a cop, so Quinn still considered them plenty dangerous.

He eased off the throttle but kept the bike moving around forty miles an hour as he neared the man who'd climbed out the driver's side of the Subaru—the shooter. The man from the red pickup was already engaged in a shouting match with the Subaru passenger, who'd made it out first. Quinn saw the gun in the Subaru driver's hand when he was still fifty feet away. The sneaker-like Truants would allow him to fight and run better than his usual motocross boots, but he wanted to tenderize the men as much as possible before he even got off the bike.

Quinn goosed the throttle, closing the distance in an instant, bringing the aluminum bottle up just in time to catch the driver in the side of his head with a resounding "tink." Two pounds of aluminum and fuel traveling over forty miles an hour dropped the witless shooter in his tracks. Quinn let the bottle go the moment after impact, grabbing a handful of brakes and skidding the bike to a hard stop along the asphalt shoulder. He drifted the rear wheel during the slide to bring the back end of the bike around so he was facing his threat.

He got the Beemer stopped in time to watch the driver of the red pickup, an older man with a tweed driving cap, slap the Subaru passenger in the ear with an open palm, driving him to his knees. The female passenger from the Subaru threw her hands in the air, wailing and cursing as if she was being beaten herself, but giving up immediately. Quinn drew his Kimber 10mm from the holster tucked inside the waistband of his riding pants and scanned the area.

The man in the driving cap had drawn a gun of his own and now trained it on the downed Subaru passenger.

"Jim Hoyt, DEA," he shouted to Quinn. "Retired."

The driver of the Subaru, a skinny twenty-something covered with meth sores, looked up at Quinn from were he sat against a slab of rock, a bloody hand pressed to the side of his head. "You could have killed me," he said. "I don't know who you are, but I'm gonna sue the shit out of you, mister."

"Hell of a thing," Hoyt said. "You'd think a little shitass cop shooter who got smacked from the back of a moving motorcycle would be a little more sedate."

Quinn raised an eyebrow, wondering how Hoyt knew a cop had been shot.

"Got a scanner in the truck," Hoyt said. "Heard the description go out about the same time this rocket scientist flew past me."

There was a no-nonsense air about the Jim Hoyt that made Quinn wonder just what he'd done for the DEA—and how long he'd been retired. A tall woman with long, silver hair and a sliver gleam in her blue eyes introduced herself as Mrs. Hoyt. She'd moved their pickup out of the roadway and now stood beside the open door, arms across the large bosom of her fleece vest. She looked at her husband and shook her head, giving a resigned sigh—certainly a policeman's wife, accustomed to his behavior.

Quinn and Hoyt worked together to pat down the occupants of the Subaru, lining them up face down in the grass along the shoulder of the road. Bad guys secured, Hoyt stepped up to Quinn, keeping an injured elbow tucked in tight against his body. His cheeks were flushed, and he was obviously in pain judging by the way he treated the elbow. Pain or not, his green eyes sparkled with a mischievous grin. His jacket fell open when he extended a large hand toward Quinn, revealing a sweatshirt bearing a blue Air Force Academy Falcon logo.

"That was some good work back there pitting these guys, Mr. Hoyt," Quinn said, nodding to the man's shirt and giving him a knowing wink as they shook hands. "*Fast, neat, average . . .*"

"Ah." Hoyt returned the wink with one of his own. "*Friendly, good, good,*" he said, providing Quinn with the second half of the phrase used by one Air Force Academy graduate to identify another. Taken straight from the Mitchel Dining Hall comment card, *Fast, Neat, Average, Friendly, Good, Good* were the only acceptable critique freshman cadets were allowed to give on the mandatory Form 0-96.

Hoyt stepped back to give Quinn a more thorough up-and-down look. "Class of seventy-five."

"Two thousand and two," Quinn said.

"Oh." Hoyt rubbed his elbow. "That class."

"Yeah," Quinn said, "that class." He decided to steer the subject away from the fact that he'd graduated from the Air Force Academy the same academic year Al Qaeda brought down the Twin Towers and crashed a plane into the Pentagon. "You sir, are a good guy to have around."

"That was hellacious!" Hoyt grinned, shooting a glance at his wife. "Work as long as you can, son. Retirement's not all it's cracked up to be."

Quinn chuckled, rolling his shoulders to relieve the pain in his ribs as he nodded to the Hoyt's elbow. "You should probably have that looked at."

"Don't worry about him." Mrs. Hoyt gave a little good-natured scoff. "He'll be glowing about this for days," she said. "Best thing in the world for him, getting to mix it up with some bad guys. Makes him realize he's still relevant."

A white Alaska State Trooper SUV approached from the north carrying Ronnie Garcia in the passenger seat. Quinn could tell immediately from the frown on her face that something was terribly wrong.

"What is it?" Quinn said when she opened her door. "What's the—"

Half in, half out of the car, Ronnie waved Quinn over. "Jericho," she said. "You need to come hear this."

Chapter 3

Nome, Alaska, 3:52 ***P.M.***

Dr. Kostya Volodin inhaled the smell of popcorn and freedom as he left the windy tarmac along with the other eight passengers and entered through the metal doorway to the air-charter office. The buzz of people chattering in English made him feel heady as if he'd suddenly had a great weight lifted off his chest.

Dressed in a threadbare woolen blazer with patched sleeves and light wool traveling slacks that were half tucked in to ankle-high hiking boots, Volodin looked like the professor he had been and not the defector he had become. Gaunt and stooped, Volodin appeared to be much shorter than his six foot two inches. Numerous cowlicks caused his wiry head of gray hair to grow in all directions at once, leaving it in a perpetual state of bedhead.

Across the cavernous hanger, a smiling American Immigration and Customs official sat at a lone metal desk. Russians were accustomed to queuing up for bureaucrats so the other passengers who'd come across the Bering Sea with Volodin lined up without direction. Kaija stopped directly ahead of him, her head moving back and forth, birdlike. He could not blame her. This was her fist trip to America. There was a lot to take in.

At twenty years old, his dear daughter could pass for a much younger woman, but he would always think of her as a five-year-old with a skinned knee, before her mother had taken her away for all those excruciating years. The tail of her blue wool shirt hung to mid-thigh of her faded skinny jeans. Her sleeves were too long and frayed at the cuffs where they swallowed up her tiny hands. Red ankles were dry and chapped above thin canvas sneakers. He could have afforded more, but she would hardly accept a kopek from him.

Youthful lips trembled when she turned to look him in the eye, obviously frightened by something she'd seen. A black wool watch cap topped straw-blond hair that hung around narrow shoulders, framing a stricken oval face. A pair of white earbuds perpetually connected her to the music on her mobile phone, but even in her terror, she refused to remove both of them, leaving one in her ear and the other trailing down the side of her neck. She shook her head, mouth hanging open, the way she'd done when she was a small child. She'd borne the same expression the day her mother—Volodin's dear Maria—had died.

"What is the matter, *kroshka*?" Volodin whispered. He put a hand on her shoulder. She was trembling and it broke his heart.

Kaija cast a hurried glance toward the door.

He followed her gaze but saw nothing but a handful of Native people, all dressed in wool and fleece and fur. He saw a few men, but mostly there were smiling women with round bodies and Asian eyes sitting on shabby furniture next to boxes of diapers and cases of canned soda pop in the open bay of the charter office that served as a combination waiting and cargo area.

Fluorescent lights hummed in the high ceiling of the tin building, barely cutting through the thin fog of dust that rose into the chilly air.

"We are safe now, *kroshka,*" he said. "I will inform the Customs Inspector we mean to defect to the United States. He will escort us to the proper authorities. He will give us something to eat and warm clothes."

Kaija clenched her eyes as if she was about to scream. "They are here, Papa."

"Who?" Volodin shook his head, still holding the poor girl's trembling shoulder. "Who is here?"

Kaija brushed a lock of blond hair from her eyes and tucked it up under the wool cap. She'd not been one to worry much with her hair after her mother died the year before. Volodin wondered for a time if she'd even bothered to bathe.

Kaija glanced toward the front of the building again, past the rows of customers waiting for their small charter flights within Alaska.

"You do not see the men?" Her breath came in short, tremulous gasps. "Outside. They are waiting for us. I am sure of it. Colonel Rostov has wasted no time in finding you."

Volodin chanced a quick look at the door. The front window of the air charter building was covered in grime, but there were indeed two men outside, smoking cigarettes and chatting in the light swirl of blowing snow. The menace in their faces was all too evident. Of course they would be here, ordered to force him back—or kill him, which was the highest of all possible probabilities considering the man who sent them.

Volodin looked at the head of the line. There were now only six passengers between Kaija and the uniformed Immigration agent.

"Do not worry, my dear," Volodin whispered, leaning down and forcing a smile for his daughter. "This man will protect us."

"How can you be sure, Papa?" Kaija said. "Is it not possible he has been paid to detain us? He could at this very moment be in league with the men outside."

Volodin rubbed a tired hand across the stubble on his face. The girl was as wily and wise as her mother. She made a valid point. Americans were brought up to trust people in uniform. In Russia it was quite the opposite—and sadly, the Russian perspective was often the correct one. Anyone could be bought.

It was a Herculean effort to look nonchalant as he scanned the air-charter office for anyone who might be waiting to shoot him in the back of the head. A bullet to the back of the head—that's the way they'd done it in Mother Russia since the beginning of bullets. Considering the awful things he'd been a part of, a quick shot would be a merciful way to go. That time would come soon enough, but for now, he had to stay alive to take care of his daughter.

Volodin snugged the wool jacket tighter around his neck and used the tip of his finger to push a pair of thick, tortoiseshell glasses back on a large nose. He tilted his head, trying to get a better look out the window without being too obvious.

"You are right, Kaija," he whispered. "It is KGB." He kept his voice low in the unlikely event the Immigration officer was one of those rare Americans who spoke something other than English—or was indeed in league with the men waiting outside to shoot him in the head.

Kaija's already pale face fell ashen. "What did you say?"

"I said you are right, my child," Volodin said, working to control his breathing. He felt as if the entire world was leaning sideways, and he found it difficult to remain on his feet. He put a hand on Kaija's shoulder, more to steady himself than to comfort her. "The KGB. They have come for us. I have no idea how they arrived here so quickly."

Kaija's gaze dropped to her feet. The fear in her face had been chased way by a look of shame. Instead of someone in mortal danger, she'd become a child whose father made her uncomfortable.

"How is this not embarrassing to you?" She whispered, suddenly much less terrified of the men outside.

A fluttering twitch blossomed in Volodin's left eye. What was she saying? KGB thugs or not, he hated to embarrass Kaija.

He could see she was still upset but working to control herself. "I am sorry, Papa," she said. "But there is no more KGB."

Volodin groaned. *What had he said*? "Of course I know there is no KGB." His face flushed red at the foolish mistake. "I meant to say FSB." The runaway twitch forced Volodin to clench his eye shut. He removed his glasses, and rubbed it with his palm, willing the possessed thing to be still. "FSB . . . or more likely Army. Colonel Rostov's goons from GRU." He pronounced it *GuRoo*.

"What should we do?" Kaija said. Her emotions could change so quickly, from anger to embarrassment to an abject willingness to do whatever he said. Her mother had been just as mercurial.

"I suppose this was always a possibility." Volodin shoved a shock of gray hair out of his face and replaced his glasses. He glanced toward the front window again.

The taller of the two men waiting to capture or kill them held his cigarette pinched between his fingers the way few Americans would. The other, an older, stockier brute had a tattoo that peeked from the cuff of his tight, European leather jacket when he gestured at his partner, pointing with his own cigarette to make some point. Such tattoos and jackets were favored by members of Russian organized crime. Mafia thugs or government operatives—the titles were not mutually exclusive—the men seemed oblivious to the blowing snow, chatting with each other and conspicuously ignoring the arriving passengers.

Volodin looked up at the round clock above the gate agent for the fifth time in as many minutes. Bony knuckles on long and slender fingers turned white as he grabbed the rumpled canvas duffel and moved forward a few steps with the line.

Kaija had retreated to her music, but her eyes still flicked around the room, a frightened fawn, frozen, but looking for a way to run. She gave a small start when he put a hand on her shoulder again, slowing her long enough to let another Native woman and her two children move ahead of them in the line. His mind was suddenly foggy, and he needed a little time to figure out how not to get shot in the head.

Kaija toyed with the dangling earbud. "Please, tell me you have a plan."

"I know this must seem odd to you," Volodin said, keeping his voice low. "But understand, *króshka*, the colonel has eyes everywhere. It is not outside the realm of possibility that he has KGB assets already in Alaska."

"FSB, Papa," Kaija said, muscles in her cheeks tensing. A spark of impatience flared in her green eyes, then subsided.

"Yes, yes, yes . . . FSB," Volodin muttered. He tried to wave off the mistake but inwardly cursed himself for getting it wrong again. "That is what I mean."

Kaija took the remaining bud out of her ear and

stuffed the white cord in her pocket. "Do you think it is wise to trust this American agent?" Her nose turned up, clearing demonstrating that she did not.

Mind racing, Volodin looked around the hangar for any alternative. The professor knew he'd reached a point of no return. There was no flight back to Providenya. The die was cast, and he had crossed his Rubicon, his only choices now to move forward or perish.

His scientific brain, fevered and worried as it was, began to shuffle and sift through the possibilities, while his eyes dissected the architecture of the hangar. Kaija was maddeningly correct. It would be gambling everything to place his trust in the lone government agent seated at the table. The man was young, with honest eyes—but he also wore a ring, and with a ring there was the likelihood of a family—and with a family came responsibilities, which meant he would need money and might be ripe to accept a bribe to simply look the other way when two KGB . . . FSB operatives dragged away an old Russian scientist and his terrified daughter and stuffed them into the belly of a waiting airplane bound for Russia.

Volodin fought the urge to hyperventilate. Trusting a stranger at this point was far too dangerous. And still, they could not simply walk out the doors and into the waiting guns of Rostov's thugs.

Still scanning the room for a way out, he followed the line of the high ceiling to a set of washrooms located along the wall that divided the area where they now waited from the adjacent hanger he'd seen as they'd disembarked the airplane out on the tarmac.

He put a hand on his daughter's arm. Only one more person stood between them and the Customs official. Volodin gave a slight nod toward the far wall. Kaija followed his gaze. He did the math in his head to convert to Alaska Time—twenty hours ahead of Providenya. "It is almost 4:00 P.M. here," he said.

Kaija gazed up at him, eyes wide. The little girl waiting to be told what to do had returned.

"It will be a risk," Volodin continued, "but I believe it to be our only option. After we clear Immigration and Customs—"

A muffled gasp rose from the travelers crowded in with their bags around the ticket counter thirty feet away. Volodin looked up to see a Native woman carrying a baby throw a shocked hand over her mouth. All eyes in the room turned to a television mounted on the wall above the popcorn machine.

The news feed at the bottom of the screen said the shaky images were streaming live from Texas. Hundreds of people ran, trampling others, as those around them fell dead and dying from some unseen force—all amid the pageantry and waving flags at an American high school football game. News commentators stammered, trying to make sense of what they were seeing—but Volodin knew. His heart was a stone in his chest. This was his doing, his fault. He fought the urge to vomit.

Machinelike, he pushed his duffle bag forward with his foot and shoved his passport onto the simple wooden table. He doubted the Customs agent would make a scene in front of the other passengers, even if he were in league with the men outside. But the situation had suddenly changed with the awful scenes unfolding on the television. He and Kaija might make it past Colonel Rostov's thugs, but if the Americans ever discovered *Novo Archangelsk* was his creation, they would stop at nothing to find him. He'd been certain he destroyed it all. And yet he was obviously mistaken. A batch had gotten away from him. His mouth hung open as he watched the horrible footage on the screen. Only a very few people even knew of the existence of New Archangel gas. Fewer still had access to his lab—but one of them had smuggled some to America. Volodin closed his eyes as a cold reality washed over him. The real question was not how they had taken the New Archangel, but how much.

Chapter 4

Dallas, Texas, fifteen minutes earlier

The interview with Allen Lamar's high school teacher took less than twenty minutes—but it had scared the hell out of FBI Special Agent Joel Johnson.

Now, as he slammed the door to his forest green Dodge Durango and ran across the rapidly filling parking lot toward a packed football stadium, he wondered if five agents were going to be enough. The brassy blare of two high school bands greeted him on the crisp air of the Texas evening.

One of the two supervisors assigned to the Dallas Area Joint Terrorism Task Force, or JTTF, Special Agent Johnson had done time in Pakistan, Central America, and a couple of refugee camps in Europe. He'd seen enough despair, madness, and evil that he was not an easy man to scare. Social media would have everyone believe that armed terrorists were lurking behind every rock and tree—a fact of life that only made it difficult to root out the real threats. But the teacher who called in the tip wasn't some paranoid conspiracy theorist. Sixteen-year-old Allen Lamar appeared to be the real deal.

The teacher had recounted the cold hard facts of the boy's downward spiral, how she'd watched Lamar change from an introverted math genius with few friends to a popular thug, disdainful and threatening to everyone in the school who wasn't a member of his select group of acolytes. Allen's new friends called him Tariq Mohammed—and he made it clear that this was his *war name*.

Allen's teacher had seen this sort of behavior before—youth finding themselves, experimenting with boundaries and new sets of friends. She'd been ready to write the behaviors off as teenage angst—difficult to watch, but not out of the norm.

And then she'd found the manifesto. Her jittery principal, fearful of another "Clock Kid" scenario and the legal battles that went with it, was furious when she'd contacted the FBI directly instead of the boy's parents. Agent Johnson felt an overwhelming sense of foreboding when he'd read the letter. Peppered with the hateful regurgitated spewage of at least three well known Internet Imams who had close ties to the Islamic State, Lamar/Mohammed detailed, in his awkward handwriting, his fervent wish to kill as many infidels as possible.

The JTTF was comprised of representatives from federal, state, and local agencies and ordinarily capable of standing up a large surveillance operation at a moment's notice. But late afternoon on "Federal Friday," when agents tended to disappear early from the office, were problematic, even when stopping a suspected terrorist. Most of the agents, troopers, deputies, and detectives who made up the task force had families and all the attendant commitments that went along with them.

Countless high school kids followed the Hate-America

crap that slimed the feeds of a dozen social media sites. Standing up a rolling surveillance on one of them at the last minute seemed a futile waste of a weekend. It was all too easy for otherwise good people to become cynical under the constant barrage of reports regarding sleeper cells of bearded men, strange women wearing hijabs at Walmart, and radicalized teens about to ship off to join the Islamic State. Johnson was on constant guard to make sure the bona fide threats didn't get buried in the noise.

To make matters worse, Lamar was already on the move by the time the teacher called in with the tip, giving Johnson zero opportunity to brief his team—or put a real team together. It was like some unwinnable test scenario from the Bureau's supervisory selection process. Everything had to be done on the fly, utilizing agents who were available rather than those who were chosen for their superior abilities. Johnson had been lucky to find five warm bodies who would answer their cellphones.

Nearing the stadium, Johnson stepped from the asphalt parking lot to the concrete sidewalk that led to the long bank of ticket booths. He lived just five minutes away from this very field, but his boys were too young to play football so he'd never been inside. A pressing crowd teemed like thousands of salmon trying to swim up four narrow streams. Static crackled in the tiny, flesh-colored bud in Johnson's ear as he slowed with the crowd to funnel through the stadium gates. Hidden by shaggy blond hair, a clear plastic "pigtail" ran from the earbud and disappeared into the collar of the agent's black leather jacket and the neck of a burnt orange University of Texas sweatshirt. The shirt was a size too large but covered the Glock .40 on his hip should he need to loose the jacket. A voice-activated microphone, sensitive enough to pick up his mumbling curses, was pinned inside that same collar, also out of sight. This surveillance kit negated the need to go all Hollywood and lift a hand to his lips each time he needed to communicate or, worst of all, touch a finger to his ear. A cellphone would have been even less conspicuous, but encrypted radios allowed each member of the team to hear the conversation of all parties in real time.

"I got eyes on," Andrea Lopez said, sounding breathless and a little too eager over the radio. She was fresh meat, just four months on the job and still covered with the entire can of whoopass they poured on new agents before they left Quantico. Her training report noted that one of the male agents in her class had made the mistake of calling her Betty Bureau Blue Suit during defensive tactics training and earned himself an "accidental" elbow to the jaw. She could handle herself but she was a hair too aggressive for Johnson's taste. Blind aggression combined with inexperience was a good way to get hurt in this line of work.

"He's inside the ticket gate," Agent Lopez continued. "A second male just walked up to him. Olive skinned, wearing a red hoodie. I'm moving closer so I can try to identify him."

"Negative," Johnson snapped, drawing a wide eye from the blue-haired grandmother who happened to be walking next to him. He lowered his voice. "Just keep your distance for now."

"Welcome to the party, Joel," a second female said over the radio. This one was much calmer, more seasoned. At fifty, Angie James had recently become a grandmother while working undercover inside a violent splinter group of the Black Israelites in Harlem. Fifty was the new thirty, she often said, and where Angie James was concerned, Johnson was inclined to agree. It was she who had guessed Allen Lamar was going to a football game after he'd left his house. She'd been ahead of the game since Johnson had given her a thumbnail brief and made it to the stadium less than two minutes after the boy pulled up in his mom's Corolla.

"Our rabbit's walking toward the concession stand," James said. *Rabbit* might sound odd to anyone who overheard the conversation, but it was much less prone to inducing fear than *target*.

"Concessions under the grandstands?" Johnson's New York accent made him immediately identifiable to his team on the radio. He shoved a twenty-dollar bill under the glass at the ticket booth and shuffled impatiently while he waited for his change.

"That's negative, sir," Andrea Lopez stepped on Agent James as both women tried to broadcast at the same time, sending a garbled mess across the air.

"Talk to me, Angie," Johnson said, calling the agent he wanted by name, and at the same time shutting down the jittery Lopez. He used plain talk instead of radio codes, so the two guys from Dallas PD assigned to the JTTF who were already inside would be on the same sheet of music.

"West end of the field," Angie James came back. "Concession stand is a series of trailers, located just past where the band lines up to go through the gate at halftime."

"Copy that," Johnson said, falling in with a river of football fans streaming toward the bleachers on the home-team side.

The smell of popcorn and chili warmed the crisp Texas breeze. Parents, brothers and sisters, grandparents, church leaders, scoutmasters—all wearing jackets and sweaters of bright red, the color of the Fighting Rams of

Reavis, Texas. A larger-than-normal press gaggle milled along the track—four from local news affiliates and at least two from major cable networks. It seemed like a lot for a local high school football game, even in Texas.

Johnson stopped in his tracks, thinking, letting the current of red booster jackets flow around him. "Why are there so many cameras?" he asked over the radio, to no one in particular but expecting one of the DPD detectives to answer.

"It's an underdog story, boss," Lopez came back, breathless, like she'd been running . . . or was just excited at the prospect of tailing a bona fide terrorist. "Reavis High just got big enough to make AAAA status. This is their first year to compete with larger schools. It's getting them some real national attention."

The knot in Johnson's gut tightened. Huge crowds, nonexistent security, and media attention were just too juicy a venue for a radicalized teenager who appeared ripe to go over the edge.

A shorter, squarish man with dark hair shoved his way through the crowd and fell in next to Johnson. His tailored gray sports coat and black open collar shirt made him look like a New Jersey wise guy. Johnson felt a flood of relief. Special Agent Dave Gillette would make seven on the surveillance. It was almost getting doable.

"I thought your kid had a baseball game?" Johnson said, still processing the realities brought on by all the media attention.

Gillette raised dark eyebrows and scoffed. "It's T-ball, and he's not very good. I got your message a few minutes ago and then headed this way when I heard the radio traffic."

"Well, I'm glad you're here." Johnson resumed walking toward the concession stand. He didn't relax, but felt better. With Angie James and Dave Gillette they might actually make it through the evening.

Both former street cops—Gillette in Miami and Johnson with NYPD, they'd been assigned to NYFO—the New York Field Office—as their first duty station, then gone their separate ways before drawing the Dallas office by chance. Each of them had been promoted to supervisory agent but over different squads.

"What do you think?" Johnson said as they walked through the crowd.

"I think I could use a hot dog."

"I mean about the kid," Johnson frowned.

"I don't know." Gillette shrugged. "He's fresh, isn't he? Not likely to do something right away. Maybe he's just coming to meet some friends at a ballgame."

"What if we're the ones who are fresh?" Johnson said. "Maybe this kid's been under our radar for months blending in."

"Or maybe he's just a kid at a football game." Gillette rubbed his face. "I read your briefing notes. The teacher said he was a normal little socialist shithead until two months ago."

A line of Reavis High School cheerleaders, all red faced from the chilly evening air bounced and tumbled on the track in front of the band at the end of the grandstands nearest the gates. Young and pretty, their short uniforms allowed them to show a great deal of leg while still maintaining their apple-pie wholesomeness—the way only a high school cheerleader could. The Reavis High School band's section belted an explosive drum-and-horn challenge that carried across the field to the rival school.

"That gets the blood up," Johnson said nodding toward the band.

"*El Degüello*," Gillette said. "Santa Anna played it before he stormed the Alamo. Means '*Slit Throat*.'"

Johnson released a pent-up sigh. "Let's hope that's not Allen Lamar's theme music.

A line of twelve young women dressed in crisp white skirts and matching sequined cowboy hats twirled large flags in Reavis High colors, moving in perfect precision with the band. The drill team, blaring band, the smell of frying food in the air—it was like a county fair, about as American as a place could be.

Gillette ran a hand over his hair. "You think two months is long enough to radicalize a kid?"

Johnson scoffed, picking up his pace. "I think a shitty two-minute Islamic State video is enough to radicalize someone who already believes all this is an abomination." He shook his head. "Lopez, what's our guy up to?"

"Still at the concession stand, boss," the agent said. "He's getting nervous though. Keeps looking over his shoulder. Maybe he's looking for—"

She fell silent for a moment. Johnson froze midstep, half expecting the jittery Lopez to come back and say she'd been made.

"They're coming your way now," Robinson, one of the DPD detectives said at length. "Rabbit bought a can of potato chips and a Coke."

"See," Gillette said. "Told you he was just here to watch the ga—"

"Hold on a minute." Angie James came over the radio, tension putting a quiet hush on her voice. "The guy who sold Lamar the potato chips and Coke just came out of the concession trailer and joined them. Looks Middle Eastern, but I can't be sure from this vantage point."

"All three of them are walking east," Lopez said. "They're on the sidewalk between the bleachers and the fence that runs along the field."

"We're moving up too," Robinson said. "If you're coming toward concessions, we should all meet somewhere in the middle at the foot of the stands."

"Keep your distance until Gillette and I get there," Johnson said, the pit in his stomach growing deeper. He used his peripheral vision so as not to look at Lamar directly. Animals and humans alike were wired to notice if someone was looking directly at them. A tiny difference in the amount of white around the iris was enough to spook someone from a block away. "Maintain a loose tail. I've got them in sight. Lamar's in the middle in a white sweatshirt . . . passing two little kids playing catch."

"That's them," Angie James said. "Hang on . . . Are you seeing that?"

"I am," Johnson said, breaking into a trot. Lamar was still a good fifty yards away.

The two other youths fanned out, one on either side of Allen Lamar, backs against the fence, facing the bleachers—as if preparing to protect him.

There came a time to bring people in—before they had a chance to shoot up a football game. Johnson intended to do just that until a crowd of Reavis High School alumni came stomping down the stadium stairs to stop directly in his path. The announcer had everyone stand for the National Anthem—completely blocking any view of Allen Lamar and his two friends. "Can you see him?" Johnson snapped, clenching his teeth to keep from shouting.

"Nope," Gillette said, shouldering his way through the crowd.

"He's just standing there, Joel," Angie James said. "All three of them appear to be looking at the flags."

"For the Anthem?" Gillette said. "That doesn't sound like a terrorist."

"I don't mean the American flag," Angie James said. "The drill team flags—like they're checking wind direction and speed. I don't like it, Joel. That's something I would do before I took a shot."

"Converge," Johnson said, knocking a bleached-blond Reavis alumni into the fence. "Everyone move in." He made it to within fifty feet of Allen Lamar before the boy opened the cardboard cylinder that looked like a potato chip tube and dropped in the soda can like a mortar shell. White foam began to bubble over the top of the cylinder, like an open soda can after it had been shaken.

Red and white drill-team flags fluttered behind the boy, snapping in a gentle Texas breeze that blew directly toward the grandstands.

Chapter 5

Khabarovsk, Russia

Legs crossed at his desk, Rostov held the phone to his ear with his left hand and listened. Interrupting the general during one of his tirades was a good way to get shot. With his right hand, the colonel used the stub of a black pencil to compile a list of people he wanted to strangle. Judging from General Zhestakova's tone, he had his own list of such names—and Rostov was on it.

The Chairman of the *Glavnoye razvedyvatel'noye upravleniye or* GRU, Russia's Main Intelligence Directorate, Zhestakova wielded immense power. He had the direct ear of the President and, more important, the collective backing of those generals who provided the presidential muscle. Nicknamed Koschei the Deathless, after the fairytale king who rode naked on horseback through the countryside stealing peasant girls, Zhestakova was also a difficult man to kill.

As a junior officer with the elite Special Forces Alpha Group, Zhestakova had at first been allied with hardliners during the *Avgustovsky Putch* to oust Mikhail Gorbachev. At the last moment, his boss had switched to the winning side, refusing along with other Alpha and Vympel commanders to move against the Soviet White House as had been planned. The coup failed, and Zhestokova won promotion over prison.

He had enjoyed a noteworthy and even prosperous career since that time, always seeming to be on the winning side, if not necessarily the right one. He made it very clear that his fortunes would not be the only ones to change should the situation with Novo Archangelsk not resolve immediately.

"Do you not see the magnitude here?" Zhestakova asked. It was his first actual question in five minutes, and Rostov paused to make certain it was not rhetorical.

Judging Zhestakova's pause long enough to warrant a reply, Rostov decided to reply, but carefully. "I do understand, General," he said. "The American's are touchy. If they were to link the Novo Archangelsk attacks to Russia—"

"And therein lies my point," Zhestakova said, his voice breathless as if he were running in place while he talked. "The President is about to give the preparatory command for Full Combat Readiness."

Rostov held his breath. Full Combat Readiness was equivalent to what the American's called DefCon 2—with forces from all branches prepared to mobilize at a moment's notice. The president did it periodically. A trigger-happy Turkish government, an overly independent Ukraine—there had been many reasons for the elevation in operational tempo. But, such escalation came with a price, invariably rattling neighbors who wondered about hidden intentions.

"The Americans will ask questions," he said, regretting his words immediately.

"Are you suggesting that we not protect ourselves?" Zhestakova said. Then, calming some, "We will blame our escalation on preparation for similar terror attacks."

"Which is plausible," Rostov said, showing that he was in full agreement. "U.S. sources say the perpetrator in Texas was an Islamist. Russia is also a target—"

"Which brings to mind several other questions the President would like you to answer." Zhestakova cut him off.

"A question for me personally?"

"Indeed." Zhestakova gave a quiet chuckle, as if were watching an old enemy roast on a spit. "The questions are for you personally, Colonel Rostov."

The fact that the President would speak of him directly made Rostov's head throb. At times of crisis, anonymity was far better than heroism.

"For instance, how did Novo Archangelsk end up in the hands of Islamists?" Zhestakova said. The sound of shuffling papers came across the line, then the tap of a computer keyboard. "And who do you have in command in Providenya?"

"Captain Evgeni Lodygin, sir."

"That little shit," Zhestakova said. "Was he not sent to Providenya because of some unpleasantness with a subordinate's teenage daughter?"

"That is true," Rostov said. "I have found him odd enough, but extremely competent and trustworthy."

"Yes, quite," Zhestakova said. Rostov could almost hear the saliva dripping off Zhestakova's teeth as he dragged out the word. "Until one of our top scientists defected and a secret nerve agent turned up in the hands of terrorists under his watch."

Rostov knew any indictment of Lodygin was an indictment against him as the commanding officer of the entire Novo Archangelsk project. "I assure you, sir," he said, "trusted operatives are even now about to return Dr. Volodin. I, myself, leave within the hour for Providenya to oversee a thorough investigation of everyone with access to the laboratory."

"Including Evgeni Lodygin?" Zhestakova said. "An investigation takes time . . ." He was breathless again, sounding like Rostov had imagined Koschei the Deathless when he was a small boy. "It might interest you to know that the President and I often find the simplest solution is often a bullet to the back of the head."

"Of course, General," Rostov said, dropping his pencil.

"Do you know how they did it, Ruslan, back in the Soviet days?" The general had never before addressed Rostov by his given name and to hear it spoken in that breathless hiss made it difficult for Rostov to swallow. Of course he knew how they did it. He'd done it himself.

Zhestakova told him anyway. The words brought a flood of memories that Rostov had worked very hard to suppress, particularly after the birth of his daughter.

"It begins with a surprise visit from a superior," the general said. "A quiet walk down a dead-end hallway—and an unexpected bullet. Many progressives view the practice as barbaric, but I have always thought it kind—a tender mercy—quick and without the unseemly snot and fear on the part of the condemned. But then, I have always tried to be kind in my dealings with subordinates. Have I not, Colonel?"

"Yes, General," Rostov managed to reply. He wondered if the reference to the bullet in the head was a suggestion on how he should proceed or a thinly veiled threat. In the end, he knew it was both.

Chapter 6

Dallas

Special Agent Joel Johnson was fifteen yards out when Allen Lamar dropped to his knees, still clutching the cardboard tube the FBI agents had mistakenly thought was a can of potato chips. The boy pointed the canister toward the crowd like a mortar tube. Even from that distance, Special Agent Johnson had a clear view of Lamar's face. His eyes had gone glassy, looking past the crowd in an unfocused, thousand-yard stare.

Agent Johnson's breath caught like a stone in his throat as he watched the foam pour over the lip of the container in a seemingly endless flow. For the first time, he realized Allen Lamar was wearing latex gloves.

Gillette moved left toward the bleachers, vaulting a short fence to get a shot at Lamar without the stadium behind him. This new angle gave him a better target but put him downwind from the foam. He fell before he could raise his sidearm, knees slamming against the concrete walk, before pitching face-first into the fence he'd just jumped. His contorted face pressed against the chain links.

"Stay back!" Johnson shouted to the rest of his team as he himself rushed forward. His heart told him to rush toward his friend and save him, but his instinct told him he had to stop the threat.

Four seconds after Allen Lamar activated the cardboard tube an elderly man in the first row of bleachers began to laugh uncontrollably. A child of five or six seated next to him dropped a bag of popcorn and stared transfixed before throwing up and toppling sideways. Spectators all around the laughing man tried to get to their feet and put some distance between themselves and the vomit. Other bodily fluids were spreading among the crowd like a fast burning fire. Unable to control their muscles, those affected fell like ragdolls on the people below them. Some became hysterically angry, tearing at their clothing and screaming nonsensical threats into the night air. Eyes grew bloodshot in an instant. Mucous streamed from noses.

Muscles began to spasm, causing people to arch violently backward, throwing them down in a human blossom as if a powerful wind had been aimed directly at the grandstand. Allen Lamar and his two compatriots fell moments later, overcome by their proximity to the fumes pouring out of Lamar's canister. The invisible cloud moved on the breeze, felling everyone it touched.

Spectators began to stampede, back pedaling away from their dying neighbors, yanking at spouses in a frantic effort to get ahead of the unseen monster attacking the stadium. Terrified parents grabbed their younger children and fled, slipping on the vomit of the person next to them, clutching their throats as they ran. The band fell silent and the air was filled with mournful wailing and the pounding of feet on aluminum stadium seats.

His back to the wind and still a dozen yards away

from Lamar, Johnson pulled up short. He caught sight of Andrea Lopez running directly toward him. Of course she would be the one who disobeyed his order. She had an ass-magnet that pulled her toward danger with the gravity of ten thousand suns.

A father and his teenage son stumbled directly in front of her, and then fell headlong into the paved walkway. Lopez hit the invisible cloud at a sprint, chest heaving, drawing in a lungful of whatever deadly stuff this was. Her legs gave out as if she'd been hit in the head with an iron bar. Forward momentum carried her skidding across the concrete nose first. Her hands dangled at her sides on useless arms. Legs writhing, she struggled, trying in vain to rise.

Johnson slammed the top of the chain link fence with both hands, fighting the urge to rush in. It was much too late to save her—and there were hundreds more lives to consider. Instead, he vaulted over the fence and onto the track that surrounded the football field—pushing dumbstruck cheerleaders and the flag-waving drill team back farther, into the wind.

Angie James's voice crackled across the radio. "Lopez is down—"

"Stay back, Angie!" Johnson screamed, for the benefit of his agents as well as all those around him. "Everyone stay back! This is gas! Repeat. We're dealing with poison gas!"

The press gaggle, there to do a story on a state football championship, smelled something much more tempting in the carnage. The reporter's mantra, "If it bleeds, it leads," drew them toward the danger as surely as it had poor Lopez. One of them, a balding guy with a hefty belly, rushed past Johnson in the melee to get a closer look. His camera fell from his grasp moments later as he sagged to his knees, clutching his chest and staring at the night sky in shock. A group of four other cameramen watched him fall and skidded to a stop, deciding it was best to keep their distance.

"Are you getting this?" Johnson heard a female reporter ask one of the photographers.

"Oh, hell yeah," the cameraman said, the giddiness in his voice belying the carnage spilling across the field. "We're live."

The death blossom grew as the invisible poison moved through the grandstands, felling everyone it touched.

Johnson looked back and forth, wracking his brain for some kind of plan. Well over a hundred killed by an unseen and apparently unstoppable force, their horrific deaths streamed on live television.

It was the stuff of terrorists' dreams.

All the girls on the drill team but one dropped their flags and fled to the far side of the field. The remaining girl stood frozen in place, eyes glazed at the sight of so much death—the false maturity of high school draining away to expose the face of a frightened little child.

Her flag popped and waved in the breeze, folding in on itself as the wind shifted—to blow back toward the field.

In the stands, spectators broke in a full stampede, pushing and shoving, jumping over the dead and dying, trampling the small and weak, anything to escape—anything to live. A referee, not two steps away from Johnson, fell where he stood, laughing hysterically and ripping away his striped shirt. Beyond the ref, the Reavis High student dressed as the red-and-white ram mascot swayed on his feet before toppling at the sidelines. The gigantic horned head rolled off to reveal a shock of blond hair and the stricken face of a young man.

Johnson's hands tightened reflexively into fists. A

heated knot seethed low in his belly. For a fleeting instant, he wondered if it was the poison gas or anger. He decided he didn't care. Taking three quick breaths, he ran for the horned head of the ram mascot, jumping the lifeless body of the referee on the way. Holding his breath, he scooped up the hollow costume head and carried it toward the cardboard canister that still foamed and spewed its deadly contents into the air from the grass beside the arched body of Allen Lamar. Johnson did his best to approach from upwind, and dropped the giant ram head over the canister like a lid in an effort to contain the gas. He thought it worked until he noticed the cartoonish screen mouth the mascot used to see through. Exertion and adrenaline worked to deplete his body of oxygen. His lungs screamed for air.

With no clear vision of what the threat actually was or where it was coming from, people ran in every direction. Some even stampeding across the field, street shoes slipping in the fresh grass, floundering to their feet and running on. Some were in a panic, hoping only to save themselves. In others, humanity bloomed, and they risked their lives to aid those falling victim around them. One of every two who got within fifteen feet of the spewing canister fell in their tracks, even now that it was covered with the costume ram head.

A half second before his lungs convulsed and forced him to draw a breath, Johnson stripped off his leather jacket and draped it over the mascot, plugging the screened opening.

The muscles in the agent's back tensed as soon as he breathed, yanking his head back as if some unseen hand grabbed a handful of his hair. A searing pain ran like an electric current up both sides of his spine—a Taser jolt that didn't abate. He fell backward, balanced for a long moment on his heels and the back of his head, his eyes wide and staring up at the stadium lights. The muscles in one side of his back overpowered the other, convulsing even harder so he fell sideways. He struggled to regain his balance, to push himself up, but there was nothing there. It was as if something had been scrambled between his brain and the muscles he wished to control. The tension in his back grew until he thought his bones would crack, but the pain eased, and he suddenly felt the uncontrollable urge to laugh. He lay on his side now, the cool grass of the football field pressed against his cheek. From the corner of his eye, he could just make out Andrea James directing people away from the overturned costume head. She must have seen him cover it and knew the threat was there. Johnson tried to close his eyes, but even the muscles in his face rebelled, drawing back into a grimace that he was sure looked like a terrifying grin. His chest heaved as if crushed by an unseen weight. Spasming lungs made him begin to giggle uncontrollably, even as a single tear escaped his eye and ran down his stricken cheek and into the trampled grass of the football field.

Twenty yards upwind, a slender brunette woman wearing a red fleece jacket and matching hat used two fingers on the screen of her phone to zoom in on the picture of the downed FBI agent. "This is gold," she said to the cameraman beside her. "Tell me you're getting this . . ."

Chapter 7

Alaska

Quinn brought up a live stream from Dallas on his phone while he listened to the breaking news on the Hoyt's truck radio. He'd spent enough time in Iraq to know the devastating effects of poison gas when he saw them.

An Alaska State trooper and three uniformed officers and a handful of detectives and brass from Anchorage PD rolled up but let the cop shooters sit handcuffed on the side of the road. Everyone stood in the shadow of the mountains alongside the Seward Highway, glued to their phones as the news of the terrorist attack unfolded.

Seeing enough, Quinn checked for traffic and trotted across the two-lane, pressing #2 on his speed dial as he slid his way down the gravel ledge on the other side of the highway. He came to a stop beside a set of railroad tracks that ran on a raised gravel bed between the highway and the ocean. The metal rails provided a convenient and relatively indestructible target for the toe of his riding boot and he kicked at them repeatedly while he waited for his phone call to jump through the series of towers, switches, and cables that would connect him to the White House. Ronnie Garcia followed, surfing down the incline on the loose gravel, one foot in front of the other to come to a stop beside him. Turning her head just right for the afternoon light to catch it, she gazed out across the frothy chocolate waters of Turnagain Arm.

"No answer," Quinn said, looking at Garcia. A stiff sea breeze blew a thick strand of ebony hair across a deeply bronzed cheek. She didn't bother to move it. If he'd had time, he would have told her how incredible she was standing in the wind wearing full motorcycle leathers.

Garcia shrugged, wonderfully oblivious to her own beauty. "Probably that whole National Security Advisor thing. I'm sure he's busy."

Quinn kicked harder at the rails and ended the call, redialing immediately.

This time, a female voice answered on the first ring. It was Emiko Miyagi, Quinn's martial arts teacher and friend. The mysterious Japanese woman also happened to be Winfield Palmer's right hand. The two were as close as people could be without being romantically involved. They'd even had that for a time, when they were younger, until Miyagi had decided Palmer knew far too much about her past.

Quinn was surprised to hear her voice. She'd been out of the country, trying to locate her daughter—and it had not been going so well.

"Quinn san," she said. Miyagi was normally curt, wasting little time on pleasantries, but now she seemed strained. Quinn chalked it up to the futile search for her assassin daughter. "He is on another line at the moment. May I take a message?"

A message? Quinn shook his head in disbelief. This

was a first. When Quinn needed briefing on something important, Miyagi was, more often than not, the one who read him in. They'd been through far too much for her to shut him out with the *we'll get back to you* line.

"I'll hold," he said.

Winfield Palmer must have snatched the phone away because he came on the line a half moment later.

"Quinn," he said, his voice a detached whisper. "I'm not sure if you're watching the news, but we're in the middle of something here."

"That's exactly why I'm calling, sir," Quinn said. As much as he respected Palmer, he couldn't remember a time in the three years they'd known each other that either man had called the other just to chat.

"I have your latest physical pulled up on screen right now," Palmer said. "You're barely even cleared for light duty."

"I'm fine," Quinn said. "And more than willing to take the risk."

"This isn't about you," Palmer said. "I can't run the risk of letting one of these bastards slip away because you're not completely healed from your last endeavor. Don't forget, you're not our only asset. Now take the time to heal, and let me get back to work. That's an order."

"Boss," Quinn said, coming as close to pleading as he ever had in his life. "I know my capabilities, and I am fine. Honestly. Let me help."

"And how about Garcia?" Palmer asked. "She was still in a sling when I saw her a month ago. Are you telling me she's good to go?"

"That's a difficult issue, sir," Quinn said, deadpan. He reached to stroke Garcia's hair, knowing she might never let him touch her again when she found out what he was doing.

"Is she with you right now?"

"That would be correct," Quinn said, still forcing the smile. He pressed the phone to his ear to make certain none of Palmer's gruff voice spilled out for Garcia to hear.

"I'll make this easy for you then," Palmer said. "Yes or no? Has she healed enough to go back to work?"

"I don't believe so, sir," Quinn said. He sighed, watching Garcia absentmindedly massage her injured shoulder. She'd unzipped her riding jacket midway down her chest, making it difficult for Quinn to concentrate. The rich black leather was a perfect contrast to her deep coffee-and-cream complexion.

"But you're good to go?"

"I'm afraid so," Quinn said.

"Well, hell," Palmer said. "Let me talk to her then."

Quinn held his breath as he passed Garcia the cellphone. He could only hear Garcia's end of the conversation, but that half told him it was Palmer, and he was in serious trouble.

"I'm fine, sir," Garcia said. "Thank you for asking . . . No, sir, still some soreness, but I am definitely fit and ready to work . . . Quinn? No, he's in good shape. I would not hesitate for a minute to put him in . . ." She gave Quinn a grinning thumbs-up. "Okay, sir."

She handed the phone back to Quinn.

"Pack a bag," Palmer said.

"Where to?"

"Still trying to figure that out," Palmer said. "You interested to hear what your partner said about your fitness for duty?"

"I heard it all, sir," Quinn said, feeling gutted.

"I'll call you back with more news when I have it. The President wants to brief the nation within the hour."

That's fast, Quinn thought, but didn't say it.

"We have damn little actionable intelligence as of yet," Palmer said, as if reading Quinn's mind, "but POTUS feels the American people need to know he's ready to act the moment we have anything to go on. The markets are going to tank when the opening bell rings tomorrow, and he wants to do something to keep them from hitting bottom."

Quinn nodded, thinking that through. Terrorists committed violence in order to destabilize nations—to tear the underpinnings out of a culture they didn't agree with. President Ricks had vowed not to let that happen on his watch. A retired Navy Admiral, former SEAL, and recent Chairman of the Joint Chiefs, Ricks struck Quinn as a man who knew where the keys to the Tomahawks were located and wasn't afraid to use them. He'd taken the reins from the disgraced former president Hartman Drake in what had amounted to a necessary coup just months before, vowing to lead the American people with a reasoned but firm hand until the next election. Ricks had no ambitions when it came to politics—which made it much easier for him choose to do what was necessary rather than just politically prudent.

Quinn had met the new president only once since he'd taken office. He was tall and gave the impression of a man in uniform even when wearing a business suit. The ribbons and medals of his combat experience on land and sea were etched in the creases of his face and the gleam of his eye. The new president had stood from behind his desk in the Oval Office at that first meeting, extending his hand to Quinn and looking him up and down as he nodded in approval. "So," he'd said. "This is my star henchman."

Quinn liked him from the start. He'd never considered himself a henchman, but, he supposed, it was an apt description depending on your point of view. In fact, Quinn didn't really care what anyone called him so long as he was henching for the right side.

Palmer's patrician voice yanked him back to the present. The national security advisor liked to hear a certain amount of feedback when he talked on the phone, even if it was nothing more than a grunt. Quinn had been listening silently for too long.

"Hello?"

"I'm still here, sir," Quinn said.

"I'm sure I don't have to tell you this," Palmer said, "but we are in a shit storm of unknown dimensions here. I'll get back with you shortly."

Garcia worked to put on her helmet, wincing from the pain brought on by the angle of her shoulder. At first she slapped Quinn's hand away, like a child wanting to zip her own coat, then grudgingly accepted his help. "What did he say?" she asked as he fastened her chinstrap.

"He said to pack." Quinn slid the phone in his pocket and climbed aboard the BMW. He wracked his brain for an easy way to tell Garcia he'd thrown her under the bus just moments before she'd lied through her teeth to say he was okay. He planted his feet in the loose gravel and waited for Ronnie to climb on behind him—harder now with her bum shoulder.

"You sure know how to show a girl a good time," she said, clenching her teeth to try and hide the fact that she was in pain.

"Are you going to have trouble hanging on?"

Garcia recoiled at the sympathy. "You just ride the bike. I'll be fine."

Quinn nodded. "We've still got dinner in a couple of hours at Marx Brothers.

"Seriously?" Garcia said. "I thought we had to pack?"

"We also have to eat." Quinn shrugged.

She leaned forward as if to put her arms around him, then sat back suddenly, flipping the visor on her helmet. "Wait a minute," she said. "He's not calling me in, is he?"

Quinn shrugged. "I'm not sure." Lie number three.

He pressed the start button, feeling the big Beemer's familiar sideways torque as he revved the engine.

"Good to go?" He checked in one last time via the intercom, hoping for some sense of understanding.

"I told you I'm fine," she snapped, in a voice that said she was anything but.

Quinn groaned. He'd planned this day to perfection. The gorgeous ride down his favorite mountain highway, a dance recital with his daughter, and a date with Garcia to a five-star dinner at his favorite Anchorage restaurant. But the ride had been cut short by the arrest of the cop shooter, and Quinn had ended up begging his boss to bring him in like some kid asking to join a ballgame. And now he had to make the hour ride back to Anchorage wearing a very angry woman like a backpack.

Chapter 8

Providenya, Russia, 2:21 p.m.

Where American military aircraft were refined pieces of sleek equipment, they were also finicky and prone to sucking up runway debris. Russian military aircraft were engineered like tractors, capable of operating in the most austere of battlefield conditions—like the Providenya airstrip.

A steady rain pounded the drab gray buildings of the old MIG base by the time the Su 35 carrying Colonel Ruslan Rostov rolled to a stop over the gravel and decaying concrete of the Providenya military airstrip. The landing was timed to fall in between American satellite passes and across the bay from the village so as to be out of the way of prying eyes. The two-seat "trainer" version of the Sukhoi allowed Rostov to make the trip from his office in Khabarovsk to Providenya in just over two hours. The dart-like fighter jet could have traveled faster, but for the two additional external fuel tanks required to make the 3500-kilometer journey.

Captain Lodygin waited at the edge of the runway in an ancient black ZiL sedan, made clean and shiny by the rain. He emerged from the car wearing a gas mask and handed one to Rostov as soon as his feet touched the ground from the small boarding ladder. The colonel slipped it on over his head, feeling foolish since the pilot went about the business of fueling without one.

"Is this still necessary," he said, glaring through the foggy lenses at Lodygin. "Has not the rain cleared the air?"

The captain shrugged. "Perhaps, perhaps not," he said. "But the winds are notoriously unpredictable here between the mountains and the sea. Who knows what has happened to the residual gas . . ."

Rostov pulled the elastic strap tight behind his bald head.

"I assume you've heard about the attacks," the captain said.

"Attacks?" The colonel sank into the tired leather of the ZiL's rear seat and shut the door.

Lodygin made his way around the sedan and got in beside the colonel. His voice was hollow as it passed through the filter of the mask, like a science-fiction movie villain. It was impossible to tell behind the filter and rubber seal, but it looked as though the man was grinning. "The second attack was in Los Angeles—also on live television. Hundreds are dead from an unknown nerve agent. The way it moved so effectively through the crowds, it has to be Novo Archangelsk."

"So it is beginning to surface . . ." Rostov had been shouting so much over the last two hours that he could muster little more than a croak. "Volodin must have put it on the market for sale to the highest bidder."

"Someone has," Lodygin said. "The formula for Novo Archangelsk is unknown to the Americans. Perhaps—"

"It *was* unknown to the Americans," Rostov said,

letting his head fall back against the headrest of his seat. "It will not take them long to analyze samples in the lungs and tissue of the victims. Do the Americans have a suspect?" Rostov asked.

Lodygin's shrug was almost lost on his narrow shoulders. "Another high school student they believe to have been radicalized by Muslim extremists, much like the attack in Texas."

"More damned jihadists!" Rostov pounded the armrest. He could picture General Zhestakova inviting him on a walk—down a dead-end hallway.

Lodygin interrupted the terrifying thought. "Perhaps these attacks will buy us some time to find Volodin while the Americans lick their wounds."

Rostov scoffed. "Americans are not known for sitting back while they lick their wounds. They will be hungry to punish someone—and if they find the New Archangel leads back to Russia . . ." He shook his head, unwilling to even speak the thought. He looked at the driver, a young soldier who also wore a gas mask. "Take us directly to the laboratory."

Lodygin's eyes flicked back and forth, buglike behind the lenses of the mask as they rode together in silence. It occurred to Rostov that Volodin was not the only one capable of selling this new nerve gas to the highest bidder.

Still wearing the mask out of precaution, Rostov stalked toward Dr. Volodin's office the way he went everywhere, leaning slightly forward at the waist, bald head pointed bulletlike at his intended target, steel-blue eyes slicing their way through everything in their path. The sociopath Lodygin's heels clicked on the polished tile floor as he scrambled up from behind to step deftly around and give a discreet flick of his fingers. He motioned the guard to unlock the door to Volodin's study. In point of fact, Rostov would have been put out had the Captain not stepped up in such a way.

The private leaned in just enough to turn the knob before snapping to in a hasty salute.

"As you were," Rostov said over his shoulder, leaving Lodygin to shut the door behind him. The captain was four inches shorter than Rostov's two meters. Hunched and narrow shoulders made him look smaller and caused his uniform tunic to sag in the center of his chest creating a loose pocket Rostov was surely big enough to hide a small cat. A flap of black hair was plastered across the man's pallid forehead as if he'd never seen a photograph of Hitler. Rostov could not help but think there was a need for greasy instruments like Captain Lodygin, so long as they were kept in a different box and weren't allowed to sully the other tools.

"Dr. Volodin is not very tidy for a brilliant scientist," Rostov noted, standing just inside the door and letting his eyes play around the room. The office was a mirror of the man, furnished with a fine leather couch and a desk of rich mahogany—both covered with a thin patina of the glacial dust that seemed to coat everything in eastern Siberia. Microscopes, gas burners, and glassware of every shape and size occupied a row of metal tables running down the center of room. Several dark circles discolored the tile below the tables indicating mishaps with chemicals or even small fires. Computers and other scientific instruments both large and small occupied various stations along the sidewall opposite the mahogany desk, which seemed more fitting for a world leader than a cloistered chemist.

Three orange suits of thick rubber hung like skinned beasts on pegs along the far wall. Beside the suits, situated at waist height, ran a long window of reinforced glass looking into the pressure-sealed work lab complete with rows of stainless steel rabbit cages. But for all the cutting-edge scientific equipment, the most prominent fixtures in the room were the piles and piles of paper, some starting on the tile floor and reaching Rostov's waist. One instrument that resembled a microwave had become home to a frayed stack of folders held together with several fat rubber bands. Volodin's scrawled handwriting covered every scrap of paper in mathematical equations and drawings of chemical compounds. Oddly, a stack of neatly rolled woolen socks was stacked in the metal in-basket atop the doctor's desk. A wicker laundry hamper sat off the end of the desk stacked with printouts of time sensitive e-mails and other important correspondence.

Rostov had been to the lab before and seen firsthand the scientist's unorthodox and erratic behaviors.

"There is an extremely fine line between brilliance and madness," he said, more to the stacks of paper than to Lodygin.

"A necessary risk, I suppose," the captain said.

"I don't remember it being this bad," Rostov said, turning to shoot an accusatory look at Lodygin. This had, after all, occurred on his watch. "How long has he been living like this?"

Lodygin shrugged, affecting the narrow-eyed, deadpan drawl that made Rostov want to put a bullet in the back of his head. "To one degree or another . . . since well before I arrived, to be sure. The man's methods are odd, there is no disputing that, but lately it has been difficult to tell where his mind is. But his methods produce results."

"I'll give you that," Rostov nodded, beginning to pick through the piles of paper. "In a war, results are all that matters, I suppose . . ." He spun to face Lodygin. "But there are no results now that you have let him sell or destroy the entire supply of the gas!"

"There are other scientists in Russia," Lodygin said, still unaware of how close he was to a concrete floor and a killing chair. "Might we not find someone else to decipher the doctor's notes and manufacture more of the New Archangel without him?"

"Tread lightly there," Rostov said, as he took a seat in Volodin's chair and began to go through desk drawers. "The fewer people that know of this debacle the better. I am quite certain that I will be called back to Moscow at any moment."

He flipped through the contents of the lap drawer, which consisted mainly of foil gum wrappers and broken pencils, preferring to think rather than speak any further to Lodygin. The man's voice was like some toxic resin on his ears and it made him physically ill to listen to it for long. Or perhaps, Rostov thought, he was ill because he knew what his reception would be should he not have any answers before General Zhestakova summoned him to Moscow.

There were many in the Kremlin who had supported his idea to develop New Archangel—but in the end, all they would remember is that Rostov was in charge, and that he had failed.

The failure had not come because the gas was used against the United States. That had always been the idea. Even the use of cut outs in the form of radical Islamists had been discussed at length—on the right timetable, with the necessary backstops in place to keep blame from falling into Russia's lap.

Captain Lodygin's sullen voice pulled Rostov back

to the present circumstance. "I'm certain there are other chemists who would do the job quietly . . . with the right . . . incentives." The man spoke as if he relished the thought of applying said incentives, the more heavy-handed and cruel the better. "Do you wish me to begin at once?"

Rostov ignored him, removing a stack of shipping labels from the lap drawer, and ran a thick finger down the pages as he read the carbon copies of previous labels, ignoring Captain Lodygin. "This is interesting," he said. "Volodin has been making shipments of what he labels "Vitamin supplements" to someone named Petyr Volodin in New York City."

"A brother?"

Rostov shook his head, perusing the slips. "His son." The consummate scientist, Dr. Volodin had even kept notes on his correspondence. *Shipped eight canisters BGH to Petyr*, the latest entry noted. Rostov flipped through the pages of the journal until he found another entry where Volodin had written out *Binary Growth Hormone*, rather than BGH.

Lodygin held up his mobile phone to show the Internet search image of a shirtless, muscular man with spiked black hair. He had a tattoo of a grinning skull on his belly and an eight-pointed star on the front of each shoulder, just above his chest.

The captain released a poisonous sigh. Rostov couldn't help but wish he'd put the gas mask back on to hide his hideous grin. "Petyr Volodin is a marginally successful cage fighter who trains at a gym in Brighton Beach." Lodygin sneered. "Apparently, he calls himself Petyr the Wolf."

"He is *Vory*." Rostov nodded at the star tattoos. "Those must be from time spent in a Russian prison,"

"It would seem so," Lodygin said.

Rostov mulled this over. If the Bratva—the Russian Mafia—were involved in the theft of New Archangel, there was a chance the burden of blame would fall somewhere else. Rostov might actually be on the other end of the gun during that long walk down the dead-end hallway.

He glanced up at Lodygin.

"Brighton Beach, you say?"

The captain licked his lips as he perused the Internet information regarding Volodin's son. "Yes. In New York City."

Rostov thrummed his fingers against the counter, thinking of ways he might avoid a bullet. "We must send someone to visit this Petyr the Wolf."

Chapter 9

Anchorage, 5:30 p.m.

There were countless times when Quinn and Garcia had been supremely content to sit together and say nothing at all. This was not one of those times. Thankfully, Quinn's daughter jabbered away nonstop all the way to the dance recital in the backseat of the crew cab GMC Quinn had borrowed from his mother.

Outside the pickup, gray clouds loomed lower and darker than they had during the earlier motorcycle ride—threatening an all-out storm, just like Garcia's demeanor.

Mattie had just finished telling them about a new boy from school named Zane who only ate peanut butter sandwiches, when they pulled up in front of his parents' house. The story made Quinn wonder what kind of a father he'd be when she started dating. Luckily for the boys who were sure to fall in love with her, he probably wouldn't live that long.

The front door opened as soon as they drove up. Kim walked out, making her way toward the driver's side of the pickup, waving serenely at Jericho. She wore a zippered white hoodie jacket, open at the front despite the evening chill and threat of rain. Her blue

Alaska Grown T-shirt was tight enough to show off her trim figure. Gray capris revealed the metal works of a high-tech prosthetic leg fitted to her above-the-knee amputation. The sniper who had shot her was dead, her neck broken by Quinn in Japan, but that didn't excuse him from being the reason that sniper had come after Kim in the first place. Still, enough time had passed that Kim appeared to have forgiven him, or at the very least, nacred over any anger she still harbored like a pearl formed over a nasty irritation.

Mattie unsnapped her seatbelt and leaned in between the bucket seats. Deep brown curls fell across her face as she look back and forth between Quinn and Garcia. But for the dark hair she'd inherited from Jericho, she was a mini-me to Kim. "Are you guys having a fight?" she said, swaying back and forth between the two seats. Like her father, she'd never been one to sit still. "Because it seems like you're having a fight."

Garcia looked out the window, nodding toward Quinn's ex-wife. "It looks like Kim wants to talk to you," she said. Her passive-aggressive expression brightened as she turned to give Mattie a wink. "How about you play me that song again on the piano?"

Mattie shrugged. "Yep," she said. "You're having a fight all right."

Quinn pressed the button on the armrest. The driver's side window came down with an electronic whir. Mattie stopped to talk with her mom for a moment before dragging Garcia inside the house by the hand. Window down, a moist evening breeze hit him in the face, carrying the beginning mists of an approaching rain and the familiar scent of the towering blue spruce that dominated the Quinn's front yard. It had seemed so big when Jericho and Bo were boys. Over the years, the brothers had lost at least two good hatchets, countless knives, and a half dozen of their father's screwdrivers, throwing them at targets set up with the spruce as a backdrop. Now as tall as the chimney, the tree cast a huge shadow across the two-car driveway. Its rustling boughs sheltered Kim from the brunt of the north wind.

"Don't you have dinner reservations?" Kim asked, leaning in so her forearms rested along the doorframe.

Quinn let his head loll back against the headrest. "We do," he said, raising his wrist so he could see the time on his Tag Aquaracer. "Marx Brothers. In a little over a half an hour."

"I love that place," Kim said. "Great Caesar salads."

She rested her chin on her arms, looking up at Quinn with the big blue eyes that had caught him back when they were still in high school. She stood in silence for a long time, working up to something. Quinn was used to it. There had been many silences between them over the years. Most of them, he deserved. The tiniest hint of a smile perked her lips when she finally decided to speak.

"From the look on your face I'm guessing you haven't asked her yet," she said.

Quinn sat up, gripping the wheel and looking directly at his ex-wife. The only other person he'd told about the ring was Jacques. His line of work had trained him to be an incredibly skilled liar, but he and Kim had too much history. She knew all his tells. Quinn decided to draw on his SERE training and stick with the original lie no matter what tricks the interrogator pulled. "Ask her what?"

"Come on, Jericho," Kim said, her face serene. He knew a look of pity when he saw it. She gave a slow shake of her head. "There's only one thing in the world that can make you jumpy—and that's getting serious with a woman. I know, cause I was there the first time you ever got serious."

Quinn fell back in the seat, surrendering to Kim's wiles. "I have not asked her," he said. "Not yet, anyway. I'd planned to, then things got . . . complicated."

"I saw the news," Kim said. "Figured they would." She pushed off the door so she was standing up, her face level with Quinn's now. She bounced her fingers on the doorframe, swishing air back and forth in her puffed cheeks the way she did when deciding whether to say something that she'd been holding back. "I gotta say, Jericho, you are hands down the best human being I know." She peered at him, head tilted to one side so her blond hair pooled around her neck, still deciding. A resigned sigh told Quinn he was about to get an earful. He knew her tells too. "But I have to admit, there is a righteous stubbornness about you that made me want to pull your hair out a million times over. Lord knows I have no right to give you relationship advice. If I had it to do all over again, I'd try not to be so bitchy while you were out doing whatever it is you do. But I own the choices I've made." Kim wiped away a tear with the forearm of her hoodie and stepped back from the window. The front door slammed as Garcia and Mattie come out of the house. They held hands and skipped toward the truck, jumping the cracks in the sidewalk, singing some nonsensical song.

Kim sighed. "You deserve a little happiness. I think you can have it with Ronnie. Just be patient with her. Because as righteous and perfect as you are, loving you is an awful hard thing to do."

The boughs of the big spruce whispered and groaned as the wind shifted, bringing great drops of rain to spatter against the windshield. Mattie threw back her head to catch the rain on her tongue.

"She learned that from you," Kim said. "I never can get her to come in out of the rain—no matter how cold it is. I think she'd rather freeze to death than miss something fun."

Quinn watched as Garcia stood beside his little girl, head tilted back to catch raindrops on her tongue as well.

Kim patted the doorframe. "Your life is always going to be complicated, Jer. Just do what you need to do. If you wait for it to calm down, it's going to be a long wait."

Kim made her way around the truck to walk back inside, expertly navigating the wet pavement on her prosthetic leg, ignoring the rain. She gave Garcia a hug, then shooed Mattie toward the door. For that brief moment Quinn had a view of both women together. He and Garcia had fought, and bled, and even killed side by side. They had shared emotions and events that few human beings even discussed. And still, no one would ever know him as well as Kim.

For all his pitched battles and bloody hand-to-hand fights, Quinn could imagine nothing quite so fraught with danger as proposing marriage to Veronica Garcia. Since taking up martial arts in middle school, he'd approached everything in his life with the same strategic mindset: prepare daily to meet his opponent, then, when an opportunity presented itself, move directly to contact.

The evening had fallen from chilly to cold, along with Garcia's mood. A pelting rain creased the windshield and turned the asphalt streets of downtown Anchorage into shimmering mirrors of neon lights. Sitting across from Quinn in the plush leather passenger seat, Garcia faced away, staring out the window. She'd hardly said a word since they'd left the house, and Quinn couldn't help but wonder if he was about to walk into an ambush of emotion.

Three elderly couples in brightly colored rain jackets—the last of the tourists until ski season kicked in—walked from the corner of Fifth Avenue and H Street, toward the Glacier Brewhouse. Even inside the pickup, the smells of wood-fired salmon and hot bread made Quinn's mouth water. It was a fine restaurant, but his parents had taken him there with Kim to celebrate the night they'd gotten engaged. That alone was enough to make Quinn choose a different place to propose to Ronnie. Marx Brothers was more elegant anyway, tucked into a tiny house on Third Avenue, a little over two blocks away.

Quinn waited for another group to cross at the intersection. These were locals, judging from their uniform of Helly Hansen rain gear over fleece jackets, blue jeans, and XTRATUF rubber boots. The windshield wipers thwacked back and forth, adding to the intensity of the silence inside the pickup. He was warm and dry, but Quinn wondered if he might not be happier riding alone in the rain.

He'd purchased the ring nearly two months before, while Garcia was still in the hospital. It started to burn a hole in his pocket immediately after he picked it up, but he knew the time wasn't right. Ronnie Garcia had a prideful streak. She could take being slapped around by the bad guys, stabbed, or even shot, but she would not accept pity.

So Quinn had been patient, playing a game of watchful waiting, looking for the moment when she felt good enough about herself to feel good about them. In preparation, he'd brought her to Alaska to spend more time with his parents and the wild state that had raised him.

She and Mattie hit it off like long-lost friends. Quinn's mother spent an entire day with her shopping in downtown Anchorage and getting pedicures together—which to Quinn's mom had always been a right of passage for any of her sons' girlfriends. Quinn's old man, who had never been much of a talker, had invited Ronnie into the sanctum of his mancave, going so far as to open his walk-in gun safe and show her his prized Holland & Holland double rifle. A match to Theodore Roosevelt's .500/450 Nitro Express, "Big Stick," the rifle, was worth well over a hundred thousand dollars. Few people outside the family even knew of its existence, let alone got to hold it in their hands. The old-school double barrel was once tough and ornate, functional and elegant, and a perfect metaphor for the elder Quinn. The fact that their father hunted with a rifle that had no scope and was easily worth twice what he'd paid for their house had caused many a hushed discussion between the two brothers as they grew up. The sacred but old-school Holland & Holland was a personification of their father, and there was a considerable amount of contention between Bo and Jericho over who stood to inherit it.

Quinn's phone started to buzz inside the pocket of his leather jacket as he pulled alongside the curb in front of a parking meter on Third Avenue a half block from Marx Brothers.

Quinn sighed and answered the phone while Garcia gathered up her purse and raincoat. She'd wait for him to come around and open the door, as was their agreement when they weren't on the job.

"Hello."

"Hey, Chair Force, you go through with it yet?" Jacques Thibodaux's rambunctious Cajun voice spilled out of the phone. Extremely intelligent, Thibodaux had graduated cum laude from LSU and was fluent in French and Italian. Some who didn't know him took his hulking size and Cajun accent for a sign that he was slow—they were universally mistaken. If Quinn hadn't known the giant was a square-jawed brute, straight out of a United States Marine Corps recruiting commercial, it would have been easy to picture him as the energetic and bouncy Tigger from the Winnie the Pooh stories he read to Mattie.

"Did ya? Well, did ya?" Thibodaux's words bounced over the phone. Quinn pressed the device to his ear so they didn't keep bouncing and wind up in Garcia's ears. "If you didn't, you're a coward, and if you did, you're an idiot."

"No," Quinn said.

"No, you just haven't gotten around to it yet?" Thibodaux said. "Or no, you've come to your senses?"

Quinn gave a wan smile to Garcia, who was hopefully getting only his side of the conversation.

"Not yet," Quinn said, keeping things noncommittal.

Thibodaux snorted. "Them's the words of a man who feels compelled to walk up the gallows steps without bein' ordered to."

"The arrangement seems to be treating you all right," Quinn said. There was no need to remind the big Marine of his supremely happy marriage and seven sons.

"It do, it do, l'ami," Thibodaux said. "But what's good for the goose . . . well, you know the rest—"

There was an audible click on the line and Thibodaux's voice cut out for a moment. Quinn looked at his phone and saw it was a call from Palmer.

"I gotta go."

"Okay," Thibodaux said. "But seriously, I'm happy for you, beb. Just don't want you to come crawlin' to me down the road and say I didn't give you no warning."

Quinn ended the call and felt a creeping twinge of dread as he answered the next one. The national security advisor to the president wasn't calling to encourage him on his date with Garcia.

"Ready to go?" Win Palmer said.

"That depends on where I'm going," Quinn said.

"Don't you people have television in Alaska?" Palmer said. His voice was pinched and more than a little annoyed.

"I'm not sure what you're talking about, sir."

"There's been a second attack," Palmer said.

Quinn held the phone away from his ear so Garcia could hear.

"Another deployment of lethal gas," Palmer continued. "This one happened during the taping of some kind of celebrity-dating reality TV show in Los Angeles. A hundred and three dead at last count—cast, crew, and much of the studio audience. Cameras caught the whole damned thing on live television. It's not enough that these bastards attack us at home. They have discovered the extra boost of terror from keeping the attacks in the media from the start. Every network and cable channel is running an endless loop of death and carnage—giving them hours of free publicity."

"I'm with Garcia now," Quinn said, waiting for the next shoe to drop. Palmer didn't call just to give him news.

"I may have something for her," Palmer said. "But I want her back here until we get a better read on her shoulder."

Ronnie closed her eyes and groaned at the confirmation that she was on the injured list.

"Quinn." Palmer plowed ahead. "There's someone I need you to meet."

Quinn looked at his Aquaracer. "We can catch a flight to Seattle in a hour and a half. Should be able to get a red-eye to DC or Baltimore."

"Don't bother," Palmer said. "She's already en route to you."

"Coming to Alaska?" Quinn said. Garcia cocked her head to one side. Thick black hair pooled over her injured shoulder throwing her already dark face into deeper shadows.

"ETA at JBER is just before midnight Alaska time." JBER was Joint Base Elmendorf Richardson, adjacent to the city of Anchorage. "In the meantime, I need you packed and ready to fly to Nome."

Quinn shrugged to Garcia. This was odd. Nome, Alaska, wasn't exactly the cradle of terrorism.

"We're still putting everything together," Palmer said. "I'll brief you all at the same time. I'm not sure how long you'll be out, but be prepared to act as a guide for a Russian speaker who has never set foot in Alaska. I've arranged for a C12 to take you to Nome tonight."

"Is Jacques coming?" Quinn asked.

"I have Thibodaux working on another matter," Palmer said offering no more on the subject. "Be ready by 2100."

Quinn returned the phone to his pocket, next to the lump that was the engagement ring.

Garcia turned in her seat so she faced him. "Why do

you think he wouldn't tell you who he's sending?" she said. "What's up with that?"

"I am not sure," Quinn said working through the possibilities.

"Well, I'll tell you what I'm sure of," Garcia said, her full lips set, absent their normally humorous perk at each corner. "Palmer knows I speak Russian, but for some reason he has decided I'm not fit enough to go on this mission with you."

"They nearly killed you," Quinn said. "You know he'd bench me too if the roles were reversed."

Garcia scoffed. "No, he wouldn't. He hasn't. I've seen you beat to hell, and he still let you work." Her amber eyes narrowed, thick, black lashes fluttering with tension. "What the hell, Jericho? I can play through the pain as well as anyone. And I don't need you and Palmer to coddle me."

Quinn bounced the back of his head on the seat, watching rivulets of rainwater braid and crease the windshield. Garcia was right. He'd fought on after being shot, having his ribs broken, even after having a toe snipped off with pruning shears—all without Palmer so much as flinching.

"I guess we're both just sexist pigs," Quinn said.

Garcia nodded slowly then turned to stare out the passenger window. She rarely turned away during a conversation, and Quinn had learned to pay attention when she did.

Quinn felt the evening he'd planned so meticulously slipping away. He lived the kind of life where dinner plans were often interrupted or postponed, but he couldn't help but feel like this was something beyond that. He started the truck and did a quick head check over his shoulder before pulling back out into traffic.

"Being overprotective is in my blood," Quinn said. "I do it with my brother. I do it with Jacques. There's zero chance I can turn it off when it comes to you."

"I know," Garcia said, still looking away. "And that's becoming a real problem."

Chapter 10

New York City, 9:50 p.m.

Deputy U.S. Marshal August "Gus" Bowen made his way through a narrow kitchen corridor, nodding to his new set of eyes. Bowen had befriended Bruce, the fat little sous-chef, earlier that evening with the gift of a couple of Cohiba cigars that he'd scored from a deputy working the Dominican protection detail. Bruce had balked at first, looking sideways at Deputy Bowen's black eye and his raw and swollen nose. The split in his upper lip really required stitches but Bowen didn't have the time for that. Anyway, it was beginning to scab already. His neatly trimmed salt and pepper goatee covered some of the damage to his face, but there was no way of hiding the fact that he'd been the recipient of a recent beat down.

His hair had gone prematurely silver following his last tour in Iraq, an outward sign of what his Army shrink called "a bevy of unresolved issues." The shrink had advised him to take up quiet hobbies to relieve the stress in his life. He already sailed most weekends and had been drawing since junior high. The doc said he should do more of both if he didn't want to hang up his gun—or worse. So he'd drawn more pictures of boats, and did his best to chill. He eventually moved on to drawing people—and it turned out he was a pretty good artist. He wasn't about to quit his day job, but he gave away at least one sketch each week to someone he met in the course of his duties.

Bowen would never admit it, but those same unresolved issues were what earned him the beating the previous night. He'd ended up telling his detail supervisor the injuries were from a bar fight over a beautiful woman—which wasn't too far from the truth—except they hadn't been in the bar and the girl a long way from beautiful.

The Dominican cigars and a quick pencil sketch of the sous-chef standing over a simmering pot had earned Bowen that valuable set of extra eyes in the hotel kitchen. Contacts in the backrooms and basements of hotels and restaurants were priceless sources of information, and Deputy Bowen shamelessly curried favor with as many as possible when working this kind of job. The more eyes and ears he had working for him, the safer his protectee would be.

Department of State Diplomatic Security Agents attended enough formal functions that they were allowed to voucher the purchase of a tuxedo. The United States Marshals Service had experience protecting witnesses and federal judges, so they helped out State every year during the United Nations General Assembly. Doorkickers didn't see much use for tuxedos so Bowen was told to voucher the rental of a nice black one for the evening. Accustomed to wearing khaki slacks and polo shirts—or at the most, an off-the-rack suit—the tux made him feel oddly out of place and stood in stark contrast to his injured face. Bowen was in his mid-thirties, a hair over six feet, and trim, with the powerful shoulders of a boxer.

Enough visiting federal agents needed formal wear for just a few functions that several tailors in Manhattan ran thriving businesses renting custom slacks with invisible slash pockets and belt loops—unheard of on regular tuxedos. Under his jacket, he carried a small Motorola radio, a Benchmade automatic knife, handcuffs, an expandable baton, a .40 caliber Glock, and two spare magazines. The gear made him look slightly less streamlined than James Bond, but his trim appearance helped to smooth the lines. He normally carried a second, smaller Glock of the same caliber in an inside-the-waistband holster near the small of his back. This arrangement proved too bulky for the tux so he made do by putting the second gun in an ankle holster—giving him a loadout of fifty-six rounds of ammunition. Considering the "friends" he'd made over the past year, Bowen knew even that might not be enough.

Dignitary protection was a matter of securing concentric rings—like the layers of an onion. NYPD handled the outer ring, blocking streets, placing extra patrol in the area, deploying truckloads of highly trained ESU tactical units to both preempt and deal with attacks. Bowen's job was the middle ring, looking outbound from the protectee and checking the pulse of the people working at the event. He made his way down the line, relaying his information to the Diplomatic Security agent in charge who worked the innermost ring up in the dining room with the rest of the detail protecting the Uzbek foreign minister.

A light static crackled in the deputy's clear silicone earpiece. "Babayev Advance, Babayev Advance, Babayev Shift Leader." It was Special Agent Hancock, second-in-command of the protective detail for Uzbek foreign minister, Shuker Babayev.

"Babayev Advance here." The deputy spoke into the small microphone pinned to the inside of his tuxedo shirt collar. "Go for Bowen."

"Switch to Foxtrot 6," Hancock said, using code to direct the conversation away from the open channel shared by the twenty-four other State Department protection details assigned to one of five different frequencies.

"I got a guy who wants to see you," Hancock said, when they were both on the same channel.

Odd, Bowen thought. Visitors were not the norm while on an active protection detail. He assumed it was one of the two dozen deputy marshals assigned to a different delegation who wanted to bullshit about the latest drama going on in Marshals Service HQ.

"You got a name?" Bowen asked.

"What's your location," Agent Hancock said. "I'll send him to you."

Bowen told the DS agent where he was then asked for a name again.

Hancock remained coy. "Big dude. Kind of scary lookin'. He says you two are friends."

"Okay . . ." Bowen felt his hackles rise. This was straight-up weird, and his gut told him that weird could only mean one thing.

"Azam is bringing him your way right now," Hancock said. "I think our Uzbek friend is getting hungry and wants to sample the menu."

The Uzbek minister's single native security agent was a giant teddy bear named Azam. He seemed too gentle a man for his chosen profession but was big enough that Bowen wouldn't have wanted to see him angry.

"Roger that," Bowen said. "I got a guy here who

will fix him something to tide him over until they feed us."

Bowen had made it past the twin doors of a large walk-in freezer at the back of the kitchen and turned to hunt down the fat little sous-chef.

Steam snapped at the lids of a half dozen five-gallon soup pots sending the heady odor of lobster bisque into the air, already full of the cursing and tension that went along with feeding three hundred of the world's elite including the U.S. Secretary of State.

Agents from several other details filtered in and out of the kitchen, feeding information to their respective detail bosses—but none of them had Bruce in their corner. Bowen asked for some bread and cheese for Azam. The sous-chef gave him a hearty thumbs-up, smiling as if he was part of a conspiracy, then shouted orders to his brigade of prep chefs who chopped, sautéed, and stirred the various sauces and side dishes that were being served at tonight's banquet. One of them peeled away to see to Bowen's request.

Bowen felt his stomach growl and looked at his watch. It was no wonder Azam was hungry. Bowen had come on shift at 0700, and he was starving. He was sure the Uzbek had been on the clock long before that, seeing to the needs of his boss, the Uzbek foreign minister, and working through the daily schedule so he could liaise with the DS agents about timing and routes. Dignitary protection required a certain artistic fluidity, often necessitating a move from one location to another at a moment's notice. The Uzbek minister was a compulsive shopper during these trips to New York and had kept the eight people charged with protecting his life on the move all day. Bowen and the others on the detail had been able to wolf down a quick slice of pizza over the hood of the armored limo while the minister was inside being fitted for new suits. Other than that, it had been go, go, go all day long and none of them—including Azam—had had anything to eat but for the odd Skittle or breath mint they'd found hiding in a suit pocket.

New Yorkers seemed to have an affinity for late dining, but this was ridiculous. The Sultan of Brunei had spent the last two months vacationing in Hawaii and was accustomed to Hawaii Time. Since the Sultan was host and footing the bill for this event, he deemed it appropriate to eat when his internal clock said it was time to sit down to dinner—five p.m. in Hawaii was eleven in New York. And protective agents always ate after their protectees. Bowen felt his stomach growl again and thought how nice it must be to be a bazillionaire.

The annual General Assembly of the UN or UNGA, offered most of the one hundred and ninety-three member nations' top diplomats an opportunity to visit New York City on an all-expenses-paid shopping trip. But one man's boondoggle was another man's opportunity for overtime, so Bowen had jumped at the chance when offered one of the few U.S. Marshals slots to assist Diplomatic Security protective details. Considering the ever-growing threat of terrorism, there was a fair bet the overtime would not be the relatively easy standing post and "smokin' and jokin'" of times past. With attacks on American soil moving up the scale from possible to probable—Bowen's chief had chosen him specifically for the assignment. Bowen's experience in Iraq had earned him a Silver Star, along with silver hair and the "bevy of unresolved issues." It had also made him one of the go-to deputies in the Marshals Service when it came to boots-on-the-ground tactical knowledge.

After the gas attacks in Dallas and Los Angeles, there was buzz that the Secretary General of the UN would pull rank and cancel, or at the very least postpone the late-night Plaza dinner. Many of the delegates agreed with the threat assessment, but none of them wanted to appear weak so they kept quiet. Ousted by the former President, Melissa Ryan, long-time romantic partner to the national security advisor had been reappointed Secretary of State by the new president. She'd arrived ten minutes before Bowen left to check the kitchen, flanked by a dozen dour DS agents who glared as if they viewed anyone who got in their path as food.

In the end, one hundred and sixty foreign minsters and their guests had weighed the possibilities of a gruesome death from poison gas against the benefits of a free meal and were now crowded into the Plaza Hotel's Grand Ballroom listening to a very talented Chinese woman play the cello. For the poorer countries' delegations, Bowen suspected this would be the most lavish meal they would have in their lives. For some, accustomed to living off the backs of their people, lobster bisque and macadamia-crusted halibut was nothing out of thc ordinary.

"Bread and cheese is for pigeons and rats," Bruce the sous-chef said in a heavy Brooklyn accent, waddling up to Bowen with a plate of halibut, a folded linin napkin, and a fork. "I want that you should have real-people food."

"I appreciate it," Bowen said as he saw Azam round the corner beside the walk-in freezer. "It's not for me. It's for a friend—" Bowen gave a slow nod when he saw the man walking behind the Uzbek.

Now it all made sense.

* * *

Jacques Thibodaux gave Bowen's face a sidelong look with his good eye. The other was covered with a black patch that only added to the menacing demeanor of the gigantic Marine. "Oh, yea, yee!" He said under his breath.

Where every other person at the Plaza Hotel event was wearing either formal attire or a hotel uniform, the massive Cajun had shown up in a skintight T-shirt and faded blue jeans. He carried a heavy leather jacket draped over his arm. "I thought I'd find you were out sailing around the world and instead I see you been playin' it rough with somebody. What in the hell did you do to your noggin, cher?" he asked.

Azam stood by, smiling happily while he munched on his plate of food. He spoke excellent English and appeared as interested in the story as Thibodaux.

Jacques nodded toward the bloody knuckles of Bowen's right hand. "You know, I delivered my fourth kid on our living floor so I'm pretty much a doctor. Let me know if you need me to take a look at that hand."

Bowen chuckled, hoping to move on with whatever spy games had brought the big Marine his direction. Men like Jacques Thibodaux didn't just drop by to catch up. "It wasn't much."

"Pshaw!" Thibodaux scoffed. "You forget that I've seen you fight. Ain't nobody get that many licks in on you without bein' on the receiving end of a good ass whippin'."

Bowen sighed, knowing he'd have to tell the story before Thibodaux would get to his reason for coming.

"I was walking back from the Waldorf yesterday after the night crew relieved us and happened on this guy who was beating the shit out of his girlfriend on 50th."

Thibodaux gave a somber nod. "Must have been a big guy, judging from the looks of your swollen beak."

"Big enough," Bowen said. "Some kind of bouncer from the way he slammed my face into the sidewalk." The deputy shook his head, remembering the fight in a whirlwind of painful detail.

Thibodaux's eyes narrowed as if he was trying to come to grips with the story. "Don't you marshals ever call for backup?"

"That's the policy," Bowen said.

"Why didn't you then? Hell, cher, this is Midtown Manhattan. The place is crawlin' with cops."

Bowen shrugged. "The math just didn't work out."

The Marine's brow crawled above his black eye patch. "What's math got to do with it?"

"Well," Bowen said, as if it was all so clear, "You know what they say, 'When seconds count, the cops are only minutes away.' Every second I don't step in, this guy puts another smack on his girlfriend."

Thibodaux nodded. "So you just waded in amongst this big sombitch, and he gave you a fat lip . . ."

"Not quite." Bowen gave a sheepish chuckle. "The girl gave me the fat lip while I was putting handcuffs on her boyfriend. No good deed goes unpunished, you know."

"You're a good shit, Deputy Gus Gus," the Cajun said. "Oh, yes you are." He turned and gave a wink to Azam. "You mind givin' us a minute?"

The Uzbek shot a glance at Bowen, as if to ask if he was okay to be left alone with the big Cajun.

Bowen gave an almost imperceptible nod. "I'll be fine, my friend," he said.

Thibodaux leaned in after Azam had stepped around the corner. He kept his voice low. "Remember that little *fais do-do* we got you involved in a few months back?"

"You mean when we committed a bunch of felonies and were nearly thrown in front of a firing squad?" Bowen scoffed. "Yeah, I seem to recall something about that."

A contagious grin crept across Thibodaux's broad face. "That was some fun, don't you think?" He gave Bowen a mock punch in the arm. "Anyhow, just for grins, what would you say to a little more of the same? Minus the firing squad part."

"I'm in the middle of an assignment."

"Well, cher," Thibodaux said. "As it happens, my boss is talking to your boss even as we speak."

"Your boss . . ."

"Ain't it convenient?" The big Cajun grinned. "My boss is your boss's boss's boss. Looks like you and me gonna be partnered up for a while."

"Okay, then," Bowen said. "I'm guessing this has something to do with the poison-gas attacks?"

"It do indeed." Thibodaux turned his head slightly so he could look Bowen up and down with his good eye. "I hope you got extra clothes, cause right now you look like you were pretending to be James Bond and got your ass kicked for it."

"Of course I have other clothes but they're all at the DoubleTree."

"We'll swing by your room then." Thibodaux rubbed his belly with a hand the size of a shovel blade. "The rubber chicken I had on the plane ain't sittin' right. You can change your clothes, and I'll take me a tactical dump."

Chapter 11

Brighton Beach, New York, 11:05 p.m.

Petyr "The Wolf" Volodin stood naked in front of the grimy bathroom mirror in his filthy apartment and wondered when they would come for him. He was sure it wouldn't be long. Mr. Anikin was a brutal man who surrounded himself with brutal associates. Their business was pain and they were extremely good at their job.

Petyr flexed his muscles, bouncing the eight pointed star tattoos at the top of each pec. The tats had gotten him into a world of trouble, but they drew attention to his muscular shoulders. Most guys worked too much on their biceps. That was all well and good, but in a fight, strong shoulders were all important. Petyr had heard somewhere that shoulders were the human equivalent of antlers on a bull elk, demonstrating social status and the ability to gather a harem.

"That's right." Petyr sneered at his own reflection, trying to psych himself up for what he knew was coming. "I got me some antlers, baby, and I'm gonna kick your ass . . ."

He stepped back and rubbed a swollen hand over

two days of stubble on a blocky jaw. His girl, Nikka, pissed and moaned like he'd shot her whenever he went a day without shaving. She was just too stupid to get his fight philosophy through her dense skull. An opponent could grab a long beard and turn it into a murder-handle, but give 'em a rake with the bristles of an unshaven face and it was instant rug burn. Some fighters called the rake a bitch move, but in Petyr the Wolf's mind, if it won the fight, there was no such thing. Nine times out of ten, the other guy flinched himself right into an arm bar or rear naked choke. The Wolf shaved his head three days before a fight for the same reason. The tactic wouldn't go in the big leagues, but in the places he fought, the refs could be persuaded to look the other way at a little stubble.

Even under the looming threat, Petyr took the time to admire his impressive muscles. At six three and a hulked fighting weight of two-forty, his shoulders were massive. A thirty-two inch waist and sculpted obliques made him look even broader than he was. Admiring his muscles he couldn't keep from thinking about the tattoos—and the world of shit they'd gotten him into. His shoulders sagged and his wide face fell into a dark frown.

He never should have let stupid Nikka talk him into getting the tats. Nikka had some issues—there was no doubt about that—but she was incredibly hot, and life was just easier so long as she wasn't angry. So, he'd gone to her tattoo guy and got the ink she wanted him to get. It had seemed cool at first. The Wolf was "a tough Russian son of a bitch," Nikka told him, and tough Russian sons of bitches had tattoos of eight-pointed stars on their shoulders and grinning skulls on their bellies. It was true. She'd seen it on TV.

And everything had been good for a while. The tats

actually bought him a little deeper street cred. Then the scary looking dude with a tattoo of a spider crawling up his bony throat had come up ringside two nights earlier and pressed his ugly face against the ropes. The guy proceeded to machine-gun him in Russian with questions that were all but lost in the clamor and shouts of the crowd. It was loud, but Petyr was pretty sure he heard the word *Vory*—a thief. Still flushed with adrenaline from the beat-down he'd given his opponent, Petyr had waved Spider Neck off, thinking him a crazy Russian alky. There were plenty of those in Brighton Beach.

That had been a big mistake.

Now Petyr leaned in over the sink, closer to the mirror and touched one of the many scabs on his muscular chest. This one was between the fourth and fifth ribs—directly over his heart.

Petyr was big enough to intimidate most who would even try to cross him outside the ring. A simple glare from the dark shadows of his eyes was usually enough to send even the roughest gangbanger running for his mama. For those few who were ignorant enough to face him, Petyr had the youthful strength of his twenty-six years and the skills gained from expending gallons of sweat and blood in the gym—not to mention the potent elixir his chemist father whipped up for him that worked better than any steroids he'd ever tried.

None of that mattered to the Spider Neck. He'd waited in the alley behind the locker room, leaning against the brick wall when Petyr ducked out the back door after the fight.

"Hey!" the man said, not moving from his relaxed position against the wall. Night shadows fell across his face, giving him the appearance of a gargoyle on some creepy building. "You are thief-in-law?"

It was not a question, but a challenge. The eight pointed stars were tattoos of *vory v zokone* or thieves-in-law. Spider Neck wanted to know if he'd earned them the proper way, by spending time in a Russian prison.

Though Petyr outweighed him by at least eighty pounds, Spider Neck hadn't been the least bit intimidated. Petyr hadn't seen him move until it was too late. The man seemed to be everywhere at once, swarming all over the place like an entire hive of wasps. By the time he was still, the skeletal Russian had cut Petyr in at least two dozen places. All the wounds were superficial, slicing only skin and sparing the muscle underneath—but he'd made his point: if Petyr resisted, death was a forgone conclusion.

Spider Neck shoved him against the brick wall and delivered a message from Anatoly Anikin, a local who called himself a Pakhan or captain in the Russian mafia. Mr. Anikin was one of the few former guests of Russia's infamous Black Dolphin prison who had been released in something other than a pine box. He was the real deal as far as criminal thugs went, but Petyr doubted he had any ties with the mob in Russia. More likely he was one of the many freelancers vying for positions of authority in the underbelly of Brooklyn, which probably made him even more dangerous.

According to Spider Neck, Mr. Anikin had caught a glimpse of Petyr's tattoos during a recent mixed martial-arts fight that had been streamed online. It didn't help that Anikin had bet on the other fighter and Petyr had won.

Spider Neck demanded to know how long Petyr had been in prison and where he'd done his time. The dude was scary enough but his face had twisted and darkened even more when Petyr admitted he'd never been in any prison other than the 60th Precinct lockup in Brooklyn due to possession of steroids. Nikka bonded him out after only two hours so he'd never even made it past the holding cells, but he kept that little factoid to himself.

Spider Neck had just looked at him and glared, turning the blade so it glinted in the scant light of the alley. "If you arrived in a Russian prison with ink that had not been earned, the men there would cut out your liver . . ."

He had gone on to explain that since they were in America and not a Russian prison, Mr. Anikin had graciously given Petyr forty-eight hours to have the stars and the laughing skull covered or removed. He also ordered Petyr to take a fall during his next fight. It was implied that if he chose not to comply, Spider Neck would remove the tattoos for him.

But two days came and went and no one came to cut out his liver. The more time that passed from the incident in the alley, the more of his bravery, however misguided, seeped back. Petyr hadn't spent years training to fight in the octagon to run scared from some ugly dude with a bug tattooed on his throat. By the third morning, he reasoned that if this Russian mob boss wanted him dead, he would have killed him already. The *Bratva,* or Brotherhood, was into stolen credit cards nowadays. They didn't go around whacking people over tats. By lunchtime, he'd felt ready to kick Spider Neck's ass for treating him with such disrespect. He was The Wolf. Nobody treated The Wolf like that.

But a shadow of doubt crept into his bravado, diminishing his swagger now that almost seventy-two hours had passed. Petyr nearly jumped out of his skin when someone began to pound on his door. He leaned around the corner from the bathroom and stared hard at the knob, as if he had some kind of X-ray vision, trying to figure out who it was on the other side. For a moment he held onto the hope that it might be Nikka, but the banging was much too hard for her little hands. He thought about looking through the peephole but decided against it. Spider Neck would just shoot him in the eye as soon as he saw the shadow pass across the lens.

The banging got louder, like the person doing it owned the place, then suddenly stopped. The doorknob jiggled. Petyr froze. Metal scraped against metal as someone inserted a pick set into the lock.

Petyr shot a gaze at the back window. He'd already packed a bag with the important stuff—a change of underwear and the rest of the juice his father sent him. He could hit the fire escape and be gone in a flash. But if it was Anikin's men, they would be expecting that. They'd make a big show of trying to get in, only to have Spider Neck waiting for him outside to cut out his liver as soon as he dropped off the fire escape. The door would have been easy enough to kick in if they'd really wanted to. No, this was an ambush. They expected him to run.

He took a long, calming breath, and then ducked back in the bathroom so he could get another look at himself in the mirror. He'd do the last thing they expected—meet them head on.

Slipping a loose cotton shirt over his head, he picked up a baseball bat he kept beside the door and held it over his head like an ax. Spider Neck had thrashed him so well the last time, Petyr doubted he'd brought more than a couple of helpers, and those just so he'd have an audience. Keeping well to the side of the doorframe in case someone out there had a shotgun, he reached out and flipped the lock before putting his hand on the knob, ready to fling it open.

Spider Neck had caught him off guard once. He wasn't going to let that happen again. All he wanted was to be left alone to fight in the octagon, but if these guys wanted to mess with The Wolf, they'd feel his teeth.

Chapter 12

Joint Base Elmendorf Richardson, Anchorage

Quinn felt his phone buzz with a text message at the same moment one of the two young airmen pushed a black button on the back wall of the cavernous hangar. The button activated the floor to ceiling doors, opening the entire north wall so they could drive the tug out and pull in the aircraft with Quinn's mystery guest who had just arrived from Boling Air Force Base. Metal doors rumbled on their tracks as they began to slide across each other, yawning open to reveal the black of an Alaska fall night. Blue and green lights winked in the chilly air beyond the approaching airplane. It seemed extra dark in contrast with the bright and sterile interior of the hanger.

Quinn looked down at the text and chuckled. Garcia was standing next to him and raised a wary brow at the message.

"Who's that from?"

"Jacques," Quinn said, still chuckling.

"Is he talking about me?"

Quinn cocked his head and looked her in the eye.

"Didn't your mother ever tell you it's not nice to read over someone's shoulder?"

"I work for the CIA," Garcia said. "It's my job to read over people's shoulders." She took on Thibodaux's Cajun accent as she read the text aloud. "'*Watch your ass, l'ami. The woman is batshit crazy.*' What the hell is that supposed to mean?"

"My guess is he's talking about whoever's on this airplane," Quinn said, nodding to the phone. "He left me a voicemail. Maybe that explains it."

Quinn called his voicemail but kept his eyes on the Challenger while it taxied with a high whine toward the hanger. He took a calculated risk and left the phone on speaker so Ronnie could hear. She was already what Thibodaux called "level-ten pissed," so there wasn't much of a chance she could get any madder than she already was.

"I don't have much time, Chair Force . . ." The Cajun's tone was dead sober, absent its customary irreverence. "You're about to meet my cousin, Special Agent Khaki Beaudine of the FBI . . ." He stopped, taking a long thinking pause, odd for a man who never seemed to be at a loss for words, even in the middle of a running gun battle.

Ronnie's eyes widened at the news. Quinn knew Thibodaux's cousin was with the Bureau, but other than the fact that she was getting a divorce, the big Cajun had kept anything else about her to himself.

"Khaki's a good kid," the message finally continued. "But she has some . . . well, cher, she's plum *bracque*—loony—and I ain't just sayin' that because she grew up in Texas. She's been through some horrible shit . . ." There was a muffled sound on the other end, as if someone else was trying to talk to Jacques while he left the message. "Dammit, I gotta scoot." His voice grew hushed, imperative. "You watch yourself with her, Jericho, no foolin'. I'm serious as nut cancer."

Quinn watched as the two airmen marshaled the tug and waited for the floor-to-ceiling hanger doors to slide to their stops and lock open. Outside, starkly white against the darkness, the Bombardier Challenger 601 nosed its way toward the hanger. The beefy business jet was ostensibly assigned to the FAA but was in actuality at the beck and call of Winfield Palmer. This off-the-books aircraft allowed him to move operatives and human assets around the world without resorting to commercial aircraft or infighting between government agencies.

The Challenger rolled to a stop twenty meters from the open door, and twin GE turbofan engines whined down.

The spacious hanger off the end of the Elmendorf flight line could easily hold three planes the size of the nineteen-passenger aircraft, but the National Security Advisor to the President of the United States had enough pull that they had the entire place to themselves. Even the tug driver and his spotter disappeared down the hallway to the front offices as soon as they had the airplane chocked and the hanger bay secured.

The pilot stepped to the aircraft door as soon as it opened, lowering the folding stairs himself. He caught Quinn's eye immediately, smiling a tight-lipped smile as if there was something he needed to apologize for. The first officer, a man with sandy hair, followed him off the plane. Winfield Palmer handpicked his pilots from Air Force Special Operations Command, and Quinn recognized the first officer as a former AC-130 “Spooky” gunship pilot out of Hurlburt Field.

“She does look a little crazy,” Garcia whispered as a small woman with a frosted blond pixie cut stepped to the aircraft door and stopped, her neck moving bird-like, as she looked around. Quinn estimated her to be about five three.

Standing shoulder to shoulder with Garcia, he leaned his head sideways, his eye still on Beaudine. “What do you mean?”

“I got ways of picking up on these things,” Garcia said. “Jacques is right. You should watch yourself.”

“It’s her figure, isn’t it?” Quinn said, earning an elbow in the ribs. “You’re jealous because she’s in shape.”

Garcia assured him she wasn’t the jealous type—but Quinn knew she didn’t relish the idea of him traveling into bush Alaska with a woman who wore a pair of Wranglers as well as Khaki Beaudine.

Along with the form-fitting Wrangler jeans, Jacques’s cousin wore a black turtleneck that highlighted her athletic build. Quinn felt the same way about turtlenecks as he did neckties, which was to say he hated them both. They made him feel as though a small and sickly child was trying to choke him to death. Khaki Beaudine wore hers well enough to earn an extra moment of glare from Ronnie.

Beaudine carried an earth-tone 5.11 backpack in her hand like a briefcase. She had a black parka shell draped over her left arm, exposing a Glock pistol, two extra magazines, handcuffs, and a gold FBI badge on her belt.

She nodded at Quinn as if she recognized him. Her eyes were bright aquamarine under the harsh light of the hangar, but they did not look particularly happy to see him.

"FBI." She stuck out her hand. "Khaki Beaudine." Quinn noticed a heavy twang, but wasn't sure anyone in the world could say the words "Khaki Beaudine" without having an accent.

"Welcome to Alaska." Quinn smiled, sizing her up without staring. "You're Jacques's cousin?"

"That's right." A half smile pulled into a pinched grimace as if she'd caught the odor of something unpleasant. "I can only imagine the things he's told you about me."

"Just that you were related," Ronnie said, covering for Jacques.

"Well, I guess I got more to worry about than a tale-tellin' cousin." Beaudine dropped her backpack on the hanger floor and fished out a small tablet computer. She wagged her head at Quinn while she slid the computer from a black neoprene case and folded out the screen. "Truth be told, I never wanted anything to do with you spooks. Bureau counterintelligence is like a bunch of English professors who see some hidden meaning in every damn thing. 'The whale represents evil . . . the whale is Ahab . . . the whale is a quest . . .'" Beaudine scoffed. "No Counter Intel secret squirrel mumbo jumbo for me. The Violent Crime Squads, they know how to handle their shit. Call stuff what it is, straight up—a dangerous whale that needs to be hunted down and killed."

"I see," Quinn said, wondering if she'd ever even read *Moby Dick*.

"Anyhow," Beaudine said. "I've got orders to link up with the national security advisor as soon as I'm off the plane."

Beaudine typed a password on the tablet, then consulted a small key fob from her pocket for the numbers she'd need to get through the second layer of security.

This passcode changed every sixty seconds and only worked once she'd logged in with her password. The tech was years old, but the cumbersome nature of it made it secure, and changing the methods of the largest federal law enforcement agency in the country could be glacially slow.

Winfield Palmer's ruddy, pixilated face appeared on screen a moment later. With the intense look of a man with heavy purpose, the national security advisor sat behind his expansive mahogany desk. Quinn recognized the off-site office he kept near Crystal City, Virginia. Still inside the Beltway but across the Potomac from DC proper, the quiet shopping district was a stone's throw from the Pentagon and a dozen different intelligence and law-enforcement agencies.

"Here's what we know," Palmer said a few moments later. "Preliminary test results on the stuff used in Dallas show it's a binary nerve agent akin to VX and Soman—maybe one of the Russian Novichok agents that have worried us for the last decade."

"Newcomer," Garcia said, translating the Russian.

Special Agent Beaudine nodded at the translation.

"Correct," Palmer said. "Only our guys say this stuff looks to be at least a dozen times more powerful than Sarin. It's made of two relatively harmless components, but they become a fulminating compound when mixed, producing a heavy and lingering vapor. Extremely toxic stuff."

"Twelve times as powerful?" Garcia frowned.

"At least," Palmer said. "They're telling me that if *Aum* would have had this stuff in the Tokyo subway attack in '95 most of the thousand injured would have died instead of just twelve."

"Not easy to manufacture, I'd imagine," Quinn mused. "At least not without some serious lab equipment."

Ronnie nodded. "I doubt the Islamic State or any one of the other wannabe groups of that ilk even have the glassware to produce something like this. They'd probably gas themselves in the process."

Beaudine shrugged. "The Islamic State has been trying to recruit scientists," she said. "But we don't think they've been successful as of yet. This gas used in Dallas and LA was weapons grade, not some homemade pickle-jar variety. It takes a government facility to manufacture this stuff."

"How does all this lead back to Nome?" Quinn asked. He caught the flightiness in Beaudine's eyes. It was clear she'd rather be somewhere else.

Palmer laid both hands flat on top of his desk. The huge mahogany thing was big enough to warrant its own zip code, but he was meticulous about keeping it free of clutter.

"At any given time, the FBI keeps tabs on seventeen chemists," Palmer said. "Men and women who they believe are capable of developing sophisticated nerve agents. Some work for foreign governments, some live right here in the U.S. We're not ruling anyone out at this point."

As if on cue, Agent Beaudine pulled a light-blue folder from her pack and handed it to Quinn. It was marked Top Secret in bold letters with a red diagonal stripe across its face. "Passport records show that a little over seven hours ago one of those seventeen scientists, a Russian named Kostya Volodin, passed through Immigration and Customs at the Nome, Alaska, port of entry."

"That is odd he would come to the U.S. the day of the attacks," Ronnie said.

Agent Beaudine rolled her eyes. "That's true," she said. "We have a contact in Russia who saw the doctor some four months ago and believes he's in the early stages of dementia. The Customs official in Nome confirms that he seemed addled, which makes him an even less-likely candidate for developing a gas of this complexity. More likely he's on a holiday. Guess that's why the Bureau sent a junior agent to check him out." She gave a little toss of her head. Quinn noticed she was smart enough to keep off camera so Palmer couldn't see it.

"I thought they sent you because you speak Russian," Quinn asked.

"I guess there's that," Beaudine said, still pouting like a child being forced into a chore.

Ronnie took a half step forward, making certain Palmer could see her on the screen. "Don't forget, sir, my father was Russian. I speak the language fluently. I know I can help on this. I'm ready to go to Nome now if needed."

"*Durakov ne seyut, ne zhnut, sami rodyatsya,*" Beaudine said under her breath and off camera.

Garcia shot her a hard look but said nothing, focusing instead on Palmer.

The national security advisor rubbed a hand over the top of his head in thought. It was nearly one in the morning East Coast time, and even on the small screen it was easy to see the strain in his eyes. Quinn was sure the man hadn't had a moment to stop running since the attacks—and was not likely to slow down any time soon. He drove his people hard and himself harder.

"You're going to be with me," Palmer said to Garcia. "I have Thibodaux partnered with the deputy marshal you all worked with a few months ago."

"Gus Bowen?" It was Quinn's turn to look at Palmer a little cross-eyed. Quinn had broken Bowen's nose back when they were in college—Quinn boxing for the Air Force Academy, Bowen for Army ROTC. Neither man had been too friendly with the other since. Beyond that, Quinn didn't like the way Bowen grinned when he was around Ronnie. And the fact that he felt jealous at all made him annoyed at himself—which made him even madder.

"The marshal's a hell of a manhunter," Palmer said. "Dr. Volodin was married to a Ukrainian scientist who emigrated to the U.S. in the early nineties. They have a son together. The ex-wife passed away three years ago, but the son lives in Brooklyn. Just so happens that Bowen is assigned to New York at the moment. This may be nothing, but we have every available agent and case officer working round the clock checking every possibility. Chances are you'll run these particular leads to the ground in a few hours. Call when you do and I'll put you on something else." He gave a slight nod to Ronnie. "Five of the scientists are Russian so I can use you back in DC. I want someone I trust in on the interrogations."

"Of course, sir," she said. "I'll jump on the next flight."

"The next flight is the one in front of you," Palmer said. "Be on it." As was his custom, he signed off without another word.

Beaudine scooped up her bag and went looking for the powder room. The Challenger pilots returned from the break room. Both were aware Garcia was to be their passenger and gave her a twenty-minute warning so they'd have time to push the plane back out and refuel.

Quinn leaned against the wall by a fifty-five gallon drum of engine oil next to Garcia.

"What did she say to you?" He spoke five languages but Russian wasn't one of them.

"A Russian saying," Garcia said. "She basically called me a fool for wanting to get involved."

"Really? Because you want to help out?" Quinn groaned. "This is going to be rich."

"I don't envy you," Garica said, glaring at the doorway through which Beaudine had disappeared, before breaking into a series of Spanish epithets that seemed strong enough to peel paint. "She's one of those nails that stick up on the dojo floor that has to be pounded down . . ."

"I'll have my mom send your clothes," he said.

"I don't like her," Garcia said.

"My mom?"

"You know who I mean, *postalita*." She sometimes called him a "little postage stamp" when she was angry. Quinn could never bring himself to ask her why, figuring she could have gone with a lot worse.

She turned to face him, toying with the buttons on his shirt. "Just be careful, Jericho."

"You're the one who needs to be careful," he said. "I'm only flying out to check on a dead end. DC is a lion's den even without a bunch of nerve gas and Russian scientists."

Ronnie gave him a kiss on the lips, the first since they'd left for their afternoon motorcycle ride. "Jacques is right," she said, her lips lingering near his. "This woman is crazy."

"You know," Quinn laughed, raising his eyebrows. "He's always telling me the same thing about you."

Chapter 13

Forty-five minutes after it had arrived, the Bombardier Challenger was wheels up and winging its way back toward Washington, DC, leaving Quinn and Special Agent Khaki Beaudine alone in the hanger.

"So," Quinn said, nodding to the 5.11 backpack at Beaudine's feet, "I guess you got all the gear you need?" The tough tactical bag was slightly larger than Quinn's Sagebrush Dry pack, but his was completely waterproof. His father had told him from the time they started hunting together that the more comfortable he became in the outdoors, the less he would need to bring with him to survive. Still, Alaska was an unforgiving mistress, and some things were a necessity no matter how comfortable you were.

Beaudine looked at her watch and shrugged. "We're lookin' at nearly ten o'clock. If I forgot anything I doubt there's anyplace still open where I can go buy it now anyhow."

"True enough," Quinn said. He shouldered his pack and walked toward the truck. "Come on. We'll have to drive around the flight line and catch our ride from there. I'm sure you're fine. As long as you have some kind of knife, a light, and a way to start a fire, you should be okay."

"You didn't even mention a gun," Beaudine said.

"A gun is important," Quinn said. "But bullets won't keep you warm when it's dark and you're freezing to death."

A half an hour later, Khaki Beaudine sat with her nose pressed to the window of the Air Force C-12, watching the lights of Joint Base Elmendorf Richardson slip away beneath her. Quinn had fallen asleep as soon as they started rolling, kicked back in the worn leather seat across the aisle as if he was accustomed to flying on last-minute missions to track down Russian chemists bent on destroying the free world. There was a relaxed surety about him that could easily have come across as conceit—or at the very least intimidating. When he spoke with you, he appeared to be genuinely interested in what you said, rather than simply waiting for his turn to talk again.

Khaki had only been out of Quantico for a year, and she vividly remembered the buckets of testosterone exuded by so many of the male students itching to prove they were the best in their class of NATs—New Agent Trainees. Type A personalities were the norm in law enforcement, and the FBI in particular, but she could tell even from the short time she'd been around him that Quinn wasn't so easy to put into neat descriptive boxes and columns. She was pretty sure Myers-Briggs had an entire "Q" category developed just for him. He was driven, to be sure. Mr. Palmer had told her as much. But now, he looked like he'd been run over by a truck.

It was apparent that he would have been more comfortable working with Veronica Garcia or Jacques. Khaki knew Quinn and her cousin were closer than brothers, so she was certain they had talked despite the vague denial from Ronnie Garcia. She just wondered how much Jacques had given up. Some things you didn't even tell your brother. Quinn had his own dark secrets. She was sure of that. Everybody did, no matter how pretty and perfect their life appeared on Facebook.

Quinn must have known she was new to the Bureau. He could have quizzed her about her skills and abilities but instead decided it was best to catch up on his rest. Odd behavior for a warrior type who'd just had a new partner thrust upon him. Beaudine looked past her own reflection in the window and wondered what she would have done under the same circumstances.

The pilot climbed out to the north, banking slightly west as he flew over the Knik Arm of the Cook Inlet. A few moments later the lights of Anchorage winked out behind them as they flew into the inky blackness of Alaska. It was plenty warm inside the plane, but Khaki pulled her vest up around her shoulders and shivered. The vastness of the land outside made her wonder if there was a backpack large enough to bring all the things she might need to survive.

She'd been minding her own business, happy to be shed of her worthless husband, and working in the Washington Field Office. WFO was where the real work happened. And now she'd been sucked into this nothing assignment out in the middle of Iceberg, Alaska, chasing some Russian scientist who had, from all accounts, lost his marbles.

Her body and brain told her it was well past one in the morning, no matter what time it was in this frigid hellhole. She pushed the button to let her seat recline and let her head fall sideways to look at Quinn. His deep and rhythmic breathing was barely audible above the hiss of the aircraft ventilation. She couldn't tell if he was relaxed or just completely exhausted.

She shoved the pack in the seat beside her, trying to remember what she'd stuffed inside it when she'd gotten her orders. This was a dead-end mission anyway, and you didn't need much gear for that. It was just make-work for a brand new "breast-fed"—what her bastard ex and his cronies called female agents. She'd be in and out in a couple of hours, ready for some other no-action assignment.

Chapter 14

New York

The UN dinner broke about the same time Bowen got permission from higher authorities to leave the assignment, flooding the already choked streets with armored vehicles as he and Thibodaux left the DoubleTree on Lexington. Snaking motorcades of over a hundred delegations—each blipping their sirens and flashing emergency lights to jockey for position—turned Midtown Manhattan into a honking, stagnant sea of black sedans and yellow cabs. Native New Yorkers stood bunched up at each intersection supremely unimpressed by the red and blue lights. Bordering on angry mobs, they glared at every passing Town Car and Suburban as if they were part of an invading army. Tourists lined the teaming streets with no idea of what was going on. They hoped, no doubt, to see someone famous when a motorcade pulled up in front of a hotel. Instead, they got the foreign minister of Togo—who turned out to be a very gracious, if not famous, personality.

Thibodaux had the rental car, so he drove, nosing his way through traffic toward the Battery Park Tunnel and Brooklyn, Petyr Volodin's last known address. Bowen had changed into a pair of jeans and a navy-blue cotton polo, happy to be out of the monkey suit. He left the tail out to help conceal his pistol. A brown jacket of distressed leather gave him some protection against the chilly morning fog.

It was nearly two in the morning when they finally reached a shabby, five-story walk-up apartment building four blocks off the boardwalk in Brighton Beach.

The big Cajun pulled the rented Ford Taurus next to the curb half a block from the apartment building, across the street from a Russian grocery. He chewed on a flat wooden stir stick he'd swiped from the hotel kitchen and used it to gesture when he spoke, reminding Bowen of the way his grandfather chewed a sprig of hay on the family ranch back in Montana. Steam rose from a sewer grate in front of the car, entwining the beam of the headlights and giving the dark night an otherworldly feel.

"How do you want to do this?"

"Same way you would do it, I'd guess," Bowen said.

"Okay," Thibodaux tossed the wooden stick over his shoulder into the backseat of the rental car. Voices carried on the quiet street, so he began to whisper as he exited the car. "You knock. If our guy gives us any trouble, I'll shoot him in the face." He pressed the door closed instead of slamming it. Then turned to walk toward Volodin's apartment as if that was all there was to planning.

"Hang on now," Bowen said, trotting to keep up with the Marine. "You might want to modify your community policing style. We're in the U.S., not driving insurgents out of Fallujah."

"You think I'm bad." Thibodaux grinned, bounding

up the stoop and pushing open the glass doors. "You should try workin' with Quinn."

Bowen rolled his eyes at the mention of the name. He'd faced Jericho Quinn in a boxing ring in college—and been assigned to hunt him when he was wanted for murder. Bowen trusted the man, even respected him, but it was hard to like someone who'd done such a good job of breaking your nose. "How about we just show Petyr our credentials and see where that takes us."

"Flash him your U.S. Marshals creds," the big Marine said under his breath. He ran a thick forefinger up and down the lobby mailboxes, studying the names written on peeling masking tape. "Marines don't need no stinkin' badges."

"I thought Palmer had worked it out so you were on loan to OSI," Bowen said. "Didn't they give you a badge?"

"I got one, but I don't like to use it." The big Marine gave a mock shudder. "It makes me feel . . . I don't know . . . all Air Forcey."

Apartment 307 was located at the end of a short and dimly lit tile hallway to the left of the stairs.

Thibodaux stopped when he got to the top and sniffed the air.

"What?" Bowen said.

"Blood," the Cajun said, closing his good eye while taking a deep breath through his nose. "And other stuff."

Bowen nodded. Thibodaux was right. Amid the decaying smell of mothballs and peeling paint, the unmistakable copper tinge of blood stung his nostrils. Only someone who knew the smell of slaughter would recognize it, but the presence of "other stuff" hung heavy in the air. Bowen found the first blood smear half a minute later on the chipped tile floor outside of Petyr

Volodin's apartment. There was no more than a teaspoon worth, dark as chocolate syrup, pooled in the shadows below the mouth of the garbage chute. On the tile beside it was something more sinister, a fragment of bone, moist and pink, and about the size of a dime.

"Wonder if that's a chunk of our guy's skull?" Thibodaux whispered, tossing a look over his shoulder at apartment 307.

Bowen stepped to the side of the frame to take himself out of the line of fire should anyone inside decide to shoot through the door. Thibodaux took up a position on the opposite side, back a step. When the Marine nodded that he was set, Bowen reached across and pounded three times with the heel of his left hand, expecting a neighbor to come out at any moment to confront them for the noise at this time of night. If anyone was upset, they kept it to themselves.

"Want me to huff and puff?" Thibodaux said when no one answered, backing off another half step like he was going to boot the door.

Bowen shook his head and took a black leather pouch from the inside pocket of his jacket. He opened it to reveal a half dozen slender metal shims—his lock-picking tools. "Watch my six," he said and had the door open in twenty seconds.

There is a particular stillness to a vacant house or apartment. For safety's sake, Bowen assumed there was a bad guy hiding in some closet waiting to blow his brains out, but he could almost always feel it when there was no one home. Both men entered with pistols drawn anyway, rolling around the doorframe and doing a quick sweep for threats—stepping over and around the copious pools of blood and bone as they moved.

Petyr Volodin was long gone—judging from the carnage, probably long dead.

The overwhelming odor of dirty gym socks and the dead-animal flatulence of a gym rat on a steady diet of protein powder hung in an invisible cloud. Someone had done a cursory job of cleaning up, but there was enough blood and what Thibodaux called "spatter matter" on the tile floor to lead to the logical conclusion that Volodin—or someone—had been killed just inside the door. A bloody baseball bat lay on the floor next to the radiator, encrusted with matted hair. Bone does a lot of damage to wood and jagged shards were embedded up and down the business end of the bat. There was a divot in the tile where the killer had overshot his mark and hit the floor instead of his intended victim.

Bowen looked at the bat and closed his eyes, remembering too many bloody scenes from his time in the Middle East. Rage did terrible things to people. He'd once seen one man beat another with so much vigor he'd broken the handle off a claw hammer in the process.

"You okay?" Thibodaux said, snapping his fingers to break Bowen's trance.

The deputy exhaled quickly, coming back to the present. "I am outstanding," he said. "Thanks for asking." He left the bloody bat where he'd found it.

The apartment was small, consisting of a living room and kitchen just inside the front door. The bathroom was tucked in behind the kitchen, adjacent to a single bedroom. The kitchen was tiny—what Bowen's Coast Guardsman father called a one-butt galley. Thibodaux alone took up the entire space. Considering the piles of dirty laundry, porn magazines, and video games that covered the floor, the bedroom was too small for both men to stand in at the same time.

"Gallons of blood here," Bowen said, looking across

the empty apartment toward the door. "And blood on the garbage chute."

"I know," Thibodaux said. The big Cajun gave a sour grimace, as if he was sick to his stomach. "I guess we should go look in the basement. What you wanna bet we're gonna find our shitbird down there with his head stove in . . ."

The darkness of the basement was greasy with diesel fuel and the sour stench of garbage from the twenty-four apartments on the floors above. Deputy Bowen reached around with his left hand to search inside for a light switch, pistol at waist level and standing outside the fatal funnel of the metal threshold. Jacques Thibodaux was two steps behind him. Some people liked to search an unknown area with flashlights, but in most cases, Bowen preferred to throw as much light on the matter as possible right from the beginning. The odds that anyone would hide where they'd dumped a body were long, but Bowen had never walked into any dark basement including his own without feeling there was something lurking in the shadows.

And there was—a black rat the size of a small dog. The thing looked up with pointed eyes and made a little phhht sound that Bowen imagined was the sound rats made when they were disgusted. It didn't seem too fazed by their presence but waddled off, raising its tail toward the two men in what must have been the rat version of flipping them the bird.

"I hate rats," Thibodaux muttered.

"I got more blood," Bowen said, pointing with a bladed hand to the garbage chute above a rusty, powder-blue dumpster as soon as his eyes adjusted to the light.

They made a quick sweep of the room before stopping to investigate the blood, checking the double doors across from the Dumpster where the garbage truck would back up from the alley. It was secured with a padlock, but the dented metal man-door beside it swung freely, with nothing but a hole where the knob was supposed to be.

"Puddles of blood, rats, and lord knows what else," Jacques said, taking a quick peek into the alley. "This place is spooky as shit. Apparently, the management feels that no one in his right mind would come in here to steal anything."

Satisfied they were safe from ambush, Bowen held his breath and leaned over the lip of the Dumpster to find two bodies partially wrapped in blood-soaked sheets.

"Neither one of these looks like Petyr," he said.

"Holy hell." Thibodaux came up behind him to see for himself. He gulped, eyes glued to the carnage. "Neither one of 'em look much like anybody anymore," he said.

The Cajun was right. Whoever bludgeoned the two men had left little to identify their faces. It was no wonder there was so much evidence of a violent death upstairs in Petyr's apartment.

"I'm pretty sure they're dudes," Thibodaux said, regaining his composure by slow degree. "Middle Eastern maybe, but that's about as far as it goes. Let's get a couple of photo—"

The almost imperceptible scuff of a footfall on concrete drew both men's attention toward the stairs. Thibodaux put a finger to his lips and drew his Kimber and pointed it toward the doorway. Bowen's Glock was already in his hand. Bowen nodded that he understood and took up a position to the right of the door while the Marine stepped to the left, angled to avoid crossfire. Pistol muzzles angled toward the floor, both men froze, waiting. Bowen knew it was likely the super or someone else connected with the building but after seeing the bludgeoned faces, neither he nor Thibodaux was willing to take any chances.

The scuff of another footstep whispered down from the stairwell, followed a few seconds later by a third—then silence. Bowen was just beginning to wish he'd left the lights off when the point of a leather boot, followed by a knee, crept slowly into view.

Because of their angles, Thibodaux was closest. He gave Bowen a wink, and nodded to the Glock while he holstered his Kimber. Bowen understood immediately that he would provide lethal cover while the big Marine, one of the strongest men the deputy had ever seen, would grab whoever came through the door.

They didn't have to wait long.

A glimpse of brown flashed through the doorway. Thibodaux pounced, snatching what appeared to be a sleeve. He ended up with nothing but an empty corduroy jacket. Whoever was on the other end turned and tore back up the stairs, heavy boots slapping the concrete steps in an all-out sprint.

"*Cochons*!" Thibodaux said, drawing his pistol and doing a quick peek around the threshold before bolting through the door and up the stairs. Bowen followed a half a step behind, catching just a glimpse of a bearded runner before he rounded the landing above, swinging himself around the steel railing with one hand as a pivot.

"I . . . hate . . . stairs . . ." Thibodaux ranted as he ran, in perfect time with his feet hitting the steps.

The bearded man hit the fire door hard at the top of the landing, shoved it open and ran onto the roof. The heavy door slammed shut behind him, echoing in the concrete well like a gunshot.

Faced with the closed door, both Bowen and Thibodaux slowed. Each knew better than to rush out into the unknown. The metal door opened outward. Crouching in the stairwell, Bowen tipped his head toward an exit sign above and frowned.

"Fire exit," he said, catching his breath.

"Great," Thibodaux said. "Our turd's just waltzin' his way down the fire escape while we're trying not to get ourselves killed."

"Or he's waiting right outside the door to shoot us," Bowen whispered. He glanced at the door handle, which was nearest to where Thibodaux stood. "What do you think?"

The Marine flung open the door in answer. Bowen did a quick buttonhook, rolling around the threshold to allow Thibodaux fast access behind him. It was too easy to get bunched up and play Keystone cops going through a door with a man as large as the big Cajun.

Through the blue darkness between the night sky and the black tar roof, the arched supports of a rusted fire escape ladder over the lip of the building squeaked and moved under the load of someone climbing to the ground. Bowen ran to the edge and peered over, just in time to see the bearded man jump into the passenger side of a dark sedan that waited on the street below. They sped away without any lights.

"Tell me you got a good look at him," Bowen said as Thibodaux came up beside him.

"Oh, hell yes, I did," Thibodaux sighed.

"It wasn't Petyr," Bowen said, waiting for Thibodaux to confirm what he already knew.

"Not unless he's grown a black beard, lost fifty pounds, and turned into a track star."

Bowen bounced his fist on the lip of the waist-high cinderblock parapet that ran around the edge of the roof. "I'll get with NYPD. They may have some cameras down on the stree—"

The metallic squeak of the stairwell door sent a chill down Bowen's spine. He froze, shooting a sideways glance at Thibodaux and held his breath. The quarry gone, both men had relaxed too quickly.

Somewhere in the darkness behind them, Bowen heard the unmistakable snick of a rifle safety coming off.

Chapter 15

Nome

A howling wind blew in from the Bering Sea, shoving at Volodin like the horns of an angry bully. Kaija stood hunched over as she worked on the man door to the hangar, assuring him over the screaming blizzard that she could get past the combination lock. He had thought the lee of the metal building would block the storm, but the wind seemed to come from every direction at once. There was no hiding from it. Crystalline snow scoured the exposed skin of his face and neck, forcing him and his daughter to withdraw into their scant clothing like tortoises in a sandstorm.

It seemed impossible, but the attack he'd seen on television was of his creation. Someone had sold or given away New Archangel. Only he and Lodygin had the codes to the lab, so it had to be Lodygin. If the Captain was involved, then so was Colonel Rostov. Evgeni Lodygin was a vile thing to be sure. Volodin warned Kaija to stay well away from the pervert. But from what Volodin had seen, the Captain would not so much as get a haircut unless he had the approval from his boss.

His back to the wind, Volodin pounded at his forehead with a palm, trying desperately to fill in the growing black holes that seemed to be taking over his mind. He knew he was a bad man. Chemical weapons had been called "a higher form of killing," but Volodin knew that was a lie. There were no high and low killings. Only killing. It made no difference if it was for money or patriotism. Anyone who would create a substance as deadly as New Archangel had made a deal with the devil. Volodin cursed himself at the thought. He could not remember making the deal, but he must have. And if he made a bargain so vile, what else had he done?

"It is open," Kaija said, entering the hanger without looking back. Her anger toward him was palpable. And why shouldn't she be angry? It was his fault they'd been forced to hide for hours in the cramped attic above the lavatories of the air-charter building. They were unprepared, and they both knew it was his doing.

They'd waited another hour after the building had closed, moving only when they heard the last of the employees lock the door to the charter office.

It was Kaija who located another hangar where they could spend the remainder of the night. She was a supremely intelligent girl, and had, Volodin supposed, spent enough time around him to know that people, even smart ones, tended to write down things like door combinations. This one was scratched into the paint of the metal siding a few feet away from the push-button cypher lock.

Volodin lit a match as soon as he entered the pitch-black hanger. Kaija was quick to blow it out, using the light from her mobile phone to point to three high-wing bush planes and the assorted fuel cans stacked around them.

"Papa," she said, shaking her head and glaring with

her small mouth set in a hard line, the way her mother had looked when she was cross. "This is not a place to light matches."

"Of course," Volodin said, tapping at his forehead with an open hand again. "I should have known better. I am sorry, child."

Kaija led the way across the rough concrete floor. A metal desk, a filing cabinet, and a small refrigerator set one area of the open bay apart as an office area. Thankfully there was a stack of candy bars and four plastic bottles of water inside the fridge. Kaija scooped them up along with something wrapped in white paper that turned out to be a pastrami sandwich.

Kaija cut the sandwich in half and handed part to Volodin. "Eat this," she said, biting into her half. "It will help you get your strength back."

They ate in silence for a time, with Kaija playing the light of her phone around the huge space, past shelving piled high with airplane parts and winter gear.

"I need to know something, Papa," Kaija said at length.

"Of course," he said. He'd dragged her this far. What else could he say?

"The spill into the river," she said, eyes piercing even in the dim light of the phone. "What were you thinking?"

Volodin sighed. He'd taken only two bites of the sandwich before his stomach began to rebel. He carefully wrapped the rest and set it on the corner of the desk so Kaija could eat it later.

"Honestly," he muttered. "I do not know. It seems to me that the entire lot of what I have done should be destroyed. I must have thought that if I released the chemicals one half at a time, they would be inert and cause no damage."

"They would have, Papa," Kaija said, frustration showing in her twitching brow. "But for some unknown reason you decided to release both components within minutes of each other. Had you not rinsed out the original batch you would have been killed when you simply flushed the second set down the drain."

"Perhaps that would have been better than what is happening to me now," Volodin said, hanging his head.

"We have been rushed, Papa," she said, stating the obvious. But perhaps he needed the obvious. He certainly made enough mistakes. "Rushed into fleeing our homeland when we are unprepared."

"I know this," he whispered.

"Do you, Papa?" She was fuming now. "Do you understand how important it is that we discuss big decisions? There are many places in the world I would have wanted to go besides the United States. Your foolishness has put us in jeopardy. You have put everything in jeopardy."

"I am a horrible man, *kroshka*. Tomorrow I will turn myself in to the American authorities. I will tell them you had nothing to do with this, and they will give you asylum. Perhaps you will like America." He smiled. "It is not such a bad place. They have excellent universities"

"I do not wish to live in America!" Kaija screamed. "We will be at the mercy of filthy, thieving *zhid*!"

Volodin slapped her, hard, bringing a trickle of blood to the corner of her mouth. "Never use that word," he said. "Your great-grandmother was a Jew."

Kaija rubbed her jaw, staring at him. For a moment, he thought she might hit him back. Instead, she merely shook her head. "I am very tired," she said.

"I am sorry, *kroshka*," Volodin said. "I should not

have struck you." Her mother had held such racist thoughts, and it had been a constant source of friction between them.

Kaija held up her open hand. "The fault is mine, Papa." She clearly had no remorse about what she'd said, only that she'd said it to him. "I will watch my words. We are both exhausted."

There were no cots inside the hanger, but there were several pairs of nylon wing covers, quilted bags to protect the plane from snow and frost. Two of them folded made a serviceable if lumpy mattress to keep them off the chilly concrete. And two more proved large enough to climb inside and use as sleeping bags.

"Go to sleep, child," Volodin said as he settled in against the stiff nylon. It smelled of oil and mildew, but it was American oil and mildew. "We must not be here when the owners of this place come in tomorrow."

"Papa," Kaija said, facing away in her own makeshift bag. "I am concerned about your plan to go to the authorities tomorrow."

Volodin rolled onto his shoulder. His eyes had become accustomed to the darkness, and he could just make out the lump of cloth that was his daughter in the dim glow from the computer on the desk a few feet away.

"What would you have me do?" He asked. "We cannot hide for long. Those men are surely still looking for us. I expect I will see more by tomorrow. Rostov has eyes everywhere. They will crawl through car and building until they find us."

"I am sure this is true." The heavy nylon wing covers rustled in the darkness as Kaija rolled up on her side as well, looking directly at him. "And that goes to my point. Nome, Alaska, is a very small place, barely larger than Providenya—and just as remote. We will eventually have to go to the authorities, but not here. It would be better to wait until we are in Anchorage where we have a better chance to find someone not in league with Colonel Rostov."

"Anchorage?" Volodin said. "There will be people looking for us at the airport."

"I have a friend," Kaija said. "A girl who lives in a small village northeast of here. If we can get to her, she will help us. It will be out of the way, but according to her, the authorities do not check identification on small aircraft within the state. We can get to Anchorage without raising suspicion."

"How do you know this girl?" Volodin said.

Kaija fell back in her bed, laughing. "You are such an old man, Papa. The Internet makes it possible to have friends all over the world. We will find a flight out to my friend, Polina, in the morning. She will help us."

"So I should not turn myself in?" Volodin said.

Kaija gave an exasperated sigh. "No, Papa, you should not."

Volodin stared into the darkness. She was angry with him again. They had been arguing about something, but he could not remember what it was.

Chapter 16

New York

"NYPD!"

A blue-on-blue shooting—catching an accidental bullet from another officer—was a constant danger to any law-enforcement officer in plain clothes. Bowen had been on the other end of the gun in the same situation and knew he was a hair away from catching a volley of bullets in the back. He let his pistol fall to the rooftop, breathing a sigh of relief when he saw Thibodaux was smart enough to do the same thing.

"We're on the job!" Bowen yelled over his shoulder without turning around. Considering all the blood and bone the responding cops had walked by on the floors below, there was no doubt they would be a little twitchy on the trigger.

Bowen could feel more than one officer behind him and knew even without seeing them that several muzzles pointed in his direction. He'd felt the feeling before, and it was not an easy thing to forget. Thankfully the officers were well-disciplined and absent the melee of contradictory commands that were often issued under stressful confrontations.

"Step away from the guns!" a voice barked. It was deep and sure, accustomed to giving orders. "Hands away from your sides!"

A moment later both Bowen and Thibodaux were bum rushed by a swarm of police. Bowen caught glimpses of blue windbreakers and gold shields swinging from neck chains as he was forced face down. Detectives, Bowen thought. That made sense.

"U.S. Marshals," Bowen said as the handcuffs ratcheted closed at the small of his back. His voice was muffled. He tasted tar from the roof. "My creds are in my left jacket pocket. Badge is inside my shirt on a chain around my neck."

A hand reached around to retrieved the black credential case. "Wearing your badge inside your shirt is a good way to get yourself ventilated," the authoritative voice behind him said.

"Can't argue with that," Bowen said. "This thing went from interview to shitstorm before we knew it.

"They got a way of doin' that around here," the detective said.

Bowen chanced a look over his shoulder. When no one kicked him in the head, he began to relax.

A stocky man with a flattened nose from one too many fights stood back a few feet, perusing both sets of credentials. From the way the other men seemed to look to him for direction, Bowen guessed he was the detective in charge.

"They're good." The man nodded to the contact detectives. He snapped the black leather cases closed, apparently satisfied. "Go ahead and take the cuffs off and help them up."

Bowen and Thibodaux brushed the dust off the front of their clothes and took back their credentials in turn. The lead detective raised a blond eyebrow at Thibodaux. "What in the hell is OSI?"

The Marine shook his head. "I know, right?" he said, not bothering to explain.

"Detective Sean O'Hearn," the detective said. "Sixtieth precinct organized crime squad. I'm assuming you guys came to speak to the mope in 307."

"We did," Bowen said.

O'Hearn rubbed his face. "Well, said mope has recently started keeping company with people who are on our radar." He suddenly looked directly at Bowen. "Looks like you been on the wrong end of a fist."

"You should see the other guy," Bowen said, rubbing his wrists, but deciding not to go into detail.

"What do the feds want with the Wolf?"

"Who?" Bowen said.

"It's Petyr Volodin's fighting name," O'Hearn said. "Petyr the Wolf. I know, he's a dumbass. Anyhow, what do you guys have on him? I didn't notice any warrants in NCIC."

"Oh, you know," Thibodaux gave a noncommittal grin. "National security stuff."

"Of course it is," O'Hearn grunted. He turned to walk toward the stairwell. "I got a shitload of blood in his apartment that looks like the floor of a butcher shop—and no Petyr."

"I'm guessing you haven't seen the two bodies in the Dumpster yet," Thibodaux said.

O'Hearn spun in his tracks, interested now. "I have not. The babushka in 309 was up nursing her gouty arthritis and spied you two through her peephole when you were breaking into 307. We grabbed the call from the uniforms when we heard the location was Volodin's. We barely had time to clear the apartment before we heard you two clomping up the stairwell. Is one of the bodies the Wolf?"

"They're faces are pretty caved in," Bowen said. "But I'm guessing them to be two Middle Eastern males."

"No wonder the feds are involved." O'Hearn unclipped a radio from his belt. "Ramos, do me a favor. The marshal says we got two dead in the basement Dumpster. Secure them until CSU gets here." He hooked a thumb over his shoulder, sending the rest of his squad down to help.

"Roger that, boss." Ramos's voice crackled back. "I'm on my way down there now from the lobby."

O'Hearn pointed the radio antenna at Bowen, giving him a wry look. "This leaves me wondering who it was you chased up the stairs."

"Not sure," Thibodaux said, "but he's long gone. Some dark-complected dude with a black beard and short hair. Neither of us got much of a look at him. We were hoping to grab some security video and run it through facial recognition if you have anything streetside."

"I'll see what we got as far as cameras," the detective said. "But don't get your hopes up. The local gangs take 'em out with BB guns and paintballs as quick as we put 'em up."

"Mind if we tag along on the investigation?" Bowen said. "We promise not to get fed gunk on anything."

"Fine with me." O'Hearn shrugged. "I got thirteen open homicide cases attributed to the wannabe Russian Bratva mobsters we got around here. Feel free to help me out all you want. I gotta tell you though, I don't like Petyr Volodin for this one. He's a hell of a fighter in the ring, but outside . . . he's kind of a mook."

"We need to talk to him in any case," Bowen said.

"No doubt."

"Any suggestions about where we start?"

"His girlfriend Nikka," O'Hearn's shoulders shook in a mock shiver. "She's a stripper off Surf Avenue. A place called Cheekie's. You'll want to wear protection when you talk to that one."

"Protection?" Bowen grimaced.

Thibodaux's brow peeked out above his eye patch.

The detective gave a pensive chuckle. "I'm only half kidding. This broad fights us every damn time we make contact with her. Don't tell him I said this, but Ramos—the guy checking the basement for me—he's kind of sweet on her. She'd be kind of a looker if she wasn't so mean. No kidding though, you should wear some kind of sunglasses when you talk to her. She slings spit like a St. Bernard dog when she gets mad." The detective leaned in as if to drive home his point. "And it don't take much to piss her off."

Thibodaux frowned. "Slings spit, you say?"

"Yeah," O'Hearn said. "It's really more of an angry lisp. Hissy, like a wet cat. And gets worse and worse the madder she gets. Red blotches on her chest too when she's nervous. Won't be a difficult clue to spot if you can catch her when she's working at Cheekie's. They don't leave anything to the imagination at that place."

"Hey, boss," Ramos's voice came across the handheld radio again.

"Go ahead," O'Hearn said.

"Negative on the bodies."

Bowen shot a glance at Thibodaux at the news.

O'Hearn's face darkened. "Say again."

"I got plenty of blood, and what looks like brain

matter on the floor and in the dumpster—but no bodies.

Bowen gave a slow shake of his head as he worked out the reality of what had happened. "The guy with the beard was a decoy. He drew us away long enough for someone else to move them."

"All right, Ramos," O'Hearn said into his radio. "Secure the scene and we'll get CSU down there to see what they can find." He took a business card out of his wallet and held it out to Bowen. "I'll work on grabbing security footage from any street cams that happen to be working, if you want to start looking for Petyr."

Thibodaux rubbed his palms together. "Vanishing bodies, killer Russian mobsters, and a blotchy spittin' stripper—this is liable to get interesting."

Chapter 17

Nome

It was after midnight by the time the Air Force C-12 Huron crabbed in over Nome to set down on an icy runway amid a stiff crosswind and blowing snow. The Air Force pilots handled the landing with steely-eyed grace, though Quinn was certain they wondered what was so important as to bring them out to Western Alaska in the middle of the night.

He'd been able to grab a short nap after they left Anchorage, but woke with a start an hour into the flight, his mind flooded with questions. It took him several hazy seconds to figure out where he was and what he was doing on a small plane with this blond woman who had her face pressed to the window. He found few answers even after his head cleared, so he sat with his eyes half shut, listened to the whir of the ventilation system, and rested his body, if not his mind, for the remainder of the flight.

The pilot, an Air Force Major named Sitz ducked his head to step around his seat and throw the lever for the door, before stepping back into the cramped cockpit to allow Quinn and Agent Beaudine enough room to exit.

Cold air flooded the stuffy cabin as soon as the door opened, bringing welcome relief along with the chill. Quinn was used to boarding and deplaning on the tarmac without the aid and protection of a skyway, so he'd put on his coat in anticipation of landing. Beaudine shivered and quickly shrugged on her coat. She didn't complain about the cold, a fact that made Quinn feel slightly better about going on a mission with someone he knew next to nothing about.

A white Tahoe with the golden bear emblem of the Alaska State Troopers on the door idled fifty meters off the nose of the C-12 next to the ten-foot chain-link fence that secured the perimeter of the airport. The Tahoe sat in the shadows, just beyond the reach of the hazy yellow lights behind the Alaska Airlines terminal building. Exhaust vapor swirled around the back tires for an instant then disappeared, whisked away by the wind, making it feel colder than it actually was.

Just a few degrees below the Arctic Circle, temperatures in Nome could plummet to well below zero this time of year. Quinn guessed it was somewhere around twenty degrees—balmy weather by Nome standards—but the biting wind made it feel much colder. The Bering Sea had already brought in the first big storm of the season, and knee-high drifts and plow berms edged the fences and buildings. Pockets of snow clogged the gaps in the chain-link here and there like a giant crossword puzzle, remnants of the recent blizzard.

Quinn's boots crunched as he trudged across the thin layer of crusted snow. The sea wind bit him hard on every exposed inch of skin. He resolved to get the wool liner for his jacket out of his pack at his first opportunity.

Beaudine ducked her head, a look of grim dismay seared into her face by the sudden cold.

The driver's door swung open when they reached the Tahoe, and a smiling woman in a powder blue trooper jacket stepped out and waved. Her cheeks were a healthy pink. Matching rosy lips turned up in a natural smile. Blond curls stuck out from beneath her black wool watch cap. She didn't have the battle-hardened look common to Alaska State troopers who'd spent much of their career assigned to the bush, and some might have considered her a pushover, but Quinn knew better.

"Jericho!" the woman said through her wide smile, grabbing him in a fierce hug that startled Beaudine enough she pedaled backward.

"Special Agent Khaki Beaudine from the Bureau," Quinn said. He sniffed from the cold and stepped aside, giving the two women room to shake hands. "I want you to meet my mother's younger sister—Trooper Abbey Duncan."

Just three years older than Quinn, his Auntie Abbey was really more like a cousin. The two had virtually grown up together. They'd run the Mayor's Marathon, the Crow Pass Crossing, and taken jujitsu classes together over the years. Other than harboring an unabashed hatred for motorcycles, which Quinn could partially overlook in a relative, she was the near perfect aunt. A senior in high school when he was a sophomore, she had been his first crush, though he'd never admit it. She'd stayed in Anchorage after high school, attending the University of Alaska. She'd taught middle school like Quinn's mother but ultimately decided that putting felons in jail was preferable to grading papers and dealing with snotty parents.

"Khaki," the woman said, taking Beaudine by the shoulders as if to size her up. "Is it a nickname?"

"Nope," Beaudine said. "It's on the birth certificate."

"I love it." Duncan hustled them out of the wind and into the Tahoe. "Call me Aunt Abbey." She rested her hands on the steering wheel and waited for the C-12 to taxi out to the vacant runway. "You're always into the big stuff, nephew, getting dropped off by an official Air Force plane that's doing a turn and burn just to get you out here." She drummed manicured thumbs on the wheel, glancing back and forth between Quinn, who sat in the front, to Beaudine, who was behind the Plexiglas prisoner screen.

"She's the important one," Quinn said, tossing a backward glance at Beaudine. "I came along to show her around."

"Whatever you say." Duncan smiled. She'd grown up in Alaska but for some reason had an accent like she was from Minnesota. "Anyways, you guys are lucky it warmed up. We've had one heck of a cold snap here for this early in the year. You gotta make sure you come by the house when you're finished with your secret mission. Michael would love to see you." She gave Quinn a chiding look. "Are you still riding those murdercycles?"

Quinn learned as a youngster that ignoring the question was much easier than arguing with Aunt Abbey.

"Our hotel's the other way," he said, as Duncan headed north off Seppala Drive at the end of the airport rather than continuing toward town and the Aurora Inn where he'd hoped to catch a few minutes of actual, horizontal sleep.

Her handsome face was tinged green in the glow of the dash lights when she turned to look at him. "I am familiar with Nome, my dear," she said. "But we're not going to your hotel. Not yet, anyhow. There's been a break-in at the ticket office where your scientist passed through Customs."

Beaudine poked her head through the open hatch in the prisoner screen. "You know about the scientist?"

"Hon," Aunt Abbey said, "Nome is a very small place. The checker down at the AC store probably knows about your scientist."

"Tell us about this break-in," Quinn said.

Duncan turned the Tahoe off the main road and into the lighted parking lot of the air charter business that handled trips between Alaska and Russia. Snow drifted against the blue metal building, most of which served as a maintenance hanger with the remainder converted office and terminal space. Quinn guessed it was large enough to house five or six aircraft at least as large as the C-12 or a couple of larger birds.

A dark-skinned Inupiaq man wearing a wool watch cap and light jacket stood in a pool of yellow light in front of the building, seemingly impervious to the cold. The smoke from the ember of his cigarette was whipped away into the darkness. He gave a stoic wave when the Trooper vehicle pulled up. The headlights threw his long shadow across the driven snow.

Trooper Duncan introduced him as Angus Paul, a night watchman for the airport.

"I brought the feds, Angus," the trooper said, her voice breathy against the cold air. "Show us what you found."

Angus Paul studied them for a long moment, then picked a stray fleck of tobacco leaf off his lip before turning to walk around to the side of the building. He pointed to a broken window three feet off the ground and still outside the airport perimeter fence. The area was protected from the view of anyone who happened to be driving by and a logical place to try to force entry without being detected. It was also protected from the wind. Several spots of yellow snow suggested it was the spot Angus Paul stopped to relieve himself during his nightly rounds—which was probably the reason he'd discovered the broken window before sunrise.

Quinn took a small flashlight out of his pocket and stooped to look at the ground without approaching too close. Shards of glass lay scattered in two sets of tracks in the snow—the larger, a pair of boots with a lug sole and a well-worn left heel. The other tracks were narrower and smaller all around with a circular pattern in the tread.

Quinn glanced at Angus Paul's boots.

"You won't find any of my tracks around there," the man said as if reading Quinn's mind. He lit a fresh cigarette and blew the smoke into the relative still air in the lee of the metal hangar. "Anyways, looks like more of a break out than a break-in if you ask me. There ain't any tracks walking up to the building, just the ones leadin' away. I followed 'em as far as that drift over there by the road before the snow covered 'em over."

Quinn nodded. "You're right. Whoever made these tracks was leaving, not breaking in. The glass is pressed into the snow where they stepped on top of it. You see any sign of forced entry anywhere else in the building?"

Evidently tired of talking, Angus wrinkled his nose and eyebrows, the Inupiaq equivalent of shaking his head no.

Quinn held his flashlight so the beam fell across the tread, throwing a slight shadow and revealing what looked like the imprint of a flower among the circular treads.

"You know what that is?" Quinn asked, pointing to the design.

"A girl's shoe," Beaudine mused. She squatted down beside him, careful not to disturb the tracks. "Looks like a daisy."

Quinn put his pen alongside the track for scale before snapping several photographs with his phone. "Could be," he said. "Or it could be a chamomile, the national flower of Russia."

Quinn took a couple of notes, gleaning all the information he was going to get from the few tracks outside the building by the time the emergency contact for the charter company showed up ten minutes later.

The break-in was really Nome PD's jurisdiction, but with Alaska State Troopers and FBI on the scene, they were more than happy to yield the investigation. Aunt Abbey carried in a small crime scene kit, but the building manager, a balding man named Charles with a long goatee that was crooked from sleeping, could find nothing missing. It was Beaudine who found the displaced tile in the women's restroom and scuff marks on the back of the toilet where someone had apparently accessed the false ceiling.

"Mind if I use some of your fingerprint powder?" Quinn asked.

Abbey handed over her kit. Quinn used the magnetic brush to dust the back of the toilet with finely ground iron powder, revealing the black outline of a shoe print where someone had stood on the porcelain with both feet. One of the prints was clear enough to make out the design of a chamomile flower in the tread pattern.

Aunt Abbey stood next to the toilet and peered up. “So they cleared Customs and then hid up in the rafters waiting for the building to close.”

“Apparently,” Quinn said. “Any flights leave Nome after dark?” He already knew the answer but asked anyway.

“Nope,” Angus Paul said. “Not even any charters tonight. Too windy.”

Quinn looked at Beaudine then checked his Aquaracer. He stifled a yawn when he realized it was a quarter after two in the morning. “Let’s get back to the hotel and catch a couple of hours sleep.”

“This makes no sense,” Beaudine said. “Why would someone go to the trouble of hiding after they cleared Customs?”

“You said he had mental issues,” Quinn offered. “But I’m guessing your doctor is hiding from someone other than the U.S. government. Maybe a welcome party.”

Agent Beaudine’s face fell into a thoughtful frown. “I’m wondering if that makes this more or less of a shit detail.”

Chapter 18

A stout bang on the door ripped Quinn from the blackness of his dreams and sent him reaching for the pistol he kept on a folded washcloth in the drawer beside his bed. He sat bolt upright, staring through the darkness toward the door. The nightlight from the bathroom revealed that the chair he habitually placed in front of any hotel door was still in place.

The pounding started again, followed by the urgent voice of his Aunt Abbey.

"Jericho!" she said, her voice a breathy stage whisper. "Open the door before I wake everyone in the hotel!"

There was no place to tuck the pistol since he slept in a pair of loose sweatpants, so Quinn set it back on his nightstand before opening the door. He squinted at the bright light of the hotel hallway. Abbey batted her naturally long eyelashes—dark for the blond that she was—and grinned, reminding him of why he'd always loved her. She shoved a cup of coffee in Quinn's face.

Across the hall, the door to Agent Beaudine's room opened a tiny crack revealing a tan strip of thigh and one extremely sleep-deprived eye. The door opened completely when she realized it was Aunt Abbey. She wore a pair of navy blue sleeping shorts and a simple white T-shirt that hid much less than she probably thought it did.

Beaudine ran a hand through the frosted hair of her mussed bed head. "Didn't you just drop us off ten minutes ago?"

"Hours ago, my dear." Abbey said. "Hours ago." She handed Beaudine a cup of coffee as well. "I don't know how you like it."

"I like it now," Beaudine said, taking the cup with both hands and using it to warm herself.

"It's six thirty-five, dear nephew." Abbey shrugged. "You can go back to bed if you'd rather, but I thought you might want to know we have another break-in—with the same chamomile print in the track."

"Where?" Quinn was instantly awake.

"Another airplane hangar, about a quarter mile from the charter office where we went last night," Abbey said. "Looks like your Russian scientist might have slept there. The guy who owns the place is pretty hacked off. I guess they ate the pastrami sandwich he had planned for his lunch today."

Five minutes later Quinn had splashed water on his face and stuffed his gear in the waterproof pack. Two minutes after that, he and Beaudine sat in Abbey Duncan's Tahoe heading back out toward the airport in the steel gray grip of predawn twilight.

"This your first trip to the bush?" Abbey asked, glancing at Beaudine in the rearview mirror.

"It is," Beaudine said through a long yawn.

Abbey kept her eyes forward on the snowy road. "They say you find three things out here: money, missionaries, and misfits."

"Which are you?" Beaudine said.

Abbey shrugged. "Jury's still out."

"No it's not," Quinn said.

The trooper radio on the dash crackled to life.

"Hey, Abbey," the voice said. "I got more news about those folks you were lookin' for." It was Angus Paul.

"We're on our way to take a look at the break-in now," Abbey said. "Whatcha got?"

"Just talked to Millie Beaty at Tusk Charters. She says Earl flew out to Bornite Lodge about fifteen minutes ago with an older man and a teenage girl." *Gussaq* was the not entirely friendly word Inupiaq people used for white people.

Abbey kept the microphone to her mouth, but shot a look at Quinn. "Interesting," she said.

"You better come over here," Angus said. "There's somethin' else you need to see."

Angus Paul was waiting at the perimeter fence, still wearing no more than his light jacket against the morning cold. He held the gate open so Abbey could drive the Tahoe straight inside, and then jumped in his truck to follow her across the snowy taxiway. Private aircraft heaved against their tie-down ropes in a steady breeze. A few had quilted wing covers and appeared to be well maintained. Far too many were tattered and covered in snow, icicles drooping from their props as if they were sad at being abandoned by their owners.

"How far away is the Bornite Lodge?" Beaudine asked when they'd gotten out of the car. She wore her waist-length jacket hunched up around her neck. Her thin fleece watch cap was pulled all the way down around her ears, eclipsing all but the tiniest wisps of frosted hair.

"About two hours northeast," Abbey said. She turned to Angus Paul. "You said there was something we needed to see."

Angus's eyebrows shot upward, the Inupiaq equivalent of nodding his head. A homemade sign bearing the image of a huge bull walrus hung on the small metal hanger behind him. It was the base of operations for Tusk Air Services.

He turned around without a word and started toward a bare patch of snow outside the hanger. Quinn motioned for Beaudine to follow.

"The Tusk plane was parked here when everyone got on board," Angus said, squatting low and holding an open hand over a patch of snow ground. "See that track there?"

Quinn leaned in close enough to see the faint impression of a chamomile flower in the tread. "If we're right, that's your Dr. Volodin and the girl heading for the lodge."

"That's not the most important part," Angus said. "Millie said three other guys came by right after Earl took off. She described 'em as Russian thugs. They told her they were supposed to meet a friend—some old guy. Sounds like it might be your escaped scientist."

"He didn't escape," Beaudine said. "We just need to talk to him."

"Anyhow," Angus said, giving her a wary eye that said he didn't quite believe her. "Millie feels really bad about it, but she accidently let it slip Earl was headed to the Bornite. They musta chartered Corey Morgan's plane because Millie saw 'em leave a few minutes later."

Quinn mulled over the new information. Russian thugs trying to locate a Russian chemical-weapons expert on the day after the attacks turned this into an entirely different mission.

Beaudine was on her phone immediately, talking to what she called HBO—Higher Bureau Offices. The pinched look on her face and the way she kept throwing her arms in the air said the conversation wasn't going the way she wanted it to.

The roar of another airplane overhead pulled Quinn from his thoughts. Landing lights twinkled in the gunmetal morning sky as a blue-and-white Piper Cherokee Six crabbed in, angled into the stiff wind.

"That guy's coming in early," Abbey said. She craned her head to watch the plane touch down before she turned back to Quinn. "I'll go to talk to Millie and see if I can get a better description of those three Russians."

Quinn couldn't help but grin as the newly arrived plane taxied off the runway and rumbled across the lumpy ice and snow toward them. "Actually," he said, his voice rising to be heard over the roar of the approaching airplane. "I need you to do me a favor, Aunt Abbey."

"Of course, my dear," Abbey said. "What is it?"

"We have to get out to that lodge and our ride just got here," Quinn said. "I need you to loan Agent Beaudine a bigger coat."

Beaudine was still arguing with someone in the Bureau hierarchy as the pilot of the Piper Cherokee applied the brake to one wheel and gunned the engine to spin the plane so it faced back toward the runway before coming to a complete stop. A slightly built Alaska Native girl climbed out. Her chopped orange hair, uneven as if it had been cut with a pair of garden shears, hung almost to her shoulders. A pink fleece swallowed her up, two sizes too big and grimy around the cuffs from constant wear. A black ball cap was embroidered with *LOVITA AIR* in bold pink letters. Her faded jeans were ripped above both knees in the way city girls found stylish, but Quinn knew was evidence of the intensity with which Lovita Aguthluk lived her life.

"What in *the* actual hell?" Beaudine groused, hand over her phone. She enunciated each word like the angry Texas girl that she was. "How come she gets to wear denim jeans? I thought you said cotton kills."

"All bets are off with the folks who live out here." Quinn grinned. "We're just wannabes. They're tundra tough." He nodded to the little thing walking toward them. "Especially her."

"Quinn!" Lovita squealed when she saw him, standing on tiptoe to smile and give him a stiff wave like a schoolgirl with a crush. She was the twenty-two-year-old niece of his friend James "Ukka" Perry from Mountain Village down on the Yukon River. Giddy as she was at seeing Quinn, Lovita was an extremely traditional Alaska Native woman. A prominent tattoo of three green lines ran from the tip of her chin to her lower lip, tying her visually to the ways of her Yup'ik and Inupiaq Eskimo ancestors. At the same time, orange hair and a half dozen tiny stainless steel hoops in her left ear put her squarely in the modern world of a young adult trying to make a statement about her individuality. Lovita had become a pilot as soon as she was old enough to get her license, spending every penny flying and maintaining the Piper Super Cub she'd inherited—even saving Quinn's life with her flying skill. Quinn recognized the young woman's potential as soon as he met her and took her under his wing as best he could. With his help and a healthy dose of grant money, she'd recently invested in the twenty-five-year-old Cherokee Six and started her own bush charter service.

Quinn had contacted her before he left Anchorage. The roads leading out of Nome didn't go anywhere, but there were quite a few of them and he thought a dedicated aircraft might come in handy in the search for Dr. Volodin. He figured he might as well give a little business to Lovita Air.

"That little nubbin of a thing is flying you out to the lodge?" Abbey looked up long enough to grimace before going back to rummaging through the back of her Tahoe. Every so often, she'd find something she deemed important enough to stuff into a tattered waterproof duffle.

"She is indeed," Quinn said. "That little nubbin is one of the best pilots I've ever flown with. We've been through a lot together. I trust her."

"Well that's something." Abbey paused, sniffing an extra pair of her pink wool socks before stuffing them into the duffle. "Because it looks to me like you're about to head into the bush with an FBI lady who's going to fight you every step of the way."

Quinn shot a glance at Beaudine, who stood twenty feet away, gritting her teeth and grinding her cellphone against her ear. "She's too busy fighting herself to have much of a war with me."

Lovita ran up and threw her arms around Quinn, pulling him down in a tight squeeze that lit up his bruised ribs. She smelled of cigarettes and smoked salmon and was amazingly strong for such a little woman.

"What's this?" Quinn frowned, eyeing the wad of punk ash—a mixture of leaf tobacco and burned tree fungus—she has tucked under her lower lip.

She groaned. "Don't you start with me," she said. "I'm still tryin' to quit smokin'. One thing at a time."

"Well, *quyana*," Quinn said, using the Yup'ik Eskimo word for *thank you*. He decided it was best not to hound Lovita on her tobacco use since she'd flown through the darkness to get to him. "I know it was short notice.

"It's okay," Lovita said. "I saw the biggest herd of walruses ever, hauled up on a sandbar out in the sound." She winked. "But I'm still gonna charge you for the flight."

Quinn explained the change of plans and the need to make the two-hour flight out to the Bornite Lodge rather than just flying around the Nome area. Putting her pilot hat back on, Lovita nodded quietly then pulled a small salmon-colored book from the pocket of her pink fleece. It contained descriptions of virtually every airstrip in Alaska.

"Us Eskimos got a sense about the weather, but lemme check with the *gussaq* weather guessers just in case. I'll top off with fuel." She looked at her watch. Quinn smiled when he saw it was a TAG Heuer Aquaracer identical to his. It was big for her small wrist, but she didn't seem to care.

"We can be in the air in twenty minutes," she said, checking the weather on her iPhone while she spoke.

Quinn thought about the men with Russian accents who'd just taken off in pursuit of Volodin. "Ten minutes would be better," he said.

Lovita raised both eyebrows. A silent "okay."

Aunt Abbey came around from the back of her Tahoe with a duffle in one hand and a long black case in the other.

"Take my AR-10," she said, handing the bags to Quinn. "I put three thirty-round mags in the case."

"A state gun?"

"An Abbey gun."

"Best aunt ever." Quinn grinned in spite of the uneasiness in his gut. He kicked himself for coming to the bush with nothing but his pistol. A ten-millimeter had the equivalent stopping power of a .41 Magnum, but the rifle would make him feel better.

Khaki Beaudine stomped back a moment later in her own little bubble of discontent. She looked like she could melt the snow with her glare.

"Jackasses," she muttered to no one in particular before turning to Quinn. "And, how come she gets to call herself an Eskimo? I was told they didn't like it."

"Some do, some don't." Abbey smiled. "I figure I'll leave it up to them."

"What did your brass tell you?" Quinn asked.

Beaudine rolled her eyes. "I gave my A-SAC a rundown of what we have going on." The A-SAC was the assistant special agent in charge—always spelled out with the FBI since for some reason they didn't want to be referred to as *sacks*. "Considering we got Russians chasing our guy, you'd think he'd free up some help for us. But nooooo." She wagged her head for effect. "The stupid shit said every other agent in the Bureau is too busy running down more promising leads. I'm supposed to go to this lodge and interview Volodin, then report back."

"Good," Quinn said. "We need to go out there anyway. Since you have orders, I'll let the FBI voucher out the cost of the air charter."

In truth, Quinn didn't mind not having a large group of backup agents. If Palmer hadn't ordered him to take Beaudine, he would have left her behind as well. Some things, like dealing with thugs—Russian or otherwise—were best done alone, with as few witnesses as possible.

Chapter 19

Near Bornite Lodge, Alaska

Yegor Igoshin stared at the back of the pilot's head. He would ultimately have to kill the man; that went without saying. Gachev was larger, so he sat in the front seat of the Cessna 206 to the right of the pilot, a young and underfed man who explained that he was building flight hours as a bush pilot so he could eventually work for a major airline. The idiot droned on as much as the airplane's engine. Thankfully, Gachev would be able to fly the plane out once their mission was complete.

Mikhail Orlov sat next to Igoshin in the backseat, their shoulders overlapping one another in the cramped cabin. None of the men were small, each weighing well over 200 pounds. Igoshin was the tallest of the three and as a soldier, clean-shaven. He had deep brown eyes and kept his dark hair cut close to his scalp. Gachev and Orlov were soldiers once, and like Igoshin, had enjoyed the certain loose latitudes of behavior Russian soldiering brought them. Instead of staying in when their military commitments were up, they had moved on to the more lucrative world of the professional contractor—which, it turned out, provided an even wider latitude when it came to behaviors. They had let their beards go, and their hair reminded Igoshin of two shaggy dogs. Their kit, however, the weapons and gear in the bags on the seat behind them, was in perfect condition. Igoshin's rifle, an American Remington 700 chambered for the powerful .338 Lapua Magnum topped with a Nightforce 5.5-22 power scope, lay lengthwise in a padded case in the back of the plane. One way or another, he was going to try it out on this trip, even if it meant letting the pilot make a run for the river. Igoshin made a lucky shot during his last deployment to Chechnya, killing a separatist leader with his Kalashnikov. An officer, who'd needed something positive to report to higher command, walked off the distance and announced in front of everyone that it was an 800-meter shot. It was probably half that if Igoshin was lucky, but it was enough to get him decorated so he had not argued. Russian needed her heroes—one of them might as well be him. Everyone assumed Igoshin was a crack shot and he began to believe them. He found he actually had an aptitude for long-range shooting and made an honest 1100-meter shot at the range. But he'd been sitting at a table, with the rifle resting on a bag. He'd yet to break in the rifle on a living, moving target.

Perhaps this would be the trip.

When they weren't actually on a mission, each of the three men spent their time exercising their bodies or abusing them with vodka and women. Far from the sculpted muscles of the American gym rats, these men were thick and brutish, preferring the raw power of a barbarian to the look of a body builder.

Spitting rain shot past the wings and trailed along the windows as the little airplane banked into a tight downwind on their approach. The cloud ceiling was high, well above three thousand feet, providing a clear view of the lodge nestled among the pockets of green forest and brown tundra below. Out of habit, Igoshin built a mental map as they overflew the facilities.

Five small cabins fanned out behind the main log building, each with a matching red metal roof, shiny and wet from the rain. Even when viewed from over a thousand feet up, the lodge itself was impressive for such a remote location. It was built of peeled logs well over a foot in diameter with a gabled roof and a massive front porch that ran the entire length of the building. Four balconies jutted from the second floor of what the Russian guessed was the back of the building, leading him to believe there were at least four guest rooms upstairs. A wooden deck, complete with outdoor Jacuzzi, ran between the east end of the lodge and the bank of a small tributary that connected to the larger Kobuk River, two kilometers to the north. A long, slender building that Igoshin guessed was a workshop or garage separated the lodge from the runway.

There was no sign of anyone at the lodge, but they'd met another aircraft in the air a half hour before that was heading back toward Nome. Certainly this was the one that had brought Dr. Volodin and the Chukchi girl. They had strict instructions to capture the doctor or kill him and bring back some type of canisters that they were forbidden to open. Back in Nome, Orlov had pointed out that anything they were forbidden to open was likely worth a great deal of money—and all three men were considering their options as the babbling pilot slowed the aircraft on final approach.

A tall man wearing a green raincoat and a brown slouch hat stepped out of the shop building and walked through the drizzle toward the plane as it taxied onto the gravel apron at the end of the runway and stopped.

A moment later an equally tall woman with her gray hair in long braids stepped out of the same building to join the man. The couple waved in unison.

"That's Adam and Esther Henderson now," the pilot said, peeling off his headset and hanging it over the yoke. "They're usually not too busy this time of year, but I'll wait around to make sure they have a cabin for you."

"That would be most welcome," Igoshin said. He spoke English but didn't like the taste of it.

Igoshin pulled his rifle case from between the two back seats and climbed out the side door after the others.

Adam Henderson stepped up to shake everyone's hand in turn. "I don't remember when we've had so many people come in the same day without reservations," he said. "We still have rooms in the main house. I've already winterized the cabins."

"The main house is quite acceptable." Igoshin brightened.

"I'll go put on some more bacon," Esther Henderson said, peering at the three men with narrow eyes. "You do eat bacon, don't you?" She gave Igoshin a look that said if he didn't eat bacon, he could get right back on the airplane.

"Bacon is also acceptable," the Russian said looking around. The buildings seemed bunched much closer together now that he was on the ground and not a thousand feet up. "I assume our friends have arrived before us."

"If you mean Kostya and his daughter, then yes, they have." Henderson took off his hat and ran a hand through thick gray hair, nodding his head. "I was just calling them in for breakfast. They must have taken a walk downriver a ways because I can't seem to locate them. We have a father and son dentist team here as well but they're likely off fishing somewhere and won't be back for breakfast."

A stiff gust of wind carried in the sweet smell of wet willows and brought with it a stronger squall of rain. Esther looked at the pilot. "You can't fly out in this. You may as well come in and have breakfast too." She turned to make her way back to the lodge, seemingly oblivious to the rain.

Adam Henderson snugged down his hat and hunched the rain jacket up around his shoulders. "This should bring your friends back in a hurry." He offered to help with the bags but didn't argue when the men demurred, turning instead to scurry after his wife. Corey, the young pilot, trotted up beside Henderson, and the two men began to talk of the fat grayling and Arctic char in the nearby river.

Igoshin paused to let the two men get a few yards ahead, then leaned in so only Orlov and Gachev could hear him. "This fishermen father and son could be a problem," he said. "Whatever the case, we will do nothing until we locate Volodin."

Orlov raised a thick brow and stared back, as if letting the words seep in to his thick skull. "I see no sign of the doctor or the girl. This man says they have walked away."

"They are here," Igoshin said, nodding to the scrubby trees along the water and endless miles of tundra that stretched out beyond the woods. "There's nowhere else for them to go."

"And after we have Volodin?" Orlov said.

"Then—" Igoshin gave a benign smile. "Then we will kill them all."

Chapter 20

The Cherokee Six, Lovita Air's one and only plane, was set up to carry six passengers, two in the cockpit, two facing aft directly behind the cockpit, and two more facing those in a vis-à-vis configuration. The rear seats could easily be removed to allow space for more cargo through a small door on the left side of the airplane.

Quinn sat up front beside Lovita behind a second set of controls. He didn't really care for small planes since they put his immediate destiny in the hands of someone else, but working in bush Alaska made flying a constant necessity. In any case, sitting next to Lovita was much more pleasant than being in the back with the spitfire Agent Beaudine, who, since the conversation with her boss, was engaged in what Jacques would have called one long hissy fit.

"No offense," Beaudine's voice came across the headset intercom. "Does it make you mad that they call this plane a Cherokee?"

Lovita shot a glance at Quinn. "It's a great airplane. Fast, strong, nimble. Native name fits if you ask me."

Beaudine nodded and sat back, lost again in her own world.

Quinn's leg bounced in time to the Imagine Dragons song spilling out of Lovita's green David Clark headset. Her orange hair bobbed back and forth as she mouthed the words to "I Bet My Life on You." Quinn smiled. Mattie loved that song—and it suited all three of them perfectly.

Lovita had brought smoked salmon strips—Quinn's favorite—and a plastic margarine tub of *akutaq,* also known as Eskimo ice cream. It was a blindingly sweet concoction made from whipped fat, sugar, and berries. Most people now made it with Crisco but Lovita preferred the more traditional ingredient of caribou fat. Tasting surprisingly like buttercream frosting, the rich stuff was the perfect survival food when the temperatures dipped. Beaudine turned up her nose at both treats, but Quinn had gone through a half-dozen salmon strips twenty minutes into the bumpy flight. Each strip was roughly the size of a fat fountain pen and dried to the consistency of soft jerky. A piece of silver gray skin ran up one side of the smoky, orange-brown flesh. The fish still contained plenty of its natural oil, and Quinn could feel the nutrients and energy flowing into his body with each greasy bite. Strips just like these had been carried into the backcountry by Eskimo and Athabaskan hunters for centuries. Some whites called the stuff *squaw candy*, but in Quinn's experience, calling it that was a good way to earn a kick in the teeth from a Native female.

Unable to help himself, Quinn took another strip from the plastic bag between the seats and used his teeth to peel off the skin. He held the skin out to Lovita who popped it in her mouth the same way she'd done each of the earlier strips. She seemed to love the skin as much as the smoky meat—enough to make her spit out her punk ash tobacco—and chew on it like gum while she flew the plane.

As a start-up, Lovita Air had no access to the fancy navigational aids and avionics. Her console was made up of simple analog instruments that gave her measurements like oil pressure, altitude, and direction of travel. A handheld GPS attached to the dash with Velcro provided her with a moving map, but she generally navigated with a paper chart and compass, preferring traditional navigation as well as traditional food.

Suddenly animated, Lovita's voice crackled over Quinn's headset. "Look at all those caribou off my wing." She slowly shook her head as if it was hard to believe. "Must be thousands of them."

Quinn lifted out of his seat so he could look. He turned to point them out to Beaudine who slumped in the backseat with her eyes closed. She'd taken off her headset and put in earplugs, which Quinn decided was just as well. She was looking a little green, the bumps likely making her sick to her stomach.

"Thank you for helping me out with my business," Lovita said, turning down the volume on her music. She used a paper towel to pick up an errant piece of salmon strip from her seat and popped it in her mouth before cleaning up the oily spot. "The way I figure it, I'll be able to get a loan on a second plane and hire another pilot in about three years."

"You're a good investment." Quinn couldn't help but smile at the energy that oozed from the tiny Native woman.

"So far as you know." She grinned back at him, her head almost disappearing into the neck of the well-worn pink fleece. "I joke." The traditional tattoos on her chin only added to the mischief of her grin. If anyone could grow a charter business in the remote corner of the world, it was Lovita.

"We'll be coming up on the lodge in two minutes." She leaned forward to consult the GPS, and then nodded off the nose of the aircraft. "I'll overfly it so I can make sure what the wind is doing down there and you can have a look before we set down."

Quinn nodded, turning to wave and get Beaudine's attention. "We're nearly there," he said when she removed one earplug.

"Good," she said. "Because I need to pee."

"There's another plane off the strip," Lovita said.

Quinn pointed out the window to the Cessna parked at the end of the runway so Beaudine would see it.

"That's Corey Morgan's 206," Lovita said, blushing. "He's kinda got a crush on me. Keeps tellin' me we should get together and raise lots of bush-pilot babies."

"I'll have to have a talk with the boy," Quinn said, feeling a rush of paternal jealousy.

"That's Adam Henderson going inside now," Lovita said. "He's the owner. Always feeds me breakfast when I bring clients out here. I like him."

Quinn was quiet now as he studied the buildings around the lodge and started building a map in his mind. It was fine to eat salmon strips and dream about future business plans while they were flying in, but now he needed to focus on Dr. Volodin and the dangers surrounding him. Odds were that the men who'd come after him were FSB, making certain he didn't intend to defect. A defection could make for a sticky situation if Quinn got in their way.

Things appeared to be peaceful—but questioning the way things appeared kept Quinn alive when he should have been otherwise.

"Agent Beaudine," he said. "You carry my aunt's long gun but keep it out of sight."

Beaudine canted her head and glared. "Let's remember one thing, okay. I've heard about your tactics. You're working for me out here, not the other way around. We're not going in with guns blazing."

Lovita shot Quinn a protective look, and for a moment, he thought she might climb over her seat and claw out the agent's eyes.

"Suit yourself," Quinn said. "My aunt's rifle is there if you want to use it. But good tactics are good tactics, no matter who's in charge—and out here, we are our own cavalry. No one is going to show up and rescue us."

Agent Beaudine snatched up the rifle case and slung in over her shoulder.

Quinn turned back to Lovita. "Would you mind staying with the plane until we check things out. If you hear shooting, take off and try to get a call out on the radio to the troopers."

Quinn knew the chances of getting a call out over the radio from this far out were slim to none. He also knew Lovita was so devoted that she would never leave him behind unless she had a mission—but telling her to made him feel better.

Two minutes later Lovita brought the Cherokee to a stop at the end of the gravel runway, far enough behind the Cessna that either plane could make an easy getaway without turning around. She watched as Quinn and the whiny FBI agent made their way to the front porch. The agent grudgingly carried the rifle in a flat case over her back, out of sight. Lovita could tell there was something bugging the woman, something heavy. Whatever it was, that was just too bad, because Lovita's first allegiance was to Quinn. If the grouchy agent popped off again at Quinn when they were in the air, Lovita resolved to fly loops until she puked her guts out.

Standing by her airplane, a good fifty yards away from the porch, Lovita tried to hear what Quinn was saying but the drizzling patter of a steady rain made it impossible. She didn't really care. She trusted he would do what he had to do and then come back to the plane when he was ready. She thought Corey Morgan might come out to see how she was doing, but he was nowhere to be seen. Instead, Adam Henderson came back to the door. He smiled at Quinn and waved, so Lovita turned her attention to the weather. She didn't mind flying in the rain, but the clouds to the north were growing darker by the minute. She intended to be an old pilot, not a bold pilot, and if Quinn didn't finish with his business before the front rolled in, they were all going to stay the night at the lodge.

With little else to do but wait and watch the clouds, Lovita decided to do what pilots did and try to check the forecast. She'd just reached the door of the airplane when she heard a crunch in the gravel behind her. Smiling at the thought of a chat with her friend and fellow bush pilot, she turned, expecting to find Corey Morgan standing behind her. There was no one there.

A wet wind rustled the dark boughs of the spruce trees along the runway. The few golden leaves that clung to white birch fluttered and hissed, sending a chill up Lovita's legs. A flash of movement caught her attention, and she peered into the tree line. From the time she was a toddler, her grandmother and aunties had told her stories about the *enukin,* small, gnome-like beings that dressed in caribou skin and lived in little houses beneath the mountains. Sometimes *enukin* helped stranded hunters, but they were impish in nature so they could just as easily bring misfortune.

The wind picked up again, shaking the airplane and whipping the treetops. Her back to the Cherokee and peering hard into the darkness of the forest, she caught a flit of movement—but missed the crunch of footsteps in the gravel behind her. She'd never seen one of the little people, but her granny had, and whatever it was out in the woods, it was definitely the right size to be an *enukin* . . .

Gravel crunched again, somewhere near. She cocked her head to one side, straining to figure out where the noise came from amid the swirling, moaning wind. She heard it again, coming from directly beneath the airplane. A half breath later something grabbed her by both ankles, jerking her feet out from under her. She slammed face first into the gravel. It was on top of her in an instant, pounding her face with big, hamlike fists—much too large to be an *enukin*.

Chapter 21

New York

Bowen made a quick call, then asked Thibodaux to drive directly from Petyr Volodin's apartment to the Brooklyn office of the U.S. Marshals Service. The supervisory deputy happened to be one of his academy mates, and let them in with a promise to reset the alarms before they left.

Bowen believed in gathering all the intel he could when he hunted someone, and he ran computer searches on both Petyr and his girlfriend to check national criminal histories. He'd printed two sets of everything he found, including photos, and threw together two powder-blue investigative folders. It was four in the morning when he finished, and Cheekie's was closed by the time they got there. Rather than banging on more doors and tipping their hand, they'd decided to postpone their hunt in favor of a couple of hours of much needed sleep.

Thibodaux picked Bowen up at his hotel at eight a.m. looking more well rested than he should have. The chilly morning air, along with a stainless-steel mug of black coffee, helped to make Bowen feel almost human again. By the time Thibodaux worked his way through the sea of yellow cabs and clogged morning traffic to hit the Brooklyn Bridge that carried them over the East River, he was ready for business.

A large neon sign made up of two tilted wine glasses forming the outline of a female backside, hung above the red double doors of what could have only loosely been called a gentleman's club. Nikka Minchkhi's rap sheet noted that she lived in a small apartment above the place. Thibodaux drove around the block to get a better view of the back entrance. He parked the rented Taurus along the curb a half block away beside a kids' playground that seemed to Bowen to be horribly close to a tittie bar.

"I think I'm more excited to find this spittin' stripper than I am to find Petyr the Wolf." Thibodaux tapped the steering wheel with his big hands. "He's gonna be boring next to her."

"She's our best bet to find him." Bowen leaned back in his seat and opened the blue folder to flip through Minchkhi's file.

Thibodaux stared out the windshield, deep in some thought. "She worked until the wee hours of the mornin' not counting any . . . side business. My bet is she's still sleepin' this time of day."

"No rest for the wicked." Bowen sighed. He set the file on the dash so he could check out Cheekie's website on his phone. "Apparently there's enough of a demand for skanky pole dancers during the day that they open back up in a few minutes."

He slipped the phone back in his pocket and returned to the file to learn what he could about Nikka Minchkhi.

Originally from Tbilisi, Georgia, she had apparently come to the U.S., as did many women from Eastern Europe, with the promise of a job to be a nanny that somehow evaporated when she arrived. Since then she'd been arrested nine times for prostitution, the first shortly after she'd gotten to America when she was only eighteen years old. She looked terrified in that booking photo but still relatively normal in well-kept brunette hair and a loose gray sweater that hung off a pale shoulder. The arresting officers and the prosecuting attorney had been certain the girl was forced into prostitution and basically living as a slave—but Minchkhi had steadfastly refused to give them any information. The charges had been dropped.

Something happened after that first arrest because the photos that came afterword became increasingly terrifying. Apart from her crimes in the sex trade, Nikka had a record for shoplifting, a couple of minor drug offenses, and one arrest for stabbing a fellow prostitute in the thigh with the pointy end of a rattail comb. Each time, she'd also been charged with resisting arrest and assault on a police officer—and each time, the charges were reduced to disorderly conduct.

"I'd like to see what the judges would charge her with if she attacked one of them," Thibodaux said, perusing an identical copy of her arrest record from behind the steering wheel.

Bowen chuckled. It was impossible to dispute the point.

The last five of Nikka's later booking photos portrayed a tall woman with broad shoulders caught mid-swing in a fight with the jail photographer. Bleached blond hair stuck out in all directions like some sort of Medusa. Heavy makeup ringed tired, but still crazy, blue eyes. Ruby red lipstick smeared a full mouth, as if she'd been interrupted while trying to wipe it off. In one photo, her face looked as if it had been ground against a curb, complete with a giant raspberry of pink flesh on a swollen cheek. Another showed a split lip and a broken front tooth. Black eyes and torn clothes were common to all the later booking photos—along with blotchy red flesh from beneath her sullen chin that Detective O'Hearn told them about.

Bowen looked up from the file at the Marine. "Fighting a girl is bad enough," he said. "Naked girls are the worst."

"You're tellin' me." Thibodaux shuddered. He tossed his file folder on the center console and put a hand on the door. "Guess we better get this show on the road."

Bowen sat up straighter. "I usually like to sit and watch the address for a bit—see who comes and goes."

"You kidding me, Gus Gus? Lookin' at your wounded face I'd peg you for more of a barge-in-and-see-who's-in-there kind of guy." Thibodaux checked over his shoulder out the window for traffic, ready to fling open the door.

"Depends on the moment," Bowen said. "If things are chill and nobody's getting hurt, then it's better to wait."

Thibodaux let out a deep sigh. "Sittin' and starin' at the outside of a strip club ain't much of . . ." His voice trailed off, and his jaw fell open.

Bowen followed the Cajun's gaze out the front window to see a familiar tall woman with broad shoulders unfold herself from a little red Miata that had pulled up to park along the curb in front of them. Ronnie Garcia wore the car like a cute little blouse that was a touch too tight. Full, ebony hair hung over each shoulder, dappled in the shade of a sycamore that stood like a sentinel between the playground and the strip club. Bowen couldn't take his eyes off of her as she leaned down to get her purse from the passenger seat. It was a pretty sure bet Quinn would have shot him had he been there to see him gawking.

Garcia backed out of the Miata with her purse and pulled on a zippered hoodie.

"Hey, boys," she said, after Bowen had regained the partial use of his brain and rolled down the passenger window on the Taurus. "Palmer gave me a quick brief on Nikka while I was driving over to meet you." She rolled her bad shoulder for effect. "Maybe I'm still on the injured list, but I think I can still be of some use getting information in an upstanding establishment like this."

"Palmer tell you she's a fighter?" Thibodaux said.

Garcia grinned. "*Yo también.*" *Me too.* "But I'll leave the fighting to you he-men. If we want to find out if Nikka's hiding Petyr, then we need to get inside without giving him a chance to run. Crashing in like you boys were about to do is likely to get us *nada*."

Bowen nodded and shot a quick glance at the Cajun, who'd wanted to do just that, but didn't linger long enough to gloat.

"I have an idea that will get us inside," Garcia said, throwing open the back door to climb in behind Bowen. "You boys avert your eyes a minute."

A series of grunts and cursing came from the backseat for the next few seconds, followed by a black sports bra flying forward to land on the dash. "Thanks, boys," Garcia said. "No way a girl of my . . . stature could do that in the Miata with a bad shoulder." She opened the door again and got out, stopping beside Bowen's window to draw a folding knife from her jeans. Flicking it open, she stuck the point under the fabric of her polo shirt below the bottom button, and cut a small slit. Returning the knife to her pocket, she used both hands to tear a three-inch rip in the garment—sending a shudder up Bowen's spine.

"Anyway," she said through a tantalizing smile. "I think you get the gist of it. I'll explain the rest on the way."

It stretched the bounds of believability to think that the sad-eyed waif swinging idly around the center of three dance poles was a day over seventeen years old. O'Hearn had been dead right. Cheekie's was not the sort of establishment that liked to leave much to the imagination, and the poor thing wore little but a hungry look and a back covered in fading bruises. Techno music thrummed and blared, heavy with base. Multicolored lights flashed and spun in a layered haze of cigar and cigarette smoke, smoothing out the girl's flesh and muting her injuries, but Bowen saw them clearly enough. His knuckles cracked as he clenched his fists, walking between the front row of semicircular booths that surrounded the stage, hunting for someone to punish. Two sorry looking men in their late forties slouched over half-empty beer bottles, either still glassy-eyed from a long night, or getting an early start on a day of drunken leering. Bowen considered busting a bottle over each man's head on principle alone. Ronnie must have felt him tense and let her head loll against his shoulder as they walked past the men.

"Remember," she said, "we're here to see what crawls out of the woodwork, not send everyone running. You're my manager, not Dudley Do-Right here to save the day."

"Got it," Bowen grunted. "But when we're done here, I'm smackin' the hell out of somebody."

Regaining a semblance of control over his emotions, Bowen gave a toss of his head toward a big-jawed fat man who pecked away at a laptop computer at the farthest booth from the door. The stubby big toe of a cigar smoldered in a ceramic ashtray beside the computer, providing the fat man with his own personal cloud. Greasy black hair was slicked backward from a high forehead and bristled over the collar of a dingy white shirt. A minuscule pair of reading glasses perched on the end of a large nose. The glasses didn't quite reach the fat man's ears and seemed held in place by the sheer width of his face. A green lamp sat on the table in front of him beside a stack of cash-register and credit-card receipts.

The man snatched off the glasses when he saw Bowen and rubbed his eyes between a chubby thumb and forefinger. His vision apparently cleared enough to see Ronnie and a fleshy smile took over his jowly face. His cheeks moved upward at the effort, causing him to squint.

"Word is you're looking for dancers," Bowen said over the thrumming noise. He gave a toss of his head toward Garcia.

The fat man picked up a handheld remote control and turned off the music, throwing the strip club into a startling quiet. The skinny thing on stage continued her half-hearted gyrations, and the two men in the booth behind them didn't appear to notice the silence.

"I always have need for dancers," the fat man said, his eyes crawling up and down Ronnie like bugs. "Provided price is right." He spoke with a strong Eastern European accent that Bowen couldn't place—like Russian, but not quite. "It also depends on what she is willing to do on side."

"Take a look at her first," Bowen said, imagining he was showing a prize racehorse—barely able to hide his disgust. "Then we'll talk specifics."

Ronnie winced when he took her by the arm and nudged her forward, gritting her teeth and drawing away. Bowen had forgotten about her injured shoulder, and his heart sank to think that he'd hurt her. The fat man grinned. It was common for men in this business to tenderize their female merchandise.

"I am Gugunova," the fat man said. The drooping smile on his face was absent even a shred of kindness. "Those fortunate to work for me call me Gug." He pronounced it Goog, and Bowen wondered if he knew how fitting the name seemed for his ponderous size.

Gug canted his head to one side, squinting through the smoky bar haze at Garcia. "What is your name and where are you from?"

"Veronica Dombrovski." Ronnie began to speak in halting English, playing the nervous girl fresh to the big city. "I am from Moscow, er, Drezna really. My parents . . . my brothers, they work textile mills. Very poor—"

She launched into a string of perfect Russian, presumably saying the same thing again to make sure Gug believed her story.

Bowen, who was lucky to get the grammar correct in an English sentence found himself mightily impressed.

The fat man held up his hand to shush her. "You speak English well enough for Drezna River kitten." He flicked fat fingers in a circle beside his face, motioning for her to turn around. "Let us see if you speak the important language, Veronica Dombrovski." His eyes slid up and down her body. Bowen grabbed the edge of the booth to keep from slapping the man's eyes out of his head. Gug suddenly turned to look at him, eyeing the injuries on his face.

"And who are you to her?"

"Manager," Bowen said, knowing that if he said any more he'd come unglued.

"How would someone like you manage beautiful kitten like our Veronica?" Gug scoffed. "It appears to me that you have trouble managing yourself." He looked at Ronnie again and licked his carpy lips. "The world is a mean and lowly place, *kotyonok.* I think you are in need of real manager to take care of you."

Bowen took a half step forward, but Ronnie blocked him with her hip. Her eyes flew wide, more innocent than Bowen knew them to be. "I dance maybe?" she said.

A new man wearing a tight, muscle-mapping T-shirt swaggered in through the darkness from some door beyond the leather booths in the back. Knee-length gym shorts showed off his cantaloupe calves. Obviously Gugunova's muscle, he stood behind his boss with folded arms, glaring at Bowen as if he'd been summoned to throw out the garbage. Younger than the deputy, probably not yet thirty, he wore an overconfident smirk along with the tight gym clothes. His head was shaved, his face shiny and youthful—oblivious to what he was about to get himself into. It made sense that the corpulent boss would have a duress button somewhere under the private table. Guys who called themselves Gug were not likely to stomp their own snakes.

A slender Asian woman wearing a tight halter top and white short shorts seemed to materialize from the same darkness to ask if Bowen wanted a drink. She shot Ronnie a look of pleading despair, as if warning her not to jump into this pit of vipers in which she found herself.

A tinkling bell of the front door preceded Thibodaux's entrance. The big Cajun took a minute to look around the place, as anyone would when walking into a dark strip club in a shady part of town. Apparently satisfied, he waved at the Asian waitress to get her attention, and then took a seat at the booth on the other side of the two drunks. He would have a good view of the stage and it put him within launching distance of Gug's table should Bowen need assistance.

Bowen looked back and forth from Jacques to the muscle-bound kid standing behind the fat man, before tapping Ronnie on the shoulder. "Let's get out of here," he said, loud enough for everyone to hear. "I don't trust a man who has to call in his ugly bodyguards to watch a chick dance."

Roaring with laughter, Gug smacked the flat of his hand on the table, causing the Asian girl to flinch as if she'd been slapped.

"I only have one bodyguard, Mr. Manager," the fat man said. "This new gentleman is not on my payroll. He is patron. People come to my place for entertainment. How about you let Veronica Dombrovski entertain?"

Bowen leaned in so only Ronnie could hear. "We can still stop this," he whispered.

"Let's see what happens," Ronnie whispered. "Just try not to swallow your tongue." She tossed him a mischievous wink before climbing up onto the stage.

Chapter 22

Alaska

Quinn approached the lodge quickly, wanting to cover the distance between the airplane and the front door before anyone decided to shoot him. His mother had often told him that there was "*no right way to do a bad thing*." It was a great sentiment, but the older Quinn got, the more he realized that *bad* was on a more or less sliding scale. His particular skill set dictated a job that routinely found him neck deep in things that would have made his mother weep—no small feat for an Alaskan middle school teacher. Heaven knew he'd given her enough to cry about over the years, so he tended to keep most aspects of his life to himself.

Still, his mother's credo stuck with him, and when he found himself doing something bad—or particularly dangerous—he at least did his best to do it quickly.

Moving just short of a committed trot, he kept his head on a swivel, eyes flicking across the face of the lodge as he neared the imposing log structure. Set in a gentle oxbow of the Bornite River, a few hundred meters from the Kobuk, the lodge was at least fifty feet long. It was built of peeled spruce as thick as Quinn's waist and varnished a rich honey color for protection against the bitter winters and rainy summers of interior Alaska. Four connecting balconies jutting from second-floor windows formed a porch over the front door and lower windows of the building.

Quinn trotted up the steps, wondering how many eyes had watched his approach from behind any one of eight sets of curtains.

He didn't have long to find out.

An older man who had to be Adam Henderson opened the door, moving like an automaton. Quinn didn't wait to be invited and brushed past the man to get inside. To her credit, Beaudine moved two steps to the left rather than staying directly behind Quinn after they came through the door. The warmth of the room hit Quinn immediately, along with the almost imperceptible static of fear.

An older woman with silver hair, still damp from a recent trip out in the rain, sat in an overstuffed chair with her back to a floor-to-ceiling chimney of melon-size river rock that occupied the center of the vaulted great room. Her face was slack, and she seemed to be avoiding any eye contact with Quinn. A large man with full red beard and an erect military bearing stood behind her, his hands low and behind the chair so Quinn couldn't see them.

On the far side of the fireplace, to the woman's right sat a young man with a forced smile painted on his sallow face. A blossom of bright red blood stained the shoulder of his tan Carhartt jacket. Quinn tagged him for the young bush pilot who had a crush on Lovita. It looked like he'd been shot, but he was still sitting upright and breathing. Quinn couldn't help but think he and Beaudine had interrupted a little group interrogation by the Russians.

A hallway, presumably leading to guest rooms, ran off the far end of the back wall behind the injured pilot. A stairway of split logs rose up beyond the fireplace, leading to a long balcony complete with varnished log railings. Another large man, this one with shaggy hair and a matching beard the color of a rusty nail looked down on them from the balcony. This one looked twitchy, half hiding behind a thick log support column. Quinn figured they'd interrupted him searching for Volodin on the upper floors. Like his partner, he "bootlegged" his gun, keeping it ready, but behind his thigh and out of sight.

There was no sign of Dr. Volodin or of the young girl who'd supposedly departed Nome with him. Quinn took a deep breath, noting the position and distance of each person in the room. The woman at Tusk Charters had said there were three Russians—which left one unaccounted for, a fact that added to the nagging feeling that pressed against Quinn's gut.

Once back inside, Adam moved toward his wife. Quinn caught him by the shoulder with his left hand, never taking his eyes off the big man standing at the chair.

"Stay behind me," Quinn said, the cold hiss of his voice leaving no room for argument.

Henderson did as directed but couldn't help but call out. "How you doin', Esther?"

The silver-haired woman cleared her throat. "Just fine, Adam," she said, swallowing hard in an attempt to get the words out.

Hearing the terror in his wife's voice was too much for Adam and he started to move again. Esther tried to rise and go to him, but the bearded Russian grabbed her shoulder and yanked her back into the chair. He looked up at Adam and bellowed: "Stay back!"

"You son of a bitch." Adam's voice boiled over in a mixture of rage and unsteady terror. "Take your hands off my wife or I'll—"

"Oh, Mr. Henderson," the man said, his voice thickly Russian. "My friends and I have little problem." His eyes narrowed, his voice grew more intense. "And now our problem has become your problem."

"Now y'all just hang on a second!" Beaudine said, lifting her hands. "My mama always told me that you don't so much solve a problem as work it through—"

"You are not in charge here," the man behind Esther Henderson said, letting his gun swing out ever so slightly from behind the chair to drive home his point. "Little lady," the Russian said, imitating Beaudine's Texas accent. The man on the balcony joined him in a derisive chuckle. "Some problems, they are more difficult to solve than—"

Action was always faster than reaction so Quinn knew he had to make the first move. He'd left his jacket unzipped, his shirttail pulled up over his pistol. All he had to do was sweep and draw. His hand moved toward the Kimber while the two Russians were still making fun of Beaudine's drawl.

Quinn's first round caught the man behind the chair directly in the forehead. He rushed his second, catching the man on the balcony in the knee. He followed up with a third that took him center mass. Both men crumpled to the floor.

"Problem solved," Quinn said.

"What the hell?" Beaudine stared at him in horror.

Quinn ignored her, moving to grab Esther Henderson and pull her back toward her husband. His eyes followed the muzzle of his Kimber as he swept the interior of the lodge for other threats. There was still one Russian unaccounted for. He motioned the young pilot toward him with a flick of his hand. "Where's the third one?"

The kid shook his head, looking like he was about to cry. He looked at both the men Quinn had shot. "Do you think they're dead?"

"Pretty sure," Quinn said. "But it wouldn't hurt my feelings if you went upstairs and kicked the gun away from that guy." Quinn nodded toward the kid's wound. "Are you able to do that?"

"I was feeling woozy." The young man nodded. "But I think I'm okay now."

Beaudine moved to check the dead man behind the chair.

"Any idea where the third Russian went," Quinn said to no one in particular. He kept his Kimber up, moving it back and forth from the balcony above to the hallways below.

"He ran out the kitchen door right after we heard your plane touch down," Esther said.

"Lovita!" Quinn said under his breath.

"Hang on," Corey said, starting after him, but swaying in place and cradling his wounded arm. "You mean Lovita flew you in?"

"She did," Quinn said, already moving toward the door.

Corey gave a pitiful groan. "Then that other guy's out there with her."

The front door flew open an instant before Quinn reached it. The third Russian was darker and even more menacing than his friends. Clean-shaven and broadly muscled, he looked like some sort of super soldier. He strode into the room giving orders and spewing angry demands. It apparently hadn't occurred to him that anyone besides his two comrades might be the ones shooting inside the lodge. He had a pistol in his hand, but it dangled down by his side like an afterthought.

The bellowing Russian charged when he realized his friends had been shot, bending low for a double-leg takedown. He was much too close for Quinn to bring his weapon to bear. The point of his shoulder hit Quinn in the belly, driving him backward and slamming the Kimber out of his hand. Quinn reacted without thought, letting his body bend forward naturally from the impact. Face down against the Russian's broad back, he wrapped his arms around the man's chest and let his legs collapse, allowing the Russian's forward momentum to roll him backward onto the floor. He landed between the two overstuffed chairs in a jujitsu throw called *tawara gaeshi.* Ignoring the searing impact of the unforgiving hardwood against his bruised ribs, Quinn grabbed one fist with the other as he rolled, pulling the monstrous Russian against his belly and bucking his hips to roll him feet first and on his back. The Russian crashed against a wooden coffee table beside a startled Esther Henderson, reducing it to kindling.

Quinn kept moving as he heard the table splinter behind him, scrambling sideways and working to regain his bearings. Stunned but not out, the Russian had lost his pistol as well and now knelt on all fours, blinking as he pushed himself up. Quinn beat the man to his feet and drove a quick knee into his face. The blow should have ended the fight but the big Russian absorbed it like he took knees to the face for breakfast. Instead of reeling back, he exploded upward, roaring at Quinn and coming in for another charge. Quinn was more prepared this time and stepped offline like a matador, slapping the Russian in the ear as he plowed by, stunning him further, but still not putting him down. The

Russian was larger, more powerful—and not weighed down with fatigue and injury. Quinn knew the man would eventually kill him if they simply traded blows.

But there was a lot more to a fight than a simple contest of size or strength. In fact it was not a contest at all. A contest would have implied that there were rules.

Crouching next to the fireplace now, Quinn snatched up a wrought-iron poker. When the Russian turned to come back for more, Quinn bent the metal bar around his face. The big man staggered sideways, still not out, so Quinn hit him again, this one sending him careening headlong against the stone hearth. His eyes rolled back in his head and blood covered what was let of his demolished face.

"Holy shit," Agent Beaudine whispered, her voice a little shaky. "This escalated quickly." She let her gun hand fall down by her side, blue eyes locked on the Russian's battered skull as she spoke to Quinn. "I'd like to see how you fight when you're not on the sick list."

Chapter 23

Corey Morgan flung open the front door and staggered out to check on Lovita. Quinn wanted to follow but didn't dare leave until the situation inside the lodge was completely secure. He retrieved his Kimber from where it had come to rest under one of the chairs, returned it to the holster over his kidney, then stooped beside the big Russian. The man stirred when Quinn began to go through his pockets, laughing a slurred laugh as if he held some great secret that Quinn wasn't privy to.

Stifling a groan from the tremendous pain in his side, Quinn ignored him and did a quick search for more weapons. He found a vicious little hawksbill karambit-style knife that thankfully the Russian had been unable to snatch from his belt during the fight.

"You are dead man," the Russian slurred, blood and spittle hanging in ropy lines from his tattered lips.

"How's that?" Quinn said, looking at the depression in the man's skull. The orbit of his right eye was now more octagon than oval. The fire poker had done a number on him and without medical attention the swelling in his brain was likely to kill him during the night.

"Americans think you are so smart . . . we are not the last." The Russian began to laugh again. "You will never see him coming . . ." He lapsed back into Russian before falling back against the floor, panting, squinting up at Quinn as if he was having trouble keeping things in focus.

Quinn glanced at Beaudine. He counted his breaths to consciously slow his heart rate. The fight was over, but their mission had just moved up several notches in priority. He stood and moved away from the Russian before he spoke, not wanting to put all their cards on the table.

"You get anything new from what he said?"

"Something about a wolf hunter and the moon," she said. "He could just be babblin'. You cracked his head a pretty good one."

"Maybe," Quinn said, working through the possibilities. In his experience, babblers often gave up actionable intelligence. It was just a matter of sifting through all the garbage. "In any case, I think we know that Volodin's visit is more than a coincidence. We need to give your people a heads-up. The Russians want him bad enough to send out a plane full of gun thugs."

Beaudine brightened at the thought. She took the satellite phone out of her jacket pocket and unfolded the antenna, heading toward the door.

"Won't work," Adam Henderson said, nodding at the phone. "I suppose you can try, but we're so far north the satellites are too low to get a signal most of the day. It might work later this evening. The radio's usually the best option but these bastards smashed ours up right after they shot Corey."

"We'll try and call out from the plane," Quinn said. "I'll get someone here to take care of these bodies as soon as we're in the air—"

The clomp of footsteps on the porch turned everyone's attention to the front door. Lovita came in a moment later, pressing a wadded pink bandana to her bloody nose and clutching Corey's good arm. He was obviously feeling woozy again and Quinn couldn't tell who was holding up who.

"I'm fine," she said, before Quinn could ask. "Not much of an Eskimo to let some *gussaq* creep up on me like that though . . ." Her eyes played around the room until they fell on the battered Russian who slumped beside the fireplace. Beaudine had cuffed his hands behind his back, but Lovita stayed well away from him.

"That's the one who hit me," she muttered, nodding. "Serves him right that you broke his head."

The Russian glared, spitting disdainfully at her.

"Somebody gonna tell us what this is all about?" Esther Henderson said, collapsing into the recliner farthest away from any dead bodies.

"FBI," Beaudine said, making the rookie mistake of believing that was an explanation.

Adam's face screwed into a half frown. "What's the FBI doing way out here?"

"There's another Russian man here who came in with a young woman," Quinn said. "We need to speak with them."

"Take them with you," Adam said, hand on his wife's shoulder. "I got no use for guests who bring this kind of shit rainin' down on us."

"They're gone anyhow," Corey Morgan said, looking toward the door. "I just watched them leave in your boat, heading downriver toward the Kobuk."

Adam stepped out to the porch and returned a moment later. "The kid's right," he said. "They took my damn boat."

"It's very important that we find this man," Beaudine said, her Texas accent coming on strong as she poured on the charm. “Do you happen to have another boat we could borrow?”

“Not one that works,” Henderson said.

Quinn looked at Lovita’s swollen nose and frowned. It had stopped bleeding, but jutted to one side, clearly broken. Her top lip was swollen and blue, ruptured where it had been caught between her teeth and the big Russian’s fist.

“Are you well enough to fly?”

“She’s not flying anywhere!” Corey said.

Lovita shot the boy a withering look. “You speak for your own self,” she said. “I been hurt worse than this from a mosquito bite.”

“I’ll fly you where you need to go,” Corey said, blinking back his dizziness. “I won’t even charge you, but she needs to see a doctor.”

“Forget about a doctor,” Lovita said. “I grew up in the village. My head’s harder to crack than that. You’re hurt worse than me.” She looked at Quinn. “Anyways, I’m not gonna get left out on your manhunt.”

“Maybe Corey’s right,” Quinn said, gingerly touching his rib to check for more damage. A punctured lung was not out of the question. “I know from experience how hard that guy can hit.”

“And see,” Lovita said. “You’re not givin’ up. Come on, Quinn, you can’t shut me out ’cause some Russian son of a bitch punched me in the nose. It ain’t my fault.” For the first time since he’d met her, the tough little Eskimo looked like she might cry. “We been through too much together for you to scrape me off like mud on your boots. Haven’t we?”

“I’m not scraping you off, Lovita.” It was impossible for Quinn not to remember how he felt when Palmer had threatened to bench him. Still, Quinn knew himself—and the risks that went along with charging in half broken.

Lovita put a hand on his arm, squeezing. Her eyes gleamed with welling tears—tears of tension, not pain. "Seriously, Jericho," she whispered. "I'm okay."

He sighed, throwing a glance at Beaudine, who just shrugged.

Quinn turned away, ignoring Lovita's plea while he made up his mind. Corey could hardly stand up, so he wasn't flying them anywhere, but it remained to be seen if Lovita was in good-enough shape to get behind a yoke. He decided to search the dead Russians while he mulled it over. They were following Volodin, maybe they had some information about where he was going.

"Tell me exactly what happened, Lovita," he said as he worked.

The Native girl sighed, eyes on her boots in embarrassment. "I got lazy, that's all, and let that stupid *gussaq* sneak up and punch me in the face."

Quinn stooped over the first man he shot to begin going through his pockets. "Did he knock you out?"

Lovita paused, touching the bandana to her split lip.

"Were you unconscious?" Quinn asked. Contrary to the movies, getting knocked out was a big deal. It left you wobbly and disoriented for some time and could very well mean a concussion.

"He hit me, and I fell on my ass, okay?" She threw her hands in the air. "I saw stars, but that's it. I'm sure he intended to kill me, but the next thing I knew, you guys started shootin'. I guess he came back here to check it out."

Quinn stood, stretching his sore back. He wondered if he really had an alternative. They had to follow Volodin. He climbed the stairs to search the second dead man, mulling over the decision as long as possible.

Each of the three Russians carried forged identification as oil workers from the North Slope. They had American names like Tony and Gary. According to his Louisiana driver's license, the guy slumped by the fireplace was A.J. The IDs looked convincing but were most certainly forged. Each man had been armed with a pistol as well as a blade similar to A.J.'s hooked karambit.

"That one brought in a rifle," Adam Henderson pointed at a padded canvas case leaning against the far side of the fireplace hearth. Slightly tapered and the length of a rifle, the case was olive drab and equipped with carrying handles as well as backpack straps. Quinn recognized it immediately as a drag bag. He unzipped it far enough to see it contained a Remington bolt-action rifle and a Nightforce scope with extreme long-range turrets. The Nightforce alone cost over two thousand dollars. This setup was a serious sniper weapon.

Tapping the case in thought, Quinn turned to Beaudine.

"If they're sending a sniper after this guy, they think he's a valuable target—and if he's valuable to them—"

"He's valuable to us," Beaudine said, finishing his sentence.

The Russian leaning against the fireplace began to laugh, staring at Quinn. His eyes were wild and slightly askew from the beating with the fire poker.

"Fool," he chuckled, slowly shaking his head as he lapsed into Russian.

"He's still talking about a hunter," Beaudine whispered. "And wolves."

"Hey, girly," the Russian called out toward Lovita. "You had better run if you know what is good for you." He followed with something that sounded neither Russian nor English. Whatever he said sent a terrified Lovita fleeing back behind Quinn's back.

Quinn turned and put a hand on the terrified girl's shoulder. "What's the matter?"

"He spoke in Chukchi," Lovita said, "It's close enough to Alaskan Yup'ik that I understood. He says there is a bad man coming for us."

"A bad man?"

Lovita nodded. Her wide eyes gleamed like a frightened child's. "The elders tell stories of a hunter who comes across the water from Siberia," she said. "They say this man hunts our hunters when they are out on the ice. They say he is a giant with eyes as white as a winter blizzard. The old women call him Worst of the Moon. I always thought the scary stories were to make little kids stay close to camp when we're out picking berries." Lovita peered at the Russian over her wadded bandana. "I never heard no *gussaq* talk about it before, though."

"Worst of the Moon?" Beaudine mused.

"Listen," Lovita said, shooting a worried glance over her shoulder as if she expected some monster to burst through the door. "I know this sounds crazy to you guys, but weird shit happens out here in the bush. The tundra, these forests . . ." She looked at Quinn for support. "Tell her. You've been out here long enough to see it with your own eyes."

"I have seen some odd things," he said, "all over the world."

Lovita gave a fast nod, thinking she'd found an ally. "I think I even seen an *enukin* just before this guy attacked me."

"Wait a minute." Beaudine put up her hand. "What's an *enukin*?"

"Like a Native leprechaun," Adam Henderson said. "Usually harbingers of bad as far as I can tell, but they've been known to help folks in trouble."

Quinn rubbed his eyes. "Let's focus on this Worst of the Moon character."

Lovita shivered. "It's what my people call February, the cruelest time of winter. He ain't been around since ancient times like the *enukin* or the hairy man. My granny started puttin' Worst of the Moon in her stories about eight or nine years ago."

The Russian threw his head back as if to howl at the ceiling. Instead, he grimaced against what had to be an agonizing headache. The worst of the pain apparently ebbing enough for him to talk, he began to babble in Russian. Quinn recognized one word he used over and over—*okhotnik.* Beaudine told him it meant *hunter*. The Russian's eyes flicked open. One of them stared directly at Lovita. "The stories are real, girly. *Okhotnik* is real."

Quinn took a moment to load a full magazine into his Kimber. He stuffed the partially used one in the pocket of his jacket, resolving to top it off as soon as he got back to the plane and his backpack. This was no time to be walking around with a half-empty gun. Everything this guy said made sense. Most of Russian operatives Quinn knew were meticulous in their thuggery. If they wanted one of their own scientists dead bad enough to send a sniper team to America, they were certain to have a backup plan. Quinn couldn't help but glance out the window to make sure Spetsnaz paratroopers weren't at that very moment dropping into the skies of Alaska Red-Dawn style.

Beaudine folded the satellite phone and returned it

to her jacket pocket, apparently satisfied that it wasn't going to work. "Okay, Quinn," she said. "You're the Alaska expert. What are you thinking?"

"Nearest settlement is Needle Village," Adam said. "Not quite thirty miles up the Kobuk. If they go downriver they'll be out on their own for a couple of days and neither one of them look like they were dressed for a night in the bush. The weather's supposed to do nothing but get shittier."

"They might not even know where they're going," Beaudine offered.

"They know," Corey said. "They told me. And I'll tell you, but you have to let me fly you. Have you looked at that storm coming in from the north? I don't want Lovita out in it in her condition. Let me fly you, and I'll tell you where they went."

"Oh, *hell* no." Beaudine walked up to the boy with a swagger to match her Texas accent. She thumped him in the forehead with her index finger. "We got no time for games, son." She hooked her thumb toward Quinn. "Do either of us look like we bargain much?"

"Okay." Corey rubbed his head, shying away as if he were afraid she might thump him again. "The girl said her friend worked here at the lodge. Said they wanted to surprise her."

Esther Henderson looked at her husband. "She had to be talking about Polina."

"Polina?" Quinn said.

"A Russian girl," Esther Henderson said.

"One of those mail-order brides," Adam Henderson said.

"We don't know that," Esther chided her husband. "Married to a school teacher upriver in Ambler. She comes out and does deep cleaning for us a couple of times a month."

"When was Polina here last?" Beaudine asked.

"Two weeks ago," Mrs. Henderson said. "She was supposed to be back next week but she's having some troubles with her pregnancy."

"Where does she stay when she's here?" Quinn asked.

"Usually in one of the cabins," Henderson said. "But she's six months along. Esther insisted she stay here in the main lodge the last couple of times—so she could be closer to the radio." He walked to a knotty-pine door off the back corner of the lodge's great room, opposite the fireplace, and pushed it open. "This is where we've been putting her."

"Does she leave anything here?" Quinn said. "In between visits, I mean." He stepped past Henderson, scanning the room. It was rustic but cozy with pictures of loons on everything from the duvet to the hand towels outside the private bathroom.

Henderson shrugged. "A few toiletries and some rain gear I think so she doesn't have to haul it back and forth from Ambler. She got a package last week." He stopped short, pointing to a short table at the end of the varnished log bed frame. "I'll be damned," he said. "It's gone."

"What's gone?" Quinn asked, though he already knew the answer.

"The box," Henderson said. "I left it right there."

Beaudine stood in the doorway, keeping an eye on the wounded Russian. "What was in this box?"

"Polina sometimes had packages delivered here," Henderson said. "She told us they were her special cleaning supplies from Russia, but I'm guessing that's not the case."

"Not likely," Beaudine said. "Did Polina take it the last time she was here?"

Henderson shook his head. "It came last week. She hasn't been out here yet. Come to think of it, that girl was puttering around back here. She must have taken it."

"It's been a while since I've been out this way," Quinn said. "Ambler is up river past Needle, right?"

"Another forty miles or so," Henderson said.

"That puts it what, seventy miles from here by water?" Quinn said, picturing the winding Kobuk River. He'd taken a three-week fishing trip from the headwaters to Kotzebue with his brother, Bo, and their Aunt Abbey when he was in high school.

Henderson gave a non-committal nod. "Closer eighty by airplane. Over a hundred by river because of the oxbows."

Quinn remembered the Kobuk's meandering path very well. In some places the river turned back on itself so sharply, he had Bo had been able to scramble up one bank and look over the top to see the portion of the river they'd be paddling on two hours later.

Quinn looked at his Aquaracer. "Fiver hours of daylight," he said. "Plenty of time to fly ahead to Needle and then on to Ambler."

Lovita squealed, uncharacteristically giddy. She jumped up and down like a schoolgirl, causing a thin trickle of blood to weep from her crooked nose. "I wanna be where you are if Worst of the Moon is comin' after us." She grinned at Quinn around a chipped tooth he hadn't noticed before. "You won't regret this, Jericho."

"Worst of the Moon," Quinn muttered, pulling the straps on the drag-bag containing the sniper rifle tighter onto his shoulder. He regretted his decision the moment he opened the door. A bank of thick clouds rolled in from the north, black with trailing green edges that meant hail. Lovita marched past toward her airplane, seeming not to notice the storm moving directly into their path.

Chapter 24

New York

August Bowen chewed on the inside of his cheek and thought of angry nuns, dead kittens, anything to try to keep his brain in focus while Ronnie Garcia climbed the narrow wooden steps. It didn't help.

The sultry Cuban took the stage like she owned it. Her back to the audience, she moved only her hips and arms at first, starting slowly, and half a beat off the music. It didn't matter. Bowen doubted anyone in the club could hear anything but the sound of their own throbbing pulse. Far from tentative, Garcia's every movement was relaxed and natural, as if she were dancing alone and for herself rather than the pitiful audience. Somehow, she had the uncanny ability to make the men in the room believe she was actually enjoying herself, a fantasy they all gripped as fast as their beers.

Bowen folded his arms across his chest and leaned back against the edge of the padded leather booth next to Gug's table. A cold surge of empathetic embarrassment for Garcia washed over him when he thought she might actually take off her clothes. Then he realized it made no difference. Veronica Garcia didn't need to strip to send every jaw in the room dropping to the floor. The sad-eyed waif who had held the stage before her even stopped to watch, bony arms dangling, head shaking in disbelief that this fully clothed woman had stolen the eyes of what had been her small audience.

The younger girl's head snapped up suddenly, looking offstage. She peered through the darkness behind Ronnie for a moment, then down at her own bare feet. Something had startled her, and that something was walking toward Garcia.

A tall woman wearing a gauzy red robe and matching princess slippers stopped next to the gleaming stripper pole on the far right of the stage. Blessed with the same curvy body type as Garcia, this new woman walked with a heavy, cowlike gait, unable to carry the thickness around her hips and chest with the same ease and grace. She stopped for a moment, folded arms pushing up an ample chest, with her hips and a single knee cocked to one side. Her black hair was cut in a twenties-style bob—short in the back and slightly longer in the front. It shimmered under the glaring stage lights as if it had been combed with oil. Pink blotches of skin covered her neck and chest, making her look like she'd just run a mile. Her face was flushed as red as her robe.

Her hair was different from any of the booking photos, but there was no doubt that this was Nikka Minchkhi.

"And who ith thith?" the woman bellowed, pointing at Ronnie with a forefinger that bore a costume-jewelry ring the size of an apricot.

Bowen shot a quick glance at Thibodaux, nodding toward the woman in red.

Gug stopped the music with the remote and raised his eyebrow as if interested to see what was about to happen.

"I athked you a quethchon?" Nikka said, wiping the spit from her mouth with the sleeve of her robe.

"A new dancer?" Gug said, shooting a conspiratorial glance at Bowen. It killed the deputy inside to think that this slob believed they were on the same team.

Nikka leaned in, glaring. "Well, she can't come into our plathe and danth with clothe on. Itth. Not. Right."

"This is tryout," Gug said. "She'll get there soon enough." His eyes went back to Garcia, and Bowen went back to wanting to knock the guy out.

Garcia stopped dancing and leaned against the center pole, rolling her eyes at the woman.

"She ith too clean," Nikka stammered. "I thay she thmellth like a cop."

"You are jealous of my new kitten, dear," Gug said. "I've never seen a cop dance like this."

Thibodaux took the opportunity to walk up and ask Gug where the toilet was.

"Saba," Gug said to the muscleman behind him, flicking his fat fingers. He was more interested in the women on stage than some customer who needed the john.

Saba frowned, put out at having his attention drawn away from the women, but stepped forward to point out the small neon sign in the back corner that led to the restrooms. He shot a quick glance at the big Cajun but waved him past, a hyper-inflated ego binding his mind like his bulging muscles tied up his body.

Bowen made his way up on stage as if to escort Ronnie off, but turned midstride to face the lisping stripper.

"Turns out you're right," he said. "U.S. Marshals, Nikka. We need to talk to—"

Minchkhi's face screwed up like a red raisin. She clenched her fists like a child throwing a tantrum.

On the floor, Saba took a half step forward but stopped in his tracks when the twin barbs from Thibodaux's Taser caught him, one in between the shoulder blades and one at the fold where his butt cheek met his right thigh. His muscles knotted and he fell like a stiff pine board, bouncing off the filthy carpet nose-first.

Gug raised his fat hands. "I not move," he said. Thibodaux drove the contact points at the end of the Taser into the man's neck, shocking him on general principle. The barbed prongs, still buried in Saba's tender parts, conducted the second shock as well, keeping both men compliant.

The two drunks sipped their beers, blinking sleepily as if this was all part of the show. The Asian waitress smiled at Thibodaux, looking like she wanted to kiss him.

Nikka's entire body shook so badly that Bowen thought she might be having a seizure. She shot a glare down at her boss, before turning back to the deputy. "I cut your heart!" she screeched. Slinging spittle, she launched herself toward him.

Bowen moved to one side, preparing to snag her as she came by but Garcia swooped in out of nowhere, catching the screaming woman with a devastating palm heel to the chin that slammed her teeth together with a loud crack. Nikka had obviously been hit many times before, and the blow dazed her but didn't stop her. Stunned but still furious, she ramped up her attack, bright red fingernails clawing the air. Using the woman's own momentum against her, Ronnie grabbed a handful of hair and yanked, pulling Nikka face first into the nearest stripper pole with a sickening metallic thud. Nikka slid down it to land in a heap of red silk and blotchy flesh, finished fighting, but still muttering lispy threats.

“That’s the trouble with you good guys,” Ronnie said, winking at Bowen. “It’s hard for you to really hit a girl like you mean it. Even if she’s trying to gouge your eyes out. Me, I’m an equal-opportunity ass kicker.”

“That was pretty damn smooth, Cheri.” Thibodaux grinned, still holding the Taser above Gug’s neck. He used his free hand to take a flat toothpick from his mouth and pointed it at Garcia, wagging his head as he spoke. “But mercy! The next time I gotta watch you dance like that, I’m puttin’ in for danger pay.”

Chapter 25

Gug and his goon, Saba, slouched on the grimy carpet with their hands cuffed behind their backs. It took two pair of cuffs linked together to get Gug's arms behind him. Three would have been better, but Bowen didn't really care if the fat slob was uncomfortable or not. The two drunks had been shown the door, and the Asian waitress and skinny dancer now sat together in one of the booths, wearing thick terrycloth robes while they wolfed down bowls of stew Gug had been preparing in the kitchen for his lunch.

Nikka Minchkhi sat in the center stage where she'd fallen when Ronnie decked her, knees up, legs splayed, her red lace robe blossoming like a trodden red thistle flower. Garcia had secured the spitting dancer's hands behind her around the stripper pole to keep her from flying off the handle again. One of her red princess slippers had come off during her rant, revealing a hole in her pink stocking through which poked a stubby big toe, pedicured, but blackened on the bottom from dancing barefoot.

Thibodaux stayed down by the two male prisoners

while Bowen and Garcia stood on the stage around the sullen dancer, arms folded, waiting for her to answer their questions.

"I do not know what you are talking about," she said, refusing to look either of them in the eye.

"Are you saying you don't know Petyr Volodin?" Bowen said, shaking his head in disgust. "Everybody we talk to says you two are an item."

"Then everybody you talk to ith misthtaken." She tried to throw her head back in a scoff, but accidentally banged it against the stripper pole in the process. The blotches on her chest flushed to a bright crimson.

"We're not the regular cops, you know," Bowen said. "It's against the law for you to lie to us."

"Tell us where he is and we're outta here," Ronnie said. "You get on with your life or whatever it is you call what you do."

"I do not know where he ith," she said.

"Lithen thweety!" Thibodaux raised the brow over his good eye. "Get your stories straight. You don't know him or you don't know where he is?"

"You are not copth." Nikka glared back at him. "You will only try to kill my Petyr, but you will never find him."

Gug craned his fat neck as best he could. "Hey," he said, getting Thibodaux's attention. "Why you not tell me you are looking for Petyr. She's one of his girlfriends."

Nikka screamed. "His only girlfriend, you piece of—"

"Shut up!" Garcia stepped closer to cut her off. "I'm sure your man is completely faithful, chica."

"Seriously," Gug said, putting on a somber bargaining face. "I have information on my computer to help you find Petyr. Maybe you could do a little to help me."

"I cut you for thith," Nikka spat. The red blotches on her chest began to move up her neck.

Bowen hopped off the stage and moved to the booth where Gug's computer sat on the table by the smoldering stub of his cigar.

Bowen snapped his fingers at Gug. "Give me the password."

"Petyr isth not an idiot," Nikka screeched through clenched teeth. "He knowth anyone would come here to look for—"

In the back of the club, the kitchen door swung open to the sound of someone whistling, loud and off-key.

"Hey, *Zaychik moy,*" a young and muscular man said as he rounded the far booth. He wore a white wife-beater shirt under a maroon velvet tracksuit. A large yellow duffle bag hung from a beefy hand. Earbud wires trailed from both ears, rendering him oblivious to the fact that he'd stumbled into his girlfriend's interrogation. It had to be Petyr Volodin.

Apparently used to seeing his girlfriend tied to a stripper pole in the middle of the day, he hardly gave her a second look. His eyes instead fell to Ronnie as a lascivious grin spread across his face. "Lucky I got here in time," he said. "Let's see some of that ass, sweet—!"

Nikka screamed, yelling a warning in Russian. His head snapped up and he turned on his heels to run. Bowen caught him with a well-placed snap kick to the groin.

The Wolf's eyes rolled back in his head. The duffle slid from his hand. His knees buckled and he toppled over sideways, green around the gills.

Bowen couldn't help but chuckle when Nikka threw back her head in exasperation at the stupidity of her boyfriend and banged her head against the stripper pole.

"Too smart to come here?" Bowen mused.

"You son of a bitch," Petyr groaned.

"Hey!" Bowen cut him off. "There are women present."

"Strippers!" he said, breathless. "I think they've . . . heard it . . . before. They are whores . . ."

Bowen gave him a smack in the back of the head. "Language," he said.

"Okay," Petyr said, curling up from the pain.

"Just don't kick me in the ba . . . in the privates again . . ."

"Privates," Bowen laughed. "That's fitting. I call mine 'the generals.' "

Volodin's head sagged, resting against the filthy carpet. He moved his jaw back and forth like he was about to vomit.

"Well, ain't this a surprise," Thibodaux said, looming over Petyr and pulling him into a seated position to pat him down for weapons.

"It's no surprise," the younger man groaned. "You obviously expected me to be here."

Thibodaux gave a genuine belly laugh. "No, sir," he said. "We expected to have a little chat with your spittin' stripper girlfriend. We honestly had no idea you were such a dumb shit."

"Go ahead and do it then," Volodin said. His entire body slumped as if he'd given up.

Bowen shot a glance at Garcia, then Thibodaux. "Go ahead and do what?"

"Kill me." Volodin shrugged. "Isn't that what Mr. Anikin sent you to do?"

"We don't aim to kill you," Thibodaux scoffed. "Unless you start in with that whistlin' again. That was some awful shit."

"Why does this Anikin guy want to kill you?" Ronnie asked.

Volodin looked at Garcia, then looked away as if afraid Bowen might kick him again. "Vory would never allow a woman to ask your questions."

"Vory?" Bowen looked at Garcia. "Whatever that is, we're not it."

"*Vory v Zakone,* Russian prison gang," Ronnie said. "What have you done to piss off the Vory?"

Volodin pulled back one shoulder of his tracksuit jacket to reveal the eight pointed stars tattooed on his shoulders above the neck of the wife-beater shirt.

"Listen up," Thibodaux said, "We could give a shit about your fictional ink. We need to talk to you about your daddy."

Volodin's head snapped up. "My father? Is he all right?"

"You're close to him then?" Bowen asked.

"Not close." Volodin shook his head. "I guess he wants to make amends for abandoning me and my mother years ago. He's some kind of scientist so he helps me out with Russian body-building supplements." His eyes turned pleading. "He swears it's all legal shit."

"When's the last time you talked to him?"

"I don't know . . . an email about two weeks a—"

A heavy rapping at the front door cut him off.

Thibodaux moved to Gug's computer and checked the surveillance cameras outside the building. "Four dudes with guns," he said, looking at Petyr. "I'm bettin' these are the Russian mob boys you're worrying about, coming for your fake ink."

"You led them here!" Volodin fumed. "That's the only way they could find me so fast."

Nikka rolled her eyes at his stupidity, clunking her head a third time on the stripper pole. "You are idiot," she said. "I am your girlfriend. This is first place anyone would look for you."

"I should go," Volodin said, grabbing the yellow duffle and pushing himself to his feet.

"Sit your ass down," Thibodaux snapped.

The banging grew louder, followed by a loud crash as the door gave way.

The Asian waitress and the bony stripper both ducked out of sight under their booth. Gug and Saba knew enough to roll to the floor, but Nikka was a sitting duck ziptied to the stripper pole. The pop of small arms fire rattled down the front hallway and bullets began to thwack against leather upholstery and wooden rails. Two of the stage lights exploded in a shower of sparks. Petyr fell, face forward, doing a pushup over his yellow duffle.

"Get her down from there!" Bowen yelled at Ronnie as he moved in a crouch around the end of the stage toward the door. He returned fire blindly down the entry hall, hoping to hold the attackers at bay long enough for Garcia to cut Nikka free and move her out of the line of fire. Minchkhi was a hateful woman, but few people deserved to be gunned down while chained to a Cheekie's stripper pole.

"One of the four just turned tail and ran," Thibodaux said. The big Cajun had drawn his weapon but he'd turned the computer around so he could scan the camera feeds while keeping an eye on the back entrance to the club. "Conserve your ammo, Gus Gus," he said.

"Thanks, Gunny," Bowen shouted over his shoulder, sending three more rounds down the hallway. "But this isn't my first prom."

"Never mind," the Marine yelled back. "I keep forgettin' you were Army. You're not apt to hit nothin' anyhow."

Ronnie came up beside Bowen and tapped the elbow of his support arm. "I cuffed Minchkhi under a booth. We're good," she said. Her tight clothing had made carrying impractical during her dance, so they'd agreed beforehand that he would loan her his ankle gun if things turned rodeo. Now that Minchkhi was out of the way, he passed Garcia the baby Glock 27.

Between the two of them, they were able to lay down a steady rate of fire that didn't burn up their meager ammunition supply.

"Looks like they're haulin' ass," Thibodaux said, watching the computer.

Bowen took a deep breath, heady from the gun battle, not to mention the proximity of Garcia. Her chest heaved beside him as she worked to slow her breath now that the shooting had stopped.

"How about the back door?" Bowen yelled over his shoulder, thinking the shooters might have circled around.

"Nope, Gus Gus," Thibodaux said. "They've definitely hauled . . . What the hell?" The Cajun jumped to his feet and pounded the table with his fist.

Bowen turned to find nothing but scabby carpet in the spot with Petyr Volodin used to be.

"Damn this eye patch," Thibodaux said. "That meatheaded son of a bitch took advantage of my blind side and beat feet while I was lookin' at the screen."

He hit the table again, his face as red as Nikka's at having let the prisoner escape. "I am gonna beat his ass for sure."

"That's enough playin' around," Thibodaux said to Nikka ten minutes later. "You need to do yourself a favor and tell us where your boyfriend went."

"I want lawyer," the woman said, before breaking into a litany of slobbering Russian.

"What's she sayin'?" The Cajun asked, looked at Garcia.

"You know how your wife only gives you five non-Bible curse words a month?"

Thibodaux nodded.

"Well," Garcia said, raising her eyebrows, "the words she's using would probably cause a Bible to catch fire."

Thibodaux's huge jaw clenched tight. His face was red, still steamed from letting Petyr Volodin slip away.

Bowen sat at the center booth, going through a pile of papers he'd grabbed from Minchkhi's room. The pile was mostly made up of lottery tickets and receipts from her doctor for STD treatments, but he'd learned over years of fugitive work that tiny slips of paper often caught very bad men.

"I think I might have something here," Bowen said, holding up a training schedule for a fight gym in Spanish Harlem. There was a phone number scribbled on the back as well as the cost of a cot and showers. He showed the flyer to Garcia who read it over before passing it to Thibodaux.

"You think it could be that easy?" she said. "Surely he would run further than Harlem."

Nikka's head snapped up when she heard the mention of Harlem. She'd not been able to see what they were looking at, and it had taken her by surprise.

"He'th not thtupid enough to go there." She twisted sideways, trying to conceal the blotches on her chest that were a sure indicator that she was upset. "It ith next plathe anyone would look for him."

Thibodaux rolled his good eye, grinning now that he once again had hope for catching Petyr the Wolf. "Yeah, and this is the first. And he sure enough showed his brilliance by not showing up here."

Chapter 26

Alaska

The Piper Cherokee jumped off the gravel runway and banked to the left, with Lovita bringing it around to the north as she climbed.

A shaken Adam Henderson had promised to take care of the wounded Russian until Quinn could make contact with a passing airplane or pick up a signal with the satellite phone and get more authorities out to the lodge. Corey Morgan stood on the porch and held himself up against a log pillar as he watched his would-be girlfriend fly away.

The wind had died down but the boiling storm loomed like a black wall to the north, throwing the vast tundra below into muted shadows. A drizzling rain, pushed ahead in advance of the larger storm, streamed along the airplane's windows and peppered the dozens of tiny, unnamed lakes. A small herd of about forty or fifty caribou strung out in a long line were moving at a good trot along a gravel moraine that formed a natural highway on the boggy tundra.

"*Enukin* are real you know," Lovita said, turning to face Quinn as she flew. With her big green headset and dyed orange hair, the little woman looked pretty impish herself. "They're strong enough to lift a whole caribou over their head and run with it. My friend Jason's a bush pilot and he's seen it happen—caribou traveling along the tundra on their sides . . ."

"I'm not arguing with you," Quinn said. Running through plans and possibilities of the pending confrontation with Volodin and what had to be a box of deadly nerve gas, little imps were the furthest things from his mind.

Lovita's shoulders relaxed when Quinn didn't call her crazy. "You guys should try some of my *akutaq*," she said, changing the subject. She leaned forward and gave one of the gauges a little tap with the tip of her finger. "I picked the berries and caught the caribou myself."

Quinn couldn't help but smile in spite of the situation. He'd always liked the way Alaska's Yup'ik and Inupiaq Eskimos referred to hunting as catching instead of killing. Caribou and seal were *caught* the same way you *caught* a fish. And he'd eaten enough traditional Native dishes to know there wasn't much that went unused. From fish eyes to seal guts, most of any animal could be turned into what someone somewhere considered a delicacy.

Lovita licked her lips and looked sideways to wink at Quinn. He caught the glint of something in her eyes that he couldn't quite make out. If she'd been any other person, he would have said it was worry, but Lovita wasn't the type to fret over much. "Man that bou had some nice backfat," she said. "Whiter than Crisco—"

Beaudine's muffled voice interrupted her. She'd forgotten to put on the headset again. Instead of taking his off, Quinn pointed at the set hanging off a bungee above her armrest.

Lovita fell silent waiting for Beaudine to speak. Quinn pressed his nose to the window, studying the terrain below. They followed the twisting silver snake that was the Kobuk River. Row after row of oxbow lakes, left isolated when the river had changed its meandering course, bracketed the slow moving water in countless parentheses of green and gray. Beyond the river the tundra turned to forest, and the forest rose into green hills that nestled into the lap of the Kobuk Mountain Range a dozen miles to the north. Lone spruce trees shot upward spirelike, here and there, from thick stands of willow. They dwarfed their tiny tundra cousins and choked the riverbank in thick green and yellow.

"What do we do when we find them?" Beaudine asked once she'd situated her headset.

"We'll find a place to land," Quinn said, scanning the water for any sign of Volodin or a boat.

"Are there any?" Beaudine asked. "Places to land, I mean."

"A few," Lovita said. "Not right here on the river, though. We'll have to go up and look around some when we spot them." She gave the temperature gauge another tap and then looked at Quinn. "You want to try the radio again?"

"Whoa," Beaudine said. "Are those what I think they are?"

"Depends," Quinn said, twisting in his seat to look out Beaudine's window. "If you think it's a brown bear sow with a couple of two-year-old cubs, you'd be right."

"She looks like she could take care of our Dr. Volodin problem," Beaudine said under her breath.

Quinn shrugged. "We're part of the food chain up here."

He keyed the radio mike and tried to hail a passing

plane, with negative results. No one else was foolish enough to be out with the approaching storm.

Lovita tapped the gauge harder this time—the way pilots did when they sense something is wrong but don't want to believe it.

Quinn snapped the mike back in its clip on the console. "Okay," he said. "You're about to knock that gauge through the firewall. Want to tell me what's up?"

"We're runnin' a little hot," Lovita said, chewing on her bottom lip the way she did when she held something back.

"Hey," Beaudine said, her voice buzzing as she pressed her face against the window. "I see them. I see the boat!"

"Keep an eye on them," Quinn said, eyes still fixated on Lovita. "How hot?"

"Just touchin' the redline," Lovita said through clenched teeth. She shot a worried look at Quinn, the thin vertical lines of chin tattoos quivering slightly as she spoke. "But the needle's still climbing."

"What do you think it is?" "Quinn asked.

"Engine's not getting' enough oil," Lovita said.

Quinn's ears began to pop as she put steady backpressure to the yoke, adding just enough power to keep them climbing.

"I need to climb higher," she said. "Look for a place to set us down if it doesn't correct itself."

"Wait. What?" Beaudine poked her head up from the back seat. "What has to correct itself? Why are you taking us higher if we need to land?"

A sudden thought crossed Quinn's mind. "Could you have been unconscious long enough for someone to mess with the engine?"

Lovita began to chew on her lip again. She said

nothing, nodding instead as she took the plane up through four thousand feet.

Beaudine pounded on the backseat. “Somebody better tell me what’s goin’ on!”

Quinn rummaged through the pocket in the door beside him, finding the chart for the area he believed they were flying over. He unfolded it while he spoke, knowing it would do no good to scold Lovita now. She needed all her attention to fly the airplane.

“Any ideas of where to put down?” he asked, running a finger over the paper chart.

Left hand on the yoke and right on the throttle levers, Lovita scooted forward in her seat. She peered over the console, then glanced back and forth out the side windows. She looked incredibly small in her oversized pink fleece jacket, like a child in charge of the airplane—and all of their lives. But as small as she was, she was handling this emergency like someone with twice her flying experience.

“That’s not good,” Lovita muttered, half to herself as a spider of black oil began to crawl up the windscreen. There was a loud pop and an instant later oil covered the screen completely, robbing her of any forward visibility. She checked her console, then looked at Quinn.

“I was hoping we’d make Ambler or at least Needle, but that’s not going to happen.” She banked the plane slowly to angle farther north, away from the river—into the storm. “There’s a little mine about three miles up.” Lovita’s teeth were beginning to chatter from nerves, but she continued to fly the airplane.

Quinn found the airstrip on the chart noted by a single line in a circle—which told him it was at least 1500 feet long. “How much room do you need to put us on the ground?”

"About a thousand feet," Lovita said without looking at him.

Quinn looked over his shoulder at Beaudine who'd buckled herself in and sat on both hands staring out her window. "See if you can get a call out on the sat phone," she said. "We need to report our position." He gave her a weak thumbs-up in an effort to let her know everything would be okay—which was a bald-faced lie. Things were completely and hopelessly out of his control. He could not remember a time when things had been much further from okay.

"Quinn!" Lovita said, drawing his attention back to the front. She nodded toward a trail of thick gray smoke pouring out of the engine compartment, streaming down both sides of the plane. A terrific clattering noise rose from the engine. Quinn stifled a cough as the entire cabin filled with the acrid smell of burning metal.

"We're not even going to make it to the mine," Lovita said, banking slowly to the left, nose against the side window. "Looks like a wide spot in the gravel by that stream below us. I'm gonna get set up for a crash while I still got an engine."

Chapter 27

Quinn knew how to do a lot of things, but flying an airplane was not one of them, so he left it to the twenty-two-year-old expert. The way Lovita managed the airplane—and herself—during the middle of a life-and-death crisis made him hope his daughter Mattie would be able to keep her cool in such a way. Mattie. Of course he would think of her at a time like this. She was the one and only constant in his life.

The airplane went suddenly quiet as the engine locked up, starved for oil and pouring smoke but yet to catch fire. Absent the roaring noise of engine and propeller, the whir of wind and spatter of rain seemed deafening against the thin metal fuselage. Quinn's stomach rose in his chest as the bottom of the plane seemed to fall away and they dropped toward the hills three thousand feet below.

"Make sure you know how to get out of your seat-belts," Lovita said through clenched teeth. Her knuckles were white where she gripped the yoke. "Good chance we'll have a fire with this much fuel. Get out quick."

The Inupiaq girl moved like a machine, making minor adjustments to her aircraft. With her windscreen completely obscured by thick black oil, she slipped the plane sideways every few seconds, crablike. The maneuver sacrificed altitude and airspeed but gave her tiny increments of forward visibility.

Quinn caught the glimpse of a silver ribbon of gravel out the side window during one of her slips. The tundra was rising up quickly to meet them. Green hills and now treetops loomed out the windows, shooting by at an alarming rate.

To her credit, Agent Beaudine kept trying to get through on the satellite phone through the entire process.

"Everybody hang on," Lovita said raising her chin and looking out the side window as she slipped the Cherokee sideways one last time. She straightened out the nose a moment before touchdown.

The last clear picture Quinn had before impact was the bright orange of the Eskimo girl's hair resting on the dingy collar of her pink fleece. It brought back memories of the year before, when she'd saved his life flying a Piper Super Cub.

The plane hit hard, slamming Quinn forward against his shoulder harness, before bouncing and driving him back into his seat. Behind him, Beaudine gasped but didn't scream. Quinn reflexively gripped the narrow leather grab strap on the door. Lovita continued to fly the plane without a word.

A loud bang split the frenetic air followed immediately by the groan of protesting metal as the nose gear snapped off, and the airplane's belly gouged into the earth. Quinn was vaguely aware of being thrown sideways, then up, and then sideways again. Smoke choked his lungs and seared his eyes, making it impossible to see. Everything was a blur—the console, the trees whipping by outside the window, even Lovita beside him.

Yanked back and forth, he felt as if he was caught up in the jaws of a great bear that was shaking him to death. The pressure of the harness against his chest combined with the thick smoke to choke the life from him. His head bounced off the window post as metal screamed and groaned.

And then they were still.

Quinn wasn't certain if he'd been unconscious for minutes or moments. He could hear the static chatter of electrical circuits arcing somewhere in front of him. His head felt oddly heavy and it took him a few precious seconds to realize he was upside down, trapped in his seat harness. Through the smoke he could see Lovita hanging beside him, the arms of her pink fleece trailing above her head, hands in the rising water. The creek outside didn't look deep, but the plane must have dug a trench as it slid to a stop in the gravel bed, a trench that was now filling rapidly with water.

Quinn braced himself against the dash so he didn't break his neck, and then popped the release on his harness. His ribs lit up with pain as he slammed against the ceiling, shocked into full consciousness now by the incoming hiss of freezing water. Floundering in the overturned airplane, jammed between the dash and the backrest of what had once been his seat, Quinn peered into the back passenger compartment to find Agent Beaudine also hanging upside down in her harness, arms trailing above her head as if she were riding a roller coaster. Blood covered her face like she'd been scalped.

"Hey!" Quinn shouted. "We have to get out of here!" Beaudine moaned but didn't move.

It was often necessary to triage medical patients

during an emergency, prioritizing the nature of their wound or illness by urgency of treatment. Quinn had no idea which of the two women had the most severe injuries. The dead often moaned, and for all he knew they were both gone already. But if they weren't dead yet, they certainly would be in moments if the water covered their faces before Quinn did something about it.

Lovita was the shorter of the two, which gave her marginally another few seconds over Beaudine, who hung lower in the water. Quinn left Lovita were she was and went for Beaudine first. Ducking his head underwater, he wriggled along the ceiling between the headrests. The release on her harness gave way as soon as he touched it, and he did his best to break her fall. Her head went under but he brought her up before she could suck in any water. A quick dunk in the river water momentarily exposed a deep gash across her forehead and nose. Typical of a head wound, a curtain of blood washed down her face a moment later. She stirred, blinking and sputtering.

Quinn gave her a pinch on the back of her upper arm to get her attention. She winced, opening her eyes long enough to look at him.

"Wait here!" he said, propping her against the side window of the airplane. The water was to her waist, and still rising, but she could breath. In another ten seconds, Lovita would not have that luxury.

Quinn didn't wait to make sure Beaudine had heard him. He wriggled backward, crawfishlike between the headrests, making it to the front as Lovita took a last desperate gasp and the water rose above her face.

Quinn took a deep breath and ducked under beside Lovita's face, covering her mouth with his to give her a rescue breath as he reached up to release her harness. She fell away in his arms and he pushed her to the surface, kicking at the passenger door again and again until it finally opened enough to pull her out.

Fuel dripped from the shredded metal sheeting. Steam rose from the engine compartment, but so far at least, the initial splash of impact had extinguished any flames.

Sliding and slipping over snot-slick rocks, Quinn cradled Lovita's limp body in his arms and carried her to the gravel shore twenty feet away. Her breath was shallow, but she was still alive. Quinn got her situated as best he could on the damp ground before sloshing quickly back into the icy water, moving on autopilot to retrieve Beaudine.

From the perspective of even this short distance, Quinn wondered how any of them had survived. The Piper looked more like a crushed beer can than an airplane. He smiled in spite of himself, chalking it up to Lovita's ability to fly all the way to the bitter end. She was a tough girl, and she'd saved his life again.

Cursing spilled from inside the plane as Quinn made his way toward the rear cargo door. That was a good sign. Deeper water piled up in the trough of gravel behind the wreckage and shoved him sideways. The fuselage was badly twisted and Quinn was unable to pry open the rear door, even when hooking the fingers of both hands inside the lip. Beaudine was on her belly, already working her way forward by the time Quinn made it around to the front door. Leaning inside and half submerged in the freezing water, he grabbed her flailing hand and fell backward, pulling her under the headrest and through the narrow crack in the door like he was delivering a newborn baby. He floundered in the stream with Beaudine on top of him.

"You okay?" she sputtered, clamoring to her knees. Achingly cold water rushed in around them, and she had to hang on to Quinn's shoulder to keep from being upended in the current. A cloud of white vapor blossomed out of her mouth with each unsteady breath when she spoke. A nasty mixture of drizzling rain and wet snow began to fall, peppering the river and making it feeling even colder.

Outside of the shadowed interior of the plane, Quinn was able to get a better look at the nasty gash that ran down Beaudine's forehead, splitting her left eyebrow and bisecting the bridge of her nose. River water and blood plastered sodden hair to her face. The wound didn't look like it went to the bone, but it was deep enough that they would have to do something about it.

Beaudine swayed as she struggled to her feet, rapidly falling into shock. Unless they did something to get dry, hypothermia would follow in a matter of minutes.

"Lovita?" she said, her teeth chattering in time with the raindrops. She pushed sopping wet hair out of her eyes and then held up her fingers to look at the blood.

Quinn nodded toward the bank. "The crash knocked her out," he said, panting. Water dripped from the end of his nose. "But she's a tough kid." He held Beaudine by the arm as they walked, bracing her against the shove of the icy current. If his assistance bothered her now, she didn't mention it.

"Am I hurt bad?" Beaudine said, dabbing at the wound again with her fingertips as they staggered into the shallows and up onto the bank.

"It'll be . . . a cool . . . scar," Quinn stammered. His teeth chattered so badly it made his jaw sore.

Slogging out of the water, he dropped to his knees beside Lovita. Water drained from his clothing. His soaked wool shirt had grown several sizes too large and his sleeves hung past his hands.

Lovita's eyes fluttered at the growing intensity of

the rain. She turned slightly at the crunch of gravel to look up at Quinn, her lips pulling into a tight grimace from even that slight movement.

"Hi, Jericho," she whispered, licking chalky lips.

"Hey, kiddo." Quinn peeled off his jacket and draped it over her. It was wet but would provide some protection from the drizzle. "I'm going to get us a shelter put up. We need to get you dry and warm—"

She reached for his arm but missed, flailing feebly at nothing but air. He took her hand in his and patted the back of it.

She opened her mouth to speak but broke into a series of ragged coughs that wracked her entire body. Her face seemed to grow even paler than it had been. "Stay," she whispered once she regained control, swallowing hard. "Please, just stay with me."

Quinn nodded. "But just for a minute," he said. "I need to get a fire going."

Lovita's eyes rolled back, and then fluttered shut. She struggled to swallow again, then gave his hand a weak squeeze. "I think I broke somethin'." She used the grimy fingers of her free hand to point at her left shoulder.

Beaudine staggered up beside them to collapse in the wet gravel, legs akimbo, hands cradled in her lap. Quinn was afraid she might fall forward on Lovita, but her body listed heavily to one side. Her eyes drooped as though she might pass out at any moment. "Can . . . I . . . help?" she asked.

"I don't know," Quinn said, fighting back a futile panic that pressed at his chest. He brushed a matted strand of orange hair out of Lovita's eyes. "Okay, hon," he said. "The pain, you say it's in your shoulder?"

"Uh-huh," Lovita whispered. She strained to roll

toward him to take the pressure off her shoulder blade, like she was attempting a sit-up but couldn't manage it. Tears welled in her eyes. Her tongue flicked over pale lips. She was beginning to hyperventilate.

The fact that she complained of pain in her shoulder but was still able to move both arms sent a flood of worry over Quinn. This was something far worse than a broken bone. Hoping he was wrong, but knowing he was not, he moved to unzip the pink fleece jacket, and inadvertently brushed Lovita's abdomen. He barely touched her, but she recoiled, screaming the unintelligible noises that humans make when pain or fear was too overwhelming for them to form words.

Quinn's heart fell when he lifted the tail of her shirt. Her belly was tight and distended, an ugly purple bruise forming a donut around her navel. The harness should have prevented such an injury, but Lovita was so small she'd had to scoot her seat forward to reach the airplane's foot pedals. This put her dangerously close to the yoke during the crash. Intense pain in the left shoulder after impact very often meant a damaged spleen. It was called Kehr's sign. Quinn had seen it far too many times when vehicles hit IEDs and the driver was slammed against the steering wheel. Lovita was bleeding inside—and bleeding badly. Quinn put a hand to her neck. Her pulse was fading fast, hardly even there.

Stifling a scream, Quinn fell back on his knees and squeezed a handful of gravel in his fist until his hand shook. A man of action, the tremendous weight of helplessness pressed him down, threatening to grind him into the earth. Three years of tactical medical training, dozens of real-life operations as a Combat Rescue Officer in some of the most austere and dangerous environments on earth—and he could think of absolutely nothing to do. There were really only two options with traumatic internal bleeding—transport to the nearest surgeon . . . or stand by and wait for his friend to die.

Lovita reached for his hand again. Her breath came in short, shuddering gasps now. Eyes clenched, her small, almost Asian face twisted from the unbearable agony as blood filled her gut. Quinn smoothed the hair out of her eyes, gently resting the back of his hand against her cheek. He was covered with oil and his hand left a black streak across her copper skin.

"I'll stay right here beside you," he said, willing his teeth not to chatter, his hands not to shake. "I promise."

The wind kicked up from the north, and the drizzle turned into heavy snow.

Beaudine's mouth hung open. Her eyes grew wide and stricken as the gravity of the girl's injuries dawned on her.

"I'm . . . sorry, Quinn," Lovita whispered. She tried to cough but couldn't summon the energy. "I guess that Russian *gussaq* . . . he did knock me out . . . long enough . . . to mess with my airplane . . ."

The wind stiffened, and snow began to fall in earnest.

Snowflakes landed on Beaudine's hollow face and stayed there, her skin too chilly to melt them quickly. A tear creased the grime on her bloody cheek.

Lovita's lips drew back with another wave of pain. Slowly, the grimace fell away and she relaxed, grinning. She looked up, seeming to focus on the falling snow. It was her old grin, the one she'd give Quinn when she joked and called him names or tried to feed him her strange Native foods. "You know what I always wished, Jericho Quinn?" Her gaze fell back to him. She sounded amazingly calm—her normal self.

"What's that?" he said, forcing words from a throat so tight he could hardly breathe.

"I . . . wish . . . you woulda been about ten years younger . . ." Her tiny hand gave him a final squeeze and then fell away.

Quinn felt for a pulse again. He collapsed back, slouching in the wet gravel when he found none and stared up at the falling snow.

He knelt there beside his frail little friend for some time, letting the silent rage close in around him with the cold that seeped through his soaking wet clothes. Soon, even anger was not enough keep him warm, and he began to tremble from grief and exposure. At length, he folded Lovita's hands across her chest and climbed to his feet with a low groan.

Beaudine looked up at him with drowsy, unfocused eyes, chin against her knees. Her hair was covered with a cap of fresh snow.

Quinn's feet crunched in the gravel as he slogged over to her. Her lips and the backs of her hands were blue.

"Hey," he asked, reaching to touch her forehead. "Can you remember what happened?"

"Do what?" Beaudine jerked her head away. "Of course I remember what happened. What kind of dumb-ass question is that?"

"Hypothermia," he said, struggling to stay on his feet. "Your skin is cool and clammy . . . and you're even more irritable than normal. You are still . . . shivering, so it's not as bad as it could be." He turned toward the river.

"Where . . . are you . . . going?" Beaudine gasped through ragged, shaky breaths.

"Back . . . to the plane . . . to get my pack." Quinn's chattering teeth were now so out of control that any conversation was difficult. Physically and emotionally spent, instinct alone carried him forward.

He'd just reached the water's edge when he heard a sickening moan behind him, like a beached fish croaking for air. He turned in time to see Beaudine topple over.

Mechanically, he staggered back up the gravel incline and dropped to his knees beside her. He made certain she was still breathing, then got his jacket from where he'd left it over Lovita's body. Dragging it across the snow and gravel by one sleeve, he made it back to Beaudine and draped it over her shoulders. She stirred at his touch. Her eyes blinked half open and then flicked back and forth, confused.

"Hang on . . . a . . . couple . . . minutes," Quinn said, trying desperately not to crack a tooth. He knew he should probably say something more, something to try to rally her hopes, but he had little hope left himself. Any time now his core temperature would fall so low his body would lose the ability to warm itself. One thing was sure; if he hoped to save Beaudine, he had to save himself first.

Struggling to his feet, he slogged back down to the bank. His arms dangled and flopped at his sides, far too heavy to lift. His legs barely obeyed his orders to move. Memories of the crash, his mission, even Lovita's death, slipped from his mind. A single truth drew him forward, through the cold water and into the darkness of the mangled plane—without a fire, both he and Beaudine would be dead by nightfall.

Chapter 28

New York

Ronnie Garcia found a bottle of aspirin in the first-aid kit mounted to the wall in Gug's kitchen and marveled that even a skanky strip club like Cheekie's was subject to OSHA rules. Bowen talked on the phone with his people, securing babysitters to keep Nikka and Gug under wraps and ensure that no one tipped off Petyr about their new lead to the MMA gym. Thibodaux sat in Gug's booth, a cell phone pressed to his ear, trying to get in touch with Palmer. Elbow on the table, he rested his chin in his hand, still brooding over letting Petyr slip away.

Garcia rubbed her aching temples and washed down the aspirin with a glass of water—knowing it might calm her headache, but wouldn't even dent the pain in her shoulder. Attempting an erotic dance on a strip club stage in front of your friends was about as exhausting as running a marathon. It was no wonder the poor girl dancing naked had such a desiccated look to her soul.

Ronnie had seen the way Jericho hobbled around early in the morning as the wounds on his body woke up one at a time. He often joked that the injuries he got in China stayed on Beijing time and took a while longer to loosen up than the ones he obtained in the good old U.S. of A.

Ronnie smiled, remembering how she'd take a Sharpie and threaten to label the geographic location of each place he'd earned a scar. Since so many were from growing up in Alaska, she made it a point to work in reverse alphabetical order, beginning with a knife wound on his right bicep from a short stint he'd done in Yemen. She'd pretend to label a bite wound on his forearm from the UK, a gash from a broken bottle in Turkey, before moving to an interesting half moon arc an inch above his bellybutton from a mission in Thailand. It took him a year to tell her about that one.

Garcia closed her eyes, imagining she wasn't in this stinking strip club but back with Jericho when *he'd* held the Sharpie. He always started with the scar she'd earned in Afghanistan, and when he started there, the game moved away from the marker in short order . . .

"Hello, Boss." Thibodaux's deep Cajun drawl jostled Garcia out of the pleasant memory and back to the sad reality of the strip club. Thibodaux flicked his fingers to motion her closer. The President's national security advisor was a bombastic man in word and action, so she had no trouble hearing both sides of the conversation when she plopped down in the booth next to Thibodaux.

"Situation report?" Palmer said. He was never one to chitchat, but his tone was even more brusque than usual. The tap of his computer keyboard was clearly audible in the background.

"Sounds like you're busy," Thibodaux said. "I'll call back." The big Cajun had a pet peeve against people typing or scrolling the Internet while he talked to them—on the phone or in person. Ronnie gave a silent chuckle, surprised he'd enforce such a notion on a man who was the right hand of the President of the United States.

The tapping stopped.

"As a matter of fact I am extremely busy, Gunny," Palmer said, giving an exasperated sigh. "We have five chemical weapons experts in custody—two Russians, a Pakistani, a Kuwaiti, and a card-carrying member from the Sword of God's Chosen from some place in Idaho. Every one of them is capable of manufacturing the stuff behind these attacks. I've got six more chemists who have dropped off the radar, not including your guy's father. So how about you tell me some good news?"

"Well," Thibodaux said, "it looks like Petyr Volodin is in the grease with the Russian mob so we're not the only ones lookin' for him. You want us to come in and help follow up any of those other leads?"

"No," Palmer said. "Stick with him until we hear back from Quinn. He's yet to find Dr. Volodin, and the kid may know where he's going. Quinn can tell us when we can close the book on this trail."

"Roger that," Thibodaux said.

"How's Garcia holding up?" Palmer asked, sounding genuinely concerned.

Thibodaux grinned and gave a thumbs up for Ronnie's benefit. "She's good to go, Boss," he said. "Doin' great. Any word from our little buddy?" The Marine asked the question about Jericho that was ever on Garcia's mind.

"Nothing since this morning," Palmer said. "When last we spoke he was about to follow Volodin out to some remote fishing lodge with Special Agent Beaudine."

"Oh ye yi!" Thibodaux gave an audible shiver. "I feel me some sorry for Chair Force if he's gotta fly anywhere with my crazy cousin."

"Are you saying she's not capable?" Palmer said, his voice tight and annoyed.

"Oh, she's plenty capable, sir," Thibodaux said. "But that don't mean I'd want to spend a day in the woods with her."

Chapter 29

Alaska

Quinn made it a practice to carry an extra set of wool long johns in a vacuum-sealed bag whenever he went into the woods. Inside the same bag he kept a box of windproof matches, a candle, and a baggie of cotton balls. Thankfully, his aunt Abbey had grown up in Alaska and shared the same sentiments. She had stuck a similar sealed packet of extra woolies in the duffle she'd thrown together for Beaudine.

The snow came down hard now, driven by a stiff north wind. What had been a barren gray gravel bar just minutes before was now covered in white. Beaudine, cloaked in the same blanket of snow, no longer stirred. Quinn wasn't even sure she was still alive, but it would only waste valuable time if he stopped to check. Without a fire, there was nothing he could do for her anyway. He estimated the temperatures to be in the high twenties—not particularly cold for interior Alaska—but the wind chill on wet skin was sucking the life out of both of them. With most of his blood rushing to warm his core, Quinn's hands were little better than useless claws by the time he'd dragged enough standing dead wood to start a fire beside a large boulder, away from the cold sink of the stream bed. He staggered up and down the bank, swinging his arms in an attempt to drive blood into his extremities while he searched for a dead black spruce that was small enough for him to push over in his weakened condition. He located one the diameter of his ankle and wiggled the spiky gray trunk back and forth. Thankfully, it was easy to tip out by the roots in the shallow topsoil. It was a poor excuse for a tree, but Quinn didn't care that it had few limbs bigger than a pencil. He was looking for the nestlike crown of needles and twigs the sorry spruce wore like a ratty wig.

Dragging the tree to the flat spot beside the boulder, he dropped it next to the rest of the wood he'd already gathered. Exhausted, he sank to his knees in the snow. His hands shook so badly he thought he might drop the four cotton balls he'd taken from his survival pouch. Leaning over the spruce nest to shield it from falling snow, he stuffed the cotton at the base of the twigs that made up the crown of the little tree. The simple act of grasping a match between his fingers was a Herculean task and he wasted three matches, dropping them into the snow with his clumsy efforts. Delirious, he laughed out loud that his life could hang in the balance over whether or not he had enough dexterity to hold on to a two-inch sliver of wood. The fourth match ignited before he dropped it, landing in the spruce crown rather than the snow. In a state of near euphoria over the tiny flame, he slowly, carefully, began to nudge the match close enough to catch one of the cotton balls. Thick, gray smoke seared Quinn's eyes and threatened to choke him, but he didn't dare move for fear that blowing snow would put out the feeble beginnings of the fire. Damp twigs in the spruce crown sputtered at first, but in no time the entire sappy mass burned as if it had been doused with gasoline. The flames cast long shadows in the cold gray twilight, illuminating Lovita's lifeless body. Quinn wiped a tear from his eye with a trembling hand and allowed himself a moment of melancholy, thinking of how Lovita often said, "turn on" instead of "light" the fire.

Quinn piled on pieces of kindling no bigger than his thumb at first, allowing the fire to dry and ignite them before adding several more the size of his wrist, eventually forming a knee-high teepee around the blazing spruce crown.

It was all Quinn could do to keep from squatting down and letting the warmth of the flames overwhelm him. Still, the notion that a fire was there warmed him mentally, allowing a small sliver of hope to creep back into his mind. Forcing himself to leave the warmth, he half dragged, half carried an unconscious Beaudine to the fire.

Less than ten minutes later he'd stretched a silicon treated nylon tube tent on a piece of parachute cord strung between two likely spruce trees near the fire. When weighted down at the corners with stones from the riverbank, the single tube of waterproof cloth formed a triangular shelter that was open at both ends. Roughly three feet high at the center and seven feet long, the open end nearest the fire caught the warmth of the blaze as it reflected off the split boulder some ten feet away.

Quinn stripped out of his wet clothes now that he had someplace that would offer a relatively dry shelter. Popcorn-size snowflakes gave wet kisses to his shivering body as he hurried to pull the fresh wool underwear over clammy skin. Like pulling a dry sock over a wet foot, convulsive shaking made it even more difficult. He was panting by the time he finished, but he could think, and his hands were working again.

Wearing nothing but the black long johns and his unlaced boots, he was still shaking as he pulled Beaudine's jacket up over her head. Then he used his teeth to tear open the vacuum-sealed bag Aunt Abbey had sent along. If it made Beaudine angry for him to make suggestions about tactics, he could only imagine how she'd feel when she woke up in the tent and realized he'd changed her into dry underwear—assuming she ever woke up.

The job done, he shoved and prodded the still unconscious Beaudine into the tent, taking care not to rip the fabric. He was sure Lovita carried several sleeping bags in her plane, but he'd only been able to find one in the wreckage, sealed in a compression bag under the co-pilot's seat. Rather than risk more time in the icy water, he'd decided to make do with the one sleeping bag and a large Mylar survival bivy sack. The outer layer of the bivy was bright orange to make it easier to spot and facilitate a rescue. The inside was lined with reflective foil and large enough for two people to share, maximizing body heat in an emergency.

Quinn knew the cold ground would suck away massive amounts of body heat so he spread their only sleeping bag as flat as he could get it to give them some measure of insulation and padding. He put the bivy on top, rolling Beaudine's body into the foil envelope. Her skin was blue and cold. The periodic rise and fall of her chest was the only thing that told him she was still alive. The hollow hopelessness of complete exhaustion fogged Quinn's brain. He collapsed against the relative softness of the sleeping bag, giving in to the painfully overwhelming urge to sleep. The tension in his muscles began to fade, but the moment he closed his eyes, the thought of a faceless Russian killer crept in through the fog. Groaning, he pulled the bivy over Beaudine, and rolled over once again to crawl back out of the tent and through the blowing snow to the pile of gear he'd left by the boulder. A howling wind turned the fire into a forge and Quinn piled larger pieces of wood onto the blaze, knowing it would burn down all too fast. He grabbed the small Tupperware bowl of Lovita's rich *akutaq* from his pack and picked up the rifle, dragging it back to the tent. The last of the gray was fading from the sky by the time he once again wiggled and crawled his way into the bivy bag. Lying on his side, he popped the top off the plastic tub and sucked a big glob of *akutaq* off his fingers. He could feel the fatty stuff begin to warm him at once, maybe even enough to keep him and Beaudine alive through the long Alaska night—if Worst of the Moon didn't kill them in their sleep.

He pulled both their shirts up high so they were belly to belly and wrapped his arms around Beaudine, drawing her to him. Her skin was cold and clammy and he nestled in as close as possible, offering what little warmth he had left, and hopefully, at some point, drawing some back from her. Sleep was the enemy when hypothermia loomed—too many people dozed off and never woke up. He should have tried harder to wake her, but his mind was too frazzled to focus. Exhaustion finally pushed him under, the last thoughts in his mind of Lovita's grin and the sweet taste of *akutaq* on his lips.

Chapter 30

The three stubby candles Kostya Volodin found in the deserted cabin did more to remind him it was dark than provide any usable light. Little more than a pile of decaying logs and earth, the place offered no more than a spot to get out of the wind. They were fortunate to have even seen it tucked in along the banks of the river through the blowing snow.

Volodin stooped under the sagging roof and shook out a tattered wool blanket in front of him. Rodent droppings clattered against the rough wooden floor like BBs. A red-backed vole glared sullenly from the corner, flicking its little ears at every noise. Tiny black eyes glistened with accusation at the theft of its nest.

An incessant wind howled through numerous cracks in the log walls, bellowing the blue tarps that had been nailed over the collapsing window holes and nudging the piece of heavy carpet that hung from a wooden crossbeam over the flimsy door.

Even in this sorry condition, the cabin had seen recent use. A grease-spattered rectangle on the dusty shelf showed the place where someone, presumable hunters judging from the pile of caribou hooves outside, had used a small camp stove. The smell of fried meat and cheap whiskey mixed with the odor of humans living in close confinement made the windy drafts a welcome addition to the sour air.

The five crumpled blankets the hunters had left behind were long past their prime. Volodin was elated at first, but when he shook out the vole droppings, he discovered it would take at least three to make sure none of the rips and holes overlapped. He kept the two that were in the worst shape and handed the others to Kaija who accepted them without a word.

They hadn't eaten since leaving Nome. A narrow escape from the lodge left them unprepared, and this blizzard soaked them to the skin by the time they reached the cabin. Volodin didn't feel it prudent to start a fire. There was too great a danger that the smoke would give away their location even with the storm. A relatively dry place out of the snow and wind would have to do.

Thankfully, he and Kaija had been outside when the three Russians arrived at the lodge.

He'd not gotten much of a look at the men at the lodge, but they were surely sent by Rostov to bring him back—or perhaps just kill him. Poor Kaija. She had been terrified when the plane landed, but insisted on running back inside to retrieve her black plastic case. He'd not noticed it when they left Providenya, but his mind was slipping. He had not noticed many things. They'd fled to the river, hiding in a small building that contained fishing equipment.

When the second plane landed, presumably with reinforcements, Volodin saw the boat was their only means of escape. Kaija directed him where to go. She was such an intelligent child. Her friend would help them, she assured him, sitting at the bow of the boat clutching the black case in her lap.

Now Kaija stretched out on one of the two plywood beds ten feet away, facing the wall. She'd gone silent once they were on the river, brooding like the approaching storm. She blamed him, and he certainly deserved the blame. This mess was of his creation. He longed to talk with her, to explain, if only to hear a few accusatory words. But she'd put in her cursed earphones. When she listened to her music, he might as well be on another planet. Perhaps the battery on her mobile would die soon, and they would have a chance to talk, father to daughter, before they reached civilization—if they reached civilization.

It killed him inside to put someone he loved so deeply in such a dangerous and uncomfortable position. He folded the remaining two blankets on a rough wooden bench beside a crude wooden table so he'd have some padding to sit on. Kaija had left the case on the floor beside her bed. Perhaps, he thought, they had packed some food that he'd forgotten in his foolish stupor. Kaija didn't stir as he picked up the case. The pulsing music pouring through her earphones rendered her as good as deaf.

He was surprised to find the case so heavy. It must have been important for them to have dragged it all the way from Providenya—but try as he might, he could not recall what was inside. Made of hard plastic with what looked like a waterproof seal, it looked like an expensive suitcase—the kind in which engineers or traveling photographers might carry delicate equipment. Touching it did bring back a faint memory. Perhaps he'd had enough forethought to bring food after all. He flipped the latches and lifted the lid, inexplicably worried that his daughter might turn over at any moment and catch him. To his amazement, he found a selection of a dozen metal canisters, each about the size of a soft drink can. A hard plastic divider separated six blue canisters from six yellow ones, identical but for the color. A vision of the proteins and growth hormones he'd prepared for his son, Petyr, suddenly rushed back to Volodin. The supplements were powerful stuff if he remembered correctly, packed with enough calories to see them through until they made it to the village the next morning.

"I have found us something to eat, Maria," Volodin said, smiling at his luck. "This will keep you warm, my love." He held two of the canisters, one blue, one yellow. There were no instructions, but the binary nature made it easier for him to get past U.S. Customs Inspectors. He remembered that he had to mix them.

"I am Kaija," the young woman on the cot said without turning around. "Maria was my mother."

"Kaija?" Volodin's heart sank, but at his absentmindedness and the fact that he would not see his dear Maria. "Of course," he whispered. "I knew that. You are my daughter." He clanked the canisters together. "Kaija, my dear, help me find a pan and we will have our supper."

Kaija sprang from the bed in an instant. Her lips pulled back in a horrifying scream and she flew at him, yanking the canisters out of his hands.

"You are such a fool!" she spat. "What could you be thinking?" Her chest heaved. She was angry with him—again.

"What's wrong, Maria?" Tears welled in his eyes.

"Kaija!" she screamed. "You would have killed us."

"Killed us?" Volodin fell back, collapsing on the bench stunned by his daughter's outburst. "This is the same protein and growth supplements I have sent to Petyr."

"You sent this to Petyr?" Kaija held up a canister in each hand before returning them gently to their respective spots in the plastic case.

Volodin nodded. "It is the least I could do as a father. Your half brother has so little, my dear."

"Oh, he has something if you sent him this?"

"Petyr works very hard at his fighting. You should not begrudge—"

"Are you certain you sent him these?" Kaija groaned. "Yellow and blue?"

"Yes," Volodin said. "Although that is odd. I used to label them red and white. I wonder why I changed the coloring . . ."

"How much?" Kaija said, fuming.

"Why does it matter?"

"Because, Papa." Her chest heaved and spittle flew from her lips as she screamed at him. "This is Novo Archangelsk. It is the reason we are here in this forsaken place. These two canisters alone would release a cloud of enough deadly gas to kill us and anyone who passed by on the river for days—anyone who came in this cabin for the next ten years."

"Oh . . ." Volodin buried his face in his hands. The uncontrollable twitch returned to his left eye. "Novo Archangelsk," he whispered. "Do you think Petyr even knows what he has?"

"I doubt Petyr knows what day it is at any given time," Kaija scoffed.

"I am awful human being." Volodin rocked back and forth, head still in his hands. "But why . . . why would I bring such a thing as this with me? I thought I destroyed the remainder of the stockpile."

"You did not bring it, Papa." Kaija stood in front of him, vapor blossoming around her head in the candlelight with each exasperated breath. "I did."

"Why?" Volodin said. "Oh, my dear, what do you plan to do?"

"Go to bed, Papa," Kaija said, panting as her rage began to ebb.

"Are you angry with me, Maria?" An inexplicable melancholy gripped Volodin's heart. He'd done something to make her mad. "I am sorry I didn't bring us any food."

"Kaija," the girl said, her voice soft now. "I am Kaija, Papa."

"Right," Volodin smiled. "Do you think there might be some food in that case?"

Kaija shook her head. "No," she said, snapping the latches on the black plastic case and carrying it to bed with her. "There is nothing but clothing in here. I've already looked. Go to bed, Papa. We have a long way to go in the morning." She lay down in her tattered blankets, replaced the earphones, and turned to face the wall with her body between him and the plastic case. Her slender chest still heaved from something he'd said or done. He was such a fool to keep calling her by her mother's name.

Without taking his eyes off his daughter, Volodin took the fountain pen from the pocket of his shirt and wrote "Kaija" on the inside of his wrist. Perhaps that would help him remember she wasn't his Maria.

He settled his weary bones onto his own rude bed and drew the tattered blankets up around his chin. Kaija was still angry with him. The heaviness of it filled the dark cabin. He certainly deserved it. His mind was slipping, he knew that, but he couldn't help but feel he should have been angry with her as well.

Chapter 31

Providenya

Ruslan Rostov slammed the phone back in its cradle, an angry, drowning man. Lodygin sat across the office, pale fingers to his lips as if to physically stop himself from saying something he might regret. It was his desk and his phone. Rostov picked up the phone so he could slam it down once more, glaring at the greasy captain, daring him to protest. He was a senior colonel in the GRU. He had every right to take over a subordinate's office and set his phone on fire if he wanted to.

Lodygin sat in the corner, a visitor in his own office. The man had a habit of crossing his legs, knee to knee, in a feminine way that Rostov despised. It looked affected for a man in uniform and made Rostov want to beat him to death with the phone. In fact, the whole office was too girlish for Rostov's way of thinking. They were leaders of men. A competent leader's office should reflect the odor of leather, the color of flags, and the instruments of bloody war. It should be sparse and clean and slightly uncomfortable, demonstrating a clear preference for the field of battle over an easy life in a garrison.

Lodygin's office was highly decorated with nesting dolls, ornate copies of Fabergé eggs, and even woodblock prints of two Orthodox saints on either side of the requisite photograph of Putin. A scented candle did little to mask the stench of his moral decay.

"I assume it was bad news," Lodygin said, both hands on his knee, drawing small circles in the air with the toe of his polished boot.

Rostov put both hands flat on the desk in an effort to compose himself. "General Zhestakova is not a patient man," he said. "I will be summoned to the Kremlin at any moment."

"Today?" Lodygin said.

"No," Rostov said, wondering if he would ever see his wife and daughter again. "Not today, but soon." He glared at the captain. "I should take you with me."

"Perhaps you will be able to reason with the general," Lodygin said. "The events in America . . . they are not exactly contrary to the hopes and dreams of the Kremlin. Are they?"

Rostov's head snapped up. He'd only heard half of what the idiotic captain was saying. "What?"

"The directive to develop New Archangel came from the Kremlin, did it not?" Lodygin gave a flip of his hand. "You and I are both aware of the strategic plans—keep the Americans busy fighting a war on their own soil so the Motherland has time and room to become the world power we deserve to be." He shrugged. "Is that not exactly what is happening now?"

"Apparently, General Zhestakova does not take the same optimistic view," Rostov said. "Perhaps he has taken the time to think through the Americans' reaction when they discover this gas is tied to Russia and not some cretin jihadist from the Middle East."

A vaporous smile spread over Lodygin's face as if he'd won an argument. "One man's cretin jihadist is another man's operative."

"Shut up," Rostov said.

The captain did have a point. Someone had smuggled the New Archangel out of Russia. It was not beyond the realm of possibilities that this same someone was an agent of the Kremlin. Lodygin had remained much too calm throughout the unfolding of these events, even for the sociopath that he was. Rostov glared at him, trying to see through the smarmy façade. Lodygin was odd without being awkward, terrifying without a shred of bravery, and dangerous with no physical strength. He was intelligent enough to pull it off, but who in the Kremlin—or anywhere else—would trust such a vile man?

"Still no word from your *best* soldier?" Rostov asked. The last dripped with open disdain.

"None as of yet, Colonel," Lodygin sighed. "But he will contact us as soon as he is able." The captain pursed his lips. "I do have news that will certainly interest you."

"Very well," Rostov said.

"I was fortunate to spend a delightful three hours in the company of one Rosalina Lobov, a school friend of Kaija Merculief . . ." He stopped, eyes glazing for a moment as if he was remembering and savoring some sordid detail.

"And?" Rostov prodded. "Spit it out."

"Kaija," Lodygin said, "I mean to say the young woman with Volodin is not his child mistress after all. She is his daughter by a woman named Maria Merculief."

"His daughter?" Rostov mused. "That makes sense."

"There is more," Lodygin said. Rostov thought he detected a slight wag in the man's head, as if he was on the verge of gloating. "According to Rosalina Lobov, Miss Merculief is not fifteen as we had previously believed but in reality is twenty years old."

"She attended secondary school?"

"She did," Lodygin said.

"And no one at the school thought to verify her age?"

Lodygin bounced his knee. "I'm sure they did, Colonel," he said. "But I doubt that they were very thorough. Who would lie about their age in order to attend school all over again?"

Rostov leaned back in the chair, steepling his fingers in front of his face. This was interesting news. "And what of this girl's mother?"

"Maria Merculief," Lodygin said. "Deceased. Apparently she and Dr. Volodin were together for several years while he taught at the university in St. Petersburg."

"What did she do?" Rostov asked. "The mother."

"Ah," Lodygin said. "That is where it gets interesting. We have no record of her doing anything. Everyone assumed both she and the girl were prostitutes."

"But they were not?" Rostov said. "Get to the point, Captain!"

"According to Rosalina, both mother and daughter were involved with the Black Hundreds." Slender hands still holding his bouncing knee, Lodygin gloated, triumphant in this revelation.

Rostov's hands dropped to the desk again. This was news. The *Chornaya Sotnya,* or Black Hundreds, was an ultra-nationalist, anti-Semitic group from the early twentieth century. Extremely Russia-centric, they had denied the existence of the Ukraine and considered all borders of Russia prior to 1917 to be sacrosanct. In recent years a new Black Hundreds had emerged. These were as fiercely protective of all things Russian as the earlier group had been of the monarchy. They held fast to a fervent belief in a Novorossiya, free from the Zionist tyranny of the United States and the World Bank.

A fringe group to be sure, but even the Kremlin utilized their watch cry of a *New Russia* when it suited political aims.

"I want to talk to this Rosalina Lobov," Rostov said.

Lodygin's hands fell away from his knee. He uncrossed his legs. "That would be . . . I mean to say, that would not be advisable, Colonel." He gave a smile capable of curdling milk, and then steered away from the subject.

"How did you get her talk to you so openly?" Rostov looked at him through narrow eyes.

Lodygin shrugged but said nothing.

"Is she in custody?" Rostov asked.

"Of a sort," Lodygin said.

"Are you . . ." Rostov raised his hand, turning away. "I do not want to know."

"I think that is best, Colonel," Lodygin said. "Dear Rosalina did divulge to me that Kaija Merculief is quite the scientist herself, sometimes assisting her father with his work on the New Archangel."

"Rosalina Lobov knows of the work on New Archangel?" This was too much.

Lodygin nodded. "I am afraid so. According to Rosalina, Kaija is brilliant, and has a photographic memory." The captain inhaled through his nose, closing his eyes as he mulled over some delightfully nasty memory. "But I have a strong feeling the girl is holding something back."

"Where is this Rosalina Lobov now, Captain? New Archangel is a state secret. She cannot be allowed to speak of the things she has heard."

The smirk on Lodygin's pursed lips slowly crawled across his face to form a tight smile. "You have my solemn word, Rosalina Lobov poses no future risk to this endeavor."

Rostov resolved to shoot Lodygin in the face if the man ever so much as looked at his daughter. But still, there was a need for animals like him in moments such as this.

"I assume you will cover your tracks," he said, feeling the urge to wash his hands in extremely hot water.

"Of course, Colonel," Lodygin said.

Rostov drummed his fingers on the desk, his mind whirring with old problems and new possibilities. If Volodin's daughter was a member of the Black Hundreds, she was certain to have contacts around the world, contacts who could help her deploy the New Archangel in Dallas and Los Angeles. Strategically focused, such a network could be useful to the Kremlin. As it stood now, they were a liability, likely to incite an American response that could level the Russian map.

"Volodin and his daughter must be stopped," he said.

"My men will locate him," Lodygin said. "I mean to say, you have my assurance of that."

"No, Captain," Rostov said. "I am in no mood to depend on your assurances. If your men ever do get around to contacting you, remind them that Zolner is already en route. If they value their lives, they should stay out of his way."

The smile brightened on Lodygin's lips at the mention of the name. "I have always admired Zolner's work."

"I do not doubt that," Rostov said. In truth, the two men were both savages, though Zolner carried his savagery under the guise of a man's man.

PART II
ACQUIRE

Now no one learns to kill while young.
This is very short-sighted.
—Hagakure, *The Book of the Samurai*

Chapter 32

Winter 1981, Verkhoyansk, Siberia

Feliks Zolner's mother kissed him between the eyes—the only part of his skin left exposed to the freezing air. He caught the hint of black tea and wild cherry jam on her breath, felt the dab of moisture on the end of her nose. Even at the young age of nine, he knew she'd sacrificed, taking only a glass of tea and a scant spoonful of homemade jam while he ate the last of their stewed sweet cabbage and simple black bread.

She pulled the scarf up immediately after the kiss to cover her full lips, but Feliks could tell she was happy by the frosted outline of a smile on the cloth. Another drop of moisture formed on the tip of her nose, freezing immediately. She brushed it away with the back of her hand out of habit. Tucking his scarf into the collar of his wool coat to be certain his ears weren't exposed, she patted the rifle in his hands.

"Wait here, *lapushka,*" she said.

Her presence gave him warmth against the incredible cold, but Feliks thought himself well beyond the age of childish names. They were too poor to have any animals that they could not eventually eat, so he had to fill the niche of family pet. Malvina Zolner assured him that no matter how old her son became, he would always be her *lapushka*, her "*little paw.*"

It would be dark soon, but Malvina made sure to place him so the sun was at his back. Orange light filtered through the white birch forest and cast a diffused glow across her wind-bitten face. Ice-blue eyes sparkled, and her button nose, which looked much like his but for her heavy crop of freckles, wrinkled, the way it did when she concentrated hard on a thought.

A hard winter had brought marauding wolves to the birch forest around the village. Malvina said the government in Moscow called them a super-pack, estimating there were more than three hundred animals. The powerful killing machines had slaughtered dozens of reindeer in three days time, gutting many of the horses the villagers kept for milk and meat while the poor animals stood helplessly in the drifted snow. Feliks had been at once horrified and mesmerized to watch how the wolves nipped and tore at their victims' flesh, ripping away at the hams and belly until the animal lost enough blood it could no longer kick or run.

The shadow of a wolf loomed behind every tree around the village or along the snow-covered road. The blacksmith's partially devoured body had been discovered in the alley behind his shop, but it was generally agreed that he had died from an over-indulgence of vodka, and the wolves had merely been the beneficiaries of his frozen carcass. No other human deaths had been attributed to this pack, but that would not hold. There were too many children and too many wolves.

Most of the able-bodied men—including Feliks's father—had gone to fight the war in Afghanistan—leaving only those who were old or crippled—or crazy like Stas and Vladik Pervak to look after the village. The brothers lost nine ponies to the wolf pack and seemed to believe that as they had seen such a great loss, they should be in charge of wolf reprisal. Feliks did not like either of the men, who always drank too much to look after as many ponies as they had. They leered at him when he passed them in town, and often mumbled filthy comments about his mother. Even as a child he knew these men were nasty and vile.

His mother had killed three wolves that morning, shooting a big gray female from a distance of well over two hundred meters as it bounded away. Malvina Zolner was without a doubt the best shot and the finest hunter in the village now that his father was away. She should have been hailed as a hero, but if anyone else thought so, they didn't mention it to Feliks. They were jealous. That was it. She was beautiful and skilled. Feliks sensed that this combination was too much for some men to accept. Besides, they said, there were too many wolves for three to make a difference—and as the Pervak brothers pointed out, Malvina was only a woman. Instead of thanking her and seeing to it that she received the bounty for killing the wolves, they had insulted her in their drunken rage. Feliks had cried openly, earning contemptuous looks that gripped at his throat like a fist and made it hard for him to breath.

Even now, hours after the drunken taunts, his small face glowed red under the rough wool scarves.

"You must understand, my *lapushka*," his mother said, her words short and panting in the bone-numbing cold. "These men are beside themselves with fear." At seventy degrees below zero, the moisture in her breath froze the instant it left her beautiful mouth, forming ice crystals that tinkled to the ground. The old people called it "the whisper of angels."

"I know we must kill the wolves, Mama," Feliks said, jutting his chin to make room for his voice under the heavy scarf. "I do not hate wolves, but I hate those men."

"Fear often makes men the more dangerous of the two," Malvina said, patting him on the head. White crystals of frost lined her delicate eyelashes, reminding Feliks of a snow princess he'd seen in a book.

Gathering him in her arms for another moist tea-and-jam kiss, she wrapped a second wool scarf around her son's neck and picked up her own gun with her gloved hand, leaving him to sit completely still on a thick pile of hay in the loft of their three-sided barn. The crude wooden loft was low, no more than six feet off the ground. It would be accessible even to the weakest of wolves if one wanted to jump up and eat him. But Feliks was not afraid. He had his gun, and he knew his mother would come back for him once it was too dark to shoot.

She always came back.

Feliks squeezed his rifle as he watched his mother trudge past the rough ball of hair that was their milking cow, and toward the shooting hide she'd built in a tall spruce tree two hundred paces away. Her reindeer skin boots left tiny tracks in the snow. Feliks stifled a laugh at the oblong shadow cast by her ratty fox fur hat. It made her look like she had a pumpkin on her shoulders. Her wool coat hung down past her knees, but Feliks could see she was shivering. The coat was much too thin to keep her warm in such bitter cold, and it would only get worse as darkness fell. She had two good scarves, but had given her second to him.

A wolf howled to the west, beyond the house, and was immediately answered by another somewhere in the endless expanse of trees behind Feliks. It was a foreign noise, chilling yet inviting and made Feliks want to join in with the howling. The boy kept his eyes fixed on his mother but imagined the magnificent animals loping silently through the birch forest, making no sound but for their mournful cries—and the crunch of teeth on bone.

Malvina stopped as she approached the homemade ladder at the base of her spruce tree and turned slowly to study the woods to her right. Felix held his breath. She must have seen something in the trees.

Feliks kept completely still, flicking his eyes sideways, following his mother's gaze without moving his body. Why did she did not raise her gun if it was a wolf? Slowly, fluidly, so as not to draw attention to the loft, Felix brought his knees up. He crossed his ankles so he could rest his elbows on the muscles of his thigh and peer down the iron sights if his rifle. He scanned the woods beyond his mother, controlling his breath the way she'd taught him, keeping the front sight perfectly aligned with the notch in the laddered V at the rear.

Zolner was large for his age, but his mother made certain not to teach him bad habits by giving him a firearm fitted for a grown man. She'd sawed off the butt of her father's Mosin-Nagant carbine and worked down the stock to fit Feliks's shoulder and length of pull, carefully rasping down the wooden grip behind the action so his small hand could wrap around it when he placed his finger on the trigger. Malvina's grandfather had been a student of the famed Soviet hero, Vasily Zaytsev during the Battle for Stalingrad. He had survived, and taught Malvina how to shoot. She'd handed down this knowledge to Feliks, demonstrating proper breathing and trigger control. The more important aspects of shooting—the cold and calculating instincts that could not be taught—she had passed down to him with her blood.

A wolf howled again, and Felix shifted slightly, beginning to worry since his mother still stood at the bottom of her tree. She turned toward the woods and took a step away from the ladder. A lone man emerged from the forest, his hands raised as if to show he had no weapon. It was a curious thing that a full-grown man would stroll through the wolf-infested woods with no rifle at any time of the day. To do so in late evening was madness.

Feliks recognized the man by his lopsided sable hat and patched greatcoat as Stas, the larger of the Pervak brothers. Stas took a few steps toward Malvina Zolner gesturing wildly, pointing toward the trees. Malvina peered in the forest, rifle in hand. Feliks could not hear it, but he felt certain the man was speaking hateful words, as he'd done earlier in the day. Without thinking, the boy rested the post of his front sight on the man's ear. His mother should not have to hear such words. Feliks had the power to stop them. The trigger broke cleanly. The rifle bucked in his small hands, but he kept his eye on the target, watching the lopsided fur hat fly off along with a piece of skull. Feliks grinned under his wool scarf, feeling a peculiar warmth he'd never felt before. Stas Pervak would speak no more words, hateful or otherwise.

Half his head gone, the remainder of Pervak's body stood there for a moment, unaware that it was dead before collapsing into the snow in a heap of filthy rags. Malvina's head snapped around at the sound of the shot. He waved. Certainly she would be proud of him. He had taken Stas in the head from well over three hundred paces. Malvina began to run toward him, flailing her arms, staggering to keep her footing on the frozen ground.

A moment later Vladik Pervak charged out of the trees another hundred meters beyond the house. His rifle was slung over his shoulder. The lead rope of a wooly pony draped over one arm. He stopped in his tracks when he saw his brother's body and the spray of frozen carnage around it. The pony dropped its head, nibbling at the snow. Vladik began to scream. At that distance Feliks could not make out the words, but it did not matter. If a Pervak spoke, it was bound to be vile.

Feliks swung the cut-down Mosin-Nagant toward Vladik as he ran toward the body of his dead brother. He took a deep, calming breath estimating the distance at two hundred meters, and led the man like he would a running reindeer. He held a hair higher than he had on Stas, knowing the bullet would drop at least six inches in that distance.

Feliks exhaled slowly, pressing the Mosin-Nagant's crisp trigger in the moment of respiratory pause at the bottom of his breath, where his body was completely still.

Vladik pitched face-first into the snow seventy-five meters from his dead brother. Feliks had taken both men with clean shots through the head.

Nine-year-old Feliks Zolner looked down the barrel of his rifle, past the terrified face of his mother at the bodies of the two men he'd just killed—and smiled.

Malvina Zolner threw the rickety wooden ladder against the edge of the loft and hauled herself up to where Feliks sat with his rifle. Her chest heaved under the tattered coat. Her breath came in deep, wheezing croaks from sprinting through the sub-zero air. Frozen tears frosted her eyes, forcing her to keep wiping her face with the back of her arm.

"Oh, *lapushka*," she wept, "why would you? Why? Why would you shoot those men?"

Feliks pulled the rifle to his chest, hugging it tightly. "You say *why*, Mama." He smiled sweetly. "I say why not?"

Feliks Zolner looked out the window of the Cessna 185 and watched heavy snow zip by like gray bullets. His spotter, a squat but powerful man named Kravchuk, who he'd worked with for the last three years, sat in the rear seat beside a former Spetsnaz soldier named Yakibov. It bothered Zolner to have anyone sit behind him, even a man he more or less trusted, but at a height of over two meters, the front seat of the cramped aircraft was the only place he would fit. He was acquainted with Yakibov but didn't know him well enough to show his back, so he made certain Kravchuk occupied the seat behind him and put the Spetsnaz man behind the pilot.

Zolner was clean-shaven, with flecks of sliver in mouse-colored hair. A perfect crew cut lorded sternly over a brooding forehead and blocky jaw that looked as if it were carved of granite. His smallish, almost button nose looked out of place surrounded by the otherwise severely masculine face. He was a rawboned man, with a thick neck and brutish muscles. Large hands hung from the end of powerful arms. He was built much like his mother's grandfather so far as he could tell from the only photograph he'd ever seen of the man, standing beside a dead Nazi in the rubble of Stalingrad. Broad in proportion to his height, even now, his shoulders pressed against those of Ilia Davydov, who was not himself a small man. Zolner had known the pilot slightly longer than he'd known Kravchuk.

His hands were too soft to be of use for anything but piloting, but he was exact in his actions—and for now, that was enough.

"The lodge is off of our left wing," Davydov said, bringing the Cessna around in a shallow bank.

"Hopefully they are still here," Yakibov said, sneering.

Davydov gestured out the windscreen with the flat of his hand. "We are going to be here until the storm passes. The wind in those clouds would turn us on our heads."

Kravchuk scanned the area below with a pair of powerful Komz binoculars. "There is one airplane at the end of the field." It was getting dark, but the man's eyesight was almost as good as Zolner's. "Two male individuals standing in the river north of the small buildings," he said. "I believe they are fishing."

Davydov glanced at Zolner, fighting a buffeting crosswind as he brought the Cessna in line with the gravel airstrip. "We know your target came here," he said. "But what of the other team?"

"They are professionals," Zolner said. "If they have not yet reported in then something has happened to them."

"And what of the others in the lodge?" Kravchuk said.

Zolner took a long breath, exhaling through his mouth with a slight pause at the bottom, the way he did when he was preparing to shoot. Correct breathing was important in all aspects of life and helped to settle his mind.

"Do not worry, my friend," he said. "I will let you take care of them. Colonel Rostov has been very clear. There can be no witnesses."

Chapter 33

Alaska

Something heavy dug into Khaki Beaudine's rib-cage. No matter how much she willed it to move, her right arm refused to obey. Her head twisted unnaturally to one side, nose against a cold, orange blur. Beaudine briefly considered that she might be dead, and if she was dead, the fact that everything around her smelled of wood smoke and gasoline didn't bode well for her final destination—not that she was surprised. Then she realized she needed to pee. Her toes wiggled, so she was relatively sure she wasn't completely paralyzed. For one panicked moment she thought she might still be trapped in the airplane, but then she remembered the blizzard. Surely she would have frozen to death had she still been trapped in the plane. The orange blob in front of her nose smelled like a plastic pool toy and brought back distant childhood memories of trips to the lake . . . before things went crazy with her family. She had a vague recollection of Quinn dragging her through the snow.

A fire popped and crackled outside, casting dancing

shadows against the tent wall. Beaudine could feel the reach of its warmth on the top of her head. Beyond the fire, a gossamer curtain of green and purple swept across the sky, ebbing and flowing, brilliant in the surrounding blackness. The mournful howl of a wolf lingered over the lumps and shadows of the snowy ground. It was an incredible sight, beautiful despite the terror of the situation. Beaudine tried to rise, but every muscle and bone rebelled, pressing her back to the rocky ground.

Pain cleared away the fog of sleep, and Beaudine slowly came to realize the weight across her ribs was an elbow. The body connected to that elbow was tucked in beside her, breathing gaspy breaths against her neck. There appeared to a sleeping bag laid out underneath them and some sort of foil space blanket above, but it was Jericho Quinn who provided most of the warmth that enveloped her.

The longer she was awake, the more Beaudine realized how badly she hurt. Her knee was on fire. Her left eye seemed to be glued shut, and she was pretty sure she'd cracked a front tooth. Even the slightest movement of her neck sent excruciating bolts of fire arcing down her spine, but she could move it, so that was something. She knew all too well how to work through pain.

She tried to push herself up on all fours, causing Quinn to draw back his arm and roll away, not exactly in recoil, but like someone who didn't want to loose an important appendage.

"Sorry." His voice was deep and came with a phlegmy morning cough. Hearing it brought back memories of the crash and with them, images of Lovita's death. Babying her neck, Beaudine rolled onto her side so she faced Quinn. Even this small movement brought a stab of pain to her hip, but it was a worthwhile trade in order to get a better look at her surroundings in the orange darkness of the shelter.

Beaudine felt the welcome warmth of the fire reflecting on her face.

"Wait a minute," she said. "If you were still asleep, how do we still have a fire?"

"Don't worry," Quinn said, his exhausted voice muffled against his own arm. "It wasn't the little people. The storm stopped about an hour ago and I got up to add more wood then."

Beaudine relaxed a notch. She'd always thought of herself as a wilderness girl, but the woods she knew didn't come with plane crashes, creepy little goblins, or killers named Worst of the Moon.

It could be noon for all she knew. Dancing flames cast long shadows from the scrub willows onto the gravel bluff overlooking the river. Everything looked cold and sinister and much larger than it actually was. A curtain of black closed in beyond the reach of the fire, but this was Alaska, so darkness accounted for a large chunk of day at this time of the year.

Beaudine used her elbow to nudge a heavy pocket of snow that sagged the tent, sending it sliding down the fabric with a hiss to the drifts along the base. At least six inches had fallen during the night.

Quinn lay on his stomach, one arm trailing by his side, the other up under his face like a pillow against the rocky ground. Healthy black stubble from the day before had grown into a respectable beard overnight. Dark hair pushed up over his ear in lopsided bed head.

Beaudine rubbed her nose with her sleeve and suddenly realized she now wore the same type of black merino wool underwear that Quinn had on. Her life before the crash seemed much too long ago to remember what she'd been wearing, but she was pretty sure it wasn't black wool. She fought the urge to ask who had dressed her, deciding she'd rather live with the fantasy that she'd changed out of her wet clothes on her own while in some sort of stupor and just couldn't remember it.

A sudden twinge of pain above her left eye made her reach up and touch her forehead. The flesh was tender, swollen and caked with blood. The pain eased some after a moment, falling back to a sickening ache.

"We're going to need to take care of that before we do much else," Quinn said, looking at her wound, chin against his bent arm. "Do all your bones bend in the places they're supposed to bend?"

"So far," she said, clearing her throat. "Something's going on with my wrist. Hope it's just a sprain. How about you?"

Quinn arched his back, wincing slightly, but keeping it to himself if anything important was damaged.

"I'm fine," he said.

"This feels like shit." Beaudine's fingers explored the crusted mess on her forehead. "How bad is it?"

"You could see out of both eyes last night," Quinn said. "But you're going to need stitches before we go anywhere."

"I don't want to even think about that," she said, rubbing her wrist. "My watch must have come off in the crash. What time is it?"

Quinn rolled up on his side. He pulled back the edge of the tent directly over his head so he could look up at the stars. He appeared to find what he was looking for, closed his eyes and counted quietly using his thumb and fingers.

"About five A.M.," he said at length.

"You can tell by looking at the stars?" Beaudine

eyed him hard with her good eye. "Who are you—Daniel Boone?"

Quinn nestled back down in the bag. "I looked at my watch a little bit ago."

"Sure you did," Beaudine said. "Jacques told me you were Daniel Boone." She turned a little, stretching her neck by degrees, and saw the snow-covered lump in the moonlight that she realized was Lovita's body. "I'm really sorry about your friend."

Quinn rubbed the stubble on his face and stared into the night. "Thank you," he said, his voice still thick, and now with the added heaviness that comes with losing someone very close. "I can't just leave her out there on the rocks . . ."

Quinn wriggled forward, waiting to climb to his feet until he was well out of the survival bag so as not to rob Beaudine of the relatively warm bubble of air. She watched him shrug on his heather gray wool shirt and step into the unlaced boots he'd stashed just inside the door of the shelter. He disappeared into the darkness looking completely at ease in his floppy boots, unbuttoned shirt, and long johns.

He wasn't gone for more than two minutes but Beaudine felt a flood of relief when she heard the crunch of his boots on snow and gravel.

He stooped to look into the opening of the shelter, shining a tiny flashlight into the corner beside his pack. "There's some *akutaq* in that white container," he said. "It'll warm you up until I get the fire going again."

Beaudine nestled deeper into the sleeping bag, trying to take advantage of the warm spot Quinn had left. It hurt her face when she turned up her nose, but she did it anyway. "I don't think this Texas girl's stomach could handle reindeer lard and sugar."

"I'm serious," Quinn said. "I don't know what Lovita

has in the survival kit but I guarantee you it won't have as much food value as *akutaq*."

Beaudine eyed the plastic container like it might bite her.

"Caribou fat?"

"Lovita is . . . was a traditionalist," Quinn said. "It's got a lot of berries too."

"Look, I'm not trying to . . ." Beaudine shook her head. "I just, I mean . . . sugar and lard. 'Nuff said."

"I get it." Quinn shrugged, absent any malice. He seemed more interested in kicking snow away from the coals of his fire than schooling her about food prejudices. "Up to you, but we'll need our strength to go after Volodin."

Beaudine perked up and poked her head out of the thin foil bag."

"We're still going after him?"

"Someone has to," Quinn said.

"And how are we supposed to do that? We don't even know which way he went."

"I didn't say we were going to catch him," Quinn said, a gleam in his eye despite the situation. "Seriously, we know he was headed toward Needle Village before the crash. If I've got my bearings right, we're maybe ten miles away once we reach the main river."

How far are we from the river?"

"A couple of miles, I think," Quinn said, adding another log to the fire. "Lovita put us down to the south of the river, which is too bad because it's boggier on this side. The tundra around here isn't frozen yet. Two miles jumping from tussock to tussock will be like running a marathon. I think we'll have to follow the streambed all the way down. It'll be a winding route, but might be the only way without sinking up to our knees."

He looked completely at home squatting there, poking the flames with a charred piece of willow. Both their jackets had frozen into stiff wads overnight. Quinn propped both on the top of the split boulder. Steam began to rise immediately from the damp wool and fleece.

Quinn stared into the flames, shaking his head. “I’ll make another trip out to the plane and see what else we have in the way of supplies.”

“Back into that water?” Beaudine shivered just thinking about it.

“Afraid I have to,” he said.

“Well, I gotta find me a place to use the little girls’ room,” Beaudine said, stifling a groan as she finally pushed up on all fours still inside the foil bag. Cold air rushed in around her, bringing a shiver that collided with the pain in her hip. She was tempted to retreat, but nature called.

She slipped her feet into the frozen boots Quinn had staged for her inside the shelter opening, just out of reach of the snow. “I don’t suppose we have any—”

Quinn reached in the pocket of his wool shirt and held up a plastic baggie containing a small roll of toilet paper, rescuing her from having to ask for it.

“This stuff is like gold out here,” he said. “Every time we go hunting my dad has what we called “the TP talk”—makes everyone in camp promise to be a *folder* and not a *wadder*. ‘Wadders are wasteful,’ he’d say when we were kids and threaten to make us use spruce cones if we ran out.”

Quinn went back to poking at the fire, looking completely serious about toilet-paper etiquette.

“I’ll keep that in mind,” Beaudine said, snatching up the toilet paper. She turned to go, but stopped after one step, staring into the shadows. They seemed even darker now. The wolf howled again. It sounded far away, but it was impossible for her to tell in the snow. "I don't suppose you'd loan a girl a flashlight . . ."

Quinn had just finished hanging the rest of their wet clothes around the boulder when Agent Beaudine came hustling back into camp.

"I heard something out there," she said. "It sounded big. You think it might have been that wolf?" The long johns looked like yoga pants, but were made to fit Aunt Abbey, so they hung a little looser in the seat on Beaudine.

"Hmmm," Quinn mused. "Probably not a wolf."

"That's a relief," Beaudine said.

"More likely a bear," Quinn said. "We're camped right on a bear trail. I saw all kinds of tracks last night."

Beaudine's eyes narrowed. "And you didn't think to tell me this before I wandered off into the forest by myself?"

Quinn chuckled. "Did you want me to come with you?"

She thrust the plastic bag with the toilet paper roll back at him without answering. "I only used four squares, in case you're a counter."

Quinn arched his back, introducing his old injuries to the new ones he'd gotten from the crash, before looping the headlamp around his neck and starting for the river.

Beaudine looked up at him from where she warmed her hands by the fire. "Where are you going?"

Quinn sighed. In the bush, the harsh practicality often chased away the niceties of life. "I'm going to keep the ravens from eating my friend."

Chapter 34

The northern lights cascaded across the sky in dancing curtains of green and purple, incredibly bright now that Quinn had the fire behind him. He crunched the thirty feet down the gravel slope to the water, hardly looking up.

The mangled wreck of the airplane was a silver shadow in the black water. The Aurora and crescent moon reflected off the snowy landscape, giving plenty of light.

A night of snow and heavy rain upriver had caused the little creek to swell and jump its banks, changing the terrain just enough to throw off Quinn's bearings. It took him a moment to find the white lump of snow that was Lovita's body, and he was horrified to find that the stream had flooded enough to cover her legs and now lapped at her waist. It was a foolish notion, but Quinn couldn't help but worry about how cold she must feel in the icy water and moved quickly to drag her body to higher ground.

"Don't worry, kiddo," he whispered, gently brushing the snow from her face. Her body was stiff, but she looked like she was asleep. "I'll get you to your airplane until I can come back and do things right."

Quinn swallowed hard, patting his young friend on the shoulder as if to comfort her. He looked out at the water that just hours before had come to his knees. Now, it would easily reach his waist.

Shaking the snow off a nearby willow bush, he removed his shirt, and then peeled off his woolies, draping them on the bare branches to stand naked along the bank.

The frigid water pushed the wind from his lungs as surely as if he'd been hit in the chest with a sledgehammer. If there was an upside, it was that the cold numbed his feet so the stones didn't hurt quite as much. His teeth chattered, his muscles ached, but the overwhelming need to find Volodin drove him forward.

It took him five agonizing minutes standing in the rising stream to pry open the wing locker where Lovita kept the survival gear and medical kit. He grabbed the second sleeping bag as well, and his Aunt Abbey's AR-10 rifle. Frigid water shoved at his hips as a stiff current rolled loose stones under his bare feet, threatening to push him down with every step.

He had little feeling left in his legs by the time he'd carried all the gear back to shore and picked up Lovita's body for the return trip. She was light, barely a hundred pounds, but cold and circumstance had weakened him to the point of collapse. He fell twice, floundering in the icy water and nearly letting her get away from him. Shivering uncontrollably by the time he reached the door, he could just fit Lovita's body into the airplane. She was still stiff, so he had to slide her in at an angle on the roof of her airplane, between the inverted seatbacks. His brain fogged with anger and cold, he stood at the door, at a loss for what to do next. His mother would have said some kind of prayer. Instead, Quinn clenched his jaw to silence his chattering teeth and leaned inside the plane on his belly. He put a hand on his friend's cold forehead and told her good-bye.

It took another full minute to get the door bent back shut and bend the latches into the locked position with a multi-tool he'd carried out for that purpose. It wouldn't be enough to slow down a hungry bear—but he hoped it would keep her safe from wolves and ravens for a while—and it was the best he could do.

Quinn took a step toward the bank, then turned, overwhelmed with the sudden need to know what had happened to cause the crash. The aircraft had overturned on impact so he had to stoop and use the multi-tool to open the engine compartment, playing the beam of the headlamp around the charred mess. Burned oil made it almost impossible to tell one piece of the engine from any other, but the tool marks were clearly visible. Quinn had worked on enough motorcycles over the years that it didn't take him long to find the problem.

Khaki Beaudine was up and dressed by the time Quinn walked into camp wearing his long underwear and unlaced boots. He was deathly pale, and she couldn't tell if he dropped the load of gear because he wanted to put it in front of the tent, or if his shivering arms simply gave out at that particular spot. He shot a wild look at her, but didn't speak, moving immediately to squat in front of the fire, arms outstretched, as close as physically possible without bursting into flames himself. Clouds of steam escaped the fabric of the black long johns.

He'd been gone the better part of an hour, and Beaudine had spent the time watching Quinn's shadow moving back and forth in the darkness, and punctuating her worry with the few useful chores she could think to do. She'd nearly collapsed with relief when he finally switched on his headlamp. The tent was still up but she'd stuffed the sleeping bag in its stuff sack along with the folded Mylar bivy blanket. Trails of her boot prints crisscrossed the snow along the gravel bar, disappearing into the darkness where she'd braved wolves and bears and creepy little gnome people to search for firewood. It seemed silly now, but she was inordinately proud of the large pile of deadfall she'd been able to find.

Quinn looked at the wood and gave an approving nod. He opened his mouth wide, going through a series of grimaces to get the blood flowing in his cheeks, wincing as cold and numbness surely gave way to warmth and revitalizing pain.

"Give it to me straight, Jericho Quinn," Beaudine said. Her Texas accent twanged as strongly as her mama's when she was nervous. "Just how bad are we screwed?"

"Pretty bad." Quinn stood, stepping into the pants he'd left warming on the boulder, and then shrugged on the fleece jacket. Warm now, he looked at ease, as to begin going through their meager pile of gear. Beaudine watched as he opened an empty plastic bag and scooped it full of snow before setting it aside. Using the headlamp, he searched through the first-aid pack, taking out a bottle of water and what looked like a small multi-tool, and setting them on top of the rifle drag bag to keep them off the ground. "I'm pretty sure the Russians disabled the Emergency Beacon. But even if anyone is looking for us, they won't be looking for us here because Lovita had to leave her original flight path to Needle Village in order to find a suitable place to set down."

Beaudine took a deep breath, letting the reality of their situation sink in. "And we can't build a signal fire because that would just bring this Worst of the Moon guy right down on top of us."

She dabbed at the wound on her face with the cuff of her woolies, pulled down over the heel of her hand. She'd managed to get the crusted eye open but she could feel the angry flap of skin on her forehead, just above her left eyebrow. It wept blood constantly, blurring her vision and forcing her to keep wiping it away.

Quinn found what he was looking for and stood, turning to her, firelight flickering off his face.

"I think I've stopped shivering long enough to get you stitched up," Quinn said. "Then we need to pack the rest of our gear and get on the trail."

"Like John Wayne always said." Beaudine gave a nervous laugh. "We're burnin' daylight."

"Burning moonlight," Quinn smiled. "If we're not on the trail well before the sun comes up, there's no way we can catch up to Volodin before the Russian hunter gets to him." He threw more wood on the fire, and then untied the support line to take down the nylon tube tent, which he spread out like a tarp between the fire and the boulder. Positioning the headlamp in the center of his forehead, he stretched a pair of latex gloves from the first-aid kit over oily hands and sat on the second sleeping bag with his back to the boulder. The bag was still inside the vacuum-sealed wrapper and formed a two-by-two-foot compressed square that made for a perfect seat cushion.

"Okay," he said, waving a gloved hand over the top of the tarp. "That should keep you dry and out of the snow. I need you to lie down here as best you can—on your back, so you're looking up at me."

Beaudine froze. "With my head in your lap?"

Quinn nodded. "That's the idea."

She moved grudgingly, maneuvering her bruised body so the back of her head rested on Quinn's thigh. She peered up at him with the eye that wasn't crusted shut. He smelled like wet wool and wood smoke—smells she'd never found particularly pleasant but were oddly comforting at the moment. He wore the headlamp but hadn't switched it on yet, and looked down at her smiling, as if it wasn't weird that he was patting her forehead in the middle of the Alaska wilderness. She knew he was merely assessing her wound, but the flickering firelight and her reclining vantage point made it feel tender, and the circles she ran in didn't offer that sensation very often.

She closed her eyes and tried to concentrate. "You ever sew anyone up before?"

"You'll make seven," Quinn said. "If you count myself, and the pig and two goats at field labs during Pararescue training."

"Two people?" Beaudine said, her good eye flicking open. "You mean to tell me you've only stitched up two live people?"

"I've practiced on a lot of pig feet," Quinn said, winking. "Look, stitches are a last resort in the field. We should really wait until we get back, but you'll need both eyes for the work we have ahead. There's superglue in the kit, and I'll use it when I can, but it's not likely to hold up on the deeper areas." He held his hands back away from her face as if to get some sort of go-ahead to continue.

Beaudine sighed. "Well, two is two more than I've ever done, so I guess you're the expert."

"I am," Quinn said, sounding sure enough of himself to calm her nerves a notch. He held a small syringe over her face so she could see it. "I need to irrigate the wound. Make sure we got all the crud out before I close it. I can probably get by with six or seven stitches above your eye and close this one over your nose with butterfly strips or glue.

"There a mirror in that kit?"

"It's pretty small." Quinn rifled through the pack that sat on the tarp beside him until he found a two-by-three Lexan mirror with a signaling pinhole in the middle. "You want to look at it before and after so you can sue me for malpractice?"

Small or not, the mirror did the job. Beaudine flinched when she saw the angry gash that ran in a diagonal red line across the bridge of her nose and up to her scalp. It was a scar she'd live with the rest of her life—and it was eerily familiar.

"Well, hello there, Merline," she whispered.

Quinn had waited much too long to clean the wound and had to use several canteen cups worth of watered down Betadine and the syringe to work loose all the dirt and debris that had made it inside. He knew it must have been extremely uncomfortable, but Beaudine lay quietly as if she were napping.

"I got a feeling this is where it's about to get real," she said when he stopped irrigating. "Aren't you supposed to give me a bullet or something to bite on?"

Quinn held up the Ziploc bag of snow so Beaudine could see it without moving her head. "You'll still feel the sutures," he said, "but the cold should numb the area up a little."

As gently as he could, he held the baggie to the tender skin over the worst portion of the gash, just above her eyebrow. He took her hand and moved it on top of the bag so she could keep it in place before turning his attention to the small wax-paper envelope that contained the sterile cutting needle and suture material. There should have been a hemostat in the kit, but if Lovita had ever had one, he couldn't find it. He'd have to make do with the tiny Leatherman Squirt he carried is his pocket virtually every day of the year. Absent a hemostat, the small pliers would serve as a passable needle driver.

Quinn pinched the curved needle with the tip of his Leatherman. Just under an inch in length, it was sharpened to cut rather than merely pierce, and attached to a foot and a half of black monofilament suture line. He moved the bag of snow and turned Beaudine's head slightly, putting the wound perpendicular to his body to make it easier to work.

Beaudine's good eye popped open and looked up at him. Her lips trembled slightly as she spoke. "I know this is gonna hurt," she said. "But I'm pretty good when it comes to pain. Pain was a pretty normal thing in our house when I was growing up."

"Who's Merline?" he asked to pass the time.

"My mama." Beaudine's voice was stretched tight, as if he'd hit a nerve with more than the suture needle. "I was sure Jacques told you."

"He said you had a rough childhood."

"Did he tell you my daddy shot my mama in the head when I was eleven?"

"He did not," Quinn said, needle poised a fraction of an inch from Beaudine's wound. So that was what the cryptic message was all about.

"Just sew, okay . . ." Beaudine closed her eyes and fell back limp in his lap. "I guess that pretty much sums up all there is to know about me."

"I doubt that, Khaki," he said, driving the blade of the needle into pink skin along the center point at the deepest portion of the wound.

Beaudine's lips trembled, but she didn't flinch.

"She forgave him, you know," Beaudine continued with her life story as if the telling of something so awful might ease the pain of her present situation. "Can you believe that? The son of a bitch shot her in the head, and she forgave him. Bullet went in over her left eye and sorta skirted around under the skin but didn't go through the skull." Beaudine gave a little shrug, almost causing Quinn to stick her with the needle where he didn't intend to. She must have felt him pull back. "Sorry," she said, looking up through a watery eye. "I'll be still. Anyhow, Daddy did two and a half years in Angola state pen for attempted murder, but the parole board let him out on accounta Mama bawled her head off at his hearing. Worst part about it—well not the worst part, but a bad part anyhow—me and Jacques, we used to be really close, you know, when we were kids. My mama and his mama are sisters. But after my daddy got out of prison, Jacques's father wouldn't let my family come around. And who can blame him?"

Quinn kept sewing, unwilling to step into whatever this was with a question.

"They're still together, you know, if you can believe it." Beaudine tried to shake her head at the thought of such a thing and tugged against the needle, causing her to wince in pain. "Sorry," she said again. "I guess it's no wonder I'm a bitch . . ." She suddenly looked up at Quinn, both eyes wide the way he imagined she might have looked as a frightened little girl. "Sorry for vomiting up my past like that. Could you please talk for a while? Mama used to say words to me when things got really bad, it didn't even matter what the words were, as long as I had something to hang on to during the worst of it."

"Okay." Quinn said, relieved to change the subject. He was sure Beaudine's family issues would come up again. Beaudine's problems were far too complicated for a hit-and-run conversation. Old wounds had a way of opening up in times like this, especially if they had festered. On some level it hurt Quinn to see another human being carrying around that sort of pain, but he'd never been much good at providing more than a listening ear—surely one of the many reasons his wife had given him the boot.

They were both quiet for a time while Quinn tried to think of something to say. He used the tip of the Leatherman to throw near perfect surgeon's knots with surprising dexterity considering how long it had been since he'd sutured a comrade at arms. It took a certain kind of detachment to cause pain to a friend in order to help them. Detachment—now there was something he was good at.

"It looks like Lovita's plane was sabotaged," he said at length. "Someone crimped one of the oil lines."

"Had to be that big Russian bastard who came in last," Beaudine said. "Glad you clobbered him with the fire poker. I'm surprised her instruments didn't tell her anything."

Quinn used a small pair of scissors from the trauma kit to cut the monofilament after he completed each suture. The longer he worked, the more he came to realize this was going to require more stitches than he'd originally hoped. He kept up his pace without mentioning it, thinking it better to finish the most painful part of this gruesome business as quickly as possible.

"Lovita's a great pilot," he said. "But the saboteur was tricky. She would have thought we had oil pressure when she did her run-up before takeoff, but with no way to circulate, the engine overheated and eventually blew. We're lucky we didn't burst into a ball of flames."

Firelight reflected off Beaudine's face, but her eyes remained closed. Quinn of all people knew the tremendous amount of trust it took for someone in her line of work to close her eyes and let a near stranger get near her with a sharp metal object.

She gave a small shake of her head, barely moving at all. He wouldn't have even noticed it had she not been nestled against his thighs. "Doesn't make any sense," she said. "Why sabotage the plane if they planned to kill us all anyway before we got in it to fly away?"

"Good point," Quinn said. "But killers can't afford to have any loose ends. They couldn't account for every guest. The big guy who hit Lovita was outside taking care of the oil line before he came in and saw what was going on. Half the people in Alaska have some sort of pilot's license. Say those guests who happened to be out fishing turned out to know how to fly—or even Volodin for all we know. The sabotage would have eventually taken care of them even if they were able to slip by the Russians. Burning the plane would have thrown up a fireball that risked drawing a passing aircraft to the lodge."

"I guess I can buy that," Beaudine said.

Quinn's needle pierced a piece of inflamed skin, and she gave a real flinch for the first time since he'd started the process. A tiny tear formed in the corner of her good eye. "Women cry from tension, you know," she said, staring at the sky. "Not because we're weak."

"So my mother, ex-wife, seven-year-old daughter, and girlfriend tell me," Quinn said, smiling and thinking of the four women.

"How much longer?"

"We're not quite half-way there," he said.

Beaudine took a series of long cleansing breaths, like she was going into labor, and settled in again. "All righty then," she said. "What say you teach me how you tell the time with the stars like you did."

"I can do that . . ." Quinn resumed his stitching as he spoke, using low, even tones. "Big dipper rotates counterclockwise around the North Star like an hour hand on a twenty-four hour clock. Midnight is at that top, with one, two, three, and so on running around the left side of the circle."

"Counterclockwise." Beaudine said, eyes closed, as if repeating the line from a bedtime story.

"Right," Quinn said, snipping the ends of another surgeon's knot. "You draw a line from the North Star through the two pointer stars on the cup of the dipper. That line points to the correct time on the circle March sixth of every year."

"Do what?" Beaudine stared at him, seemingly oblivious now to the pain from the cutting needle. "What happens if you want to know what time it is on the other three hundred sixty-four days of the year?"

"Ahh," Quinn said, tying another knot. "You can do that, too. All it takes is a little math—"

"I'm gonna stop you right there, mister," Beaudine said. "Khaki's brain doesn't respond so well to mathematical things."

"Funny," he said. "I'll bet you do math every day and don't even think about it."

"Not this gal, sweetheart," she said. "Me and math, we got us an understanding. It leaves me alone, and I leave it alone. There's a reason I went to law school instead of becoming an engineer."

"No worries then," Quinn said. He smiled as he snipped the line on the twelfth and what he hoped would be the final suture. "We're not likely to use too much math on the rest of the trip."

Quinn returned the needle to the paper envelope and finished off the wound on either end of the stitches with butterfly bandages and superglue. He covered the entire length of the wound with a thick line of antibiotic ointment and then taped on a gauze bandage before patting her gently on the shoulder.

"What?" she whispered, eyes closed, sounding sleepy.

"You can get up," Quinn said. "We're all done here."

"Dammit," she said, still not moving. "I should have had you teach me the math."

Quinn looked at his watch, too tired to bother with the stars. "Less than two hours until sunrise," he said. "Time to start walking if we want to catch Volodin alive."

Beaudine sat up, running a hand down the front of her jacket to compose herself. "You sure it's safe to hike out there in the dark with all the wolves and bears and et cetera?"

Quinn knelt by the tarp, cataloging their gear in his mind as he divided it between their two packs.

"I'm not worried about wolves or bears," he said. "It's the et cetera that will kill us."

Chapter 35

The hardy, weather-bitten souls who lived in Siberia were fond of saying that there was no road, only a direction. To Feliks Zolner, there was no direction, only pursuit—whichever way it took him.

He woke well before dawn, having slept the deep and dreamless sleep known only to men who possessed no conscience. Zolner and his men had left only the fool, Igoshin, and the pitiful couple who owned the place alive. They had killed the fishermen and young pilot quickly and without fanfare. Zolner had chosen the largest suite on the top floor. The room the Hendersons reserved for special guests, it boasted a king-size bed with an enormous down comforter and enough feather pillows to smother a horse. His profession made sodden sleeping bags the norm during a chase, when he was fortunate enough to have a bag or sleep.

A hunter at heart, Zolner lived a life of purposeful stoicism. He relished the small, relative comforts of a leaky shelter during a downpour or a warm parka against the teeth of a blizzard. Clean, Egyptian cotton sheets were a seldom-seen luxury, and he was happier that way. In truth, the softness of the lodge ran contrary to Zolner's nature. A life of ease rendered people lazy, careless, and prone to mistakes. Extravagance made one soft, and to be soft was to be dead. Hardship sharpened the intellect and the body like grit polished a stone. His mother had been the best hunter he'd ever seen, and as far as he knew, she'd never eaten anything richer than wild cherry jam. He was certain the poor woman had never owned more than two pairs of socks at any given time.

Cold gray eyes flicked toward the sound of creaking wood—someone heavy plodding down the hallway in bare feet. It would be Kravchuk, up to take a piss. Zolner had warned him about keeping company with prostitutes. The man's prostate could no longer last two hours, let alone an entire night. Zolner hated the thought of training a new spotter. Sitting in a sniper hide with someone who had to urinate every other moment was impractical. Zolner eyed the Grach 9mm pistol on the varnished pine night table beside his bed. As if on cue, Kravchuk's graveled voice carried in from the hall on a series of coughs. A smart man, he did not want to be mistaken for an enemy and shot through the wall.

"It's just me boss, going to the toilet."

As large as the bed was, it was almost too short for Zolner. At a brawny six feet eight, his heels came within inches of the footboard.

Zolner threw back the covers and swung long, powerful legs off the bed. He'd showered the night before, putting on a fresh set of wool underwear so he could be ready to move at a moment's notice.

Igoshin had thought to ingratiate himself by telling Zolner all about the dark and dangerous man who'd beaten him up with the fire poker. Quinn, that was his name. According to the babbling Russian, the blond woman traveling with him was FBI, which was curious.

In Zolner's experience, American policemen traveled in packs, and then called in even more reinforcements at the slightest provocation. These two were hunting Dr. Volodin, so FBI or not, that made them a problem.

Foolishly believing that he and Zolner were operating on the same team, Igoshin bragged that he'd sabotaged Quinn's airplane, swearing through broken lips and a swollen face that it had to have crashed somewhere in the bush not long after takeoff. Zolner had allowed the buffoon to remain alive only because he might remember some significant information during the night. In Zolner's world one did not ingratiate himself by getting beaten by the enemy. Weakness was to be weeded out, never tolerated. Wolves did not accept excuses from one of their own if it was injured and unable to hunt. Useless members of the pack became a valuable food source and were simply eaten for the good of all.

Zolner planned to question Igoshin once more before he left and then put the useless man out of his misery. He hadn't decided yet what he would do with the old couple—if they were even still alive. Yakibov, the former Spetsnaz soldier, had made it clear that he considered the woman a spoil of war. Zolner thought his spotter to be a sadistic bastard, but Yakibov appeared to have even Kravchuk beaten in that regard.

Seated on the edge of the soft mattress with both feet on the floor, Zolner rubbed a large hand over the bristles of his salt-and-pepper crew cut, then down across his face, feeling the stubble and the small scar that ran across the bottom of his chin. He had few external scars, and the man who had given him that one had paid dearly for the privilege.

Rolling off the bed to drop facedown to the cool wooden floor, he pushed himself into a plank position.

His dear mother had told him when he was very young that her grandfather had done fifty push ups each morning before anything else, even over the long and tortuous months of the Battle for Stalingrad. Zolner had followed in his great-grandfather's footsteps, finding a routine of morning exercise got his blood moving and made him immediately more alert.

Zolner performed each pushup with the same exactness that he did everything. Afterward, he took himself through a series of stretches, some seated, some standing, always paying particular attention to his breathing. Some would have called what he did yoga.

Kravchuk's cough in the hallway drew his attention toward the door.

"Boss?"

"What is it?" Zolner said, bending at the waste to touch the flat of his palms to the ground. His thick chest pressed against his thighs.

Kravchuk coughed again, a habit even more problematic than the overactive bladder. "Davydov has the plane ready to go at first light . . ."

"And?" Zolner said. With Kravchuk, there was always an "and" of late. The man could never get to the point without a lengthy preamble. Zolner expected his pilot to have the plane ready to go the instant he wanted to leave. There was no reason to inform him of that fact.

Kravchuk coughed again. "That guy, Igoshin, he has been begging to talk to you. He says it is important."

"Of course he does," Zolner said. Igoshin had surely spent the fevered night mulling over dozens of scenarios where he could trade information for his pitiful life.

* * *

Zolner's hunting boots were waterproof and quiet, making little noise on the polished wood as he trotted down the stairs and into the lodge's great room fifteen minutes after he'd finished his morning stretches. He carried his rifle loosely in his left hand. It was pleasing to see that Kravchuk had a fire going in the stone hearth, adding a small element of cheer to the otherwise dreary mood in the log interior.

Zolner's camouflage clothing and freshly shaved face combined with his rigid posture to give him the look of an officer in some elite unit. In truth, he'd never been a part of the actual military, working instead on contract for specific generals and colonels who could get their hands on enough money to meet his price.

Zolner folded out the aluminum legs of the bipod and set the rifle on the long wooden table so the weapon rested upright, protecting the three-thousand-dollar 12-52X56 Valdada scope. Both the rifle and the attached suppressor were covered in a white and gray "Yeti" Kryptek camouflage pattern, perfect for winter stalking.

Kravchuk slid a bowl of cooked oats across the table—as was expected of him first thing in the morning.

Igoshin slumped where Zolner had left him, in a large leather chair beside the fire, panting heavily, a bag of frozen vegetables pressed to the bloody mess that had once been his face. He'd been dozing, or maybe half unconscious considering the extent of his head injuries, but he glanced up at the noise of the bowl sliding on wood and tried to push himself to his feet.

"Please," Zolner said, "stay where you are."

Igoshin fell back with a low groan, vegetables to his face.

Henderson, the lodge owner, sat tied to one of his

high-backed wooden dining chairs. His wrists were red and torn from struggling against the ropes. His shirt torn, Henderson's head lolled in a state of near insanity, half teetering between consciousness and complete madness. His eyes were swollen shut from crying. Blood and spittle drooled down his grizzled chin, smearing the pale flesh of his shuddering chest. He'd no doubt heard the incessant screeching from his wife as Yakibov demonstrated the special techniques a disgraced Spetsnaz soldier had at his disposal for the treatment of a female war prize.

Kravchuk must have told Yakibov that Zolner was up, because he dragged the shattered woman in by her hair before Zolner even had time to take a bite of his oats. Zolner nodded to another of the high-backed chairs and Yakibov shoved her into it.

"We're not complete animals," Zolner said, wiping a bit of milk from his lips with a paper napkin. "Allow the poor woman to sit by her husband."

Yakibov grunted, sliding the chair and the women across the room. Zolner wondered if he'd even taken the time to sleep.

Mrs. Henderson's eyes were open but catatonic, staring a thousands meters into the distance, unfocused. There was nothing left of the fiery spark they'd held when Zolner and his men first arrived. It was unlikely she recognized her own husband or even knew where she was anymore.

Everyone sat in silence as Zolner finished his oats, picking up the bowl to drink the last of the milk. Without warning, he slammed his fist on the table, rattling the bowl and causing Igoshin to nearly jump out of his skin across the room. Mr. Henderson's eyes opened, but he was too exhausted to flinch. Mrs. Henderson just continued to stare.

"So," Zolner said. "You wanted to speak with me?" He remained at the table, his back to Igoshin. One hand rested on the cheek piece of his rifle while he flipped up the bolt with the other, inspecting the chamber.

"I had hoped you would send word to Colonel Rostov," the wounded Russian said. "Inform him I am here so he can send an extraction team to take me home."

Zolner moved slowly around the table so the rifle was between him and the squirming Russian. "What do you think of my weapon?" he said, looking up at Igoshin with the full force and effect of his gray eyes.

Igoshin opened his mouth as if to speak, but produced only mumbles. When he finally rallied his words they came in nervous stops and starts. "I . . . it . . . I . . . it is exquisite."

"I think so as well," Zolner said. He patted the stock as if it were a beloved friend. "She is chambered in 375 CheyTac and built especially for me." He ran a hand from the muzzle up the fluted barrel toward the action. "Aluminum stock, adjustable for pull and cheek height, she weighs nineteen pounds without the Valdada scope." He gave a chuckling nod, as if both men shared a secret. "Some people of weak constitution might say that a rifle that pushes a 300 grain bullet at over 3000 feet per second needs to be heavier." He gave a disdainful flip of his hand as if shaking off a thought he felt was unclean. "But I am a man, and men are not bothered by a small amount of recoil."

"Of course not," Igoshin muttered.

Across the great room, standing beside the catatonic Mrs. Henderson, Yakibov smiled.

Zolner released the CheyTac's box magazine into his hand, then used it to gesture toward Igoshin as he spoke. "Colonel Rostov informed me that one of the men in your team was trained as a sniper. Decorated in battle."

Igoshin moved the frozen vegetables away from his swollen face. His nose was split across the bridge and hung more off than on. "That was me," he said, nodding his head emphatically, apparently thinking the two had found some common ground. "The colonel was speaking of me."

"Well, that *is* good news," Zolner said. Kravchuk passed him a plastic container of ammunition and he began to press rounds into the magazine one at a time. Loaded with a projectile of a solid copper nickel alloy, the rounds were huge, each nearly as long as his ring finger. Zolner pushed seven of them into place with a series of resounding clicks. "I consider myself fortunate when I am able to speak with another professional shooter." Zolner looked up. "May I see your rifle?"

Igoshin hung his head. "I no longer have it," he whispered.

"I did not quite hear you." Zolner pressed the loaded magazine back into the rifle, driving it home with a firm smack. The bag of frozen vegetables slipped from Igoshin's hands with the sudden noise.

"The dark man took it," Igoshin said.

"Quinn?" Zolner said. "I see. This dark man must have been highly trained in order to shoot two of Colonel Rostov's men and beat you to death. It takes an especially skilled man to steal the one thing that a professional sniper would never allow himself to lose."

"He—"

Zolner pounded the table again. "The one thing!" he roared, glaring at Igoshin with dead gray eyes.

"He is—" Igoshin repeated himself.

"You have already told me about him," Zolner said. He gave a nod to Yakibov and Kravchuk. "In fact you've proven yourself quite a talker. I want to know what you told this man about me."

"I told him nothing," Igoshin said. "I . . . I swear it. He is surely dead in any case."

"People like this Quinn are cockroaches," Zolner said. "I will assume they infest my life until I feel them crack under the heel of my boot." He sat at the table and swung the rifle around so it was pointed directly at Igoshin, fifteen feet away. The buffoon began to hyperventilate, casting battered eyes around the room looking for any ally, any route of escape.

"I ask you again, my friend." Zolner kept his voice low, almost consoling. "What do this dark man and the FBI agent know of me?"

"There was an Eskimo girl with them," Igoshin said. "She had heard stories about you. She told everyone who listened that you are a ghost, a great hunter who steals her people away when they are out on the ice."

Zolner smiled as if this pleased him. "These Natives, they fear me, then?"

Igoshin nodded so emphatically it looked as though his head might fly off the end of his neck. The movement must have put him in great pain considering the injuries to his face, but it didn't stop him. "You scare the shit out of them, sir. They are terrified of your hunting skill."

"That is good to hear," Zolner said.

"They have a name for you," Igoshin said, caught up in the act of pleasing his captor, oblivious to the futility. "They call you Worst of the Moon."

Zolner's smile was genuine this time. "Worst of the Moon," he said, considering each word. "I like that very much." The smile vanished from his face, and he leaned forward against the rifle's stock, working the bolt to feed a round into the chamber. The action was butter-smooth and hardly made a sound. He flicked his free hand, motioning his men to drag the Hendersons' chairs so they were seated directly in front of the table, lined up shoulder to shoulder between the muzzle of the CheyTac and Igoshin's heaving chest.

Zolner put his eye to the scope. The view was extremely blurry, as he knew it would be. At this close range, a blurry reference was sufficient. The bullet would rise as it flew from the barrel so he lifted the butt of his rifle slightly, placing the center of the crosshairs on the fuzzy patch of cloth three inches above Mr. Henderson's elbow.

Rising from his chair, Zolner stepped back to study his targets, hands together, thumbs to his lips, as an artist might consider a work in progress.

"The question remains," Zolner said at length. He moved around the table to reposition Mrs. Henderson's chair so her right shoulder touched her husband's left arm. If the woman knew what was about to happen, she gave no indication. "How did this Eskimo girl know I was coming? How did she know she should be afraid of me?"

Igoshin appeared to sink into the stuffing of the chair, defeated.

"How long until sunrise?" Zolner said taking his seat back behind the CheyTac.

Kravchuk looked at his watch. "Fifty-one minutes, boss," he said.

"Very well. I am almost finished here. Inform Davydov I wish to be in the air before sunrise—as soon as it is light enough to see the ground as we fly."

Zolner peered over the top of the scope at the dejected Igoshin. "I will shoot only once." His eyes shifted to the Hendersons, his voice a piercing whisper. "Think of it—bone, lung, heart, lung, bone, bone, lung, heart, lung, bone . . ."

Igoshin pressed his eyes together, beginning to weep.

"It is possible that it will strike a rib or even a spine and stop somewhere along the way." Zolner settled in with his cheek pressed firmly against the stock. "But you and I both know that is highly unlikely." At this distance, he didn't have to worry about his breathing—but he did anyway. Every shot must be perfect. His mother had taught him that.

Chapter 36

New York

Petyr Volodin loved the pop and whir of the thin plastic jump rope as it snapped against tile and sped past his ears. Knees bent, ankles loose, the balls of his feet barely left the floor. He breathed through his nose, keeping his heart rate slow. Sweat rolled down a hairless chest, soaking the waistband of his gray sweatpants.

The clientele at Ortega's ran the gamut of prospective fighters. Street kids got a break on a locker and lessons for a flat forty bucks a month. Petyr paid half again that just for the locker—but that's all he needed. It was the steady stream of corporate warrior types who paid the rent. These were the executive fighters—the mortgage brokers, investment bankers, and accountants. They didn't fight to find a career. Hell, virtually everyone who stepped in the cage got a trophy, win or lose. But there was something about the smell of spit buckets and liniment, the taste of sweat and blood that added some missing element to their mundane lives.

There were plenty of other fight gyms around Manhattan, but the men and women who ventured into Ortega's in East Harlem seemed to believe that working out in a gritty gym would give them a competitive edge over guys who trained at more glitzy, upscale places.

Petyr liked East Harlem because it was one of the few places left in the world where he could still get a little respect. The guys at Ortega's had no idea his tattoos were fake. Here, he was a bona fide ex-con from some brutal Russian gulag they'd seen on the Discovery Channel, one of the Thieves, an Eastern Bloc badass, the real deal. This was one of the few places he could still grab a workout with no shirt on and not have to worry about somc guy with a spider tattooed on his neck shivving him in the liver.

Petyr often used the time he spent skipping rope to try and sort out difficult problems—like these stupid tats. Damned Nikka and her bright ideas. Mr. Anikin wanted him dead. The guys who showed up to kill him at his apartment had made that obvious. Beating them to death had been self-defense, but who was going to believe that? Now he had a murder rap to figure out piled on top of everything. He made a mental note to give Nikka an extra smack when he saw her again, for talking him into getting the ink. And then there was the shit at Cheekie's. What was that all about anyway? He couldn't quite get his head wrapped around the big southern dude and his mean-ass little friend with the battered face. They'd apparently taken over the place from Gug. They acted like cops, but seemed more interested in his father than him—until he'd popped off to the steamy little sweetmeat dancing on the stage. Then they'd gotten all up on him, focusing their self-righteous rage at his behavior. Petyr sped up his rope work, letting the whir and slap console him as he pondered over the situation. Last he checked, Cheekie's was a titty bar where you were supposed to go to watch naked girls dance. Kicking him in the nuts like that was a bitch move. They'd caught him by surprise, that's all. Given the chance at a fair fight, he'd mop the ring with either one of those guys. And then their bootylicious girlfriend would be all alone and with no protection from whatever pimp racket they had going. Then Petyr the Wolf would show her what a real man was like.

The throbbing rattle of a speed bag brought Petyr back to reality. Maxim, one of the two Ortega brothers who owned the gym, stood at the front counter. He tried to fix a broken credit-card machine by prying off the back with a screwdriver. Maxim, also known as Maxim the Minimum, was the smaller of the two Ortegas at just under five and a half feet tall. He had a neck like an ox with shoulders to match. It was common knowledge that he was not the smarter of the two brothers. The screwdriver had him baffled so there was not much hope for the credit-card machine.

It didn't take long for Maxim to lose patience and drive the screwdriver through the card reader, as if trying to stab it through the heart. He threw the whole broken mess under the counter and scrawled a sign on the back of a cardboard protein supplement box that said "CASH ONLY."

Cash. That was exactly what Petyr needed. He had to get his hands on some money one way or another. Unfortunately, his talent for making money was no better than Maxim Ortega's handyman skills. The bastards at Cheekie's had kept him from getting to the emergency stash he kept hidden at Nikka's place.

All he really knew how to do was fight.

Good fights took time to set up, the ones with decent purses anyway, and Petyr found himself in a bad spot professionally. He'd lost too many bouts to get a shot at moving out of the mid-level ranks without beating one of the big names. And he'd won too many for a big name to want to meet him in the ring. If a ranked fighter beat Petyr, he would not move up in the rankings, but if he lost, he could certainly move down.

That left few options—at least any that let him retain his dignity. Petyr quit skipping with a flourish of rope swings on either side of his body, just in case another fighter happened to be watching. He grabbed a towel off a peg along the wall and replaced it with the jump rope. Wiping the sweat off his face, he caught Maxim's eye. The brothers ran a little side business that could make him some money if The Wolf didn't mind sacrificing a little bit of his integrity. He shot a glance at his yellow duffle on the floor below the rope pegs. Integrity. That was a joke. His girlfriend was a junkie stripper, and he juiced regularly on Russian 'roids his chemist father sent him. He didn't have much integrity to lose—and anyway, integrity was a hell of a lot easier to sell when you needed some cash. He picked up the duffle and carried it with him when he went up front to work out the specifics with Maxim. The stuff his father sent was hard to come by. He had to stretch it out. Make it last.

Where he was going, he'd need all the help he could get.

Chapter 37

Alaska

It was still dark when Quinn shoved the last of the gear into his drybag and zipped it closed. Beaudine was already packed and had borrowed the toilet paper to head into the brush one last time before they hit the trail.

Quinn's pack wasn't particularly large, and he had to tie the sleeping bag on the outside, horseshoe style over the top. Quinn's old man was known to venture into the woods with nothing more than a hatchet and an attitude.

Garcia had a tendency to surf the web at night to wind down after a stressful day. Such browsing only made Quinn angry so he usually read or studied Chinese or Arabic flashcards. Still, if Ronnie stayed away from political rants, she sometimes found the odd kernel of interest and shared it with him. She'd once shown him a site with the laughable array of what people put in a go-bag, popularly called the SHTF bag because it was supposed to contain the gear vital to survival when the proverbial "Shit Hit The Fan." Many such bags looked as if they were kits prepared for all-out war—but included few of the necessities for the inevitable lull between battles. Some had a couple of axes, a folding saw, three or four handguns, multiple pocket knives, push daggers, machetes, road flares—all of it useful gear in the right situation. Quinn could hardly judge. He was rarely without two guns and two blades—but a good go-bag had to contain some beans and Band-Aids to go with the bullets. Quinn found himself amazed at how few bags contained toilet paper.

He started any kit with his EDC, his everyday carry. Unless he happened to be swimming, it was a rare moment that found Quinn without at least three things: a knife, a light source, and something to make fire. In this case, he had his Zero Tolerance folding knife, an orange zippo lighter—less *tacticool* but harder to misplace, the Leatherman Squirt, and a SureFire Titan flashlight. Smaller than his little finger, the light ran on a single AAA battery. The satellite phone was somewhere underwater inside the airplane. Quinn and Beaudine both had cellphones, but they would do them no good until they reached a village, almost all of which had a cellular tower. His custom Kimber 10mm rested in a leather Askins Avenger holster on his strong side, balanced by a spare magazine and the thick piggish blade of his Riot sheath knife. The hot 10mm round gave him similar ballistics to a .41 Magnum, but he was still happy to have his Aunt Abbey's AR-10. Quinn was certainly not against handguns—having used them to great effect, but if things devolved into chaos in the woods as in an urban environment, a handgun of any kind was merely the weapon used to fight his way to a rifle.

The most basic kit for any bush venture added a

headlamp and at least fifty feet of parachute cord. Quinn wore his headlamp now to make sure he didn't inadvertently leave behind anything important but planned to turn it off once they started to move, preferring to navigate by natural light. Wearing a beacon on your skull was a good way to get turned into a bullet sponge.

Inside his pack, Quinn carried a second flashlight because, as he'd learned from hard experience, *Two is one and one is none* when it came to critical pieces of gear. The second light was larger and used two of the ubiquitous 123 lithium batteries. A small plastic case contained spares as well as an extra photo battery for the Aimpoint Patrol sight mounted on Aunt Abbey's rifle.

The cold weather had both Quinn and Beaudine layering in virtually every piece of clothing they had, including Lovita's pink fleece that he'd dried by the fire and given to Beaudine. Freedom of movement made large parkas impractical, but Quinn felt relatively comfortable with his waterproof Sitka shell layered over a fleece jacket, the wool shirt, and wool long johns. Aunt Abbey had provided Beaudine with much the same system. As with the woolies, everything was a little large, making the FBI agent look as though she was dressed in her big sister's clothes. She didn't seem to mind. Warmth beat style every time in the bush.

Both Quinn and his brother had worn Mechanix gloves for years, first when working on their bikes—long before they had fallen into favor with the tactical community. He kept two pair of the lightly insulated gloves in his pack year round.

Quinn carried his personal trauma kit, but augmented it with bandages and some extra QuiKclot gauze from the plane. He gave the high-calorie energy bars from the aircraft to Beaudine, preferring the taste of Lovita's salmon strips and fatty *akutaq* to the cookies that tasted like coconut and sawdust.

Gorilla Tape, a hundred feet of 550 cord, Quinn's Vortex binoculars, and the Russian's .338 Lapua sniper rifle rounded out their gear. Quinn figured they each carried around twenty-five pounds, not including the long guns—sickeningly light since it was everything they had.

Beaudine came in from the shadowed timberline and crunched across the gravel as Quinn pulled the last tab tight to secure the sleeping bag. She must have gone down the stream and washed away the blood and grime from the crash. Her face was now clean and pinked from the cold water.

She handed him the toilet paper.

"Keep it," Quinn said, waving away the baggie. "I found another roll in the survival kit.

Beaudine thanked him and shoved the new treasure in her pocket before looking up at him. He flipped up the lens on his headlamp so he didn't blind her.

"Sorry about getting all weepy before," she said.

Quinn shrugged. "It happens."

"Not with me," Beaudine said. "I was raised under the iron notion that only my pillows should see my tears."

Quinn kicked snow into the fire, throwing the camp into darkness and sending up a hissing cloud of steam. "You're like your cousin in at least one respect," he said, chuckling.

Beaudine's brow furrowed, lopsided because of her wound. "How's that?"

"You both get philosophical when you take toilet paper into the woods." Quinn shouldered his pack and then picked up the rifle.

"I spilled some pretty gnarly details about my family," she said, falling in to crunch along beside him in the dark. "It doesn't make you worry about working with me?"

"Makes me worry for the other guys," Quinn said. "I don't know, maybe we really do heal stronger in the broken places."

"Math and Hemingway," she said. "You must have done well in school. Anyhow, that's a nice platitude. My grandma used to say stuff like that—'The good Lord won't give us a trial we can't handle.' Well, the good Lord must think I'm a badass."

"I know what you mean," Quinn said, eager to move past the philosophizing. It was easy to see that Beaudine and Thibodaux shared the same blood.

Beaudine stopped when they slid down the gravel to the edge of the swollen stream. She peered into the darkness down the rough animal trail. It was little more than a depression in the snow that ran next to the stream.

"I get a definite vibe that you really like this stuff," she said. Vapor clouded her face in the chilly blue reflection from the snow.

"Guess I'm just used to it," Quinn said.

"Well," Beaudine continued, "remember how I told you that the FBI had the lead on this so I'm the one in charge?"

"I do." Quinn raised both hands. "Loud and clear."

"Turns out this wilderness stuff scares the shit outta me," Beaudine said. "I am officially putting you back in charge."

"We're after the same thing," Quinn said. "Who's in charge matters a lot less than who's still alive when it's over."

"And that is exactly why you're in charge," Beaudine said. She nodded toward the gun slung over his shoulder as they wove their way around snow-covered willows. "Now, tell me about the gun you took from the Russian. I know a sniper rifle when I see it. Can you shoot it well enough to protect us from this Worst of the Moon?"

"I hope so," Quinn said. "It's a chambered in .338 Lapua Magnum. Awesome round. My ex-wife was shot with one just like it."

Beaudine gave a low whistle. "We all got stories, I guess."

"Yes, we do," Quinn said. "Anyway, it'll shoot further than I'm capable of."

Beaudine stopped in her tracks and looked at him. The stitches he'd given her crawled diagonally from her eyebrow nearly to her hairline like a dozen tiny black spiders. "But you *can* shoot long range, right? I mean, you have experience with that kind of thing?"

"I can and I do." Quinn gave her what he hoped was his best calming smile. "But it's going to involve some math—weaponized math . . . but it's still math."

"Of course there would have to be math," Beaudine said. She took her frustration out on a scrub willow, knocking off the snow with her fist as she turned to continue down the silver ribbon of trail. "Yet one more reason you should be in charge."

The sun was just a pink line over the eastern horizon fifty-five minutes later when they broke out of the willows onto a wide gravel flat at the confluence of the creek and the Kobuk River.

Each step had seen them slogging through loose gravel, powering through mucky, boot-sucking tundra, or leaping between the sometimes knee-high hills of grass and relatively dry ground Quinn called tussocks. Beaudine had to concentrate to keep from wheezing.

In the lead, Quinn paused while still in the cover of thick willow and alder scrub, holding up his fist to signal that he wanted to stop. He'd warned her that there would likely be a fish camp at the confluence of the two waterways and that they should stay quiet on approach. He needn't have worried. Just when she'd found a guy that was worth talking to, she didn't have the energy to say a word.

Snow sifted down through frozen leaves as Quinn drew back an alder branch so Beaudine had a better view in the direction he was looking. He pointed across the creek with the blade of his hand.

Tattered blue tarps hung on a weathered plywood shack, heavy with snow in the windless gray dawn. Three bare wooden frames, cobbled together from old two-by-fours and sun-bleached spruce poles, stood in front of the main shack on the wide gravel bar. It made her colder just looking at it. "That's a fish camp?" she said. "I don't know why, but I was expecting some kind of lodge, or at least a real cabin."

"Not out here," Quinn said. "Plywood is sixty bucks a sheet if they can get it. This is actually a pretty nice setup."

Quinn squatted at the base of the alder, slowly turning his head to scan up and down the far bank. "No smoke," he said. "There's a boat pulled up by the shack. It's covered with snow, but it still bothers me a little."

"You think it could be Volodin?"

"Could be," Quinn said, panting in the cold air. He unzipped his pack to retrieve the binoculars.

Beaudine took off her glove and dabbed at the wound on her forehead with the tip of her finger while she caught her breath and gazed across the river. The fish camp, such as it was, was no more than a hundred meters away. A layer of fog hugged the river, and everything above it was covered in frost or snow, making it difficult to pick out much detail in the flat morning light.

"You ever play Kim's Game?" Quinn's voice was muffled against his hands as he peered through the binoculars.

"Can't say as I have," Beaudine said. This guy was even more of an enigma than she'd been told. He'd hardly said a word of conversation through their entire walk and now he wanted to talk about some game.

Quinn passed her the binoculars, then leaned away slightly to give her a clear view. "Look it over like you would a crime scene for a minute or two."

Beaudine wiped the moisture away from her eyes and looked through the binoculars, careful not to touch them to her wound. She swept back and forth a couple of times before attempting to hand them back to Quinn. "That was a fun game," she said. "We'll have to play it again sometime."

"Okay." Quinn gave her a quiet smile, the kind of smile you give a child when you have the upper hand. "Tell me what you saw."

Beaudine sighed, exasperated. "I don't know. A ratty old shack with a bunch of ripped tarps for a roof. It looks vacant though. Like you said, no tracks."

"Did you see the sheet of plastic they're using for a window?"

"I saw it," Beaudine said. "It looked exactly like a sheet of plastic."

"Did you see the frost on it?"

Beaudine raised the binoculars again, taking a better look this time. There it was, a layer of frost—*inside* the plastic sheeting. She glanced sideways at Quinn, suddenly glad that they were still hidden in the willows. "Frozen vapor from somebody's breath?"

"Breath and maybe a propane heater," Quinn said. "There's definitely someone in there."

Chapter 38

Quinn squatted in the shadows, going over the various routes of approach in his head while Beaudine continued to scan with the binoculars.

"Why did you bring up that . . . what did you call it? Kim's Game?" she asked.

"It's from my favorite Kipling book," Quinn said. "Kim, the boy, is training to be a spy in British India. He plays a game where he looks at a tray full of stones of different size and color for a given amount of time. His teacher covers the tray, and Kim has to recite what he saw. Snipers use the same kind of game for observation training. Makes you pay attention to detail."

"I've played that before," Beaudine said. "You mean to tell me we played sniper games at my friend's bridal shower?"

"Pretty much," Quinn said. "My daughter and I play it all the time—when I'm around anyway."

"The things you learn sitting in the woods spying on a fish camp," Beaudine said, still looking through the binoculars. "Someone . . . or a few someones are in that camp. What's your plan?"

Quinn gazed to the east. Morning light filtered through

the trees, casting long shadows across the windblown snow. "First, we hurry and get across before who ever it is wakes up and shoots us."

"I'm with you there," Beaudine said. "I don't think my face could take another hit."

Quinn led the way back a hundred meters upstream from the camp, keeping to the alders and willow scrub until he found a spot where the water spread out to a width of about thirty meters. Crossing here would put them in the open for much longer, leaving them naked and vulnerable to any would-be attackers, but wide water had a chance to slow down, often making it relatively shallow. Even at this wide spot, the swollen stream reached their knees. Quinn pushed his way through the current, dragging his feet and slowing just enough so that he didn't loose his footing on the slick melon-sized rocks that rolled along the streambed with a periodic audible clatter. He walked upstream from Beaudine, shuffling his numb feet in the freezing water and doing his best to block the current so she wouldn't fall.

The main shack sat in a clearing on a low bluff overlooking an open gravel bar as long as a football field and half as wide. Scoured clean every spring by great slabs of river ice during breakup, the gravel was barren of all but a few tiny scrub willows that had to start over again every year.

Quinn sloshed out of the freezing water, moving up the bluff where a dark pocket of stunted spruce trees offered some semblance of concealment if not actual cover. Water squished from his boots with every step. Dry socks would eventually become a necessity, no matter the rush. He'd suffered from the agony of trench foot once before on a hunting trip with his brother, Bo, and once was plenty for a lifetime. Ever immortal in their own minds, the brothers had tried to tough out cold and wet boots for two full days on Kodiak Island. The week of red and swollen feet that followed was enough to make them both firm believers in the value of dry socks. As his old man said, "It did zero good to hurry if you were worthless when you got there."

Snow dampened their approach on the gravel, but Quinn and Beaudine moved quickly once they left the trees, going straight to the hollow-core door without stopping. Rifle over his shoulder, Quinn held the Kimber at high ready as he booted the flimsy thing and button hooked to his left around the threshold, just inside the twelve-by-twelve-foot room. Beaudine followed him inside immediately, hooking right as per their prearranged plan. She held the AR-10 high, moving in a slight crouch, elbows tucked like a professional shooter.

An Inupiaq boy in his mid-teens lay in his sleeping bag on a rough wooden frame across the room. He sat straight up and faced the door at the thud of boots on plywood. His sleepy eyes went wide and both hands flew up to shield his face.

Quinn lowered his pistol once he saw the other two bunk frames were vacant.

"Who are you guys?" the boy said, his voice remarkably calm for being woken up at gunpoint.

"FBI," Beaudine said, lowering the AR-10.

A smile spread over the boy's face. "No crap? You guys are really FBI?"

"We're after a fugitive," Beaudine said. "Thought he might be here."

"That was friggin' awesome," the boy said. "You busted in here like a friggin' HALO game." He suddenly noticed Beaudine's wounds and gave her a somber nod. "Your fugitive do that to you?"

"Plane crash," Quinn said, wanting to speed things along. He started to tell the boy about Lovita but decided it better to wait. "My name's Jericho. Do you happen to have a cell phone?"

"Only works when I'm in sight of the village." His face brightened into a smile. "They just built a new tower out here last year." He swung his feet onto the floor. He wore dingy gray cotton socks that had once been white, green nylon basketball shorts, and a stained T-shirt of the same color. At least a dozen dark purple hickeys encircled his neck, just above the collar of his T-shirt. He rubbed his eyes, then extended a hand toward Quinn. "I'm Brian. Brian Ticket."

Quinn gave him a fist bump. "I know some Tickets. Any relation to Lawrence?"

Brian coughed, still waking up. He scrunched up his nose and wrinkled his brow, the Inupiaq equivalent of shaking his head "no." "Those are the upriver Ticketts. Upriver Ticketts have two Ts. Us downriver Tickets have one T."

Beaudine's face screwed into a grimace. "What's with all the love bites, Brian Ticket with one T? Somebody try to suck your face off?"

Brian looked at the floor without answering.

"It's a thing they do in the village," Quinn said, grinning at Brian Ticket. "I'm betting you had an away basketball game last week, didn't you?"

"Shungnak." Brian nodded. "My girlfriend don't trust them upriver girls. She wanted to let 'em know I was already taken."

"Well, she did a good job of it." Beaudine gave a low whistle, shaking her head at the hickey damage. "You're lucky she didn't decapitate you."

Beaudine used the .308 to gesture toward a stack of small cardboard boxes that were on a small wooden table, the only other furniture in the room. Quinn counted five. They were flat, about two inches thick and each about six-by-six-inches square.

Beaudine let the rifle fall against the single point sling, parking it so it hung just in front of her handgun. She picked up one of the boxes to study it. “Why in the everlovin’ hell would anyone need a bunch of wax toilet rings out here where they don’t even have toilets?”

“To patch the boat,” Brian said. “There’s a big hole in the side. Usually works great but my genius brother-in-law hit a rock and broke the shear pin on the motor yesterday. He and my nephew loaded up our other boat with the caribou we caught and went back to Needle to get a spare sheer pin. I got stuck here guarding his old piece of junk boat.

Beaudine’s hands shook as she set the box back on the table with the other four. The after-effects of the cold-water crossing were catching up to her fast.

“Okay, Brian,” Quinn said, holstering his Kimber. “My friend and I are going to hurry and get into some dry socks, and then we’re going to need to borrow your boat.” He shrugged off his pack and dropped it on the plywood floor between his feet. Sitting on the low bed, he stripped off his soaked boots to put on his last dry pair of wool socks.

Brian leaned back against the plywood wall on his bunk. “I told you guys, the boat’s broke. We have to wait for my brother-in-law to bring back some welding rod to use for a shear pin.”

Quinn wiped as much moisture out of the boots as he could with a dry bandana from his pack. “When is your brother-in-law coming back?” he asked without looking up.

“He had to cut up three caribou last night. And, he’s been away from my sister for a few days, so I’m sure he's sleeping in a little with her this morning . . ." He winked. "I joke . . ."

"This is serious, Brian," Beaudine said. She leaned back with one foot stretched out in front of her, struggling to pull the dry sock over her shriveled wet foot. "This guy we're after is a very bad man. We're going to have to try and fix your boat."

Quinn held up his hand, motioning for her to stop talking as he peeked out the window. The roar of a low-flying aircraft grew louder as it flew directly overhead. He watched through a gap in the tarp as it flew by slowly

"I counted three heads," Quinn said, throwing the pack over his shoulders. "They're following the river."

"Who's following the river?" Brian said.

The sound of the engine seemed to hang there for a moment, before fading slowly into the distance.

Beaudine brightened, shooting a hopeful glance at Quinn. "Do you think someone's looking for us? Your Aunt Abbey, maybe?"

"Not likely," Quinn said, peeking out of the grime-covered plastic to make certain no one was using the same tactics he had used to sneak up on the shack. He turned back to Beaudine. "The storm would have kept any planes trying to get out to the lodge grounded through last night. And absent a visit to the lodge, it's too soon for anyone to even know we're missing."

"So it's Worst of the Moon?" Beaudine dropped her head as if being murdered from a distance was a foregone conclusion.

"Wait, wait, wait!" Brain threw aside his sleeping bag and shot to his feet. "Did you just say Worst of the Moon? He's coming here?"

Quinn raised both eyebrows, the silent affirmative in Inupiaq culture. "That's exactly what she said."

Brian rubbed his face with both hands, looking as if he might throw up. "Holy shit . . . sorry, FBI lady. I mean holy crap, holy, holy, holiest of all craps. If Worst of the Moon is a real person . . ."

"You've heard of him then?" Beaudine said.

Brian collapsed backward to sit on the edge of the bunk again. He drew his sleeping bag around him like a security blanket and shook his head slowly, mouth hanging open. "The Elders tell us kids these stories, you know, like Long Nails, the creepy old hag who gallops around on all fours eating kids who go into the beach grass. You can hear her toenails clicking on the earth when she comes after you. I figured the stories were just to keep us from wandering off and getting hurt."

"Like the fairytales about the little leprechaun people."

"*Enukin*?" Brian looked up, deadpan. "No, *enukin* are real. My dad's seen 'em lots of times. So's my mom."

Beaudine rolled her eyes and glanced at Quinn. "You think they saw our tracks when they flew over?"

"Doesn't matter," Quinn said. "Caribou hunters are leaving tracks all up and down the river." He started for the door, nodding to the pile of boxes on the table. "Brian, grab one of those wax rings and lets go see about fixing your boat. We've got to get to Needle ASAP."

Melting snow dripped from the tarp roof, splattering into a rapidly forming moat of black mud around the heated shack. Just as Brian had said, the battered aluminum boat had suffered a gash in the hull just below the waterline. Quinn estimated it to be about eight inches long and nearly an inch wide. Smears of flaking yellow wax around the damage gave evidence that it was an old wound and plumbing material had been used several times in the past. The battered shaft of a motor that had been removed from the transom now lay under the boat, semi-protected from the weather. Quinn grabbed the badly nicked prop and dragged the motor out in the slushy snow with both hands.

He spun the prop and glanced up at Brian with a narrow eye. "Your brother-in-law do all this?"

"My sister's husband is a great hunter." The boy gave a toothy grin. "He just ain't such a good boat driver."

"Thirty horse Nissan," Beaudine said. "Tough motor."

"I know Worst of the Moon is breathin' down our necks," Brian said, "but I'm telling you it's useless until my brother in law gets back from Needle. We looked all over the place for something to use as a shear pin."

The shear pin was a piece of soft metal rod about an inch long that was soft enough to give way when the propeller struck a fixed object, preventing damage to more expensive parts of the motor. Without it, the propeller spun freely, providing no power to push the boat forward.

Quinn looked up river toward Needle, thinking, then turned to Beaudine. "You mind helping Brian push some of that wax into the hole, and I'll take a look at the motor."

"How about you patch the boat while I take a look?" Beaudine said. She took off her parka shell and spread it over a stump before setting the AR-10 on top to keep it out of the snow. "I'm not tryin' to take over again. It's just that the only good times I ever had with my daddy were when we were working on small engines. Sometimes, for a minute or two, I could even pretend he wasn't a murderous bastard."

Brian looked down at his feet, good manners overshadowing his youthful curiosity.

Quinn took the wax ring. "Be my guest," he said.

Beaudine knelt in the snow beside the motor, using her multi-tool to remove the pin and nut that held the battered propeller in place. "Shear pin's toast all right."

"Told you." Brian shrugged.

"But I can fix it," Beaudine said, leaning over to grab her rifle. "Just so happens the brass end of a rifle cleaning rod makes a perfect shear pin if I use my Leatherman to cut it down to size."

"And my aunt keeps a small cleaning kit in the butt of her rifle." Quinn gave a nod of genuine admiration. He hoped he would have come up with such a fix.

Chapter 39

Quinn and Brian Ticket dragged the aluminum skiff down to the riverbank before attaching the hundred-pound motor. Beaudine provided over-watch with the AR-10. There was little in the way of gear so it didn't take them long to load the boat. Brian disappeared into the shack for a moment, then came slipping down the muddy bank wearing his pack. His rubber boots made perfect tracks in the snow as he approached the skiff.

"Needle's only four miles up river," the boy said. "But it still takes us about twenty minutes to get there."

Quinn attached the fuel line that connected the six-gallon plastic tank to the motor. "You're not coming," he said. "It's safer for you here."

"Screw that news." Brian set his jaw in fierce defiance but softened immediately when he met Quinn's gaze. "You don't understand about Worst of the Moon. He's a giant. There's only fourteen families in Needle, and most of the men are out hunting. I gotta go back and help you." Brian stared across the Kobuk, his eyes unfocused. "A lot of people go missing out here. Could be the land that takes 'em, or maybe it's Worst of the Moon. Some elders say he's the spirit of a dead hunter, come back to punish our people for abandoning the old ways."

Quinn shoved the stern of the boat into deeper water so he didn't break another shear pin on the gravel. He banged on the aluminum gunnel with the flat of his hand. "Get in the boat, Khaki."

Beaudine threw a leg over the side, still looking at Brian with a narrow eye. "Punish you how?"

"He hunts us," Brian said. "Like wolves. The elders say Worst of the Moon hunts on the ice or open tundra the best. You never see him coming until he's shot you in the head."

"How do they know he likes the tundra the best?" Beaudine asked.

Brian shrugged. "That's where the people go missing, I guess."

"Hang on," Beaudine said. "If all the victims are still missing, or never hear the bullet that kills them, how do you know he's a giant?"

Quinn pumped the rubber bulb on the line to deliver fuel to the motor. He could feel Volodin pulling farther away with every moment they weren't on the river.

"Homer John from down at Noorvik seen him once." Brian squatted on the sandy bank and used his finger to draw a map of the area in the dirt, like some Native women using a bone knife to illustrate stories in the sand. "Noorvik's clear down here, closer to Kotzebue. Homer was out on his snow machine last year lookin' for musk ox when he rode up on this big guy camping in the middle of nowhere. There was another man with him, but Homer said it was clear the giant guy was the boss. Homer said he had gray eyes—colder than he'd ever seen—and a tiny nose that made his face look flat. He just sat by his stove with a giant rifle in his lap and watched Homer John ride by."

"This Homer John guy," Quinn said. "He's pretty sure it was Worst of the Moon?"

Brian shook his head at Quinn. "You tell me. How'd a guy like that get out there? Where'd he come from? He didn't come through none of the villages. Like my dad says, strangers just don't show up in the middle of the tundra. They got to travel through somewhere."

"True," Quinn said.

"Anyhow," Brian said. "He let Homer John live for some reason, but two more hunters went missin' fifteen miles from that spot the very next day."

"Did anyone report it?" Beaudine asked.

"My dad says there ain't enough troopers in Alaska to take care of an area this big," Brian said, looking like he might cry. "Now come on and let me in. It's my boat, ya know."

"I'm sorry," Quinn said, giving the starter rope a yank. Smoke poured from the motor as it coughed once, then died. He pulled the rope again and it roared to life. He flipped the lever in reverse and backed out, letting the current of the Kobuk pull the boat downriver, stern first. He shouted so the bewildered Brian could hear him above the burbling chop of the engine. "We'll look in on your family." Throwing the transmission forward, he moved into deeper water before twisting the throttle to coax the little boat upriver toward Needle.

Beaudine clutched the gunnel with one hand while, leaning back to look at Quinn. "You promised to look after his family?"

"We'll kill the people that pose the danger," Quinn said, watching water seep in around the wax. "It's the same thing. But first we have to make it there."

Four miles was a long way to go for a boat patched with a toilet ring.

Chapter 40

Mitkun, Needle, Alaska

The paunchy Inupiaq man clutched a cigarette between his teeth and threw Kaija's plastic case on a metal rack at the rear of a green four-wheeler. He stacked the duffle bags on top before working to untangle a set of bright orange ratchet straps. Slightly shorter than Volodin, the man had a barrel chest and powerful hands. He wore a pair of nylon chest waders and a wool shirt. Shaggy black hair stuck out from beneath a yellow Caterpillar hat cocked back on his head as he worked. His name was Ray Stubbins, and Volodin estimated him to be in his late thirties.

The chemist folded bony arms across his chest and stomped his feet back and forth, trying to keep from shivering in the bright morning chill. Needle was set up in a long handled T, with the Stubbins' house located at the terminus of the northernmost short end. The sun was up high enough to begin to melt last night's snow from the hulks of three old snow machines rusting in front of the wind-beaten wooden home. Two little kids giggled and squealed a few feet away. Dressed in rubber boots, fleece jackets, and wool hats, they used a broken four-wheeler with no tires as a jungle gym. Neither looked old enough to attend the school at the other end of the T. Steam rose from the vent pipes of similar houses nearby, disappearing into the crisp morning air.

"We'll take you as far as Ambler on the Hondas," he said.

One of the few adult males left in the village, Stubbins had been carrying gear up from his boat when Volodin and Kaija had arrived. Kaija had wisely pointed out that they were sitting ducks when confined to the river. An overland route would make them less likely to be found—if they could find someone to sell them a four-wheeler. Stubbins was in no mood to sell his only mode of land transportation right in the middle of hunting season, but he and his brother had agreed to shuttle them for the sum of three hundred American dollars. It was a quarter of the cash Volodin had on hand, but all the money in the world would do them no good if Rustov's men caught them. Like most people in rural Alaska, Stubbins called all ATVs Hondas no matter the brand. This one happened to be a Polaris. "It's about a five-hour ride. Pretty bumpy, too."

Ray's brother, Frank, nodded at that, but said nothing, preferring to smoke his hand-rolled cigarette while he secured the load on the back of his four-wheeler. He wore a pair of gray sweats tucked into black high-topped rubber boots. An unzipped fleece revealed a red T-shirt stretched tight over a belly even larger than his brother's.

"And we only have to pay you for the one way?" Volodin said. He was becoming more unsettled by the moment, as if he might fly away in a gust of wind.

"The price covers gas but you're just payin' for one way. We'll hunt our way home." He slid a lever-action rifle into the fleece-lined plastic boot bolted vertically to the front of the ATV.

"We can reach big city from Ambler?" Kaija said in broken English.

Stubbins tied a plastic jug containing an extra five gallons of fuel to the back of his ATV. "There's a milk run flight that will take you from there to Fairbanks. You should call and get a seat now though."

"I lost ID. We have problem with security in Ambler?" Kaija asked, seeming worried, but sounding far from guilty of smuggling deadly nerve gas.

Stubbins scoffed. "There ain't no security out here. I've flown from Fairbanks to Anchorage on some of the smaller planes without them checking ID. Takes longer to get there, but they're more worried about weight and balance than who you are."

Kaija nodded, the faintest of smiles perking the corners of her mouth.

Finished packing, Ray lit another cigarette and turned to his brother. "You about ready to go?"

Frank Stubbins cocked his head to one side. "You hear that?"

"We expecting a flight in this morning?" Ray said. He took a long drag on his cigarette and gave a disgusted shake of his head, blowing smoke into the cool air. "Why do all the visitors have to come when the caribou are passing through?"

The roar of an approaching aircraft sent a sickening shiver of panic through Volodin's belly. The smile vanished from Kiaja's lips.

Ray looked at Volodin and shrugged. "No skin off my back if you want to hop on that plane," he said. "They'd probably take you to Ambler if they got seats. Be a lot quicker."

"No," Volodin said, abruptly enough to bring a narrow look from Ray Stebbins. "What I mean is, we would much rather travel overland—"

The plane came in low, clearing the housetops of Needle village by no more than a hundred feet, tilting the wings back and forth. They were clearly looking for something.

"What the hell?" Frank Stubbins yelled. "Shithead's gonna pay for flyin' that low over the village. I'm gonna kick his ass whenever he lands. What's he thinkin'?"

Ray Stubbins sloshed through the mud and snow between the houses after his brother, keeping a wary eye on the airplane as it headed toward the gravel runway at the edge of town.

Volodin looked at his daughter, trying to make sense of all the noise. Kaija winked at him, giving a quick nod toward Ray's ATV. The key was in the ignition.

"What?" He looked at his daughter in dismay. "You mean steal it? We cannot steal from these people. They were going to help us."

Kaija moved to the ATV, her long leg poised over the seat. She shot a worried glance over her shoulder toward the airstrip. "It is the FSB, father," she whispered. "They are after you. We must leave at once."

Chapter 41

East Harlem, New York

August Bowen entered the gym first, peeling right to allow both Thibodaux and Garcia to fan out behind him. Petyr Volodin was just dumb enough there was a chance he'd be inside, and the big Cajun had vowed to give him a little "layin' on of hands" when next they met.

Thibodaux paused when they were inside and took a deep and audible breath through his nose. "You smell that?" he said, grinning.

"What?" Garcia scoffed. "Old jockstraps and horse liniment?"

"No," Thibodaux said. "That's the smell of pain, cheri. And I miss the hell out of it."

Two muscular Hispanic men stood at a computer screen behind the front counter. Oddly, a large screwdriver stuck up from a broken credit card machine beside the men. Bowen recognized them from a large banner behind the counter as the Ortega brothers, the owners of the gym. Both men wore sweatpants and loose tank tops to display their impressive muscles. They were not the large mirror muscles like those found on a body builder. This was a fight gym, and the broad shoulders and thick necks of the two men at the counter said they practiced what they preached.

". . . I'm tellin' you, bro," the shorter of the two Ortegas said, chewing on the end of a plastic coffee stirring stick. His name was Maxim according to the wall banner. "Luis is gonna kill it at the shock put this year."

"It's *shot put*, dude," Raul, the taller of the two brothers said. "You're sayin' it wrong."

Maxim shook his head. "No, it ain't," he said. "And you're a dumbass. I said it that way all my life—*shock put*." He over-enunciated the *k* and *t* of each word, puffing out his chest as if he could prove himself right with bluster.

"You're the dumbass." Raul laughed out loud. His eyes shifted toward Bowen, amused. "I'm pretty sure it's *shot* put."

Thibodaux stepped up to the counter. "Do you know what you call the big metal ball they toss around in the event you're talkin' about?"

Maxim shrugged.

"The shot," Thibodaux chuckled. "Not sure if that helps."

"What the hell you want?" Maxim glared.

Raul stood beside his brother, glaring. Shot or shock, it was clear they were united when it came to outsiders.

"We're looking for a guy named Petyr Volodin," Bowen said.

Garcia moved to the end of the counter taking a quick peek behind it. They'd decided before they came in that she'd be the one to look for hidden weapons.

Maxim folded his arms across his broad chest. "Never heard of him."

"Really," Bowen said. "Is that the way you want to go, genius? Because that looks like his picture on the wall with his arm around your shoulder."

The muscles in Maxim's jaw tightened. "Are you cops?"

"They are," Thibodaux said. "I'm just their pet ass kicker." He snapped his fingers. "*Tempus fugit*, boys. Times a wastin'. When's the last time you saw Petyr the Wolf?"

"Forget it," Maxim sneered. "The gym-client relationship is *sacrosaint*. You know what I'm sayin' "

Raul threw up his hands. "The word is *sacrosanct*, you stupid . . ." He looked at Bowen. "Look, we don't talk to cops about our friends."

"Yeah," Maxim said. "There ain't no law that says we have to." His eyes played up and down Garcia. "You come back later without your pimps, chica. I'd be happy to talk to you."

Bowen reached across the counter and slapped the plastic stir stick out of Maxim's mouth. He squared off for a fight, but Garcia pushed him back.

"I really wish you tough guys would let me stomp my own cockroaches." She glared at Bowen. "Would you slap someone who insulted Thibodaux?"

"He can take care of himself," Bowen said, glaring at Maxim Ortega.

"Well guess what, *mijo*," Garcia said. "So can I."

She spun quickly, ripping the screwdriver out of the credit card machine and shoving it into a surprised Maxim's groin, denting, but not quite piercing the fabric of his sweatpants. A string of Spanish curses Bowen couldn't understand flew from her lips.

"You just insinuated that I'm some kind of whore," Garcia said in English, jiggling the tip of the screwdriver to make her point. "Is that what you meant to do?"

Maxim shook his head. Raul raised his hands. Bowen turned outbound, keeping an eye on the other fighters at the gym just in case any of them carried a sense of misguided loyalty. No one even looked up.

"No . . . no, I didn't . . . mean that at all," Maxim said. "You know . . . you guys can't be doin' shit like this if you're cops."

"Well ain't you a bona fide rocket surgeon," Thibodaux said. "We're not your average cops."

"But they are cops?" Maxim nodded, as though he'd won some debate. "And you're a cop? Right."

"Don't you worry about what we are." Thibodaux cocked his head so he could look directly at Maxim Ortega with his good eye. "You ought to be concentrating on what you are, and from where I'm standin' that's a guy with his cajones balanced on a flathead. Amazing what kind of damage a screwdriver can do in the hands of an angry woman . . ."

"About Petyr," Garcia said. "Where would we find him?"

"I got him set up in a fight." Maxim's eyes flicked back and forth, searching for some kind of ally. No one else in the gym seemed to know or care that a beautiful Cuban woman was a fraction of an inch from emasculating one of the owners.

"A fight?" Bowen said over his shoulder. "Here?"

"It's not that kind of fight," Raul said. "Petyr needs some quick cash so we obliged him, that's all. The fight's unsanctioned, so it can't be at a regular gym. Gotta be underground. We got an agreement with a guy in Chinatown."

"Who's he fighting?" Thibodaux asked.

"It's a mismatch," Raul said. "More of a spectacle, which means a bigger purse. More money for Petyr."

"And coincidentally more money for you," Thibodaux said, turning his good eye so it looked directly at Raul. "I ask you again, who's he fightin'?"

"That's still up in the air," Maxim groaned. "I thought I had a guy but he chickened out when he found out it was against The Wolf."

"I'll fight him then." Thibodaux laughed. "That would sure enough be a mismatch."

Raul shook his head. "No way," he said. "You're taller, and from the looks of you, you got better moves, but no one wants to see a mismatch that don't look like a mismatch." He nodded toward Bowen. "How about him. His face looks like he's used to getting beat on."

"That's a good idea," Maxim whispered. He looked at Garcia, brown eyes pleading. "Come on, chica," he said. "What say you take the screwdriver away from little Maximus and we talk some business? I'll forgive you for comin' in here and throwin' around your weight, and you forgive me for bein' rude."

Garcia stabbed the screwdriver back through the credit card machine.

"Damn!" Maxim said, nearly collapsing against the counter. "That. That right there is why I ain't married."

"Boxing or grappling?" Bowen said, turning around to face them now they were talking business.

"It's whatever you want it to be, man," Maxim said. "You box?"

"A little," Bowen said. He saw no reason to bring up the fact that he was an Army boxing champion.

"Okay," Maxim grinned, the color flowing back into his cheeks. "We got ourselves a mismatch and you got yourselves Petyr the Wolf. I'll draw you a map of where to meet up tonight. It's kind of . . . complicated."

Chapter 42

Needle, Alaska

"Bank to the right!" Feliks Zolner snapped as Davydov brought the Cessna buzzing over Needle Village, just meters above the corroded-metal rooftops. They were close enough that Zolner could see the fresh caribou hides that hung, bloody, flesh-side up on banisters and clotheslines. Stubby-legged village dogs looked skyward, barking and howling in protest at the noise.

Yakibov grunted from the rear seat, his face pressed to the window. "I only see a couple of men," he mused. "It is mostly women coming out of the houses to look at us."

"The men will be out hunting at this time of year," Zolner said.

"Ahhh," the former Spetsnaz commando said. "That is a fortunate development—"

Zolner glanced over his shoulder. "I was under the impression you have a wife and daughter," he said.

"What can I say?" Yakibov shrugged. "I enjoy the benefits of travel—"

"There they are, boss," Kravchuk said from directly behind Zolner. "This side of the plane, eleven o'clock."

"Come around for another pass," Zolner said, his voice calm as he pressed his forehead against the window. His eyes focused on his quarry, who now rode an ATV toward the edge of town at a right angle to the airport. From five hundred feet up, the surrounding tundra looked basically flat, but Zolner knew there would be dips and rolls to the terrain—places to hide. "Never mind," he snapped at Davydov, pointing the blade of his hand toward the gravel airstrip off the nose of the airplane. "Get me on the ground, immediately!" His eyes back on the fleeing ATV, he spoke to Kravchuk. "Pass me the rifle when we land."

Zolner did not have to look to know that his spotter was busy sliding the CheyTac from its padded case, inserting the loaded magazine and removing the lens covers on the scope. Zolner would simply need to put a round in the chamber, acquire his target, and calculate a firing solution.

The ground was not yet frozen, so the ATV was basically confined to a packed trail leading away from the village. For a brief moment, as Davydov brought the Cessna out of his downwind approach, the ATV and the airplane were moving in the same direction. Zolner looked at the airspeed, did a quick calculation and decided the ATV was doing no more than fifteen miles an hour—a mile every four minutes.

The Cessna's wheels squawked on the gravel runway two minutes from the time the ATV had left the last of the village road.

"Stop here!" Zolner shouted, reaching back for his rifle with one hand as he flipped the latch with the other. He shoved the door open with his hip. As large a man as he was, Zolner sprang out of his cramped seat backward, the moment the plane came to a stop. He threw the big rifle to his shoulder and put the crosshairs of his scope on Doctor Volodin's back.

"Twelve hundred meters, boss," Kravchuk said, looking through a laser rangefinder. "And moving away. Now twelve ten . . ." He stood beside the airplane, just behind Zolner's left elbow.

"Perfect," Zolner said, counting the clicks as he rotated the top turret of his scope.

"Wind is steady at—"

The roar of approaching ATV engines drowned out Kravchuk's words. Zolner considered firing anyway, but at over three quarters of a mile, if he shot without the correct firing solution, he might as well be pointing at the moon.

Yakibov opened fire with his Kalashnikov, taking care of the two men coming up on ATVs. A series of thwacks pinged off the metal fuselage of the airplane, followed later by the report of a rifle. The people of Needle clearly knew they were not friendly visitors.

Zolner cursed as he watched Volodin grow smaller in his scope. Instead of firing, he spun toward the sound of the oncoming gunfire.

Davydov had his pistol out and took cover behind the rear tires of the airplane. Fuel began to drip from bullet holes in the wing.

"Where are they?" Zolner said, spotting a man with a rifle as soon as the words had left his lips. He brought the scope up to his eye and set the crosshairs over the man's chest.

"Six hundred fifty-one meters," Kravchuk said, seeming to read Zolner's mind about the target that needed to be ranged. "He has some kind of hunting rifle."

"Ah," Zolner said, holding off with the marked hash marks in his scope rather than taking the time to readjust the turret for elevation. "Six hundred fifty meters may as well be point blank . . ."

The Native man continued to shoot. Bullets pinged all around Zolner and his men, but so far had only hit the airplane.

Zolner took a deep breath, thinking of the name the Native people called him—Worst of the Moon. He exhaled slowly, steadily, locking bone and tendon, letting the crosshairs of the scope settle perfectly still on the man's chest as he reached the quiet respiratory pause at the bottom of his breath.

The trigger broke with a crisp, three-pound snap, sending 350 grains of copper and nickel alloy screaming downrange at 3200 feet per second.

The Native man pitched forward an instant later, surely dead before he even knew he'd been shot.

"Worst of the Moon, indeed," Zolner whispered.

Another shot ricocheted off the gravel at their feet—this one from a second shooter who seemed intent to go for more than the airplane.

"Ten o'clock, boss," Kravchuk said. "Hiding behind that wrecked fire truck. Four six one meters." Another bullet hit a rock at Kravchuk's feet and ricocheted away with a zinging whir. Kravchuk didn't move.

"Fools," Zolner said over his shoulder as he swung the rifle toward the new threat.

"Wind is gusting north now at fifteen . . ."

Zolner shot the second man in the neck. "Four hundred meters," he spat in disdain. "These idiots make it too easy." He spun back to reacquire Volodin in his scope, but the ATV had vanished, melting into the tundra.

Chapter 43

Quinn let off the throttle immediately when he heard the shots, slowing the boat so he could hear above the burbling grind of the motor. Another band of Arctic weather rolled in from the north, but they were pointed almost directly east and a low morning sun dazzled the surface of water in front of them. With little haze in the clear air and a sun that bounced in a great arc just above the horizon, eye protection was a necessity this time of year. Quinn and Beaudine had been separated from their sunglasses during the crash and now spent a good deal of time squinting.

Quinn had to use his free hand to shade his eyes so he could see Beaudine, who crouched at the bow holding a plastic bucket. Constant vibration from the choppy river caused the wax patch to flake and separate from the aluminum. Water dripped from her elbows as she tried to stay ahead of the incoming deluge with a plastic margarine container that had been tied to the gunnel for just such a purpose.

"You hear that," Quinn said. He turned his head, birdlike, straining to hear over the idling motor. The frothy wake of brown water that spread in a giant V behind the boat caught back up to them as they slowed, sloshing and slapping against the stern. The current, slow as it was on the snaking river, caught the bow and began to turn it, shoving them back the way they'd come.

Quinn rolled on the throttle again, pointing the boat upriver again as the shots faded away. He'd counted nine. Two of them, spaced by a period of about seven seconds, were much louder than the others, and hung for some time like a loud wind in the chilly air.

Quinn gradually added more throttle, coaxing the little boat forward. It plowed the water grudgingly now, never quite getting up on step.

"Caribou hunters?" Beaudine gave a quick nod.

"Could be," Quinn said. "But the odds are against it."

"How far out do you think?"

Quinn willed the little boat to go faster, but three inches of water pooled at his boots. Even with the throttle open as far as it would go, the boat moved forward at a grinding wallow, agonizingly slow.

"I just realized this is a damn good metaphor for my life." Beaudine looked up from her bailing and shook her head at their progress. "Seems like I've been fighting against the current in a leaky boat since I was a kid."

Quinn nodded. "She's leaky," he said, "but she gets the job done. According to Brian Ticket there are three big sandbars between the fish camp and Needle." He pointed with his chin toward a long, boat-eating spit of brown that lay off the left bank like a sleeping river monster. "That's number three, if I counted correctly. That puts us less than a mile out of Needle."

Quinn cheated the boat right in a wide, slogging turn. Riverbanks that fell abruptly away generally provided much deeper water than the more gradual slopes, which could run just inches under the surface for several meters, waiting to catch a boat driver unaware. The last thing he needed was to run aground on hidden sand when they were nearly there.

Quinn breathed a little easier when they made it around the bar.

"Want me to spell you on the bucket?" he asked. "You can drive the boat."

"I'm good," Beaudine said, turning to look at him while she bailed. She'd shoved her wool hat into her jacket pocket to keep from overheating, and a gentle wind now tousled her frosted hair. Quinn made it a habit to keep an eye on her sutures, checking for any sign of infection. It wasn't hard. Sweat and consistent exertion on the water made it impossible to keep the gauze bandage in place. Beaudine had tried at first, but eventually ripped the thing off and threw it in the river.

So far the stitches were holding—which, considering how much Beaudine's face twisted into a frown or grimace, was very near a miracle. Blood matted her bangs to her forehead, and her left eye seemed to be frozen in a sort of permanent squint. "*Cyclops psyops,*" she called it, reckoning she'd get the mental upper hand against any opponent that had to look at her. Thibodaux had been right when he'd said his cousin was crazy, but the longer Quinn was around her, the more he saw it as a good kind of crazy. No one had ever accused him of being particularly sane.

"We should be there in less than five," he said. "But I'm guessing we've got over twenty gallons of water. That extra hundred and sixty pounds is slowing us way down."

"Thought I warned you about that whole math thing." Beaudine glared at him, throwing water over the side with rapid scoops from the plastic tub. "'Join the FBI,' they said. 'It'll be fun,' they said . . ."

Quinn smiled. A sense of humor could be an extremely valuable asset in a battle plan.

"Seriously," she said. "How do you want to do this if they're already shooting at each other?"

"I won't be sure until we get there," Quinn said. He'd favored strategy over tactics for as long as he could remember, preferring to work amid the big picture and let the little things flow. Explaining such a mindset so it made sense was nearly impossible, which, Quinn supposed, was why he found himself at ease working with only a handful of people, people who operated under the same philosophy and moved through life the same way. "Movements like this have to be fluid. According to Brian, the school is downriver a couple of hundred meters at the other end of the village from the airstrip. We'll park the boat there and come in as quietly as we can."

Beaudine dropped the plastic tub to the floor of the boat, trading it for the AR-10 and looping the sling around her neck. Rifle up, she took a seat at the bow, scanning the banks ahead and no doubt getting her mind wrapped around what was about to happen next. The Kobuk swept back northward, funneling them into the line of winter weather but making it easier to see without the sun directly in front of them. Above, the clouds rolled in, pushed by winds aloft, but the sudden appearance of millions of drifting snowflakes brought foreboding to the river.

"This looks so peaceful," Beaudine said, opening her hand to catch the flakes. "Like a church."

The clouds began to drop snow in earnest, large popcorn flakes. Ahead, on a low hill less than a half a mile up river, the roofline of Needle school came in and out of view. Quinn let off the throttle, slowing the boat and bringing the engine noise down to a quiet burble, barely staying ahead of the current.

"Khaki," he said, wanting her full attention.

She glanced over her shoulder. Snowflakes covered her head and shoulders like feather down. There was something in her eyes he couldn't quite make out. Not fear. This girl was fearless. It was a look of resignation. Quinn supposed it had been there all along. Life had simply been moving too fast for him to see it.

"This is going to be different than any raid you've ever been on," he said. "You know that, right?"

"I do," she said.

"I counted at least three in the plane when it overflew us at the fish camp," he said. "But we don't know how many there are or where they'll be."

Beaudine gave a somber nod.

Quinn continued. "I may have to do some things you'd normally arrest me for."

A slow smile spread across her face. "I got your back, hon," she said. "Us Texas girls can be bitches. But we're bitches you want on your side in a fight."

Quinn's head snapped up at the flat crack of two rapid gunshots. Beaudine brought the rifle up toward the sound. Quinn began to count again. He passed the two-second mark before the double thumps of two successive reports reached his ears.

"Over six hundred meters away," he said, scanning the bank up river through the myriad of flakes.

"Crack thump," Beaudine hissed, obviously recognizing the distinctive sound of rounds coming downrange. "Are they shooting at us?"

"I don't think so," Quinn said. "The bullets sounded

like they were going parallel to the river, up by the school. Our general direction, but if they knew we were here we'd probably not be having this conversation."

The thunderous thump of another shot echoed through the still air, this one much louder and absent the preceding supersonic crack. Quinn knew it was just his imagination, but the abruptness of it seemed to shake loose more snow from above.

"Bigger gun," Beaudine said.

"Yep." Quinn kept the boat mid-river, taking it well past where he wanted to land before angling toward the bank and killing the engine.

Beaudine held the AR at low ready, glancing over her shoulder at Quinn. There was no sound but for the slap of water against the side of the boat. "This would be peaceful if I didn't know they were out there." Huge flakes fell around her in the gray silence of the river, clinging to her jacket. "I can't help but feel like we're trapped inside some big ol' creepy snow globe with a bunch of killers."

"You could look at it that way." Quinn angled the skiff toward the steep gravel bank, well below the school. "But those killers are also trapped in here with us."

Chapter 44

"Do not waste your shots," Zolner said. Yakibov had seen the woman running toward the school first. She'd had a mobile phone to her ear, and the fool had thought to take her out with two snap shots from his Kalashnikov. He'd missed with both, but Zolner had taken care of her.

"There is not enough time to shoot everyone with a phone." He let the reticle of his Valdada scope settle over the gray metal box, centering the laddered cross-hairs over the thick electrical cables where they exited the housing. "Think strategically, my friend."

The cell tower was a pitifully easy shot at a scant two hundred meters from where he stood. His shot cut the power line that fed the cellphone tower with a shower of sparks. The second would destroy the backup battery, rendering the tower nothing more than a hundred-and-fifty foot piece of useless sculpture.

Davydov cleared his throat after Zolner lowered the CheyTac—a signal that he wanted to speak but did not want to disturb his boss. The pilot had, no doubt, heard stories about what became of people who spoke while he was shooting.

Zolner breathed in the smoke that drifted up from the open bolt, savoring it like a drug. "What is it?"

"The plane," Davydov said. "I can patch the fuel tanks but one of the bullets damaged the horizontal stabilizer. That will take me some time to fix."

"Unfortunately," Zolner said, "time is something I do not have." He ordered Kravchuk to retrieve his pack from the airplane then began to walk briskly toward the ATV belonging to a man Yakibov had killed at the far end of the runway. Kravchuk and the others' boots crunched in the gravel as they trotted along behind him, rifles up, watching for more gunmen as they came nearer to the village.

Zolner was cognizant of the danger, but didn't let it worry him. In his experience people ran from the sound of gunfire, not toward it. He was careful and cunning, but he was also realistic and resigned himself to the sure knowledge that he would never hear the bullet that eventually killed him.

"These people are foolishly innocent," he said as he walked. "They have taken our only clear path of escape."

"How shall we deal with this, boss?" Kravchuk asked when they'd reached the nearest ATV. It was a red Honda, newer and still idling. The body of its former owner sagged to the side, one arm draped across a rifle that was wedged against the handlebars. A think trickle of blood ran down the other arm where it hung, fingers dragging against the snow.

"Check the other machine for fuel," Zolner said, once Yakibov had pulled the dead rider to the ground and he could look at the gauges. "This is almost full but I must have some to spare."

"We will go after them on the machines?" Kravchuk said.

"No," Zolner said. "I will travel much faster alone."

Davydov ran back from the other machine with a red plastic fuel tank. It was flat, held four gallons of extra gas, and fit perfectly on the rear rack of the Honda.

Zolner took a sling from his pack and attached it to his rifle. The CheyTac was big and heavy, not the sort of rifle that was carried with a sling, but this was a unique circumstance. He replaced the covers over his scope and threw the sling over a broad shoulder so the barrel was pointed upward.

"It is imperative that no one in this village be allowed to call out for help," he said. "Their mobile phones will be of no use, but they are certain to have VHF radios with which they can communicate with passing aircraft."

"It will be impossible to locate every radio in the village," Davydov said.

Zolner cinched his pack down tight over the top of the plastic fuel canister, then glanced up at the pilot. "I only counted fourteen homes when we flew over this little shithole. Might I suggest it would be easier to deal with the handful of people here than to find all the radios."

Each of the three men gave him a curt nod. If any of them were upset about being left behind, they had enough sense not to show it.

"Very well," Zolner said, swinging a long leg over the four-wheeler. "But do not waste time. The men will be straggling back in from their hunts at any moment."

"We'll come for you once I repair the plane," Davydov said.

"Fine," Zolner said. "But the loose ends in the village are the priority. Help the others with that first. My gut tells me these agents of the FBI Ishogin told us about might still show up. Make certain they do not pose a problem for me."

The men turned to go without another word, each, no doubt, going over the possibilities of being left alone in the middle of nowhere with a captive group of women and children. Zolner gunned the engine on the ATV, taking a shallow ditch off the gravel road and onto the rutted trail down which Volodin and the girl had escaped. He came upon their tracks half a minute later. They were clean and clear, crossing patches of melting snow and depressed berry bushes, easy to follow.

Zolner glanced back over his shoulder at his three men as they walked toward the village. Yakibov had a peculiar bounce in his gate as if he were on his way to a carnival.

It was rare for Zolner to find himself disturbed by another man's behaviors—but he thought of the smile that had spread over Yakibov's face and wondered idly as he rode what kind of woman would marry, and have children with, such a beast. Women knew, even if they did not admit it to themselves, what sort of men they married. It was impossible to look into Yakibov's eyes and see him for anything other than what he was. The former Spetsnaz soldier was surely a sadistic killer and he made no apology for that fact—at least not when he was in the field. It was difficult to think of such a man cheering on his son at a football game. Most people walked through life staring down at their shoes, but someone, anyone who looked at the man's eyes, was sure to notice the blackness there.

Zolner did not see himself as sadistic. He killed, and he killed often, but death was merely the end result. The joy came from the pursuit, the science of the shot, the competition between the shooter and target, between predator and prey. He rarely gave any more thought to the actual death at the other end of his shot than he had given the bell at the top of the rope he'd had to climb in secondary school. No one cared that you had rung a bell. It was the trip up the rope that mattered.

Chapter 45

The crack of gunfire sent a quiet calm settling over Kaija Merculief. Up to now, all her battles had been fought from behind a computer or at the counter of a post office. She knew what she was doing was important. Her mother had assured her of that. But the fact that someone was actually shooting at her cemented the fact. This was real. Someone thought what she was doing was important enough to try to stop her. The idea of it only strengthened her resolve.

She'd considered pushing her father off the ATV and leaving him alone on the tundra by the time she'd made it five miles out of the village. The man was a millstone around her neck, and she would have gone through with it but for the fact that it would not do any good. Rostov's men would certainly kill the muddle-headed chemist for her, but nothing would stop them until they had retrieved the New Archangel. Kaija and her mother had not put up with years of Kostya Volodin's foul breath and awkward embraces to lose the prize at the last moment.

Rostov and his cronies at the Kremlin were weak. Oh, some of them had vision. A very few understood the path necessary to bring about a Novorossiya. Kaija's mother had known. Her mother had taught her the truth of a New Russia, a Russia free from the tyranny and oppression of the capitalist West with its embargos and sanctions. A New Russia where the Orthodox Church and its people would be pure from the money-lending *zhid*. Kostya Volodin was a bumbling fool, but his creation would be an enormous step toward real progress.

Kaija had already sent two shipments to the United States. Her mother's friends from the Black Hundreds had contacts with fishing boats that went to St. Lawrence Island in Alaska. At that point it was a simple matter to mail the two chemicals, in separate packaging, to the village of Ambler where Kaija's friend Polina had carried them down to the lower forty-eight for delivery to other Black Hundreds contacts already in the United States. It might have been easier to mail them directly, but the contacts in the States had an aversion to post offices, feeling they were death traps crawling with federal agents. The events in Dallas and Los Angeles had proven the pipeline worked.

It could have gone on forever, had Kaija's imbecile father not thrown everything away in a fit of humanity and drawn the attention of the authorities to his work with the white bellies of ten thousand dead fish. If Kaija's mother had been alive, she would have stabbed the old fool to death in his sleep.

Kostya Volodin may have been a brilliant chemist, but he was a tool of a weak state machine—and too much of an idiot to see that Maria Merculief had rejoined him with their daughter after years of separation only to gain access to his work.

Kaija's mother had taught her well. The parental love of a man for his long-lost daughter blinded him more than his feelings for his estranged love. Had Maria come back to him alone, he would have accepted her with open arms, but his rational, scientist's mind would have been skeptical of her motives. But Kaija's return chased away the last shred of doubt. To see his daughter again under any circumstance clouded the idiot's judgment. He would see things as he wanted them to be, rather than the way they actually were.

Reality, Maria Merculief had explained, had no place in a father's notion of his little girl. And Kaija planned to leverage that weakness until she had no more use for the man—a time that was rapidly approaching. For now, he provided a handy human shield in the event one of Colonel Rostov's goons got close enough to shoot at her back.

Volodin gripped the metal rack beside his padded seat with one hand and held the wool hat down on his head with the other. Kaija could hear his pitiful grunts and ooofs as she took the ATV up the rutted trail as fast as it would go. The knobby balloon tires crackled on the wet ground, cushioning some of the bounce, but throwing up an enormous amount of mud.

He shouted over the whine of the engine. "Are you sure you know where we are going?"

"No," Kaija said, not really caring if he heard her or not. She would never, ever forgive him for slapping her for simply stating the truth. She had studied a map on the wall of the hangar where they'd slept in Nome, and knew Ambler lay somewhere ahead of them, but had no idea how far. That too was her father's fault. When she thought on it, there was a lot for which she would never forgive the man. But that only made it easier to do what she would eventually have to do.

Kaija was no martyr. She was young, with hopes and dreams of seeing the New Russia herself, but her father had given her no option but to flee with the remaining New Archangel. Once they reached Ambler and Polina had taken the chemicals to where they could do the most damage to the United States, Kaija could give herself up to Rostov's men and blame the entire sordid mess on her father. He was certainly too far gone in the head to deny it. Even now, he probably believed the whole thing was his idea.

She pressed on the throttle with her thumb, taking the ATV up a low hill, chancing a quick look over her shoulder as they reached the top. Behind them, the endless tundra stretched for miles. So far so good, but one small problem nagged at her stomach. Polina had no idea she was on her way.

Chapter 46

Ilia Davydov walked a half step behind the other two Russians, eyes flitting back and forth among the weathered houses. Surely every home in this remote place had several guns. So the men were out hunting. Did it not occur to these fools that the Native women might also know how to shoot? Davydov had always considered himself head and shoulders above these cretins in brains. The way they walked so boldly into such a danger only proved him right.

All three men stopped in their tracks as the figure of an elderly woman emerged from among the houses and walked toward them amid the falling snow. Her navy blue parka was trimmed in the rich brown fur of *rosomakha*—wolverine. Armed with nothing but her righteous indignation, the old woman hobbled on elderly legs, shaking her fist at the approaching men. She spoke in a guttural Native tongue that sounded as if she was talking around a mouthful of spit.

Davydov couldn't understand her words but her meaning was clear. They were to leave her village immediately.

She made it to within ten feet of the men before Kravchuk began to laugh derisively and shot her in the belly with his rifle.

Doubling over in pain, the woman dropped to her knees. Yakibov began to laugh as well and shot her in the arm. They were toying with her.

The poor woman's face convulsed and twitched, and it was obvious she was in tremendous pain, but she said nothing, glaring instead at the men.

Kravchuk gave a heartless chuckle. "Let us see how brave you are when—"

Davydov shot the woman in the head with his pistol, ending her suffering but bringing a sneer from Kravchuk and Yakibov.

"Your heart is much too soft, my friend," Kravchuk said. "I consider it my duty to toughen you up."

Yakibov pointed his Kalashnikov toward the village with one hand, where small groups of women and children ran toward the school. "The old woman was stalling us," he said. "Kravchuk, you go ahead and secure any communications at the school. Davydov and I will clear the remaining houses, then we will join you there. If people are not already fleeing toward the haven of the school, they are still sleeping. This should go quickly." The former Spetsnaz man nudged Davydov and grinned. "Maybe we can toughen you up with a little fun and games while on the way."

Chapter 47

Quinn knelt among the thick willows beside Beaudine, peering through the dead leaves and falling snow at the old fuel shack that stood between them and the main dirt street of Needle. The village was laid out in a lopsided T with the long road stretching approximately a half mile between the small airstrip and the school. The top of the T, which was now to Quinn's left, ran up from the river in front of the blue metal school, continuing on to what looked like the dump a few hundred meters out of town. It was difficult to tell from his vantage point but Quinn guessed there to be no more than ten weathered wood-sided homes along the main street and another four or five on the shorter street beyond the school. Green hides hung over two-by-four wooden banisters in front of nearly every house. Here and there, partially butchered caribou quarters hung on wooden frames, now covered with snow.

Trails of fresh footprints led toward the school.

Quinn took a slow breath, scanning.

"We should have landed further upriver," he whispered. "The tracks would have given us an idea of how many we're dealing with."

"Or they would have heard the boat and killed us before we hit the beach," Beaudine said.

"There is that," Quinn said. He nodded toward the school as two more women hurried up and banged on the front door. A young man with a red beard and glasses waved them in quickly before shutting the door again.

"Looks like everyone's moving to shelter," Beaudine said. "That's good."

"The school is the center of—" Quinn stopped midsentence and held up a hand to silence Beaudine, tipping his head slightly toward the back of the houses on the other side of the fuel shacks. A Native girl, who looked to be in her mid-teens, dragged a small preschool-age boy through the snow toward the school. The girl crept slowly, skirting junked snow machines and sagging meat racks. Obviously terrified, she checked back over her shoulder every few seconds.

The old fuel shack was located nearer the school on the long leg of the T. A newer fuel shack—two pumps surrounded by a tall chain-link fence—had been built fifty feet upriver, likely to meet some safety code about standoff distance from the school. Quinn waited for the girl to look behind her and motioned for Beaudine to follow him, breaking out of the alders just below the new fuel shack.

Believing any threat was coming from the airport, the girl focused her attention backward and didn't see Quinn until he'd already come up behind her. He clamped a hand over her mouth and dragged her back into the alders as gently as he could. Beaudine followed with the child.

Quinn was surprised how strong the girl was. She kicked and jerked and screamed into his open hand, almost spinning out of his grasp several times. It took everything he had to keep her arms pinned to her sides without hurting her.

"We're friends!" he hissed, his lips next to her ear. "Here to help."

It took a moment for the message to sink in, and the girl snapped her head back, narrowly missing Quinn's nose with what would have been a devastating head butt.

"I'm Jericho," he said when she calmed down. The little boy fell into his sister's arms and clung to her, his brown eyes wide with fright at being dragged into the bushes. He stared at the scar on Beaudine's face, and Quinn realized he probably didn't look much better. "This is my friend Khaki," he whispered. "We're police, chasing those bad men out there."

The little boy nodded, giving Quinn a wary eye. "Like the Troopers?"

Quinn raised his eyebrows. Village kids often had no other contact with law enforcement beyond the Alaska State Troopers. "Yes," he said. "Like Troopers."

"I'm Hazel," the girl said. "This is my little brother, Herman."

"Your family okay?" Quinn asked.

"My mom works at the school," Hazel said, eyes welling with tears. "I saw those men shoot Ms. Bernadette . . . They shot her and just laughed . . ."

"How many are there?" Beaudine asked.

"Three," Hazel said. "They're big and scary. All of 'em have beards."

"Only three?" Quinn said. That was odd. According to the Russian at the lodge, Zolner was clean-shaven like a soldier.

The girl suddenly froze, eyes flicking toward the bushes. Quinn heard the wheezing grunt of someone shuffling through the snow. He turned slowly to see a lone man with a thick salt-and-pepper beard trotting behind the houses. Eyes focused toward the school, the man moved to an outbuilding behind the house nearest the abandoned fuel shack and stopped. Made of unpainted plywood and blue tarps, the six-by-six shed was not quite five feet tall. A rusted stovepipe and pile of split wood outside the door said it was a sweathouse.

The man scanned the houses in front of him, and then turned to face the side of the sweathouse. He let his Kalashnikov fall against the sling and pushed it behind his hip while he unzipped his pants.

"He's stopping to take a leak," Beaudine said, raising the AR-10. "Is that one of the men?"

Hazel nodded.

Quinn put a hand on top of the rifle barrel and shook his head. "We can't afford to let the others hear the shot."

He slipped the pack off his shoulders and stowed it with the Lapua in the willows to retrieve later. That left him with only what he had in his pockets and his war belt of the Kimber pistol, two extra magazines, and the Riot—a stubby but razor sharp sheath knife—allowing him to move quickly and, more important, silently.

"Hazel," he said. "You and your brother keep an eye on the river and make sure no one sneaks up on us."

He drew the Riot and crouched, glancing toward the airstrip to make sure his target was alone before looking back at Beaudine, directly into her eyes. "This is one of those times I warned you about.

She gave a doubtful frown. "You're going to fight him with a knife?"

Quinn shook his head. "This won't be a fight."

* * *

The silent killing of an unsuspecting enemy was conniving, cold blooded, and barbaric. Even when accomplished for a good cause, it felt an awful lot like murder. An otherwise moral man needed some kind of disconnect to kill another human being. Famed Border Patrol gunfighter Bill Jordan called it *manufactured contempt*. The memory of Lovita's death was still raw in Quinn's gut, making the total annihilation of any of the people involved an end game he was happy to work toward. Justice was just another name for societal vengeance, and Quinn had long before come to grips with being the instrument of it.

Shooting someone from even a short distance away offered a certain protective layer that cushioned and blunted the barbarity of the act. Sneaking up silently behind someone to snuff out their life with a blade was far different from pitched battle where emotions and rage boiled into the fight.

Quinn was a hard man, accustomed to violent action, but the inevitable sounds and sensations of a life seeping away put an indelible mark on anyone's mind and soul.

Snow covered the ground and filled the air, dampening the sound of Quinn's approach. His target was out of shape and breathing hard from trotting in from the airstrip. Quinn doubted he could hear anything above the sound of his own wheezing—and perhaps the spatter of his urine as it hit the side of the plywood sweathouse.

Quinn's training in both Air Force Special Operations and OSI had been excellent in all manner of fighting discipline and art, but courses in killing enemy sentries were non-existent. The only time it was even touched on, in some pre-deployment training, the preferred method was a suppressed 9mm carbine with subsonic ammunition. Emiko Miyagi, the enigmatic Japanese woman, had been deliberate and diverse in her teaching, demonstrating several relatively quiet, if extremely bloody, methods with blade and garrote. Many Internet experts revel in the philosophical niceties of the various arts of killing, but Emiko had actually done it, many times—and it brought a certain detachment to her eyes.

Quinn moved up behind the man without hesitating, knowing when he got within fifteen feet that he was too close to turn back. He snaked his left arm over the unsuspecting man's shoulder and clasped his hand over his mouth, stifling a scream before it could escape. At the same time, he drove the thick tanto blade of the Riot into the right side of the man's bull neck, just below the chin, sharp edge facing forward. Pulling back with his left hand, and pushing forward with his right, the razor-sharp Riot cut neatly through windpipe, jugular, and carotid in one quick and sickening motion.

The man's hands flew to his throat. A great swath of blood sprayed the plywood, but with his face pressed tight against his target's shoulder, Quinn heard instead of saw it. He felt no pity for the man he killed, but a great deal of pity for mankind in general that such a person ever existed at all.

In the movies, the enemy usually died instantly, but in reality, movement and noise could go on for some time. Quinn held the Russian for a full fifteen seconds until he ceased to struggle, then lowered the lifeless body to the snow. Unwilling to leave a rifle unattended, he stooped to pick up the dead man's Kalashnikov when a deafening boom caused him to duck for cover. Something hit the plywood sweathouse with a rattling splatter. Quinn jumped sideways as a searing pain stitched his thigh.

There was no mistaking the feeling. He knew he'd been shot without even looking down.

Chapter 48

Russia

The secure telephone connection between Providenya and Moscow was spotty at best, and Rostov could not tell from General Zhestakova's voice if he was still upset or if he'd grown ambivalent about the gas attacks on the United States. His sister was married to the Director of the FSB—the modern successor to the Soviet Union's KGB. Salina Zhestakova was smart, but not a particularly handsome woman. Many supposed that the union required the general to pay a large sum of money in order to make the marriage go through and unite GRU and FSB as if they were powerful clans or allied nations instead of two security and intelligence components under the umbrella of the same government. It was not uncommon for Zhestakova to borrow talented FSB agents from his brother-in-law for particular missions in which he did not want the GRU directly involved—or loan GRU operatives to FSB for their more sensitive head shooting.

Rostov drummed his fingers against the desk blotter, trying to calm his nerves at having to speak with the famously impatient head of his organization. "The

Black Hundreds would appear to want the same thing we do," he said.

"My mistress wants me to take her to my dacha on the Black Sea," Zhestakova said. "I would very much like the same thing, but I do not blather about that fact to my wife. The problem with these new Black Hundreds is that they do not know when to keep their mouths shut. They are idealistic with patriotic goals of a Mother Russia that cannot exist if we engage in a mutually destructive war with the United States. Would it be a terrible thing for the Americans to spend their resources tracking an unknown Islamic terrorist cell? Of course not, but we have seen what they do if they even have an inkling some nation is in possession of weapons of mass destruction."

"Yes, General," Rostov said, "but Russia is no insignificant desert nation."

"We are not," Zhestakova said. "But if we are honest with ourselves, we are merely a 'near peer,' not an equal. I am not saying we are weak. A smart dog can defeat a much larger wolf if he will but remember that he is a dog. Fighting jaw to jaw would destroy us. The Black Hundreds will kill hundreds, even thousands—some might even be willing to martyr themselves for the cause of a Novorossiya. The remaining zealots will bluster and rant—and then run back to you and me for protection."

"I understand, sir." It was pointless to say anything else when the general was on a tirade.

"Do you?" Zhestakova said. "Do you really? Because I am under the impression that you and Captain Lodygin have taken this for a game."

"I assure you, General," Rostov said. "I do—"

"*You* may not." Zhestakova cut him off. "But it is

clear that Lodygin does, and Lodygin falls under your command. If he is brash, it is because you allow him to be so."

"Yes, General," Rostov said. There was nothing more that he could say.

"I have a sense about him, you know," Zhestakova said. "He seems to me to be a damaged man."

"I assure you, General, he is capable." Rostov couldn't quite work up the will to endorse the captain any more than that. The truth was, Lodygin was broken. But he was loyal to a fault when it came to Rostov, and that alone meant something where jealousy and backstabbing were standard operating procedure.

"Perhaps," Zhestakova said. "But I would not put him in charge of my pigs, not to mention a program with the importance of Novo Archangelsk. How is he getting this information? Who is telling him Black Hundreds are behind the theft?"

"A school friend of Dr. Volodin's daughter."

"Are your men making progress in retrieving Dr. Volodin?"

"I was informed this morning that they are about to make contact. It is my belief that they already have, considering the time."

"Your belief?" The sound of Zhestakova's fist against his desk was clearly audible over the phone. "Do not your men have a method to communicate? It seems to me that if they were to avert a nuclear war with America they might give you a call immediately."

"Of course, General," Rostov said. "I have sent my best men. They are close. I am certain of it."

There was a long silence on the line. Rostov thought for a moment that the general had simply hung up, but he'd just been conferring with someone else in his office.

Rostov wondered who it might be, and went through a mental list of all the people in the Kremlin who hated him.

"This situation necessitates extreme caution," Zhestakova said. "The President has further questions that need to be answered before certain decisions can be made."

"Very well," Rostov said, feeling numb. When the ranking general in the GRU summoned you to the Kremlin, there was nothing else to do but comply. "I will arrange a flight to Moscow first thing in the morning."

"Do not bother," Zhestakova said. "There is someone en route to you."

"Do I know this person you are sending?" Rostov said, digging—hopefully not his own grave.

"No," Zhestakova said, "I am quite sure you two have never met."

"Tonight?" Rostov said.

"At any moment," Zhestakova said. "It would be best if you were waiting at the airstrip when my jet arrives." He ended the call without another word.

Rostov felt a cold wind blow across his neck—as if the Fates had just cut short the threads of his life.

Chapter 49

Alaska

Quinn rolled and came up with his pistol in time to see Hazel run from the willows waving her hands and shouting. An elderly Native woman stood around the corner two houses away, pointing a pump shotgun at Quinn. She eyed Quinn warily but lowered the shotgun when Hazel explained that he was friendly.

Any element of surprise evaporated with the shot. The other two Russians would come out to investigate in no time.

Quinn waved Beaudine out of the bushes, shouting for her to bring the Lapua as he retrieved the dead Russian's AK. He plugged his left ear and fired a string of three rounds, one-handed, into the snowbank in front of him. Beaudine ran up behind him. She started to talk but he held up his hand and reached for the radio on the dead man's belt. Predictably, another voice broke squelch to check on him.

"*Vsyo Kharasho*?" a deep Russian voice said. It sounded like a demand.

Quinn held the radio ready to speak, looking at Beaudine for a translation.

"He's asking if you're all good."

"How do I answer?"

"*Da, narmalna*," she said. *Yes, normal.*

Quinn repeated the phrase back, holding the small radio nearly a foot away from his mouth to add some distortion to his voice.

"OK," the other Russian said, laughing as he said something else. Quinn could hear the cries of a woman each time the mike was keyed.

"He wants to know if you had to stop to take a piss," Beaudine said.

Quinn clicked the talk button a couple of times, showing that he'd received and understood but didn't care to answer back.

The Russian spoke again and Beaudine translated. "He says they're about to finish up and will be along in a few minutes." She shook her head, obviously having heard the woman's sobbing on the other end of the radio.

Quinn wanted to check the wound in his thigh but there was no time. The Native woman had been fifty yards away and thankfully hadn't been using a rifle. Quinn estimated at least a dozen pellets of birdshot had caught him from just above the knee to the point of his hip. It was extremely painful but not debilitating.

"Sorry," the woman said, walking up with her shotgun. "I thought you was one of them." She eyed the carnage around the dead man and turned away to throw up in the snow.

"Understandable," Quinn said, grimacing as he took the Lapua from Beaudine. "We're going to have to do something to draw them out quickly," he said, "before they 'finish up' and kill someone else."

"Agreed," Beaudine said.

Quinn explained his plan, then gritted his teeth at

the new pain in his leg and moved quickly to the front of the house nearest the school. He backed up far enough from the house that he had a view—and a clear line of fire—down both the main street toward the airstrip and the river side of the houses. Then he stretched out belly-down in the snow behind the rifle. Settling in with the gun, he flipped up the scope covers, then motioned for Beaudine to fire the dead Russian's Kalashnikov into the ground. As planned, he gave it a three count, and then keyed the radio several times. Demands for a situation report barked from the other end. He said nothing.

As much as he hated to expose Hazel to any more violence, he wanted to avoid a repeat of the woman shooting him with the shotgun. He put the girl beside him with the binoculars so she could differentiate the Russians from any village men who happened to walk in front of his crosshairs.

Two men exited a house at the far end of the street just seconds after Beaudine began to frantically key the radio mike. Both carried their long guns up and ready to engage. Quinn had already estimated the distance to be three hundred meters. He rested the crosshairs over the man on the left and squeezed off a round. The shot went low, hitting him just below the knee. The gun fell from the wounded man's hand and he tipped sideways, unable to stand on the shattered leg. Quinn adjusted quickly, bumping the Lapua sideways so the second man appeared in his scope. He adjusted his aim, holding the crosshairs just over the top of the second Russian's head. The round impacted center mass, dropping him where he stood.

"I am glad you killed him," Hazel said, still looking through the binoculars. "I loved Miss Bernadette. That man shot her and just laughed . . ."

"Are you sure there were only three?" Beaudine said, coming up beside them at a crouch with the AK.

Hazel nodded. "There was another guy, but he took off on stolen Honda."

"Take your brother to the school," Quinn said, wincing at his wound as he got to his feet. "Tell the others we're here and not to shoot at us."

"I live right there," the woman with the shotgun said, nodding two houses down. "I'll go put it out over the CB."

Ten minutes later Quinn and Beaudine stood around the wounded Russian with a dozen very angry members of Needle Village. Ms. Bernadette and the Stubbins brothers all had relatives and dear friends among the crowd. Quinn had put a makeshift tourniquet around the Russian's leg and leaned him against the wooden steps of the house where he and the other Russian had only recently been terrorizing a young mother and her infant daughter. The woman was shaken but defiant and now stood over the terrified Russian with a hatchet that she looked ready to put to good use.

It took no interrogation for the man to tell them his name was Ilia Davydov, the pilot. He told Quinn what he already knew, that a man named Feliks Zolner, sometimes called Worst of the Moon, had been charged to capture or kill a scientist named Volodin. Between sobs and panting breaths, Davydov answered every question posed to him, describing what Zolner looked like, the type and caliber of rifle he carried, and even the kind of food he preferred—simple Russian tea and jam. He had no idea who had hired Zolner or how he planned to get out of Alaska now that the plane was damaged.

"He is a quiet man," Davydov said, panting. "He hires us to assist him, but we are never told the entire story.

That is his alone to know." He looked at Quinn with pleading eyes. "Please," he gasped. "I have only just begun working for him."

"You killed my friend," Hazel said. She'd ignored Quinn's directive to go wait at the school and now stood with the adults, mostly women and a couple of elderly men, who had gathered in front of the house.

Davydov shook his head. "The others," he stammered. "They shot her for sport, to wound her. I did not want to see her suffer so I ended her pain." He glanced at Beaudine, then quickly back to Quinn. "You must believe me, I try to be merciful. To kill her quickly."

Beaudine scoffed. "If you really wanted to show some mercy you could have put a bullet in the two bastards that shot her in the first place."

Quinn shouldered his pack and picked up the Lapua.

"What are you going to do with me?" Davydov whimpered. "You can't leave me here."

"What?" Beaudine said. "I'm sure they'll show you just as much mercy as you showed their friend."

Brian Ticket's brother-in-law, Ruben, had been out hunting ptarmigan when the Russians landed and made it back into town in time to see the crowd gather around Davydov. It had been his house the two Russians had first terrorized, and his wife—Brian's sister—now stood with the hatchet in her hand. Quinn filled him in about their meeting with Brian at the fish camp and explained the immediate need to follow Zolner and Volodin on the ATV trail toward Ambler.

"I got a better idea," the man said, clutching his wife and child like they might float away. "We'll take my boat. My uncle has a camp four miles upriver. We stashed a Honda out there two days ago. Keys are in it and it's full of gas. I was gonna go hunting, but if you can catch Worst of the Moon . . . Anyhow, there's an old trail going northeast behind the cabin. It cuts into the ATV road that comes out of here. You'll save a hell of a lot of time because the river bends back up that way before cutting southeast again toward Ambler. If we go now, you might even get ahead of 'em."

PART III
FIRE

Victory is reserved for those who are willing to pay its price.
—SUN TZU

Chapter 50

Beaudine carried their two backpacks down the gravel incline to Ruben's skiff, thankful that this particular boat didn't require a wax toilet ring to stay afloat. The Mercury outboard, shiny and black amid the falling snow, didn't hurt her confidence either.

She watched Quinn as he stood on the bank and tried to use snow to rub away some of the blood that covered the front of his coat and the thighs of his wool pants. It did no good, other than to leave him with a pile of pink snow and a damp jacket. Ruben had given each of them a pair of overwhites—basically a cotton parka shell complete with hood. Beaudine thought they looked like Halloween costumes made out of bed sheets but she understood the concept of camouflage.

Quinn gave up on his scrubbing, covering the stains with the overwhites instead before helping Ruben shove the boat into the deeper water of the Kobuk. Aluminum scraped on gravel as the current caught and nudged the stern. Quinn hopped over the side without a word and sat down, holding the rifle across his lap.

Not overly talkative for the two days since Beaudine first met him, Quinn had grown quieter since he killed the Russian by the sweathouse.

Beaudine had known, even as she watched Quinn creep from the willows with the knife in his hand, that the Russian had to be killed. He and his friends were marching through the village murdering everyone in their path. She was supposed to provide over-watch, ready to back up Quinn with a quick shot if things went bad, but even if it hadn't been her job she would have looked. Like the hypnosis brought on by watching a gruesome car wreck, she'd been unable to take her eyes off of Quinn as he snuck up behind the man. It seemed so innocent, one man tiptoeing up behind another in the falling snow, like a college boy playing a prank. She didn't turn away when Quinn plunged the blade into the Russian's neck. They were facing away, but the tremendous spray of blood and the silent struggle as Quinn arched his back and held the big man upright while he died . . . The brutality was unspeakably awful. Beaudine's breath came faster just thinking about it. She found herself wondering what sort of a human being was capable of committing such violence, even in the name of good. Such an act had to leave an indelible mark. The Russian would be no less dead if Quinn had shot him. It was a blot against the state of humanity, she supposed, that gunning someone down could somehow seem civilized, even when it was the right thing to do. She found herself feeling profoundly sorry for Quinn—and profoundly grateful that he was willing to do uncivilized things. The four men he'd killed in the last two days were all equally dead, no matter his method—but this last one had hurt him.

She'd grown up around the scent of death and regret. It was an easy thing for her to recognize.

* * *

Quinn gritted his teeth while he rifled through his pack for a packet of Betadine. He'd decided to use the time during the short ride to keep a painful but relatively minor problem from becoming something debilitating.

"Forgive me," he said, "but I'm going to have to get indecent here for a minute and clean up this wound."

"I think we're past that," Beaudine scoffed. "And Ruben won't mind. You think I don't realize you changed my undies for me when I was half frozen." She took the foil packet of antiseptic and knelt in the floor of the boat.

"That looks bad," she said, grimacing when Quinn dropped his pants and pulled the long johns down to expose his injured thigh. "I count twelve pellets." She bent closer squirting a little spray of the rust colored Betadine on each wound, then dabbing up the excess with a wadded piece of gauze. "They make a pattern like Orion when you add them to these other scars you have."

"Great," Quinn said.

"I'd be happy to try and dig them outta there," Beaudine said, looking up at him.

"Thanks, "Quinn said, pulling up the long johns before she had a chance to wipe up the rest of the Betadine. "I'm good. They say President Garfield might have lived if his doctors wouldn't have tried to dig the bullet out."

"Suit yourself," Beaudine said. She dipped her hand over the side to wash it in river spray, and then settled back in her seat at the bow of the boat with the rifle.

"Nearly there," Ruben said from the tiller.

Considering the gravity of their mission, the ten-minute journey up the Kobuk felt agonizingly slow.

Quinn grabbed his pack and prepared to jump the moment Ruben kicked the outboard into neutral and raised the shaft out of the water so he didn't ding the prop in the shallows. Apparently, one broken shear pin was enough for him.

The ATV was hidden in the shadows behind the rustic plywood cabin under a brown tarp and a layer of spruce boughs cut from nearby trees. Four inches of new snow added to the camouflage. It would have been impossible to see if Ruben hadn't been along to show them where it was.

In this case, the "Honda" was a forest green 400cc Arctic Cat ATV. The seat was just big enough for two, but the relatively small machine was designed for one, so Quinn kept as much weight as he could forward, lashing both packs and the Lapua rifle across the metal rack over the front wheels. This would help guard against tipping over backward when they climbed hills and had the added benefit of letting him keep an eye on his gear. Important things had a tendency to rattle off and get left behind, and out here losing a piece of equipment could have nasty consequences.

Using the mantra that if it wasn't on his body he didn't have it, Quinn kept his war belt with the Kimber and Riot around his waist and dropped five extra rounds for the .338 Lapua in the pocket of his wool shirt.

He threw a leg over the ATV and settled in behind the handlebars less than fifteen minutes after they'd beached the skiff. The Arctic Cat wasn't a motorcycle, but considering the slog through wet snow and bog that was ahead of them, he was glad to have it.

Ruben's secret trail cut north as it left the cabin with dark spruces rising up on either side from the undulating path of virgin snow to form a sort of tunnel through the forest. Behind Quinn, her arms wrapped around his waist, Beaudine hummed some nonsensical child's song. Had they not been pursuing a case of deadly nerve gas, it could have been an enjoyable ride.

It had been sometime since anyone used the trail and Quinn had to get off several times to push and tug deadfall out of the path. Eventually, they turned back to the east and broke out of the trees into the open.

The tundra wasn't frozen solid, even in the snow and cold, leaving the ground boggy and difficult to negotiate. Heavy clouds and a steady snow made for poor visibility—turning everything around them gray or white. In the open, with no trees to guide him, Quinn had to concentrate to maintain a heading and keep from getting stuck.

Beaudine's humming changed to "Froggy Went a Courtin'." Quinn wondered if she even realized she was doing it. He hadn't heard the song in ages, but the beat matched the bump and tumble of the ATV's tires on the trail and he enjoyed the break from their heavy mood. Even through the humming Beaudine kept her head up, scanning the horizon for Zolner or Volodin. Quinn could tell by the way she moved that her brain was going a million miles an hour. There was certainly a lot to think about. The U.S. had been attacked twice with poison gas. Beaudine had investigated two break-ins, witnessed bloody gunfights at the lodge and in Needle, been in a plane crash, watched Lovita die beside a lonely river, nearly died herself of hypothermia, watched Quinn tear out a man's throat—and then kill another with a sniper rifle.

"You okay?" she suddenly asked. Her voice a husky whisper in his ear.

"I'm fine," he said, wishing she would go back to humming.

"Okay," she said, sounding unconvinced. "It's just . . . stuff like that back there, it can change you. That's a fact."

"I'm good, really," Quinn said. The truth was, he felt like leaning out and puking on the trail, but he didn't have the time. He chalked it up to fatigue and pain as much as anything. One thing was certain—he didn't want to talk about his feelings.

Millions of falling snowflakes erased the horizon line leaving the white landscape to meld with a milky gray sky. They skirted dozens of lakes with rings of ice just beginning to form around their edges. Bumps of low-bush blueberry and scrub willow lined small streams, the smallest of which had already frozen over, spreading across the tundra like white veins.

"Maybe we should have just taken the river?" Beaudine nuzzled in closer to his back. "I mean, it goes to Ambler too—and we know that's where they're going."

"The river does go to Ambler," Quinn said. "But everyone says this guy Zolner is supposed to be a hunter. Volodin and his daughter might not even make it to Ambler. We need to intercept them en route. If that package Volodin took from the lodge was nerve gas . . ."

"And I thought this assignment was a bullshit job," Beaudine said. "Listen, I hate to be a nag, but when's the last time you put somethin' in your belly?" She surprised him by passing up one of Lovita's salmon strips.

Quinn thanked her and took the fish, feeling the oil warm him as he chewed. He was about to ask for another when he heard the shot.

Chapter 51

Four minutes earlier

The grizzly bear was small, not quite a year old, but even small bears could knock over an ATV—or at least cause a startled driver to do so. Kaija sped up at the flash of brown on the tundra ahead, blinking her eyes as her subconscious and conscious minds came together to agree on what she was seeing. It took her a moment more to remember that small bears almost always came with a big bear in tow, a bear with big claws and a big protective attitude about the little bear.

Kaija cut the handlebars sharply to take a trail around the cub, but the left front wheel dropped into a rut causing the nose to dip. Kaija and her father flew forward. Both were too slow to give up their grips and pulled the machine over with them as they fell.

Her father got to his knees and adjusted his glasses, wiping snow and grass off his face. Kaija scrambled quickly to peer around the overturned ATV, looking for the bear.

Still in its first year of life, the curious cub sat back on its haunches square in the middle of the trail less than fifty feet in front of the wrecked ATV.

"Go!" Kaija whispered, willing the thing to move rather than actually giving an audible command. She'd heard far too many stories of good Russians who'd been torn to pieces by the giant bears of Kamchatka. Though she was certain American grizzly bears would prove to be more puny, she had no desire to face even a lesser mother bear.

"Please go!" she said again, louder this time. She tried to add more force but the words just came out wobbly and without commitment. Adrenaline threatened to buckle her knees and she struggled to gain control. "Please . . ."

The mother bear padded across the snow toward the yearling. Her thick fur had to be three inches long, and blonder than her baby's, with chocolate legs and a dark, sincere face. Layers of fat, laid on for winter, rolled on her shoulders and buttocks as she waddled up and sat beside her cub. She turned her head from side to side, sniffing the wind and staring at the ATV with tiny piglike eyes.

"Get out of here!" Kaija said again, almost screaming now. The snow had stopped but the change in the weather brought a breeze that chilled her down to her bones. "Please, we mean you no harm."

The mother bear gave a single woof and rose onto her hind legs, forelimbs up and paws exhibiting long, scimitarlike claws.

Kaija jumped at the sound of her father's voice behind her. "Leave us alone!" he barked.

She took her eyes off the grizzly long enough to glance over her shoulder and see that he'd retrieved the rifle from the scabbard on the overturned ATV. Her hands flew to her ears as a deafening boom shook the air beside her head.

The mother bear remained on her hind legs and turned her head from side to side at the sound of the shot. The bullet had come nowhere near her. If it frightened her, she certainly didn't act like it. Dropping to all fours, the grizzly gave another woof and nipped at her cub to get it moving north at an easy, ambling gait.

Fuming, Kaija clenched her jaw and wheeled to face her father. The old fool was actually smiling. He held the rifle in front of him like some Hero of the Soviet Union.

"I have saved us, *kroshka*," he said.

"You idiot," she spat, waving him forward. "Put that gun away and help me get this machine back on four tires."

Volodin slumped. "But Kaija, my dear . . ." He looked as though he would break into tears at the slightest nudge.

"You have killed us, my dear Papa." She gave a derisive laugh. Her mother had been right about this man. He was at once the most brilliant and densest man she had ever seen. "How can you not be embarrassed? We were fortunate that the snow hid our tracks and now your shooting has told the world exactly where to find us."

Chapter 52

Quinn was off the Arctic Cat as soon as he heard the shot. He yanked the cord that held the Lapua in place and held it in one hand and the pack in the other, sprinting forward to put some distance between himself and the ATV.

"Wanna tell me where we're goin'?" Beaudine said, hustling after him with her pack and the AR-10.

"The four-wheeler isn't camouflaged against the snow," Quinn said. He tugged at the fabric of his over whites. "We are." He dropped the pack in front of him and knelt down beside it, feeling himself begin to sink into the cold wet mush of the tundra as soon as his knee hit the ground. Ignoring the chill, he put the rifle to his shoulder and began to scan through the scope in the direction he thought the shot had come from.

It was difficult to get a bearing from a single shot, especially on the open tundra where sound spread like a flooding tide across the vast openness. He went on instinct, and the direction he'd first turned his head when he'd heard the distant report. Quinn guessed it to be a medium power deer rifle, maybe a .30.30. It was absent the massive concussive boom that would have come with a round as big as the CheyTac Davydov said Zolner used. He'd heard no crack-thump, so the shots didn't appear to be coming in his direction.

"I've got him," Beaudine said from where she knelt on the tundra next to Quinn. Her voice was muffled against her gloves as she held the binoculars.

"You mean them," Quinn said, glancing over so he could see which way to swing his scope. "Volodin and his daughter?"

"No," Beaudine said, "I haven't found Volodin yet. I mean Zolner—or at least some guy setting up to shoot with a big-ass rifle."

Quinn backed off the magnification on his scope to get a wider field of view and then scanned back and forth until he found what Beaudine was looking at—a man kneeling to deploy the bipod on the fore-end of a very large rifle.

Grabbing his pack, Quinn took out a small notebook and the stub of a yellow pencil. He left the bipod on the Lapua folded flush with the barrel, opting to rest the fore-end on the pack in front of him instead. Once it was situated like he wanted it, he settled down behind the scope, belly and legs pressed against the wet snow, pencil in his teeth.

He zoomed in the magnification on the scope to get a better look now that he had a target. There was always a chance that this guy could be some Inupiaq hunter out for caribou—but Quinn doubted it.

"Follow his line of sight," Quinn said as he put the crosshairs in his reticle and counted the number of hash marks that bracketed the man's torso. The snow had slowed, but errant flakes still made it difficult to see across the wide-open space. "See if you can locate who or what he's setting up on."

"Already on it," Beaudine said, putting the binoculars to work.

"Let me know when you find them," Quinn said, running through the litany of formulas he'd learned a decade before when practicing extreme long-range shooting. The DOPE—or Data On Previous Engagements—that the Lapua's previous owner had written in the small notebook went out to 2000 meters—well within the capabilities of the rifle, but far beyond anything in Quinn's confidence level, especially now, beaten down, half frozen—and severely out of practice. For a blustering killer, Igoshin appeared to be a meticulous record keeper when it came to his shooting data. Quinn could understand the numbers but he didn't read Cyrillic so he double-checked everything with Beaudine and made pencil notes in English in the book. The DOPE was measured in meters, which was crucial to know, since that dictated the formula he would use to figure the range using the milliradian divisions on the crosshairs of his scope.

"Anything?" he said to Beaudine, in an effort to keep her relaxed and communications open while he alternately scribbled notes and peered through the scope. Zolner appeared to be going through the same process of calculating a firing solution on Volodin's position, wherever that was.

"Hold your horses . . ." Beaudine's voice trailed off as she scanned. "Got 'em. Looks like they wrecked their four-wheeler . . . ran it into a ditch or something. Too bad for us they're up and moving around though. Hard to say for sure, but it's gotta be them—older guy and a female. They're having some difficulty getting the machine pushed back onto four wheels."

"I need to borrow a sock," he said, holding out his

hand but keeping an eye on his target through the scope.

"A what?"

"A sock," Quinn said again. "It's okay if it's wet. Just hand me one from your pack. Quickly."

"Okay, okay," Beaudine said, tugging her pack closer so she could search through it. She passed him a damp wool sock and gave a slow shake of her head. "To each his own. Weird to find out you got this particular fetish now."

Quinn chuckled. "You sound so much like Jacques." He handed back the sock as soon as she gave it to him. "Do me a favor and fill that up with dirt and sand . . . anything you can scrape up and put in it. Gravel will be better, but not snow if you can help it."

Still kneeling, she snatched back the sock while Quinn watched the man at the other end of his scope hunker down beside his rifle, clearing a level spot for the bipod. The .375 CheyTac was a large gun, capable of shooting flatter and much farther than even the .338 Lapua. On open ground with nothing to use as cover except the ATV, Quinn's only chance against an experienced shooter behind such a rifle was to take the first shot and make it count.

"I think I put some caribou shit in there," Beaudine said, handing back the sock. "You can keep it after this."

Working quickly, but surely, Quinn removed enough of the slurry of dirt and rock that he could tie an overhand knot in the top of the sock. He shoved this grapefruit-size beanbag under the butt of the Lapua. With his right hand on the pistol grip and ready to work the trigger, he folded his left across his chest, gripping the sock of gravel and pulling the stock into the pocket of his shoulder. Alternately squeezing or releasing pressure on the sock, he was able to adjust his point of aim by lowering or raising the angle of the rifle.

Davydov had said his boss was a big man, describing him as two meters tall. That put him over six and a half feet. Quinn estimated someone of that height would be roughly 48 inches kneeling. Squeezing the sock, he moved the Lapua's point of aim so the crosshairs of his reticle were centered at the base of Zolner's knees, estimating the Russian's kneeling body filled nine tenths of the gap between the crosshairs and the first mil-dot.

"Now it's time for that weaponized math," he said.

"This is just great," Beaudine grunted. "And I told my teacher, Mrs. Umholtz, I would never have to use math."

"Seriously," he said. "I need your help checking my work. What's forty-eight times twenty-five point four?"

Beaudine took her cell out of her jacket pocket and punched in the numbers. "Twelve hundred nineteen point two," she said. "You're figuring how far away he is using the scope?"

"Right," Quinn said. "Now divide that number by point nine and that gives me approximate range in meters."

"Thirteen hundred fifty-four point six," Beaudine said. Groaning, she stretched out on the soggy ground next to Quinn. Both elbows on the ground in front of her, she raised the binoculars back up to her eyes.

Quinn took a deep breath. "Nearly a mile."

"Okay, I've got Zolner," she said. "So now you just dial in that distance on the scope and shoot him?"

"I wish it were that simple," Quinn said, as much to himself as Beaudine. "At this distance I have to account for a lot of variables . . . My brain is too fuzzy, so I'm gonna need you to use your calculator."

"Damn you, Mrs. Umholtz," Beaudine said. "Looks like math can be a life or death . . ." Her voice trailed off as she studied something through the binoculars. "Hang on, Zolner's up to something."

Quinn watched through the reticle as the Russian shifted his position so his rifle was pointed toward them.

"What the hell?" Beaudine said. "How could he have seen us?"

Quinn kept his eye on Zolner, who seemed to be scanning with the CheyTac's scope. "Check on Volodin and see what he's up to," he said. "But move slowly and don't stand up. There's a chance Zolner is just looking for us. The Arctic Cat will stand out, but our overwhites will make us hard to differentiate from the snow at this range."

Beaudine inched around, her belly making slurping sounds against the wet tundra as she stayed pressed flat to the snow. "Okay," she said at length. "The girl is looking in our direction through a set of binoculars. She must have been checking for anyone tailing her and saw the four-wheeler."

"And Zolner followed her line of sight," Quinn said. "Listen. Forget about her and scoot back around here to help me. Be careful you don't bump my arm. This cold is making me shaky enough as it is."

"Got it," she said, giving him a thumbs up.

"And if you don't like math you're gonna have to suck it up, because I guarantee you he's doing some pretty heavy calculating right now."

Beaudine lowered the binoculars long enough to rub her eyes before raising them again. She gasped at what she saw. "I think he's got us!"

Quinn took a deep breath, settling deeper into the freezing muck and willing his body not to shiver.

"Okay," he said. "Here we go. It's simple addition and subtraction for a firing solution from this point—and the last one to get the right answer wins a bullet."

Quinn consulted the recorded figures in the notebook, adding and subtracting clicks in elevation and windage on the numbered turrets of the scope as he worked through the variables of bullet drop, ambient temperature, air pressure, wind, bullet spin, and even the rotation of the earth. It took time, but at eight tenths of a mile, small mistakes meant big misses. Outgunned and in the open, Quinn knew he would have one chance to get things right.

"Not tryin' to make you nervous," Beaudine said. "But you better hurry up. This guy is up to somethin'."

A distinct crack slapped the ATV thirty meters to the left of where they lay in the snow—followed two seconds later by a hollow boom.

"Quinn!" Beaudine's voice rose in pitch and timbre. "He just shot our ride."

"He's going to be on us fast." Quinn took a quick glance through the scope, and then scrambled to finish the last of his calculations. "When I say move, don't ask why, just follow my lead. Fast."

Chapter 53

Zolner fired once at the ATV knowing his shot was on target as soon as he pulled the trigger. The vehicle's motor was still warm, and the stark white heat signature was easy to locate through the FLIR thermal imager. Rolling slightly away from the gun, he pressed the rubberized binocular skirt of the device to his eyes and began to scan again. Snow showed up like a negative image in the viewfinder, with things that were cold displayed as dark gray or black.

"Nice try," he muttered to himself in English when he found the shining white blobs of two human heads and shoulders. They thought to conceal themselves with camouflage. Zolner's heart-rate quickened when he saw they had a rifle and it was pointed directly at him. This was interesting indeed.

He'd ranged Volodin and the girl at 1810 meters, but whoever was following them looked to be considerably closer. Exchanging the FLIR for a laser, he ranged the other shooter at 1326 meters. He set the rangefinder on his pack and rolled in behind the Chey-Tac again. With careful deliberation, he began to make the minor adjustments from his shot at the ATV. At this distance the solid copper projectile would drop over 1200 centimeters and take almost two full seconds before impact. It was not a particularly difficult shot, but a great deal could happen in two seconds.

Chapter 54

Providenya

Colonel Rostov sat on the edge of the tarmac in the backseat of Lodygin's boxy black ZiL 41047. He'd been so concerned about putting the gas mask on when he arrived he hadn't taken the time to notice the car for what it was. A staff limousine before the captain had commandeered it from the back of a lonely fleet-storage lot outside Moscow, the teak trim had long since faded. Dark stains stood out against the tired beige leather. The scuffs of three decades of use by Soviet generals—and judging from the footprints on the ceiling, at least one general's acrobatic mistress—scarred the inside of the creaky sedan. Rostov toyed with a mark in the carpeting with the toe of his shoe and discovered it looked very much like a bullet hole. Exhausted, he fell back in his seat and closed his eyes, resting his hands on his belly. If scabby carpet and sagging leather could talk, there would certainly be some stories in this car.

Outside the ZiL, a cold gray wind blew in from the sea, buffeting the sedan. Bits of trash and gravel skittered across the broken pavement of the dilapidated airport. Rostov listened to the moaning wind and pulled his wool coat up around his ears. He leaned forward, telling the driver to turn up the heat. The slender conscript glanced in the rearview mirror and nodded, never quite making eye contact. A little conversation would have warmed the car, but officers did not speak with conscripts.

Bundled in his greatcoat, Rostov turned to stare past his reflection in the window at the lights of the approaching Cessna business jet used by General Zhestakova. His knee began to bounce spontaneously as the plane touched down. The driver, noticing the movement, glanced in the rearview mirror again, and then looked quickly away.

Rostov was not by nature a nervous man, but emissaries from the director of GRU did not come to lounge around the samovar and chat of world affairs over a tea and jam. When General Zhestakova sent an envoy, any message was most often given in what the Americans called "Blunt Force Trauma." Rostov knew this all too well. He had delivered many such messages as a young operative of GRU.

Rostov waited for the Cessna to roll to a stop and the turbofans to go quiet before stepping out of the ZiL. He stood in the wind with his hands folded in front of him, Astrakhan wool hat pulled down low over his ears. He did not have long to wait for the aircraft door to open.

Rostov's heart calmed when he saw the emissary was a woman. A redhead, which could certainly pose a problem, but still a woman—so all was not completely lost. At least Zhestakova had not sent someone to break his legs or throw him out a window.

"FSB," the young woman said when she reached the sedan. "Aleksandra Kanatova."

So that was the game, Rostov thought. The general

had sent someone from his brother-in-law's side of the house to test the waters before doing anything rash. This one was small, shorter even than his teenaged daughter and fully a foot shorter than him. Rich mahogany red hair hung in shoulder length curls from beneath her blue fox *ushanka*, in stark contrast to the crisp white of her down ski jacket. An alluring crop of freckles splashed across a button nose. Golden green eyes gleamed with an intensity that surprised even Rostov, who was surprised by little, least of all women. He wondered if they might not even enjoy their time together in Providenya.

"I am told there is a girl with information about the Black Hundreds," Kanatova said, getting straight to the heart of her visit.

Rostov nodded toward the Cessna. "You have no luggage?"

"This only," Kanatova said, holding up a brown cardboard file folder.

Rostov held open the door to the backseat of the ZiL. "We must get you out of the wind, my dear," he said.

Kanatova smiled as if grateful for the chivalry. "What you must do, Colonel, is take me to this young woman. I wish to question her at once."

The population on the dilapidated base was purposely kept small, with little movement outside prescribed times when American satellites were not passing overhead. Most of the buildings were vacant, so the handful of officers and senior enlisted men had their pick of quarters.

Captain Lodygin had chosen the wing of a deserted barracks at the back of the compound.

"This is the confinement area?" Kanatova said, nodded her head as she got out of the sedan.

"No," Rostov said, waving at the drab concrete building on the outskirts of the base. Its back to the perimeter fence and barren mountains, the barracks was separated from the other buildings by a gurgling stream that contained more sewage than water. "Lodygin is a loaner. This is where he prefers to live."

The FSB agent stopped at the bottom of the concrete steps, her hand on the peeling paint of a metal rail. "Captain Lodygin keeps prisoners at his residence?"

Rostov motioned for the driver to stay with the car, wondering how to couch his answer so he did not sound too callous and scare away the young redhead. In the end, he decided that if she was an agent for the FSB, she should be capable of handling unvarnished truth.

"Captain Lodygin is an interesting soul," Rostov said. "But his methods have, thus far, yielded results. He does not have an interrogation cell in his home so much as he lives in a room off the interrogation cell."

Kanatova nodded thoughtfully, seeming to chew on this information as she made her way up the stairs and through the twin metal doors. Their footsteps echoed down a long tile hallway that was covered with a thin patina of glacial dust and lined on either side with wooden dormitory doors every three or four meters. There was a forgotten emptiness to the place, like a condemned prison. Rostov caught a whiff of strong cleaning solution as they walked—and something else he could not quite identify.

"You have been to this place before?" Kanatova said as they neared a pool of light that spilled from an open door at the far end of the passageway.

"No," Rostov said. "The captain has only described it to me."

"Most interesting," the FSB agent said. "Where are the guards? Why have we not been challenged?"

"I am not certain," Rostov said honestly, as they reached the open door. "We will have to inquire."

They found Lodygin sitting at a small metal table in front of a bowl of soup, addressing a young woman across from him with a spoon. He was dressed in his uniform trousers and a T-shirt, but his tunic and light green shirt hung over the back of a chair beside him. The young woman across from him wore a thin cotton shift. She dipped a spoon into a bowl of soup identical to his and put it to her mouth with a shaking hand. Soup drizzled back into the bowl and she stared at Lodygin and went through the motions of eating without ever opening her mouth. Dark hair hung on trembling shoulders in greasy matted strands. Providenya saw little sun this time of year and everyone was pale, but the girl looked as though the life had been drained from her body. Her hands were free but a chain connected a bruised and bloody ankle to the leg of her metal chair. The chair appeared to be bolted to the floor.

Rostov was immediately struck with the foul odor of the well-used toilet bucket in the corner. He had to concentrate to keep from retching when he saw the metal ring affixed to the back wall above a thin prison mattress. A single filthy sheet for bedding was crumpled at the end, sopping up a spill from the bucket. Torn underwear, now little more than sad pieces of cotton and elastic lay on the tile next to the mattress. The sight of them made Rostov want to vomit.

"Colonel!" Lodygin said, jumping to his feet. "I wish

you would have informed me you were going to visit. I would have made myself more presentable." He gestured toward the girl with an open hand. "Our Rosalina has been very cooperative in the last few minutes, so she earned some much needed nourishment."

The girl convulsed at Lodygin's every word, a look of hopelessness in her sunken eyes such as Rostov had never seen. For the first time, the colonel noticed a short wooden truncheon on the table, resting on top of a pair of flaccid latex gloves beside Lodygin's soup bowl.

Kanatova ignored the girl, looking instead at the captain. "So, this Rosalina has provided you information on the Black Hundreds?"

A smile crept over Lodygin's face. He walked around the table to stand beside the girl and stroked her hair with the back of his hand. "She has told me a great deal about her friend Kaija Merculief, who is involved with this Black Hundreds."

"I do not care about Kaija Merculief," Kanatova spat, apparently lacking in patience. "We require information on the Black Hundreds group. I will need to speak with this girl myself."

Rosalina threw back her head in despair. "Kaija is a friend from school only," she sobbed. "I do not know about any Black Hundreds—"

Without warning, Kanatova drew a black H&K pistol from beneath her down jacket and shot Lodygin in the center of his forehead.

"I believe you," she said.

Chapter 55

Alaska

"Now!" Quinn said, scooping up the rifle. He grabbed the pack and sock with his free hand. "Follow me. Move, move, move!"

Quinn counted strides as he ran, knowing that each bounding step put approximately one meter of distance between himself and Zolner. He stopped when he'd widened the gap twenty more meters and immediately dropped the pack on the ground. Settling in behind the scope, he squeezed the sock to bring the crosshairs of his scope where they centered on the Russian's prone body. He took two full breaths, giving his nerves a quick moment to settle, then exhaled, pausing at the bottom to send the round in the stillness of his respiratory pause. He didn't wait for impact but worked the bolt and fired again, using the same hold.

The .338 Lapua's two-and-a-half-second flight gave Quinn time to get back on the scope before the projectile made it to the target. He'd seen Zolner fire as well, but the shot had fallen far short, kicking up a shower of snow just past the imprint where Quinn had been set up before. It would have been a hit.

"Hot damn, Quinn, you hit his rifle," Beaudine yelled, binoculars to her eyes. "Bet he's never had anybody shoot back at him like that. Have you, Mr. Worst of the Moon?"

The first shot from the Lapua sent up a splash of mud a foot in front of Zolner as he adjusted to Quinn's new location. The second, still traveling 1200 feet per second, slammed into the ground a few inches closer and then bounced, striking the big CheyTac in the metal stock. At first Quinn thought the round had been a hit on Zolner, but the greater likelihood was that the solid round had sent up spalling from the metal rifle stock on impact along with fragments of copper. It was impossible to tell through the scope at over 1300 meters, but from the way Zolner rolled away, it looked as though he'd been struck in the arm and face.

Zolner was up and running by the time Quinn could send another shot his direction. As good as he was, shooting of any kind was a perishable skill. A moving target at nearly a mile away proved to be impossible to hit. The Russian didn't even pause when he reached his ATV but sped away after Volodin.

"Can you believe that?" Beaudine said. "He just abandoned his fancy gun."

"Smart," Quinn said, sitting up to brush the tundra muck off the front of his jacket and pants. "What's the doctor doing?"

Beaudine swung the binoculars around. "They're long gone," she said. "Must have gotten their machine tumped back on its wheels."

A quick check of the Arctic Cat showed Zolner's round had come in perfectly under the front fender and clipped the oil line. The machine was oil cooled, which meant it was out of commission. There were two extra quarts of oil under the seat, but the rubber hose was too short to reuse once the damage had been trimmed away.

"I can fix it," Beaudine said, holding up one of the empty .338 Lapua cases and the file from her Leatherman multi-tool. "It'll take a minute, but I can do it."

Quinn nodded. "We can saw the end of the empty and use it as a hard splice. You're pretty handy to have around."

"Like I said, the only thing close to happy times I had with my daddy was when we were fixin' engines."

"He taught you to use the empty rifle bullet as a fix?"

"Hell, no." Beaudine frowned. "If we would have had guns and bullets around the house I woulda shot the son of a bitch a long time ago. He just taught me to use what we had on hand."

"Okay then," Quinn said. "If you don't mind doing the fixing, I'm going to pour some more antiseptic on my thigh. I'm pretty sure the stuff I was laying in back there came out of the south end of a north-bound caribou."

Beaudine handed him the brass shell casing and Leatherman. "Your hands are stronger. It'll go faster if you do it. In the meantime, drop your pants, and I'll take care of your antiseptic again. It's the least I can do since you sewed me up."

Quinn did as he was told, sitting on the edge of the Arctic Cat with his pants and long underwear pooled around his boots. He held the empty rifle case against the handlebars with one hand while he sawed first at the narrow-necked end of the cartridge with the Leatherman file. He'd work on the primer end next. Beaudine opened a new packet of Betadine and began to pour it on each spot where the shotgun had hit his thigh.

"Lucky for you, she was using birdshot."

"I'll say." Quinn concentrated on what he was doing to keep from wincing. It was not particularly delicate work, but he had to move the file evenly back and forth on the brass shell casing, working to form a tube that could be inserted in between the broken oil lines.

"You're sure you don't want me to try and get at them?" Beaudine offered again.

"No, thanks," Quinn said. "Better concentrate on fixing this. We slowed Zolner down but he's not going to be far behind Volodin and the girl. He might even catch them."

"If he doesn't bleed out." Beaudine grinned. "I still can't believe you actually hit him."

"Technically the bullet bounced into his rifle and then hit him."

"At three quarters of a mile, a hit's a hit," Beaudine said.

Quinn stopped filing long enough to look up and stare across the empty tundra. "Anyway, this Worst of the Moon doesn't seem like the kind of guy to bleed out."

Beaudine squatted beside the Arctic Cat, trimming the oil line with a pocketknife. "Everybody bleeds out," she said.

Quinn turned and looked at her over his shoulder, first at her face and then at his thigh. "We didn't."

Chapter 56

Providenya

Colonel Rostov felt as if his guts had turned to jelly as he watched a thin whisker of smoke curl from the barrel of Kanatova's H&K P7. He carried a Makarov pistol in a regulation flap holster on his hip, but the way this woman summarily shot Lodygin without warning . . . Rostov knew there was no way he could get to his weapon before she shot him as well.

Rosalina, reduced to a bundle of nerves from her recent treatment, lost control of her bladder at the gunshot, and fell forward across the table, knocking the soup bowl to the floor.

Instead of shooting Rostov as he expected, Kanatova returned her pistol to the holster and produced a handcuff key from her pocket. "Don't just stand there," she said as she stooped to free the girl's ankle from the chain. "Take off your coat."

"My coat . . . ?"

"Give me your coat!" Kanatova snapped, causing the colonel to shrug the thing off as if it were on fire. "Now turn away. The poor thing deserves some privacy."

Rostov turned slightly, but kept an eye on the FSB agent in his peripheral vision, smart enough not to show his back completely, but concerned enough that beads of sweat began to pop up on his bald head.

"Come, my dear," Kanatova said to the girl. "We must get you clean and into warm clothing. Do you live with your mother?"

"Yes." The reply was hardly louder than the peep of a bird.

"How long have you been here?"

"I do not know," Rosalina said. "Two days, I think."

Kanatova's green eyes shot daggers at Rostov. "Your poor mother must be worried sick. I will call and let her know you are with me now." Arms around the shattered girl's heaving shoulders, she turned again to Rostov. "I have seen what I was sent to see, Colonel."

"You will take the girl with you?"

"I will," Kanatova said, drawing her closer as if she were a beloved younger sister. There was a fierceness about her that made her seem to glow, even in the dimness of Lodygin's dismal room.

Rostov shook his head, feeling some measure of control return to his spirit. He was after all, a colonel in the GRU. "And what of Captain Lodygin?"

"Dump him in the sea," Kanatova said, her freckled nose drawing into a tight sneer. "I do not care. It is apparent Lodygin was a sadistic bastard and that is what I will report to General Zhestakova. The man had no business questioning young women about such sensitive subjects—much less being in charge of your project."

"I assure you, I did not know of his proclivity—"

"Is that so?" Kanatova said, tilting her head as if passing judgment. She turned to look at Rosalina. "My dear, have you ever seen this man before?"

"No." The girl shook her head. "Only the other one."

"Very well." Kanatova shrugged. "In that case, Colonel, I must ask you to return me to my plane."

Rostov put a hand on the edge of the table to keep his knees from buckling. "Of course," he said. "Yes . . . of course." He could think of nothing else to say. She had made it quick, and, in a manner, kind, when she'd killed Lodygin, just as General Zhestakova said it should be.

A stocky woman with her gray hair piled high in a tight bun swung her elbows as if she were marching when she walked out from the plane to meet Aleksandra Kanatova beside the old ZiL. The woman carried a bright blue wool blanket and wrapped it around the girl's shoulders like a loving grandmother. Rostov nearly collapsed in relief when Kanatova returned his greatcoat. The FSB would not go to the trouble of returning a coat if they meant to murder someone.

"Mrs. Dudkov will look after you, my dear," Kanatova said to the girl, patting her on the shoulder as the matron escorted the girl to the plane. "I will be along in a moment."

"Thank you for your assistance in this delicate matter, Colonel Rostov," Kanatova said when the girl was safely out of earshot and boarding the plane. "Finding information on any plans the Black Hundreds have regarding Novo Archangelsk is paramount to all else. Do you understand?"

"I do," Rostov said. Some of his bluster had begun to seep back in now that he knew he would survive this encounter. "You bought an incredible amount of trust from the girl when you rescued her from Lodygin."

"Yes . . . Lodygin," Kanatova said as if the name was bitter on her tongue.

"I assure you," Rostov stammered. "I was only interested in the information he brought me. I knew nothing of his activities with the girl."

Kanatova smiled, giving him a sly wink. "Oh you knew, Colonel. You knew all too well." The smile bled from her face. "The important thing is that you did not take part in those activities."

"Quite right," Rostov said, squirming, fighting the urge to tug at his collar for more air. "The girl trusts you now. That is good. She will tell you everything she knows, I am sure." He felt as if he was on the verge of collapse by the time she extended her hand. She was a civilian and did not salute, but it made sense that she would offer to shake hands.

Kanatova nodded a curt good-bye and turned. The same cold, gray wind that had brought the terrifying redhead to Providenya tugged at her hair as she walked back toward the aircraft. Rostov felt as if he could draw a full breath for the first time in hours.

Ten yards away, Kanatova stopped suddenly, patted the top of her bare head and turned, smiling.

"I am a fool," said. "My *ushanka,* I have forgotten it in the car."

Eager to see her on her way, Rostov turned and bent into the back door to retrieve the blue fox hat. He'd just leaned across the seat when he felt the cold steel of Kanatova's pistol at the base of his skull.

Rostov pitched forward at the shot, knees slamming against the pavement, arms trailing at his sides. The young conscript behind the wheel came around and helped Kanatova lift the body, shoving the lifeless lump into the back seat, head down on the floorboard.

"Your *ushanka*," the soldier said, nodding toward the blue fox hat, still on the seat. Wisely, he did not offer to bend forward and retrieve it.

"I have others," Kanatova said waving her hand at the ZiL. "I will leave the disposal of the body to you then."

The young soldier gave a curt salute and hurried around to the driver's seat. A moment later, the black sedan crunched away over the broken pavement, its grim interior heavier now with the stain of another dark story.

Chapter 57

Alaska

It took two hours, a cup of spare gasoline, and three tries to get the oil cleaned off the broken hose well enough so that Gorilla tape could hold both ends over the makeshift .338 Lapua cartridge splice. Thankfully, Zolner's bullet had destroyed nothing but a piece of plastic fender and the rubber oil line.

The clouds gave way to a bluebird-clear sky, but with the cloud cover went the insulation that held any semblance of warmth close to the earth. The snow began to crust under foot. Water and mud froze into solid ice. Though the sun offered little in the way of warmth, it seemed to be everywhere at once. The glare bouncing off the crystalline landscape was like a dazzling field of diamonds.

The after-effects of the adrenaline dump from the sniper versus sniper battle with Zolner began to take its toll both on Quinn and on Beaudine by the time they got the ATV started an hour later. Wet clothes and plummeting temperatures made it impossible to get warm, but Lovita's *akutaq* helped stave off hypothermia. Even Beaudine bowed to the reality that the sweet fatty confection was necessary to stay alive.

Quinn drove, grateful for the relative warmth of Beaudine's body clamped around his back as they bounced over the frozen tundra. As uncomfortable as it was, the freezing ground made for much easier going and cut the chances of getting bogged down. He intersected the trail to Ambler less than ten minutes from the time they fixed their oil line. It was easy to follow since both Volodin and Zolner's machines had passed over the mushy ground before it began to freeze. They left behind great tracks of now crystalizing mud, like a dotted line through the snow.

"You think he's still out there?" Beaudine said, arms tight around his waist.

"Zolner?" Quinn said. "I'm sure of it."

He took the Arctic Cat northeast on a meandering route over hummocks of willow and berry bush, bitten red by frost and bent with snow. The Kobuk River was somewhere to their south, blocked from view by thick pockets of spruce- and scrub-covered hills.

"He ran off and left his gun though," she said. "That's a good sign."

"Maybe," Quinn said, eyeing the wide-open tundra around them. Zolner had a duffle on the back of his ATV, and he didn't seem like the kind of man to carry a single weapon. He was still a threat that would eventually need to be dealt with.

They crossed a myriad of braided streams that tumbled down from the Kobuk Mountains to the north. Most were shallow with water gurgling under silver edges of ice that crept out from the banks. Two of the streams proved deep enough to splash over their ankles, soaking their socks and driving the aching cold deeper into their bones. With no time to stop and build a fire—and nothing to burn anyway—they pushed on, hoping Ambler, and the case of poison gas, lay within their reach.

After an hour of bone-jarring riding, the trail turned abruptly east. The willow bushes became thicker and spruce trees began to appear with more regularity. Open tundra finally gave up to thick forest as they arced gradually southward toward the river. The ruts grew deeper and side trails from other ATVs began to crisscross the main route, disappearing into the trees. The dense forest made for chilly shadows but provided welcome relief from the glare of sun on snow. Quinn rode past four deserted cabins. His body craved the warmth of shelter, dry clothes, and a fire, but he kept his thumb on the throttle. Volodin was close—and if he was close, so was the gas. The thought of Zolner waiting somewhere in the shadows was a constant worry and kept Quinn's mind off the cold.

It was late afternoon when they rode past a pair of ravens pecking at an old diaper in the Ambler landfill.

"This is where it gets dicey," Quinn said, his head on a swivel.

"Is that what I think it is?" Beaudine said, through chattering teeth, her cheek pressed against his neck for warmth.

"The town dump," Quinn said. "Keep your eyes open. Zolner has to know we're following him."

"Gotcha," Beaudine said. She pointed through the trees toward a low hill to the east. "Looks like the top of a cell tower."

A rush of hope surged through Quinn's body, like a glimpse of the finish at the end of a grueling race. Reality tamped back the elation. Survival was now slightly more probable, but they were a long way from the tape.

* * *

"Palmer," the President's national security advisor said when he picked up.

"It's me, sir," Quinn said, giving the specific and pertinent details first. In written briefs and oral situation reports, Winfield Palmer was not a man for small talk. He preferred a BLUF—Bottom Line Up Front type of report. The niceties could come later if there was time. There never was. Quinn spoke as he rode, coming into town from the northwest. He stayed right at the angled T intersection to head into the village of Ambler. A left would have taken him to the gravel airstrip.

Spattered with mud from head to foot and shivering to the point of convulsions, they drew stares and giggles from a gang of runny-nosed school children riding their bikes over a homemade jump in the snow. Quinn smiled and waved as he began to brief Palmer.

"We need fast air transport out of Ambler ASAP. Volodin and his daughter are ahead of us but we're not sure—"

"But you're okay?" Palmer interrupted him, giving an audible sigh of relief. The display of uncharacteristic emotion made Quinn grin despite the cold.

"We are both in working order, sir," Quinn said, leaving out information about Lovita's death until his final report.

"What the hell happened out there?" Palmer said. "You've been out of commo for a day and a half. In case you've forgotten, we're in the middle of a shitnado. I am in dire need of decent intel if you have any to spare."

And, he's back, Quinn thought, recognizing the brash Winfield Palmer he knew and loved.

Quinn brought the national security advisor up to

speed as fast as he could, using a considerable amount of energy to keep his cold-soaked brain in focus. For all he knew, it was all babble and Palmer was preparing to have him committed for mental observation.

He kept an eye out for any sign of Zolner or Volodin as he rode. He'd not gotten a good look at either, but suspected they would stand out as much as he and Beaudine did in a village of just over two hundred Inupiaq natives.

"I'll call you back as soon as I know more, sir," Quinn said. "I need to hunt up the local tribal or village police officer first."

"Very well," Palmer said. "I'll contact Special Agent Beaudine's supervisor so we can de-conflict and task the Bureau folks in Anchorage."

Quinn was glad to hear that the call to align different agencies and resources would come from Palmer's office. Moving assets in the Bureau could be like trying to turn the Queen Mary at full steam. It could be done, but not quickly.

"And the ride out of Ambler?" Quinn pressed.

"It may not be pretty," Palmer said. "But I'll get you something."

Quinn dropped the phone in his jacket pocket and pulled over beside two blond women walking up the road in front of a long beige building that had to be the school. One of the women looked like she could be the other one's aunt. Both were white and each wore the same type of insulated XTRATUF rubber boots. Neither looked native to Ambler.

"Hello," Quinn said, bringing the Arctic Cat to a stop and killing the engine. "Have you seen an older Russian man with a young blonde woman? They would have come into town in the last two hours or so."

Both women shook their heads.

"We just came from the school," the younger one said. She was pretty, round faced, and looked like many of the first-year bush teachers Quinn had met, exhausted but brimming with innocent hope.

Quinn nodded. "Is there a TPO or VPO in town?"

Some villages had Village Public Safety Officers trained by the state, others opted for a Village Police Officer or Tribal Police Officer over which they had a little more control. Good, hard working folks for the most part, TPOs and VPOs didn't have as stringent a background requirement and might very well be an eighteen-year-old kid—armed with nothing but a Taser and their wits.

"Hon," the older of the two women said. Quinn guessed she was in her mid forties and from somewhere in the south. "You need the health clinic, not the VPO." The longer she looked at Beaudine, the more her face pulled back in horror.

Quinn turned to check Beaudine and realized he'd become accustomed to seeing her with a black eye and what she'd started calling his "Frankenstein Treatment." He doubted he looked much better. They were both covered in tundra muck, oil, and blood.

"We were in a plane crash," he said honestly. "Other side of Needle."

"FBI." Beaudine gave the women a wink with her good eye. "If you do run into the Russian man, don't approach him, okay? Just find us."

"Is he dangerous?" the older teacher said.

"He is," Beaudine said. "Look, I don't want to be rude, but it's really important that we find a woman named Polina. Know her?"

"Everybody knows everybody in this town," the younger of the two women said. "Polina's married to our shop teacher."

"They live in a little yellow house over by L.J.'s store," the older teacher said. "He's still coaching basketball, but she should be at home." She waved at a young Native man approaching from the opposite direction on a red Honda ATV. His broad smile was framed with wispy chin whiskers, and he wore a dark gray uniform shirt that was easily three sizes to big.

"Hey, Lois," the young man said. "What's up?"

Lois introduced him as Clarence, one of her former students before becoming the Village Police Officer. From his youthful face, Quinn figured it hadn't been that long ago.

"Clarence," Lois said. "These guys are with the FBI. They need to talk to Polina."

Clarence's brown eyes flew wide. "FBI? No shit?" He grimaced. "Sorry about the language, Miss Lois."

Beaudine nodded.

"We don't get many FBI guys all the way out here," the VPO said, passive and absent any guile. "What happened to your face?"

"Plane crash," Quinn said again. He knew it wouldn't be the last time they had to explain.

"How about you?" Beaudine said to the VPO. "Have you seen a older Russian man with a young woman in the last couple of hours."

"I heard some guys at the fuel depot talking about a goofy Russian," Clarence said. "I never seen him though. Maybe he caught a flight out. We've had a couple of planes come and go today."

"How many?" Quinn asked, shooting a glance at Beaudine.

"Three," Clarence said. "One to Anchorage, one to Fairbanks, and another that flies the downriver milk-run to Kotzebue. You want me to take you to the fuel depot? Irving Briggs is the one who was talkin' about the Russian. You can ask him."

Quinn mulled over the idea of Volodin already being on a flight out with the gas. "I think we'd better start with Polina."

Beaudine nodded in agreement.

"I'll show you her house," Clarence said, preparing to make a U-turn on his ATV. "But I ain't goin' in. Polina yells too much."

Chapter 58

Homes in the Arctic were not simply weatherworn—they were weather-beaten, weather-savaged. Polina's sad frame house sat well back from the gravel street, tucked well back in the willows. The scrubby trees did little to protect the paint job from driving winds, and anything that had once been yellow was now bleached and sickly tan.

Quinn considered having Clarence watch the back door in case Volodin or Zolner happened to be inside and tried to duck out. In the end, he decided against it for exactly the same reason. The Village Police Officer seemed like a great kid, but he was young, inexperienced, and unarmed—no match for the likes of Zolner or anyone else who put up much of a fight. Quinn gave the VPO his cell number and asked him to go and check with the local air-service agent to see if Volodin or Zolner had caught one of the flights out. In truth, it was probably better to have the kid out of the way.

Quinn removed the bolt from the Lapua and shoved it in his jacket, not wanting to leave the rifle unattended with all the roving kids on bikes—or an enemy who happened to come up behind him. A weapon like the .338 in the hands of Zolner would prove disastrous.

There were several sets of tracks leading to and from the front door of Polina's little yellow house, some from different adults, some from kids.

"I got blood," Beaudine said, AR-10 in hand. She nodded to a trail of bright red droplets, stark against the white snow.

Quinn saw something else in the snow and scanned ahead looking on either side of the house, Kimber out and at his side.

"Caribou," he said, nodding to a pile of rib bones.

Beaudine gave an audible sigh of relief. "Good," she said. "I guess."

A dog that looked like a cross between a Corgi and a German shepherd trotted out from under the steps on the stubby legs common to village mutts with generations of inbreeding. Quinn dropped it a piece of salmon skin he had in his pocket and moved through the willows toward the house.

Beaudine kept her distance, moving so she could see Quinn as well as behind the house. Quinn was about to knock on the front door when a woman backed out onto the slanting plywood porch, facing the door as if to lock it as she left. She had the bronze skin of an Inupiaq. The rich purple fabric of her Native *kuspuk* was pulled tight from her pregnancy.

"Whatcha doin'?" the woman asked when she turned around, eyeing the Kimber in Quinn's hand. She was not so much intimidated by the gun as she was put out that he had it pointed toward her.

"Police," Quinn said. "We need to talk to Polina."

The woman gave a heavy sigh. "That's me," she said.

Beaudine moved up quickly at the appearance of the pregnant woman. "Is Kaija here?"

"Kaija?" The young woman held her belly when she laughed. "Kaija's in Russia."

"Nice try," Beaudine said. "We followed her into town."

"Well, look for yourself," Polina said. "She's not here. Whatever you do, I gotta sit down. My back hurts."

Quinn checked the bathroom and the two small bedrooms as soon as he walked in and found nothing but piles of clothes on top of old mattresses laid out on the linoleum floor.

Polina lowered herself onto the tattered orange couch and told them her story. According to Polina, her mother was Siberian Chukchi, Native cousins to Alaska's Arctic people. Her father had been a Russian schoolteacher who immigrated to the United States when Polina was still young. She'd known Kaija in grade school, and the two had hooked up again recently over the Internet via ICQ.

"But you haven't seen her?" Quinn asked, fighting the urge to sleep brought on by the enveloping heat of Polina's oil stove. He kept his mind awake and busy studying the girl's face for the micro-expressions that would tell him if she was lying. Her almost constant swaying movement and apparent discomfort from her pregnancy made reading her all the more difficult.

"She sends me packages sometimes," Polina said. "To the lodge where I work. But I haven't seen her."

"Why doesn't she just send them here?" Beaudine asked from a wooden chair from the nearby dinette. Quinn could see from her heavy eyes that the warm confines were getting to her as well.

"My husband gets jealous of Russian friends," Polina said. "He's a teacher at the school."

She had an answer for everything. It was either a well-rehearsed lie or the simple truth. Quinn had yet to make up his mind.

"You have no idea where she's going?" he said.

"Sorry," Polina said, stuffing a hand between her lower back and the couch.

"It would be better if you kept your hands were we could see them," Quinn said.

Polina pulled her hand back but she said nothing.

Beaudine moved forward to the edge of her seat. "We're going to nced—"

Prone to the jerkiness of the completely exhausted, both she and Quinn jumped when his cellphone rang in his jacket pocket.

Quinn answered the call.

"Is this that FBI guy?" a tentative voice asked. It was Clarence, the VPO.

"Go ahead," Quinn said.

"I got someone here you're gonna want to talk to," Clarence said.

Quinn shook his head to focus. "We'll be down there in a few minutes."

"Okay, bye," Clarence said.

"Hang on," Quinn said before the VPO could hang up. "Who is it that we'll want to talk to?"

"Tell me your name again?" Clarence asked the person he was with. His voice muffled as if his hand covered the phone. "Okay, I got it," he said when he came back on the line. "He says his name is Kostya Volodin."

Chapter 59

Chinatown, Manhattan, New York

August Bowen tipped his rickety wooden chair against the wall of the Golden Dragon Chinese restaurant and took a sip of his bubble tea. Outside, East Broadway seemed to overflow with a flood of wide-eyed tourists. A gaggle of a half-dozen blue-haired women in matching sweaters stopped under the glare of the evening streetlights to peer in through a large picture window at the split pig's head and smoked duck carcasses hanging on metal hooks. Bowen was pretty sure two teenagers were buying heroin from a tout selling knockoff designer purses right outside the door.

Ronnie Garcia sat across the table chasing a pot sticker around her plate with a pair of bamboo chopsticks. Thibodaux looked up over a steaming bowl of noodles, his visible eye blinking as if in deep thought. None of the three were the type to sit with their back to the door so they crowded in at the wooden table, yielding the actual "gunfighter seat"—the chair with its back to the wall—to Bowen since he was the only bona fide lawman of the group.

"You know you're not fightin', right?" Thibodaux said at length, pointing at Bowen with his chopsticks.

"What do you mean?" Bowen said.

"I mean tapioca bubble tea ain't a meal," Thibodaux said. "It's a damned dessert. Since you're not actually gettin' in the ring it's okay for you to eat real food."

"I guess," Bowen said, letting his chair tip forward so it was flat on the floor. "I thought I'd better be ready just in case . . ."

Garcia's eyes narrowed, all judge-like. "I get the impression you *want* to fight this moron."

"I kind of do," Bowen said, "if I'm honest. It would give us a chance to draw out whoever it is that's after him."

"He knows who's after him," Thibodaux scoffed. "We'll get that info from him directly. You gotta try some of this soup." He waved the elderly waiter over and ordered another bowl of hand-pulled noodles, this one for Bowen. He dug into his own bowl again once the waiter had shuffled off with the new order, talking in between bites and slurps, using his chopsticks to drive home his points. "We got no obligation to the Ortega brothers for this. I mean, what the hell is a mismatch anyhow? It ain't a fight, it's a circus, and Daux Boy worked out too many hours in the gym to be part of some sideshow."

"You're more fired up than I am," Bowen said.

"I doubt that, Gus Gus," Thibodaux said. "Cause I'm thinking you can't stomach what you saw goin' on with the poor girls back at that titty bar and you've done assigned a shitload of righteous blame for all of it to Petyr the Weasel."

"Maybe so," Bowen said. The big Cajun had a point. Cheekie's was nothing more than a front for the modern slave trade. There was no gray area in an operation like that.

"I get it," Thibodaux said, apparently reading the deputy's mind. "I really do. Somebody's gettin' a boot in the ass and it might as well be our boy, Pete. But MMA's different than boxing, cher. There's rules, but you don't want to be screwin' around in the octagon. You liable to find yourself with your jaw wired shut and eatin' nothin' but your damned bubble tea."

"I can take care of myself, Gunny," Bowen said.

"No doubt," Thibodaux said, pointing to Bowen's split lip with his chopsticks.

Garcia heaved a heavy sigh, and when Garcia heaved a sigh, Bowen thought, it was a magnificent thing indeed.

"You could take him," she said. "He's big, but he thinks he's smarter than everyone else."

"That ain't the point," Thibodaux said, slurping a big bite of noodles. "We're grabbin' him as soon as he shows. That's all there is to it."

"If Maxim would ever let us know where the fight is supposed to be," Bowen said. "'An undisclosed location in Chinatown' doesn't give us much to work with."

"I gave him the number for my burner." Garcia checked her watch. "He's supposed to call anytime."

"Makes sense with an illegal fight," Bowen said. "They call and let us know the when and where at the last minute. Nearly impossible for law enforcement to pull a raid together."

The waiter brought Bowen's noodles and another can of Diet Dr. Pepper for Garcia.

"Once he calls," Thibodaux said, "we'll set up outside the location and grab Petyr while he's still on the street. You're not even gonna see the octagon.

Bowen tore the paper off a pair of bamboo chopsticks and pulled the bowl closer. The soup did smell good, and if he wasn't going to get the opportunity to put some hurt on Petyr the Wolf, he might as well see what had Jacques slurping so loudly.

The Cajun's phone rang, causing everyone at the table to freeze.

A wide smile spread over Thibodaux's face as soon as he answered. "L'ami! She hasn't killed you . . . Yeah . . . Okay . . ."

The smile vanished from the big Marine's face. He grabbed a pen from his shirt pocket and took notes on a napkin while he listened to the other end of the conversation. Garcia leaned in close, trying to hear, bouncing so much Bowen thought she might fall out of her chair.

"Okay," Thibodaux finally said. "We'll make it happen. I got someone here who's dyin' to talk to you before you go . . . You bet . . . Be safe, Chair Force." He passed the phone to Garcia who snatched it away and fled to the far corner of the noodle shop.

Thibodaux leaned in, lowering his voice. "Turns out Petyr's daddy is behind the gas attacks," he said. "Or at least the chemist who's invented the gas itself. Calls it New Archangel. Quinn has him in custody. Seems Petyr's got a sister who might be runnin' the whole show. She was able to give them the slip and is on her way to Anchorage now, probably with enough gas to kill a gob of people. We're supposed to see if Petyr's tied up with her in some Russian Nationalist group called the . . ." He consulted the notes he'd scrawled on the napkin. "The . . . Black Hundreds or some shit. They could be using Islamic State proxies."

"ISIS working for Russia?"

"Not on purpose," Thibodaux said. "You know how it is, proxy warriors are always the last to know who they're fightin' for."

Bowen looked out the window, past the smoked duck carcasses, trying to put it all together. "Petyr doesn't fit the profile of a terrorist . . ."

"Maybe not," Thibodaux said. "But there's something else. I guess his daddy's mind is slippin', poor bastard. Petyr could be in league with his evil sister—or the old man might have accidentally sent him some of the gas labeled as growth hormone . . ."

"So Petyr's got some of this New Archangel stashed away somewhere?" Bowen took a deep breath. "He was carrying that yellow duffle pretty close when he came into Cheekie's."

"Odds are this dipshit doesn't even know what he's got." Thibodaux said. "He's just dammed lucky he hasn't dug into this batch of his daddy's stuff yet. His sis probably sent her Black Hundreds nationalists or Islamic State cutouts to retrieve the gas. It would make sense they'd try and cover it up by removing the bodies from the Dumpster."

"So we're supposed to grab Petyr," Bowen said. "Find the nerve gas his father accidently sent him, and pick up anyone else trying to get the gas . . .

Garcia walked up. "And we need to do it fast," she said, handing Thibodaux his phone and holding up her burner. "Maxim called. The fight goes down in some tunnel under Doyers Street—in half an hour. He's texting me directions."

"The Bloody Angle?" Thibodaux closed his eye.

"What's the Bloody Angle?" Bowen asked.

"Doyers Street," Thibodaux said, drumming his fingers on the table, thinking. "Sharp angle makes it the perfect place for an ambush. Many a Chinese gangster met his death by hatchet on that street around the turn of the century. Quinn and I did some work there a couple of years ago. We heard rumors the gangs had a bunch of old escape tunnels." He grabbed his phone and began to punch in numbers, pausing just long enough to pull Bowen's noodles away from him, tapping on the bubble tea instead. "Looks like you get your wish." He put the phone to his ear, winking at Garcia. "We're gonna need our own gang to make this work. Lucky for us, I got one on speed dial."

Chapter 60

Alaska

Captain Amy Munjares, the pilot in command of the Air Force C-21, was a slender brunette who reminded Quinn a little too much of his seven-year-old daughter, Mattie. The easy swagger with which she made her way down the boarding stairs was well earned, evidenced by the fact that she'd used every inch of Ambler's 3000-foot gravel runway to bring her airplane to a stop that didn't involve a flaming wreckage.

The C-21 was a military version of the sleek Learjet35 with wingtip fuel tanks and twin Garrett turbofan engines mounted on the rear of the fuselage. Capable of speeds over five hundred miles an hour, the plane would get Quinn and Beaudine back to Anchorage in a hurry. Landing one of the hot little airplanes out here was akin to racing a Ferrari down a dirt road. This particular plane was based at Scott AFB in Illinois and primarily used for medevac missions. It had been a rest day in Fairbanks on its way back from a training run to Yokota Air Base in Japan when Winfield Palmer had snagged it.

"Captain Quinn?" Munjares said when she reached the bottom of the stairs.

Quinn nodded. "Thanks for the pickup."

"Getting in was the easy part." Munjares gave him a sly wink. "I have to find a little girl's room and offload some coffee. We need to lighten the load any way we can if we want to make it off this little postage stamp of a runway. How many of you are there?"

"Five." Quinn nodded to Beaudine, Kostya Volodin, and an itinerant Public Health nurse he'd pressed into service to check over Beaudine's wounds during the flight to Anchorage. A reluctant Clarence had gone to retrieve Polina on his four-wheeler.

"Not a chance," Munjares said. "I'm two thousand feet shy of the runway I need to get this bird off the ground. I can maybe carry four counting the Trooper." She walked toward the lonely set of weathered buildings set just off the gravel apron. "Go ahead and board," she said over her shoulder, leaving no room for argument. "Lieutenant Halsey will get you settled in."

"Trooper?" Beaudine said about the time a tall man in the light blue uniform shirt and navy slacks of an Alaska State Trooper appeared at the door of the airplane. He situated a flat brimmed "Smoky the Bear" hat over close-cropped sandy hair and started down the boarding stairs.

"Aaron Evans," he said, hiding a grimace when he saw Beaudine's wounds. "AST. I guess I'm your reinforcement."

"They just sent one of you?" Beaudine said, shaking her head in disbelief.

"I was stationed in Kotzebue before Fairbanks so I know the folks out here on the river." Evans smiled. "And you know what they say, 'One riot, one trooper.'"

"Oh, no you don't," Beaudine said, puffing up like she might explode. "That's 'One riot, one ranger.' Don't you be co-opting Texas expressions."

Trooper Evans shot a save-me glance at Quinn. "You must be Special Agent Beaudine."

"Well, that sucks," Beaudine said, deflating at once. "You recognized the bitchy one as me . . ."

"Not at all," Evans said. "My boss told me you were injured. Before I took this job, I was a firefighter/paramedic. The powers that be asked me to ride with you and do double duty as another gun who could take care of getting you patched up. There was a whole separate aircraft with the Trooper Swat Team on their way out here, but when you sent word the Russian girl had already departed for Anchorage they got diverted down there to assist APD."

Quinn told the relieved Public Health nurse that she didn't have to fly out after all and then called Clarence on his cell. He and Beaudine followed Trooper Evans back up the stairs with a dejected Kostya Volodin between them. Lieutenant Halsey, a smallish man with a crew cut, sat in the right seat of the cockpit, reading emails on a tablet computer. He welcomed them aboard and told them to sit wherever they wanted.

The plane was set up with a single blue leather seat on either side, with the front two facing aft—back to back with the pilots—while the remaining four faced forward. The interior was comfortable but cramped, and everyone but Beaudine had to stoop to walk down the narrow aisle.

"Change of plans on Polina," Quinn said when the Village Police Officer finally picked up. It gnawed at his gut that he'd left Kaija's friend out of his sight, but he chalked it up to fatigue and the hot pursuit of Volodin.

"Good, 'cause she ain't at her house," Clarence said over the phone. "I'll check at the store. Maybe she's over there."

"Pick her up when you find her," Quinn said. "Just hold her at your office. Lock her up if you have to. We'll get another Trooper plane out here to bring her to Anchorage."

Clarence groused about it, but agreed.

Trooper Evans grimaced. "I don't envy him," he said, helping Beaudine get Volodin buckled into the rearmost seat on the right side of the airplane. "His office is just a broken desk in a leaky warehouse and his lockup is a folding chair beside that desk. And Polina's not the easiest woman to deal with." He shrugged. "You work with what you got out here in the village."

"Okay, ladies and gentleman," Captain Munjares said five minutes later from the left seat of the C-21. The twin turbofan engines whined as she back-taxied the airplane down the rough gravel to the far north end of the strip getting every inch of usable runway she could. "We're going to take off to the south. We got a little headwind so that helps. Thankfully, I burned off some fuel getting here, but full disclosure, if it looks like we're using the road at the end of the runway to get airborne, it's because we're actually using the road at the end of the runway."

Quinn took one of the seats facing aft so he could keep an eye on Volodin, but in truth he was going to have a difficult time keeping his eyes on anything. He sank into the soft leather and felt his worn-out muscles begin to relax one by one. He imagined them looking like the frayed strands of horsehair on his daughter's violin bow. The wounds in his thigh ached as if they were on fire, but the pain pushed back his fatigue and helped him focus on what he needed to do when they landed in Anchorage. Volodin sat mutely, staring out the window. The picture of a broken man, he seemed to have no idea where his daughter had gone, only that she was in possession of twelve canisters of New Archangel—which according to him, was enough to kill all the inhabitants of several city blocks.

Captain Munjares spooled up the twin turbofan engines once she reached the end of the runway, causing the little jet to rumble and shake in place. Facing aft, Quinn put on a headset and turned in his seat to watch the two pilots get ready to take off. They had their intercom isolated, so he couldn't hear them talk but watching them work together made him think they might actually get out of this alive. After going over a series of checklists and systems, Munjares craned her head to look out the front windows at the short runway one last time. She took a deep breath and gave her copilot a thumbs up. He nodded and returned the gesture. A moment later Quinn was thrown forward against his harness as the airplane rocketed down the gravel strip at full power.

There comes a moment of commitment in every takeoff when the pilot has gone too far to abort without crashing beyond the end of the runway. Munjares got her bird going so fast so quickly that she was committed from the moment she started her roll. Pedal to the proverbial firewall, Munjares yanked her airplane off the runway seconds before she reached the tree line, taking them up at such an extreme angle that for a few seconds Quinn found himself suspended against his seatbelt, looking down from above Volodin and the Trooper. Beaudine was in a similar position beside him but she kept her eyes clenched shut.

Swagger notwithstanding, the relief was evident in the young captain's face when she turned around and gave a thumbs-up to Quinn.

"That was some impressive flying, Captain," Quinn said into his microphone, meaning it.

"Thank you, sir," Munjares shrugged off the compliment.

"Don't sir me," Quinn said. "I'm a captain just like you."

"No, sir," Munjares said. "You're a captain who knows the President. He called my boss personally to get me to make this flight."

"It's the mission," Quinn said. "Not me personally."

"Whatever you say, sir," Munjares said. "I've been told to floor it. We should touch down in Anchorage in forty-one minutes. Forgive me for saying so, but you look like you could use a nap."

Quinn would have laughed if it hadn't been so true. He peeled off the headset and looked across at Beaudine. "Do you know the Special Agent in Charge of the Anchorage office?" he asked, watching the agent's eyes flutter and flinch with exhaustion and the pain that had been unmasked by the relative comfort of the airplane.

"Michele Pond," Beaudine said. "She taught a couple of classes at Quantico when I was there. Nice enough for a bosslady, I guess."

"Let's give her a call," Quinn said. "According to Palmer she's running the show in Anchorage. We need to make sure we're all on the same page when we hit the ground."

Beaudine took her phone out of her pocket and shook her head. "My battery is about toast," she said.

Trooper Evans worked his way up the narrow aisle carrying an orange plastic box marked "Trauma Kit" and knelt on the floor in front of their seats. "You're pretty dehydrated. How about I start a couple of IVs and get some fluids going while you make your calls," he said. "You both look like you're the type of people to keel over dead before you'd quit."

The Trooper was quick and proficient at starting IVs and had good dextrose drips going on both Quinn and Beaudine in a matter of minutes. Beaudine borrowed his phone, punched in the number for the Special Agent in Charge of the Anchorage office of the FBI, introduced herself, and then put the phone on speaker. She leaned back in her seat while she talked, allowing Trooper Evans to clean and dress the wound on her face.

Inside the sterile interior of the airplane, Quinn was able to catch a whiff of his own odor. He gave kudos to Trooper Evans for not gagging when he started the IVs.

A secretary answered the call, but Michele Pond picked up immediately afterward, sounding gracious and accommodating—two characteristics Quinn had not found common to high-level bosses at many federal agencies, much less the FBI. It was apparent that Palmer had told the Special Agent in Charge to bring Quinn up to speed since a person in her position would not normally brief a junior agent and the representative of another agency. It was impossible to tell from her voice, but Pond sounded professional and more "mission" than "ego" oriented.

"Kaija Merculiefs plane landed a half hour before we got your call," Pond said. "She's in the wind but hasn't boarded any planes out so we think she's still in Alaska. We've distributed a copy of her passport photo to everyone under the sun. APD has set up an incident command post. My office has committed all thirty-six field agents. We're coordinating with Troopers, DEA,

ATF, U.S. Marshals, and the Forest Service. All in all, I'd say we have nearly six hundred boots on the ground."

"What about Zolner?" Quinn asked.

"Your Worst of the Moon is cagey," Pond said. "We have a record of his charter from Ambler to Fairbanks. After that he disappeared."

"There are dozens of small planes coming and going out of Fairbanks," Quinn said, thinking out loud.

"And we'll eventually find which one he took—if he's not holed up in a Fairbanks motel with a hooker."

"I don't think so, boss," Beaudine said. "From what we've seen of Zolner, he's not the type to abort a mission until he has what he came for."

"I hope you're wrong," Pond said. "We have enough to worry about without some ghost sniper. DIA has heard of a shooter named Feliks Zolner but no known photos exist. We have a BOLO out on a six-foot-eight guy with blue eyes. So far it's only netted us a federal judge who got pretty angry when APD put him face down on the sidewalk. Anyway, that's where we are on Zolner. Our first priority is to lock down a target."

"Understood," Quinn said. "Since she can't get out of state, Merculief will want to do the most damage she can with the gas she has. That means she'll look for population density. What day is it?"

"I gotta tell you, Quinn," Pond said. "That doesn't exactly engender confidence."

"Ma'am," Beaudine said, nearly coming out of her seat. "With all due respect, it's easy to lose track of time when you've been through what we've been through."

"You're right," Pond said, showing an incredible amount of humility for someone with the terrible cosmic power of a Special Agent in Charge. "It's Friday."

"That's what I was afraid of," Quinn said. "What do we have going on as far as events?"

There was a shuffle of paper on the line as Pond referred to a list.

"We've narrowed it down to four likely targets. There's a production of *The Little Mermaid* at the Performing Arts Center, something called The American Forum for Citizenship at the Dena'ina, a punk rock concert at the Alaska Airlines Center, and an Aces hockey game at the Sullivan Arena."

Quinn glanced up and saw Volodin was listening intently.

"Doctor," Quinn said. "Did your daughter mention any of those places?"

A tear ran down the old man's cheek. "I am sorry," he said. "She did not."

"Okay," Quinn said, speaking back into the phone. "The last two attacks were televised. The hockey game will have news cameras."

"It will," Pond said. "My media liaison tells me local affiliates have news crews at both the Dena'ina event as well as the rock concert. That leaves *The Little Mermaid* as the only thing we can mark off in that regard."

"A lot of kids there," Quinn said. "Makes for an awfully appealing target even without the cameras." He resolved to call Kim as soon as he hung up and make sure she stayed home with Mattie for the night.

"Each of the other attacks used only one canister," Pond said. "We have to consider the possibility that Merculief got help. They could split up and hit multiple targets—or hit no targets at all and just wait and smuggle the gas out of state."

"True," Quinn said, knowing they weren't going to get that lucky. Volodin had been clear that his daughter hated America and capitalism in general. She would want to use the gas at her earliest opportunity, one way or another.

Volodin cleared his throat. "If I may," he said. "If my daughter does this horrible thing, it will be spontaneous, not well planned. My Kaija did not know we were leaving Russia until I destroyed some of the Novo Archangelsk." He rubbed his face, his hands still cuffed, looking like he might break into tears. "She is so full of hate . . ."

"We really have no choice," Quinn said, looking back at the phone. "We have to put people at all four events." He looked at his watch. It was five minutes to seven. "What's APD think about evacuation?"

"It's a topic of discussion," Pond said. "The fear is that once we play our hand, Merculief will deploy the gas before we can locate her. So far APD has blocked off access to each venue so no new people are getting in. Those already there are none the wiser . . . unless they snap to the fact that all the cops and federal agents at these venues have gas masks strapped to their legs."

A sudden thought crossed Quinn's mind, and he looked up at Volodin, snapping his fingers to get the dazed man's attention. "What did Kaija and Polina talk about?"

"Polina . . ." Volodin smiled. "She is a nice young woman. Very close to having her baby, I think." He gave Quinn a sly wink. "But I am not that kind of doctor."

"What did she and Kaija talk about?" Quinn asked again.

"Oh . . ." Volodin shrugged. "This and that. She did not look very happy to see us." He looked around the airplane then down at the handcuffs in his lap. "Have I done something wrong? Where is my daughter?"

Quinn turned back to Beaudine and the phone. "I'm not sure if Polina is involved in the gas attacks or if she's just helping a friend."

"I know Polina," Trooper Evans said.

"Yeah, we've met her too," Beaudine said, "and she's a liar."

Chapter 61

New York

August Bowen had carried a fight strategy of one form or another in his head from the time he started Golden Gloves in junior high school. Fighting was about working the angles, especially against a stronger opponent, but it was mostly about heart—and Bowen knew he had plenty of that. Unfortunately, brute strength and meanness sometimes trumped even the strongest heart.

It had been difficult enough to find the location for the fight, an eight hundred square-foot storage area off a maze a level below the famed Doyers Street tunnel. A rusted sewer line over a foot in diameter ran along the outer cinderblock wall. One of Bowen's high school coaches had warned him that he had a tendency to focus on the negative before a fight but the low ceilings and the lingering odor of rotten eggs made it impossible not to imagine a burst pipe. There was no way the two hundred plus fight fans who'd answered Maxim Ortega's invitation would be able to scramble out of the tunnels before the underground cavern filled with sewage and they all drowned. He kept the little nightmare to himself and tried to focus on the match.

Volodin had arrived first and had stowed his yellow duffle before anyone had a chance to lay eyes on him. Agents from several alphabet soup agencies were already filtering in through the tunnels, placing bets to blend in, and looking for the duffle. No one knew exactly how much of this New Archangel gas Petyr had, but the powers that be weren't taking any chances. As far as Bowen knew, half the people in the crowd were agents of the federal government—and that suited him right down to the bone. There was a chance that Volodin or his associates would deploy the gas at the fight but the general consensus was that the two hundred ne'er-do-wells clamoring for violence three stories under the belly of Chinatown didn't make for a very appealing target. Still, terrorists who didn't put much value on their own lives could easily deploy the gas out of desperation.

Surprisingly, the Ortegas had invested in an actual chain-link octagon and mat for their illicit operation. Twenty-five feet across, the padding on the support posts was more duct tape than foam, and the black vinyl chain-link was worn down to the steel in several places. The mat itself was far from level, with hills and valleys at each seam. Rust-colored bloodstains, from what looked like the remnants of a massacre, covered a five-foot section of the mat near the blue corner. It was a stark reminder of what was about to happen in the ring. Three portable halogen work lights illuminated the area, making it possible for the hungry crowd to see every drop of blood.

Flanked by Thibodaux and Garcia, Bowen bounced and shuffled on his feet to stay loose as Maxim Ortega introduced the fighters using a portable megaphone. Thibodaux had been right about the circus atmosphere of a mismatch. The faces in the crowd ran the gamut from Wall Street executives, Chinese business owners, and a sizable number of wise guys from Knickerbocker Village. Most of them had surely bet on Volodin, the odds on the Russian were so low that most in the crowd were just hungry for blood—and they didn't particularly care whose it was.

Maxim Ortega stood in the center of the mat as he introduced the fighters in an over-enunciated voice like he was trying to imitate Howard Cosell.

"In the blue corner, wearing black trunks, weighing in at one hundred eight-two pounds, standing five feet ten inches tall, the challenger, August, Baby Bear, Bowwweeeennn." Bowen had unwisely left his fight name up to Ortega.

Bowen's prematurely silver hair made many in the crowd call him an old man. But it was obvious from his physique that if he was old, he was in incredible shape. Well muscled, though not overly so, he was built more like a decathalete than a cage fighter. A prominent pink scar, the visible portion roughly the size of a football, covered the lower ribs on his right side—a badge of war earned from an explosion near Mazar-i-Sharif. The unseen portion of the wound covered his right thigh—and a good portion of his psyche.

Crowds don't root for relative unknowns, so even those who'd ventured a bet on Bowen, answered his introduction with a chorus of hardy boos. Thibodaux told him to forget about the rabble, and dabbed a tiny bit of Vaseline on his eyebrows while Ortega continued his blaring theatrical intro.

". . . In the red corner, wearing blue trunks, weighing in at two hundred and forty-one pounds and standing six feet three inches tall, a hometown boy from Brooklyn, Petyr, The Wolf, Voloooooodin!"

The crowd erupted, cheering for their hero as he danced around the inside of the octagon, waving massive arms over his head to egg them on. He flexed his chest, making the eight pointed star tattoos bounce on his pectoral muscles as he growled and leered, pounding his gloved hands together. Bowen was not easily intimidated, but this guy looked twice as big as when he'd come into Cheekie's.

"Whatever you do," Thibodaux said, "do not meet this clown head on."

Garcia squirted a jet of water in Bowen's mouth and stuck the guard in his mouth like she knew how to work a corner.

The brunette ring girl practically bubbling out of a red bikini held up the Round 1 card and began her circuit around the inside of the octagon. Volodin reached out with his glove to touch her but she swatted him away.

"Good luck, mango," Garcia said as Bowen spit into a bucket. "You got this."

"Don't listen to her," Thibodaux said, just before the air horn sounded. "Remember what I said. No head-on fightin'. That guy's gonna eat your children."

Bowen knew he was in trouble fifteen seconds into the five-minute round. Volodin shot in around both legs and took him straight to the mat, driving the wind from his lungs and nearly putting him in an arm bar. Bowen was able to roll out and scramble to his feet, dazed, and a hair wiser. The takedown did little but embolden the Russian, and he tried to rush in again after a couple of feinting jabs. Bowen understood feinting jabs more than double-leg tackles, and he tagged The Wolf on his blocky chin with a wicked jab hook combination. It would have dropped a lesser man, but Volodin shook it off. It was clear he didn't want to get hit again though and kept his distance, circling and looking for an opening. The two men traded jabs for a time, with Volodin executing several devastating kicks to Bowen's left knee, effectively chopping him down like a tree, one whack at a time. Each kick made the deputy feel as though he was trying to walk out a Charlie horse, all while someone was trying to take his head off.

Eventually, Volodin kicked and jabbed enough to work Bowen back against the cage. Thibodaux yelled at him to "circle out!" and stay away from the other fighter, but Bowen could hear little beyond the whoosh of blood in his ears.

Volodin used the backstop of the cage to his advantage, crashing in suddenly to smear the deputy into the chain link. With much of The Wolf's two hundred and forty pounds centered against his chest Bowen found it impossible to draw a breath. Fleeting images of sparky stars began to swirl in his head, and for a moment, he thought his entire body might be strained through the chain link like a sieve. He got his legs wrapped around the Russian's midsection and somehow had enough presence of mind to keep his hands up to defend himself, but he knew it was going to be over soon.

Bowen felt the referee's body wedging in between him and Volodin, and for a moment, thought the fight had been called. The sound of the air horn signaling the end of round one worked its way into Bowen's brain as he took a lungful of air. Volodin stalked off to his corner while Bowen clamored to his feet, certain that the reprieve was only temporary.

"What are you doin' out there, Gus Gus?" Thibodaux asked, dropping a stool in the blue corner so Bowen could sit. "I told you to roll out. No head-on shit. Got me?"

Bowen nodded, saving his breath.

Garcia gave him a squirt of water. "No word yet from any of our guys on the duffle," she said. "You still good?"

Bowen nodded, working to calm himself and take advantage of the full sixty seconds of rest. He was in better-than-average shape, but going all out for five minutes took its toll, and he could feel his legs turning rubbery. He had to do something to finish this quickly.

"Stop treatin' this like a contest," Thibodaux said. "You're job is to stay alive until we get what we need."

The warning buzzer sounded and the ring girl came through holding up the Round 2 card. In a repeat of the first round, Volodin reached out to grope her. She tried to bat his glove away, but he managed to get his meat hooks on her hips and yanked her backward onto his lap. Laughing derisively, he grabbed her breasts from behind before she was able to wriggle free and run from the ring with her card. Had it been a sanctioned event, he would have been disqualified, but in an underground fight, the behavior went largely unnoticed by everyone—except August Bowen.

Thibodaux and Garcia exited the ring and watched Bowen go straight at Volodin.

Garcia's hand shot to her mouth. "What's he doing?"

"Exactly what I told him not to." Thibodaux grinned. "My bad. Gus Gus don't know how to fight any other way but head-on. I'm guessin' the righteous wrath of

Bowen is about to rain down on Petyr the Wolf for his bad behavior."

And indeed it did. The Russian danced sideways at the deputy's rapid attack, still cocky, circling around to throw another low kick. Rather than trying to outbox him, Bowen bent his knee and let the kick slide up his leg, catching it with his left hand while he drove forward with his right, tagging Volodin in the chin. He could have executed a single leg takedown—and ended up on the ground, which was the Russian's domain. Instead, Bowen let the leg fall as he pressed in, raining jabs and hooks from a half-dozen different angles at the Wolf's head and face. Some landed, some didn't, but Bowen kept the punches coming, causing the Russian to duck and raise his guard enough to expose his ribs.

A hook shot to the liver is one of the most devastating blows in boxing. Bowen had eaten more than his share—and come away from every one thinking he'd rather take a ballpeen hammer on the chin. Digging in, he drove a powerful left into Petyr's unprotected side, digging in to the man's ribs and causing his eyes to roll back in his head. His hands dropped and Bowen hit him two more times in the face before the Russian collapsed to the mat. Bowen moved in for more but the ref waved him off.

It was over.

Thibodaux ran into the ring followed by Garcia who had a cell phone to her ear.

"They have the duffle," she said. "The Bureau and NYPD Emergency Services just sealed the exits. A couple of likely Islamic State dudes are in custody—evidently here to grab the nerve gas."

Thibodaux took a pair of cuffs out of his back pocket and pulled Petyr Volodin's hands behind his back.

"Any . . . Russians . . . in custody?" Bowen said, leaning against the ring to catch his breath while he peeled off the gloves. Ortega tried to raise his hand as the winner but the deputy swatted the man away and told him to get lost.

"Maybe Black Hundreds," Garcia said. "I'm sure our guys are rounding up more as we speak."

"Russians?" Petyr groaned, his battered face pressed to the mat. "It's Anakin's men, here to stab me in the liver."

"Well, don't it suck to be you," Thibodaux said, dragging The Wolf to his feet.

Chapter 62

"That wasn't my fault," Captain Amy Munjares said when she bounced the C-21 onto the runway at Joint Base Elmendorf Richardson. "That was the asphalt . . ."

Special Agent Khaki Beaudine looked out the window at the lights of Anchorage. The fluids and sugars from the IV had worked better than a jolt of caffeine and the jolt of caffeine from the onboard coffee hadn't hurt either. She very nearly forgot her rule about no public tears when she realized they had made it back to civilization—even if she did smell like an outhouse that had been doused with blood and oil then set on fire. Quinn sat across from her, talking to their welcoming party on his cell while Trooper Evans removed the IV catheter from the back of his hand and covered the spot with a cotton and a piece of clear tape.

"I'm assigned to the two of you," the trooper said as they taxied toward an open hangar off the flight line. "There's supposed to be a patrol SUV here waiting on us."

Both Quinn and the Trooper waited for Beaudine to exit the airplane first.

Beaudine put a hand over her brow and squinted at the incredibly bright lighting inside the hangar. The waxed concrete floor was white and immaculate, adding to the glare. She'd known Quinn's daughter and ex-wife would be there to greet him, but the way he'd talked about her, Beaudine thought the daughter would be older. To her surprise, a little girl with long dark hair waited at the bottom of the boarding ladder. A small blond woman, pretty, but with a fierce face, stood beside her. She wore long pants but the ankle of a metal prosthetic was clearly visible above her hiking shoes.

Aunt Abbey's rifle in one hand, Beaudine hitched her pack up on her shoulder and gave the women a tentative wave. She could smell the wonderful odor of shampoo and body lotion before she even reached the ground.

"We brought you some clothes," Mattie said, grinning. It was remarkable that this beautiful little girl didn't scream when she saw the horrific wound on Beaudine's face. Instead, she held out a pair of folded blue jeans and a black T-shirt. "Mom had some unopened packs at home. Daddy said you're about her size."

Kim handed Quinn a black leather jacket before pulling him in for an enveloping hug as if they were still married.

"Sorry about the stench," he said.

"You've smelled worse," Kim said, backing away, her eyes welling.

Trooper Evan's phone chirped. He picked up and then handed it off to Beaudine. "Your boss," he said.

It was Special Agent in Charge Pond. Beaudine's phone had fully charged on the airplane, but the SAIC only had the Trooper's number.

"Yes, ma'am," Beaudine said. "I'm putting you on speaker."

Pond gave a quick rundown of all the security measures that were being put in place at the last minute—a testament to the adaptability of a population of Anchorage who knew they had no one else to count on for the first thirty-six hours of any emergency.

"Still no sight of Feliks Zolner," she said. "We've blasted out a photo of Kaija Merculief over emails and internal databases. Every gun-toter in Alaska who's ever even heard of the JTTF is either standing post or out looking for this girl."

"Any luck narrowing down the venues for possible targets?" Quinn said. He kissed his daughter on the top of her head.

"The ones we discussed are all soft targets," Pond said. "What's your take on the play at the Performing Arts Center? It fits the profile of the football-game attack in Texas. The place is packed with families and kids. We're going to evacuate the building when everyone gets up for intermission in a little over half an hour."

"Good idea," Quinn said, rubbing his face in thought. "Tell me about the thing at the Dena'ina Center?"

"The American Forum for Citizenship," Pond said. "Turns out the Forum is sponsoring a state competition for youth. Something called Students for Civic Action—or SCA. About three hundred middle school and high school students from all over the state are competing—add the parents and teachers to that, and it's a pretty juicy target as well. That's the place APD accosted the federal judge they thought was Zolner."

"Is he still there?" Quinn asked.

"He wanted to stay but the Marshals talked him into leaving. Wasn't too hard when they reminded him what the gas did to the people in Dallas."

"I'd like to check out that site," Beaudine said. "The new Black Hundreds hates everything the West stands for. American citizenship and civic action seems like something Kaija would want to stop."

"She's right," Quinn said. "That would make a statement. Trooper Evans said he'll drive us. The Performing Arts Center is just a block away. We'll check the Dena'ina first, then head over and watch for her when you evacuate the play."

"Very well," Pond said, ending the call.

Quinn kissed his daughter on the head again before picking up the duffle of fresh clothes his ex-wife had brought him and heading for the men's room.

"I guess I better go change too," Beaudine said. "Hate to look at myself in the mirror though."

"Hang around Jericho for too long and you'll get wounded," Kim said.

"I'm not wounded," Mattie said, frowning at her mother.

Kim shot a glance at Beaudine. "He said you looked out for him out there. Thank you."

"I would have died eight times without him," Beaudine said.

"Maybe so," Kim said. "But it keeps him going when he has someone to save."

Two Anchorage Police officers wearing navy blue jackets and black wool watch caps against the cold October evening allowed Trooper Evans through the roadblock on D Street outside Fifth Avenue Mall. A Kevlar helmet was clearly visible inside the open door of one of the cruisers, within easy reach. Each officer had a three-foot hickory baton in a ring on his belt beside the black bag that contained a gasmask. "Hats and bats" meant they were prepared to get serious about the roadblock. Beaudine couldn't help but think how much less civilized civilization felt since she'd seen it last.

APD had roadblocks at all four possible targets, but they'd cordoned off an area of twenty-five city blocks in order to conserve manpower while grabbing both the Dena'ina and the Performing Arts Center inside the perimeter. There was still no mass evacuation at this point. They just weren't letting anyone inside.

Trooper Evans took his SUV through a secondary roadblock as he turned off G Street and parked in a loading zone on Seventh Avenue in front of the Dena'ina.

"We're dealing with nerve gas here," Beaudine said as she got out of the backseat. "We have plenty of plain clothes agents inside. There's no need for you to go inside."

"Nice try," Evans said, giving her an easy grin. "But you're not getting rid of me that easily. I'm an Alaska State Trooper. We blend in around here like the postman." He nodded to a very green looking APD officer posted at the entrance. "Plus, it'll keep you from having to show your badge all the time."

The exterior of the Dena'ina Center was essentially a wall of windows all the way up to the top floor, three levels up. Even before they went inside, Beaudine could see the crowd of people packed into the lobby and reception area. Proud parents posed for pictures with their children in front of a life-size copy of the Constitution along the far wall. Exhausted adults took the time, after what must have been a long day of competition, to drink mock champagne and recharge. Beaudine estimated there were at least two hundred people in the lobby alone. Some program must have just ended upstairs, bringing a steady flow of flushed youth and beleaguered adults down the escalators.

Quinn turned as soon as they got inside. "Who's the agent in charge here?"

Beaudine looked at the note she'd scribbled on her hand. She was so tired she didn't trust herself to remember. "Margot Fischer," she said. "A supervisory agent with the Bureau." She stood on tiptoe trying to get a better look at the faces in the packed lobby, then nodded toward the elevators just across from the entrance. "We need to get to higher ground."

"Agreed," Quinn said, pushing his way past a table of teenage boys wearing white shirts and American flag ties. "The elevators are this way. See if you can get Fischer on the phone. This place looks ripe to me."

"Think we should evac?" Beaudine asked.

"I'm all for that," Trooper Evans said. "If I was going to pop gas for maximum effect, this would be the place."

"Let's take a look from up top first," Quinn said, turning in front of the elevators. "Something's bothering me. Dr. Volodin says his daughter has become extremely anti-Semitic. From what I read on the plane, the Black Hundreds are all about a pure, white Russia." He turned to push the elevator call button. "Why would Polina help out in such a cause? And if she's so prejudiced, why would Kaija Merculief link up with a Native?"

Trooper Evans shook his head. "Polina isn't native."

"What?" Beaudine took a step back.

Evan's scrolled through his phone. "I worked the Kobuk for three years while I was stationed in Kotzebue. Polina Stewart is as *gussaq* as they come."

"She's white . . . ?" Beaudine said. "But . . . we talked to her."

"We talked to someone." Quinn looked at the trooper. "Pregnant, early twenties, little birthmark at the corner of her lip."

The elevator door opened and they stepped aside for a dozen spit-shined youth on their way to the reception in the lobby.

"That's Ruby Ingik," Evans said. "She's Polina's best friend so I'm not surprised she covered for her." He held up his phone to show a photo of a pretty brunette in front of the faded yellow house in Ambler. "This is Polina," he said. "Easy to recognize her from the half-shaved head."

Beaudine let out a deep sigh. "So we're looking for a pregnant woman with an undercut . . ."

They stepped onto the elevator.

Quinn pressed the button for the third level. "If she's even preg—"

The distinctive crack of a rifle from the floors above cut him off at the same moment the elevator doors slid shut.

Chapter 63

Quinn's hand dropped to the grip of his Kimber the moment he heard the shot. His first reaction was to try and get back off the elevator, but his gut told him to move toward the sound of the gunfire.

"Sounds like Kaija Merculief is down," Trooper Evans said, head cocked to the side, listening to his radio earpiece.

"Where?" Quinn asked. The elevator chimed as it passed the second floor.

"Bottom level," Evans said. "She was dressed like the staff serving at the lobby reception. No word who got her yet. And no sign of the gas."

"We need to evacuate," Quinn said. "And get that picture of Polina out to everyone. I'm betting she's still out there."

"Roger that," Beaudine said.

"I'll send you the photo," Evans said. Since he was in uniform, he stood at the door, ready to make a hole in the crowd that would surely be fleeing the sound of the shot. When the elevator doors slid open, it wasn't a crowd they faced, but the cold blue eyes of Feliks Zolner.

The Russian grabbed the trooper by his collar and pulled him straight into a brutal punch in the jaw. Evans sagged, staggering forward and falling to one knee as he tried to regain his footing. Directly behind him, Beaudine rushed in, knocking Quinn sideways in the close confines of the elevator. Zolner was a foot and a half taller, but he was startled by her presence and earned himself a solid slap to the ear before he was able to swat her away. The feisty FBI agent grabbed his arm, rolling up in a ball and kicking out with both legs at the Russian's exposed gut. He bellowed, more in frustration than pain and slammed her against the edge of the elevator door like a hammer, scraping her off but losing his backpack in the process.

Keeping up his momentum, Zolner rushed into the open elevator, driving Quinn backward and upward, shoving his head and shoulders through the opaque plastic ceiling. Kimber in his hand, Quinn raised both arms to protect his head and face from the metal support structure as the giant Russian slammed him upward again and again.

A thin piece of steel frame hooked on the right arm of his leather jacket, yanking the Kimber from his hand and leaving him suspended from the top of the elevator like a punching bag.

Head above the ceiling, Quinn wondered why no one was helping him. Pulling upward in a frantic effort to unhook himself, he twisted and kicked to keep Zolner at bay. He heard a chime above the throbbing of his own pulse and felt the telltale lurch as the car began to descend.

Still suspended and trapped by the heavy leather of his jacket, Quinn spun in a full circle, narrowly avoiding a slash to his own throat on the jagged plastic of the demolished ceiling. The Kimber lay right in front of him on a metal ceiling support, less than an inch from the edge, one good nudge away from falling into the elevator. Quinn knew if the Russian got his hands on the pistol while he still hung like a side of beef, it would be over in an instant.

Quinn doubled his efforts and pulled up with his right arm, straining against exhaustion and the old wounds in his shoulder and ribs. Below, Zolner must have seen blood weeping from the shotgun-pellet wounds. The Russian began to pummel him mercilessly in the thigh. Sick to his stomach from wave after wave of pain, Quinn clawed for the gun with his free hand, missing it by a fraction of an inch, but gaining enough of a handhold on an upright metal strut that he was able to unhook his sleeve.

Quinn hit the floor hard, bending his knees but feeling it in his teeth. He was able to keep his feet but Zolner towered over him, raining down sloppy but powerful blows. His back to the cold wall of the elevator, Quinn covered up, blocking the blows with his elbows and forearms. The Russian had ten inches of height, a good foot of reach, and seventy-five pounds on Quinn. A glancing right hook slid off his hand and into his forehead, staggering him and shoving him sideways. He followed the motion toward the corner, dragging his feet so as not to get them tangled in the process.

The corner could be a friend and force multiplier in close-quarter battle. It gave Zolner a diminishing V in which to attack and protected Quinn from the wide and ungainly haymakers the big Russian seemed to favor. This forced Zolner to bring his attack straight in.

When Zolner committed with a left jab, Quinn parried, stepping into the shadow of the much larger man and punching downward into Zolner's unprotected groin. The blow was surely nauseating but had the added shearing effect from the angle. The Russian roared, bending forward in pain and putting his chin in perfect line for Quinn's left uppercut. The blow would have finished the fight on a lesser man but Zolner lashed out with both hands, catching Quinn in the ear by accident with a massive left paw.

Quinn fell back to his corner arms up, looking for a new angle of attack. He caught a look of something he hadn't expected in Zolner's eyes. It wasn't fear. Quinn was not sure the big man had the capacity to fear. Zolner was unsettled. Just as a shooter needed a respiratory pause before a shot, a fighter had to be settled—fully joined in battle.

Zolner was a bully and he was big. His previous opponents were surely little more than victims of a quick gunshot or beat down. There was a good chance that no one had ever had the audacity to fight back. The taste of his own blood was something new and it was clear in the Russian's eyes that he wanted to be finished with it.

Sloppy as he was, Zolner moved like a machine, with each ungainly punch packing just as much power as the last. Quinn felt himself fading and knew he had to do something to even the odds. He'd fought taller opponents before, and found that if he couldn't bring them down to his level, he could usually use parts of their body to climb up and get a good choke or strike.

Waiting until Zolner stepped forward with another left jab, Quinn pushed off the wall to step onto the top of the Russian's exposed calf muscle, intent on climbing up his body and enveloping him in a choke. Fatigue and pain made him a fraction of a second too slow and Zolner grabbed him around the hips. Roaring what were surely Russian curses, he battered the ceiling again and again with Quinn's head and shoulders.

Shards of broken plastic ripped Quinn's jacket and cut his head and neck, raining down on Zolner. Arms up in an effort to fend off the metal ceiling supports, Quinn saw the Kimber on the third trip up.

In the fog of battle, everything but getting his hands on the pistol fell away from Quinn's mind. It took him two more trips through the ceiling, but he was able to grab it on the way back down. Without pausing, he flicked the safety down with his thumb and shot Zolner in the top of the head.

The elevator doors opened at the first floor to a phalanx of blue. APD officers in gasmasks poured in around him. Quinn let the Kimber fall to the floor and raised his hands. The hydrostatic pressure of a 10mm round through the top of Zolner's head proved devastating. Blood and bits of the Russian covered Quinn's chest and belly. Even his face felt moist. Two of the officers dry heaved into their masks.

"Federal Agent!" Quinn muttered, dazed from exhaustion and the after-effects of adrenaline.

One of the officers stepped in to grab Quinn by the shirt and drag him out of the elevator, away from Zolner's lifeless body. The officer passed Quinn off to someone else, then secured the pistol.

"Get your hands behind your back!" The second officer said, putting a thigh lock on Quinn's neck. His voice was tense, disembodied from the gasmask filter.

"I'm . . . I'm a . . . federal . . ." Quinn said, his words garbled gibberish in his ears. "Beaudine? Polina? Gas?"

"FBI!" Khaki Beaudine's Texas accent cut through the fog of Quinn's mind.

He was vaguely aware of her pushing her way through

the uniformed officers to stoop down and help prop him against the wall.

"Polina?" He asked again, trying to get to his feet.

Beaudine patted his arm keeping him down. "She's done, Jericho. She was about to deploy the gas. I had to shoot her with the .22 rifle Zolner had in his pack. It's the same gun he used on Kaija."

"Wait," Quinn said. "Zolner shot Merculief, and you shot Polina?"

"Yes and yes," Beaudine said. "Polina was bent over the gas canisters down in the lobby. I didn't have a choice. That shaved undercut made it easy to spot her." She gave a somber shake of her head. One of the sutures above her eye had pulled through the skin during her altercation with Zolner. "She's not going to make it, but an ambulance is taking her to Alaska Regional now to try and save the baby."

"The New Archangel?" Quinn muttered, feeling the dark edges of the world creeping in around him. Repeated bashing against the elevator ceiling had taken its toll.

"APD has it in hand," Beaudine said, patting his shoulder again. "With the eight canisters Jacques got in New York and the dozen in Kaija's case, that makes the twenty Volodin said were out there."

Quinn swayed for a moment, staring into her face, grinning stupidly. "Ha," he said, before his world went black. "You just did math . . ."

Epilogue

Anchorage, three days later

Quinn left his mother's pickup in the public parking lot off H Street and walked with Jacques Thibodaux up Third Avenue toward The Marx Brothers Café. Ronnie Garcia and Beaudine were already in the restaurant. The big Marine lumbered along in a relaxed gait as easy as his Cajun accent, scanning the evening traffic with his good eye. Quinn limped from the ache of the shotgun pellets in his thigh. His right shoulder hung a few inches lower than his left. Mattie called it "wonky."

Quinn had given the Troopers the location of the plane crash and they'd been able to retrieve Lovita's body. He and Beaudine would both return to the bush the following morning to attend the funeral in Mountain Village.

"I'm feelin' sorry for that Russian chemist," Thibodaux said, falling into the philosophical funk that was his custom after any mission.

"He did manufacture the most deadly nerve agent the planet's ever seen," Quinn said.

"And our scientists will reverse engineer that shit and make even more of it," Thibodaux said. "Should we go after them next?"

"I'm just saying he's not an innocent," Quinn said. "But I guess none of us are."

"It's still a shame he's losing his mind and the only kid he's got left is a useless bag o' ass." Thibodaux nodded toward the small, gray cedar shake house that was The Marx Brothers Café, suddenly brightening. "The girls are in there comparing notes on us."

Quinn laughed. Even after knowing him for three years, he was still amazed at how quickly his friend's mind could change directions. "You think?"

"Damn right, I think. It's what womenfolk do. Ain't you learned nothin' from me?" He turned his head so he could peer at Quinn with his good eye. "You gonna wait until later tonight before you pop the question to Ronnie?"

"Na," Quinn said. "I left the ring in my old man's gun safe. I'm gonna hold off on the marriage thing for a while. Don't think I could stand two failures."

"Wise," Thibodaux mused. "I guess . . . if it makes you feel lighter."

"I'm pretty sure it'll happen," Quinn said. "Just a couple of issues to work through first."

"Roger that," the big Cajun said, thankfully prying no deeper. "Just remember, none of 'em's perfect . . . except for my Camille." He patted Quinn on the back. "Thanks for arranging this meetin' so I can get reacquainted with Khaki. She's a good girl, for a Texan. I especially like that badass scar you gave her."

Quinn stopped in his tracks. "I didn't give her the scar."

Thibodaux sighed. "Look around you, Jericho," he

said. “My eye, Kim’s leg, Beaudine’s face . . . hell, even Garcia’s heart. We’re all this way on account of you.”

Quinn stood, dumbfounded. “I—”

“You’re readin’ me wrong, brother,” Thibodaux smiled, throwing a huge arm around Quinn’s shoulder and drawing him in for a crushing, sideways hug. “If it wasn’t for you, every last one of us would be stone dead. We only have these scars ’cause we’re *alive*. But I gotta tell you, I am beat. Maybe it’s time we all just step back and take some time to heal.”

Quinn worked his neck back and forth, counting the bones, muscles, and joints that hurt . . . and realizing it was easier to count the ones that didn’t. “Ronnie would like that,” he said. “And I’d be happy to spend a little more time with Mattie, that’s for sure.”

“I think the free world could get by if we rode into the sunset for a month or two . . .”

“You think?” Quinn said, pulling open the door to Marx Brothers. The smell of fresh bread hit him in the face. His heart nearly stopped when he caught a glimpse of Garcia.

“Pretty sure, Chair Force,” Thibodaux said. “And if it can’t, they know where to find us.”

ACKNOWLEDGMENTS

I am especially grateful to Brian Krosschell for engineering my first visit to the Kobuk River region of Alaska. I fell in love with the land and the people from the start. And thanks to him and his wife, Lila, for help with the Yup'ik and Inupiaq languages and culture. The village of Ambler is real, as is the surrounding terrain. Needle is fictional, but is a representation of many of the villages up and down the river.

As always, many thanks to Ty Cunningham, my brother-in-arms and jujitsu sensei for walking through the fight dynamics with me. My friend, Special Agent Michele Lakey endured several lunch meetings while I peppered her with questions about what it was like to be a female agent in the FBI. Sonny Caudill, Steve Arlow, Steve Szymanski, and Dan Cooper always provide valuable insight into the world of aviation, boats, and motorcycles. Brandon Spanos made sure I got the Russian language right. Daniel O and his buds at the Anchorage Police Department helped with the ins and outs of how APD might deal with a terrorist attack. I'm grateful to Ben O and the men and women of the OSI detachments in Yokota, Japan, and Anchorage, Alaska, for their friendship and assistance. My old friend and fellow deputy U.S. Marshal, Troy Meeks, put up with all sorts of questions about tactical medicine under austere conditions. Thanks, bud. I have to give credit to my friend Tyson Bundy for coming up with the idea to use a spent rifle casing to fix a broken oil line. Don and Nancy Finck and Justin at Anchorage Arctic Cat helped me out with questions about the effects of gunfire on an ATV—and even talked me into buying a new Arctic Cat so I could do further "research." Jim Hyde, Dusty Wessels, and the rest of the gang at Raw-Hyde have been an incredible resource as I attempt to hone my riding skills so I can write with some authority on Jericho Quinn's abilities with a motorcycle. Many thanks to Amanda Sundvor at ICON for answering my questions about Quinn's Truant motorcycle boots. She was nice and informative enough to make me want to buy a pair of my own. Readers often ask if I'm doing some sort of product placement in these books. The truth is, I always enjoyed it when Ian Fleming told us the brand of watch Bond wore, lighter he used, or car he drove. I put Quinn on a BMW because I ride a BMW. He wears a TAG because I've worn a TAG for thirty years. He uses a Cardo Bluetooth intercom because I do. He carries a Riot sheath knife and a ZT folder because those are the blades I depend on.

I am extremely grateful to my agent, Robin Rue, and her assistant, Beth Miller, at Writers House who have become good friends. My editor, Gary Goldstein, is a gem to work with—a big thanks to him and all the folks at Kensington Publishing.

And most of all, thank you to my sweet bride, Victoria, my partner in crime, writing, and adventure.